Wakefield Libraries & Information Services

SF

Bree McCready
and the
Realm of the Lost

Hazel Allan

www.stridentpublishing.co.uk

STRIDENT

Published by
Strident Publishing Ltd
22 Strathwhillan Drive
The Orchard
Hairmyres
East Kilbride
G75 8GT

Tel: +44 (0)1355 220588
info@stridentpublishing.co.uk
www.stridentpublishing.co.uk

Published by Strident Publishing Limited, 2012
Text © Hazel Allan, 2012
Cover art and design by LawrenceMann.co.uk

Typeset in MetaPro by oscarkills Printed by Bell & Bain

The publisher acknowledges support from
Creative Scotland towards the publication of this title.

For Graham and Alison, with love.

As always, I am grateful to Strident Publishing for opening the door.

Very special thanks to Alison for her friendship and support. And to Graham, who lived through the first two books with me.

Thank you Lawrence Mann for getting it perfect every time.

Love to Mum and Dad who support me in every decision I make and to Laurie who continues to motivate and inspire me in every area of my life. Thank you to my friends who have helped me climb out of Eed's prison on more than one occasion.

I am grateful to Lynn Steer for introducing me to the world of astrology and tipis.

I must thank all the amazing and inspirational people I have met along the way, especially the children who have taken my characters to their hearts and begged me for more.

Last but not least a huge thank you to Bree, Sandy and Honey who chose to take my hand and lead me through a world of wonder, terror and delight. I hope this is just the beginning for you.

"Chills in the night air are tingling skin
The veil between worlds is now growing thin
Bright spirits gather, the dead return
Drawn to the flickers where candles burn"

Louise Heyden

"Above all, watch with glittering eyes the whole world around
you because the greatest secrets are always hidden in the
most unlikely places"

Roald Dahl

HAZEL ALLAN

PROLOGUE

Bree ran until her lungs burned, following the seething crush of people through the shopping precinct. She stopped and caught sight of herself in the dark glass of a shop window. Her hair was plastered to her head and her face looked sweaty and bruised.

A brief scream of tyres was followed by an explosion of sound. Beside her, oil spread across the pavement and steam spewed from the crumpled bonnet of a car. A horn was blaring in one long, continuous monotone.

She spotted Adam amongst the crowd and relief flooded through her.

"ADAM!" she called, waving her arms wildly to catch his attention.

He was running straight towards her, his face a picture of panic. As he got closer she stepped out into his path to stop him, but he kept running and there was no time to move out of his way. She closed her eyes and braced herself for a collision. But nothing happened – just the sensation of an icy wind passing through her.

A young man and woman stopped beside her. His face twisted in despair, and the woman threw her hand to her mouth and started to cry. A feeling grew within Bree, not quite full blown panic, but something like it. She peered into the cracked glass in the car's wing mirror and was shocked to find no reflection. Wheeling around, Bree looked down to see what the couple were staring at. Horror swept over her when she saw her own lifeless body lying crumpled on the ground. The Book lay beside her, pages flapping in the wind like a dying bird.

"No!" she screamed, reeling backwards. *"I'm...I'm fine... I'm right here!"*

But the couple had gone, lost in the panicked crowd. Bree cried out for help but no-one heard. A strange feeling took hold of her, and with it came a terrible understanding.

This is how I die...

PART ONE
MANY MOONS AGO

CHAPTER 1
ALL THE FUN OF THE FAIR

Ramthorpe Funfair was not quite Disneyworld but it was pretty exciting as far as Rockwell standards went. A neon sign flashing – *Funhouse Thrills* – hung above the school gates. The playground was crammed with giant lorries, stalls and rides –Dodgems, Scare-O-Planes, The Waltzers and The Screamin' Swing (which lived up to its name). Fire-breathers and dancers twirled batons of flames, alongside jugglers, stilt walkers and drummers. The boom of music made the tarmac shake.

Although Guy Fawkes Night was still a week away, fountains of fireworks cascaded into the black night, and angry orange flames licked upwards through a giant bonfire made from planks of wood and unwanted furniture. The lights on the Ferris wheel shone out against the late October sky – Rockwell was ablaze with colour and noise.

Bree McCready and her friends, Sandy Greenfield and Honey Pizazz, were queuing at the burger van. The smell of frying onions and freshly popped corn hung heavy on the air. Sandy crunched into a toffee apple, shattering the brittle coating. He had decided to grow his short, messy hair into something of a more gothic tumble during the last few months. Now longer than ever before, it had been streaked through with red to match his vampire costume. He hadn't needed white face paint because he was always pale anyway, but Honey had done a great job with the rest of his make-up. His eyes, framed by his thick black glasses, were ringed with smoky black eyeliner, and the dark lipstick looked suitably sinister against his chalky skin.

"I don't know what all the fuss is about," he grumbled. "The lunar eclipse doesn't happen until tomorrow night."

Bree adjusted her tricorn hat, the pièce de résistance of her pirate costume.

"The eclipse is a big deal," she said. "It only happens at Halloween once every two hundred years."

"I *still* don't get why everyone is so excited."

Honey draped her arm around his shoulder, flashing a smile.

"Don't be such an old party pooper, Sandy!" she teased.

Dressed all in black, her hair was pulled up in an elegant swirl at the back of her head. Two felt ears sat on top, held in place by a hair band. The whiskers on her cheeks were drawn with shimmering black eyeliner, and her collar was a red diamanté choker. Her tail was made from the leg of an old pair of black tights stuffed with newspaper. Honey carried off being a cat with great aplomb.

As they left Honey to her purchases, Bree looked up at the moon, which was half covered by wreaths of cloud.

"We'll never see the eclipse again in our lifetime," she reminded Sandy.

"I suppose if you put it like that," he muttered vaguely. "What is taking her so *long*?"

Honey was stuffing her satchel with goodies, oblivious to the impatient groans coming from the ever-increasing queue behind her.

At last she joined them. "I simply adore being a cat," she purred, handing Bree and Sandy a cup of steaming hot chocolate each.

"The only cat to own a grotty old satchel!" laughed Bree.

"A sensible cat should be prepared for every eventuality," she said. "And we all know how handy this bag has been in the past."

A firework whizzed over the roof of the school, a tail of glitter trailing behind it. The crowd let out a whoop. "Do you think we're getting too old for Halloween costumes?" Sandy asked, his breath frosting out smokily into the cold air. "I mean we *are* at high school now."

"Nah!" said Honey, teasing a large length of candyfloss from the bag. "You're never too old for dressing up. Besides, I don't know what you're talking about, you pretty much dress like that all the time now!"

Sandy smoothed his long trench coat with fingers tipped with black nails.

"I *like* this look, plus it suits the image of the band."

"*The Successful Others*!" bellowed Honey theatrically.

"You won't be laughing when me and Adam are famous," he said.

Bree felt a prickle of happiness at the mention of Adam's name. She pushed her eye-patch up onto her forehead and studied Sandy's costume.

"You really suit being a vampire," she smiled. "In fact, I might start calling you Count Greenfield!"

"Very funny," he drawled, showing off his fake fangs. He popped something into his mouth and bit down hard on it. There was a muffled crunch followed by an explosion of red froth. Fake blood trickled from the corner of his mouth and onto his chin. The girls shrieked as he lunged at them with a ghoulish moan.

Something at the other side of the playground caught Bree's eye, and her face broke into a broad smile.

"Look, there's Meems! Over by the carousel!"

Honey turned on her heels, and signaled the others to follow. She crept up behind her little sister as she watched the merry-go-round spinning. Pink-cheeked children squealed with delight as they clung onto the animals – a white horse, a tiger, a zebra, a dragon and an exotic bird. Honey clamped her hands over Mimi's eyes and said, "Guess who!"

Mimi wriggled and giggled until she broke free.

"You look great – I like your tail."

"Why thank you," purred Honey, pretending to clean her face with a paw.

The carousel ground to a halt and the children piled off. "Which animal are you going to ride, Meems?" Bree asked.

Mimi studied the carousel carefully, and then skipped over to the white horse.

"This one!" she said, clapping with glee.

As Bree sipped her hot chocolate, hands curled round the cup, face buried in the steam, she sensed someone staring at her. A hooded figure stood perfectly still amidst the throng of activity. His hands were tucked into the sleeves of his cloak. A memory stirred at the back of her mind, but before she could pin it down the man lowered his hood to reveal a shiny, bald head. He stared at her with eyelids that showed up bright red against his chalk white skin. Black lips muttered something before he turned and walked away, melting into the crowd. Bree searched every face, but he had simply vanished into thin air.

"Right! Who's up for a visit to Gypsy Sue the fortune teller?" Honey asked.

Sandy rolled his eyes. "Cost-a-fortune-teller more like. Do you really want to pay to have some charlatan tell you that you're going to meet a tall, dark stranger?"

"Come on," said Honey. "She might tell us something we don't already know."

****

Gypsy Sue's caravan was tucked away in the far corner of the playground, near the perimeter wall and under a row of trees. Painted bright red and decorated with intricate gold leaf, the arched roof was the shade of wet moss, and the large wooden wheels were glossy white.

Bree tapped on the door and waited. She heard a shuffling noise inside, and the top half of the door swung open with a creak. A plump lady appeared, her black hair peppered with grey and mostly concealed under a shimmering headscarf.

"I am Gypsy Sue," she smiled, her hoop earrings swinging from side to side.

"Hello," Bree said awkwardly. "Can you tell me my future please?"

"Well, that depends."

She held out her hand and waved her long fingers impatiently.

Sandy whispered, "I think this is where you cross her palm with silver."

Bree pulled some coins from her purse and handed them to her.

"Please, come in."

Candles and fairy lights lit the inside of the caravan. It was a tiny space, so small that Bree could touch either side without stretching.

"Cramped but cosy," smiled Gypsy Sue.

"It's lovely," said Bree, admiring the walls, which were decorated with gold scrollwork and carvings of birds. The swirl of patterns and symbols covering the ceiling seemed to move with the flicker of the flames from the bonfire, which glowed through the window.

At the centre of the room, a small table was covered with a silk cloth weighed down by a hem stitched with gold coins. Gypsy Sue pulled out a stool and plonked her ample bottom down on it. Bree sat opposite her, and Sandy and Honey perched on the end of a bed tucked neatly in the corner. A muffled explosion of fireworks outside lit Gypsy Sue's face blue and red, and she stared at Bree, studying her closely.

"I can tell you miss someone very badly," she said.

Bree swallowed hard. Gypsy Sue's dark eyes narrowed and Bree was certain she could see right down into her soul.

"A...boy..." she said slowly. "No wait! A man."

Bree felt a painful tug on her heart. She missed her dad terribly. Not a day went by without her wishing he were alive. It was a bit strange, missing something you had never had.

Gypsy Sue gestured to a pack of cards lying face down at the centre of the table.

"Pick them up and shuffle them," she said to Bree with an encouraging nod.

Bree hesitated.

"It's natural to feel nervous," smiled Gypsy Sue. "But don't worry."

Bree picked up the pack of cards, shuffled them clumsily and put them back, face down. Gypsy Sue fanned them across the table with a graceful sweep of her hand.

"Now choose one."

Bree pulled a card from the middle of the deck. A skeleton, carrying a black flag emblazoned with a white flower, was riding a horse. Her eyes were immediately drawn to the bold lettering along the bottom. DEATH. She dropped it quickly, as if it had burned her fingers.

"I'm used to that reaction," Gypsy Sue chortled.

She placed her hand over Bree's and gave it a reassuring squeeze.

"Remember, appearances can be deceptive, this card does not represent physical death but rather an ending of sorts."

"That's a relief!" said Honey.

"Now choose another," said Gypsy Sue, nodding at the pack. "Take your time, think about it carefully."

Bree chewed her thumbnail nervously, then ran her finger along the deck, stopping near the end. She pulled a card showing a princely figure sitting in a chariot drawn by two sphinxes – one white, the other black.

As Bree tried to make sense of it, Gypsy Sue read her confused expression. "It implies war, struggle, and a hard-fought victory over enemies or the beasts within."

"So is the card good or bad?" asked Honey.

Gypsy Sue took a moment to reply.

"The only danger lies in following the wrong path and dying before your time is due."

The small flames on the candles fluttered, and Bree felt cold air brush the back of her neck.

"Let's move on," said Gypsy Sue, her eyes glinting in the candlelight. "The third card you choose will predict your future, and the obstacles that might hinder your progress."

Bree felt a tingle of excitement at the thought of discovering what the future had in store for her. *Would Adam be in it?* With renewed optimism she chose a card from the beginning of the pack. When she turned it over a horrified gasp escaped Gypsy Sue's lips, and her expression changed to one of despair and fear. Bree felt her confidence dissolve as she looked at the image on the card. Under a heavy sky, flames and smoke billowed from the glassless windows of a tall grey tower. The upper part had been completely destroyed by a single fork of lightning, and two people were falling headfirst towards the ground; their mouths open in a silent scream. Bree read the dark letters along the bottom —

CLOCKWORK BELL TOWER.

"What does it mean?"

"I...I need to close up," stammered Gypsy Sue, as she fumbled with the other cards on the table.

She lifted the corner of the curtain and peered out nervously.

"I'm sorry," she muttered, still unable to meet Bree's gaze. "All I can advise is that you make sure you choose the right path."

"But she's paid you to tell her fortune, you can't just stop now!" said Honey.

Gypsy Sue took the coins from the high shelf and thrust them into Bree's hand.

"Here, have your money back," she said tersely, opening the door.

"Hurry along now," she said, shooing them down the steps.

For a brief moment Bree met Gypsy Sue's gaze and saw panic in her eyes.

"Goodbye," she said with grave formality, before closing

the doors and bolting them shut.

The moon drenched the playground in silvery white light, and a cold wind had sprung up, stirring the leaves to dance around their ankles. Skeletal branches knocked overhead.

"What a weird woman," said Sandy. "Still, it's good to be able to stand up straight again."

He cricked his neck and rubbed life back into his legs. Bree looked down at the card in her hand.

"I forgot to give it back," she said.

What had caused such a terrible response? It was only a creepy old picture after all. She shoved it deep into her pocket and tried to forget she had ever seen it.

Honey blew out a puff of air. "Where to now?"

"Somewhere warm," replied Bree.

A chill had spread through her as solid and sharp as ice.

"I know just the place," smiled Honey. "The Hall of Mirrors is beckoning!"

****

Inside a marquee lit by pumpkin lamps, the grassy floor was bathed in an orange glow. Mirrors of all shapes and sizes threw distorted reflections back at the friends.

"Check me out!" laughed Honey, "My legs are all short and dumpy!"

Bree giggled, sticking her tongue out at a wobbly version of herself with a gigantic head and tiny body.

"This one makes me look like a giant beanpole," said Sandy, tilting his head at an elongated version of himself.

"Nah, that's how you always look," smiled Honey.

"Very funny."

Bree ducked through a flap leading to another compartment. It smelled of damp earth, and the canvas sides of the tent breathed in and out in the wind. A large mirror in the shape of a gravestone sat in the far corner. Tiny lights were dotted all around the frame, and the sign above it read:

ON HALLOWEEN LOOK IN THE GLASS, YOUR FUTURE HUSBAND'S FACE WILL PASS.

What harm would it do to take a quick peek? Peering into the glass all she saw was plain old Bree McCready. She noticed that the hot chocolate had left her with a light brown moustache. As she wiped it away with the back of her hand, a horrible vision appeared behind her in the mirror.

A bald man stood there, considering her carefully. One side of his face was covered with an angry scar, sinewy and scorched, with the mangled remains of a flame tattoo on his forehead. The scar had twisted one side of his mouth into a sneer that exposed black gums.

As she met his stare a stab of memory shot through her. Bree could hear his screams as tongues of fire consumed him, giving off the acrid stench of burning flesh.

The man in the mirror was Hallux Valgus.

CHAPTER 2
ROCKWELL REJECTS

Bree spun around to face the man who had once tried to kill her. But there was nobody there.

The tent flap gaped open with a slap of cold air. She could hear the rasp of her breath as she tried to make sense of what had just happened. She turned back to face the mirror, and was relieved to see only her pale reflection staring back at her. Gypsy Sue had well and truly scared her!

Suddenly another face appeared in the glass and Bree whirled around. Adam stood, eating chips from a paper cone.

"Hi," she stammered, still dizzy from shock.

"What's up? You look a bit pale."

"I'm fine, just a bit spooked, that's all."

"Well it is nearly Halloween!" he laughed, offering her a chip. "By the way, you look amazing."

"These boots are killing me," she sighed, "and the eye-patch is giving me a headache."

"All you need is a parrot," he said. "I mean, really, it's the best pirate outfit I've ever seen."

Bree tried to smile back but it came out all wonky and uncertain. Being this close to Adam was giving her the fizz-sparkle-bang sensation of lemonade and fireworks rolled into one.

"I didn't think you'd be into this kind of thing," he said, nodding at the message above the mirror.

"Oh, I'm not, this was Honey's idea."

"And *did* you see him?" asked Adam.

"Who?"

"Your future husband!"

She was trying to think of an answer, when Honey burst in, her eyes watering, and a strangled expression on her face.

"You've seen him too," Bree gasped.

Honey opened her mouth and there was a loud chorus of pops and crackles.

"I *love* this stuff," she said, holding up a packet. "It feels like fireworks going off in your mouth."

Bree laughed in relief.

"Who did I see, Bree?" Honey asked.

Before Bree could reply, Sandy appeared. "She got Space Dust from the burger van, some people never grow up. Let's go, I'm so bored."

Honey pulled back the canvas and they stepped out into the cold night. The atmosphere in the playground was electric.

"What next then?" Bree asked.

Honey straightened her cat ears. "Well, we haven't been on the ghost train yet."

"How scary could that possibly be?" asked Sandy. "I mean we're not five years old."

"It's F-U-N, Mr Grumble Pants," teased Honey. "Isn't it, Bree?"

But Bree had stopped listening. She had spotted something through the crowd. Something lethal.

A knot formed in her throat as she watched Alice Renshaw flick her silky curtain of blonde locks. Surely it was only a matter of time before Adam saw sense. Alice had delicate features and elegant poise, and yet Adam had chosen ordinary, mousy Bree

McCready. The thought unsettled her, made her suspicious. The beautiful girls get the gorgeous guys. That was the rule.

"Let's get out of here," she said.

But it was too late. Alice and her cronies –Vahita Stonewell, Hailey Harshwire and Perpetua Andulus – were making a beeline straight for them. She groaned and braced herself for the onslaught.

"It's only the boresome foursome," said Honey. "Stop stressing!"

"*Please* don't wind them up," Bree begged.

"Who? *Moi*?" said Honey, innocently. "As if."

Alice Renshaw stood in front of them, wearing the expression of someone who was continually being dragged into something infinitely beneath her. Hailey and Vahita stood either side of her, perfect clones wearing matching jackets. Perpetua stood at the back, head and shoulders above them all. Her rubbery lips curled into a sneer and there was a nasty glint in her lazy eye. Alice tightened her mouth into a mean little line.

She turned to Honey.

"A cat. How appropriate."

"Meow," Honey purred sweetly.

Adam cleared his throat. "Hi girls, having fun?"

Alice looked up at him through her long lashes and smiled coyly.

"I am now," she said with a lip-glossed pout.

She turned to Bree, her eyes glinting. "Aye aye me hearties. This truly is a night for freaks and geeks!"

Hailey and Vahita giggled and Perpetua smirked; a stupid, oafish grin.

Honey threw the back of her hand to her forehead and swooned mockingly.

"Why Malice, you wound us with your words!"

Alice sighed elaborately.

"You're *hilarious*. Anyway, I can't believe everyone gets this excited about a few pathetic fireworks," she droned, flicking her hair. "Well, goodbye for now Rockwell Rejects. Places to go, people to see. Some of us have a life."

Adam puffed out his cheeks and shook his head in disbelief.

"Actually, she's improved," Bree said.

"If that's an improvement, I'd hate to have seen her before."

"Mmm, if she had a brain she might actually be dangerous," Honey added.

"You're right. Anyway, I've got to get organised for band practice," Adam said. "I'll drop you a text later, Bree."

She felt her lips curve into a weak smile as she watched him wander through the crowd.

"I think the best way to forget about Alice Renshaw would be to take a ride on the Nightmare Express!" Honey said, breaking into a run.

****

Bree settled into the front carriage and Honey and Sandy sat together in the one behind her.

"I don't know why you want to sit right at the front, Bree," said Sandy.

"First in, first out."

When the train was full it shunted forwards with a rusty click-clack towards a double door with a giant, fanged mouth painted on it.

"Prepare to be swallowed!" squealed Honey.

Bree felt an unexpected rush of nervous excitement as the

doors opened and the train entered a dark tunnel. A sinister voice bellowed, *"WELCOME TO THE NIGHTMARE EXPRESS! ABANDON HOPE ALL YE WHO ENTER HERE,"* followed by a scream and evil laughter. The doors closed behind the last carriage and for a moment it was pitch black.

"Wooooaa!" moaned Honey, running her hands over Bree's hair.

"Stop it!" Bree laughed.

"Agh, look!" cried Honey.

On one side of the track a headless highwayman loomed out of the darkness.

"Shop dummy," yawned Sandy, unimpressed.

Everything plunged into darkness again as the train dipped, plummeting down a steep slope. Something hairy brushed Bree's cheek and she screamed, much to Honey's delight. Lights pumped and flickered to reveal skeletons and bats dangling from the ceiling, and Bree pushed away cobwebs and dodged giant fake spiders. A menacing-looking clown jumped from the shadows, and even Sandy screamed.

Bree was starting to hate the ride, she felt hot and squeamish. A sudden tight curve threw her sideways and she knocked her head on the side of the carriage. In the flashes of light she saw a man with oily, black hair, pitted skin and a vivid scar that ran down the length of his cheek. He grinned maliciously at her, his eyes not dull and flat, but black pools of ink. His head turned slowly to follow her before he melted into the darkness.

She started to fumble with her seat belt.

"Sit down, Bree!" shouted Honey. "We're nearly at the end of the ride!"

The carriage pushed open the doors and the warbled,

frenzied sounds of the funfair slapped Bree in the face. At last the ghost train jolted to a halt.

"I want off! NOW!"

She struggled free and stood shaking at the side of the track.

"It wasn't *that* scary," said Sandy.

Honey touched Bree's arm.

"What's wrong?"

Bree pulled away from her and started running. She wanted as much distance between her and the Nightmare Express as possible.

"Wait for us!" called Honey.

Bree ran until the cold air scoured her lungs. She stopped at the foot of the steps that led to the entrance of Ramthorpe Junior. A bitter wind tugged at the hem of her trousers.

"What's going on?" wheezed Sandy, his coat flapping open. He saw the bump on the side of her head, "Are you hurt?"

Bree shook her head. "That train ride *really* freaked me out," she said, suppressing a shiver.

"Kinda cheesy if you ask me," muttered Sandy.

"Something feels really weird," said Bree, her voice quiet.

"Check your knickers for spiders," Honey suggested.

Bree gave her a withering look.

"Not that kind of weird."

"Well what then?"

"I saw somebody in there."

"Who?" Honey asked, with a puzzled frown.

Bree swallowed hard and dropped her voice to a whisper.

"*Tanas Theramonde.*"

Sandy gasped, and Honey's mouth formed a tiny 'o'.

"You've had a bump to the head," she said. "Perhaps you

should see a doctor."

"I know what I saw!" snapped Bree. "And it wasn't just him. I saw Hallux Valgus in the Hall of Mirrors."

"B...but you told us Valgus fell from the rooftop garden," Honey said. "He couldn't have survived that. And then there was the fire at Castle Zarcalat. They must be dead. Could you be imagining things?"

Bree held her head in her hands.

"I don't know!"

"Surely...you don't think... this has something to do with The Book?" asked Sandy, who seemed as if he might be about to be sick.

Bree let the question sink in for a moment, trying not to panic.

"Well, there's only one way to find out."

CHAPTER 3
MANY MOONS AGO

"Just as well you've got the magic key," said Sandy, as he leaned against the Lost Property box outside the library.

"We'd never have got in otherwise," Honey added.

Bree remembered the words Don Daines had uttered as he handed it to her – "This should help you out of any tricky situations." She never left home without it.

As she pushed the handle down and gave the door a shove, icy air hit them. It was dark in the library, and all she could see were shadows and the dark outlines of the high bookshelves lining the far wall. She shivered when she thought about The Book, tucked away where they had left it last time – behind *Origami: A Beginners Guide,* high up in aisle 142.

"It's *freezing* in here," said Sandy, pulling up his collar.

"I guess they must have turned the heating off for the weekend," said Honey, rubbing away the goosebumps on her arms.

Bree felt her way across the wall until her hand found the light switch in the little office.

"My mum would kill us if she knew we were in here," she said, feeling a sudden flash of guilt.

"It's not like we're doing any harm," Honey reassured her. "Just checking everything's in order."

A firework exploded in the night sky illuminating the far corner of the library, and there, in one of the reading booths sat an old man with his head in his hands.

In the dim light they watched as he turned his head slowly to face them. The first thing they noticed was the monocle in his left eye and his old-fashioned suit. He was gaunt and bent, with red, wispy hair scraped away from his forehead; so greasy it shone in the reflection of the bonfire.

He stared blankly at Bree. She could see he was crying.

"Who the heck is that?" hissed Sandy, his eyes enormous behind his glasses.

The man lifted a bony finger to his lips, then dropped his head into his hands and sobbed silently.

"This library just gets weirder and weirder," said Honey.

He stopped crying and looked up at her with bleary eyes.

"I might be old, but I'm not deaf."

Bree shot Honey a disapproving look and perched on the chair next to him.

"What's the matter?" she asked softly. "Are you lost?"

He pointed to the window. Bree followed the line of his gnarled finger all the way up to the giant disc of the moon, which hung over the playground.

"The moon?" she asked.

"*I know what it is!*" he spat, slamming his fist down onto the table, the monocle falling from his eye. "*I'm not stupid!*"

"Let's get out of here," said Sandy, glancing back at the door.

The man sighed and slumped in the chair. He replaced his monocle and huffed out a stale breath.

"You all think I'm mad, don't you?" he said glumly. "You wouldn't be the first."

He took in Bree's costume and plastic sword, and smiled weakly.

"You're going to need a lot more than that when they come."

The words made her blood run cold.

"Wh...what do you mean?"

"On the eve of All Hallow's the sun, earth and moon will align exactly."

Bree nodded. "The Lunar eclipse. Tomorrow night. Halloween. We know."

The moon reflected in his eyes, turning them a strange milky colour.

He pulled a fob watch from his breeches and held it up to the light. Bree could see some words inscribed around the outer rim, but they were too small to read. He flicked a catch with his thumb and the lid opened to reveal a white face with Roman numerals. He wiped a bony finger across the glass, "Time is already ticking — the Veil between our world and the Otherworld is weakening."

He snapped the lid closed, and handed it to her; the brass felt icy cold in the palm of her hand. His attention drifted back to the window, but Bree could tell that he was not really seeing anything. She stole a quick glance at the engraving.

What really determines our futures are the actions of those who came before.

"It has already started," said the man.

"*You're right,*" Bree said, her voice nothing more than a whisper.

"You know something?"

Bree swallowed and nodded.

"You were spooked by the ghost train," Honey interrupted, "that's all."

"That's *not* all!" she said. "It wasn't just...*those people*... I saw. I saw a man with a cloak on too. He was staring right at me!"

Honey laughed in relief.

"Lots of people are wearing cloaks tonight, Bree."

"This was different," she said, her voice quivering. "He had the strangest lips."

"Black?" asked Sandy.

"*Yes.*"

"I saw him too," he admitted. "At first I thought I was imagining things but then... I remembered."

"Remembered what?" Honey asked, her eyes flitting between them.

"That I'd seen those red eyelids somewhere before. Only the last time we were standing in an arena watching *you* wait to die."

Honey staggered and grabbed hold of a chair.

"This *must* be to do with The Book!"

The man spun around in the chair, his eyes glinting in the fiery light.

"You *know*..."

Bree glowered at Honey who mouthed, "Sorry."

He snatched his watch and stuffed it back into his top pocket. "If you have The Book you must tell me," he said, his voice low and eager.

"I don't know what you're talking about," said Bree, grabbing her sword and making her way to the door.

The man rose from his chair, unfolding a body as lank as his hair. He ran his eyes up and down Honey's costume and let out a bitter snort.

"Do you actually believe you have nine lives?" he sneered.

"Let me remind you that you have only one. They're coming for The Book, and they will hunt you down like they did with all the others and me. Your life will be very short," he wheezed, his breath fading into a dry cough.

"Please stop!" cried Bree, clamping her hands over her ears.

But he wasn't listening.

"If they have already started to break through, they will not stop. If you have that book you can stop them!"

"We've tried before," cried Bree, "but they keep coming back. There's nothing else we can do!"

The man turned to face the window.

"You have to *keep* trying. Only you can stop them!"

"*How?*" asked Honey.

The man took a deep breath and let it out slowly. "With blood, sweat and tears."

"Who *are* you?" Bree asked.

"My name is Algernon Hart."

"I know that name," she said slowly, waiting for the puzzle piece to slot into place.

But Honey got there before her.

"Algernon Hart...born 1801, died 1903," she said, taking a step backwards as the realisation hit her. "We stood at your grave."

"*Grave?*" said Sandy, his face turning ghostly pale.

With sickening clarity, Bree realised they were talking to a man who had been dead for over a hundred years.

"*The graveyard,*" she whispered, scarcely believing she was uttering the words. "I remember now."

Hart turned to face her. "You must be the only ones who have visited my grave," he said sadly.

"It did look a little overgrown," Sandy pointed out.

Bree shot him a look, and he clamped his lips together tightly. She turned back to Hart and something suddenly dawned on her.

"Were you a borrower?"

Nobody would ever *own* The Book. Instead, anyone who found it would become a borrower and be granted seven wishes. Some were guided and protected as they sought to keep The Book safe, others could use its power to wreak destruction and chaos. Bree was not the first person who had struggled to keep it out of the wrong hands.

Hart closed his eyes and nodded. "Many moons ago. I curse the day I found it."

"But why?" Sandy asked. "You lived for 102 years if I remember correctly. Not bad if you ask me."

Hart glared at him, "Living that long was my punishment!" he snarled. "I lost everything because of that book."

"I'm sorry."

Hart's face softened a little, and for a moment he looked like a tired old man again.

"I gave the locket to my daughter, Lisbeth, when she turned nineteen, then I hid The Book under a loose floorboard in my house. I thought that if I kept them separate then no harm could come from it."

Honey stepped forward.

"But The Book and the locket must have found their way back together somewhere along the line."

Hart nodded vaguely.

"Each borrower leaves an indelible mark on the locket," he said. "As unique as a fingerprint. They can come back once and once only. I suppose this must be my time."

"That makes sense," Sandy whispered to Bree. "It explains

why we saw your Dad and Agora after they...you know...died."

Hart put his mouth close to Bree's ear. His breath was icy cold against her cheek.

"Don't you see?" he said, with a low, quick urgency. "It could all be over."

"What could?" she said, pulling away from him.

"All the running and hiding. The torment of keeping a secret. You could make it all stop just like that," he said, snapping his fingers.

He began pacing the floor again, tugging at his hair. He stopped suddenly and spun around.

"You won't know the meaning of fear until you've been where I've been!"

"We can help you, we can find you somewhere safe to hide."

"It's too late," he whispered with a demented smile. *"They're already here."*

****

It had suddenly become very warm.

"Who's here?" Bree asked.

Dark clouds raced across the moon, momentarily drowning out the light in the library.

Sandy wiped sweat from his brow with the back of his hand. "It's roasting," he muttered, taking off his leather coat.

Algernon Hart collapsed to the floor like a puppet with the strings cut. Bree rushed over to help him.

"Leave now if you want to live," he wailed, swatting her away.

Honey took one of his arms, Bree the other, and together they helped him back to his feet. He weighed about as much as a bag of feathers.

"Let's get out of here NOW," hissed Honey, but Bree shook her head.

Suddenly, the floor rumbled sending books tumbling.

"Mr Hart," she pleaded, "what can we do?"

A devilish smile appeared on his lips and he tapped the side of his nose.

"I have a weapon."

He bent down and produced a small dagger from the inside of his sock. It had a long, ivory handle shaped like a horn, and a short blade.

Foamy spittle had gathered in the corners of his mouth.

"The power, the cure. It's in our blood!"

Bree took a step backwards and felt something crunch under her shoe. She looked down to see Hart's monocle in pieces. He did not seem to care. He thrust the dagger at her.

"Cut me," he said.

"I...don't...understand."

A scratching, scurrying noise stopped him in his tracks.

"Cut me NOW!" he ordered, thrusting the point of the dagger in Bree's direction.

"*I can't!*"

"Leave her alone!" Honey yelled. "Can't you see she's terrified?"

"I *must* bleed," Hart cried. "But the cut cannot be self-inflicted."

As he stabbed the air with the dagger his face changed, and he rushed towards Bree.

"If you don't cut me, then I'll cut you!"

She stumbled and fell in a heap on the carpet, her hand landing heavily on the shattered eyeglass. She didn't have time to register the pain, because suddenly Hart was looming over her, the froth at his mouth turning him from a frail old man into a rabid animal. Sandy whirled his coat above his head like a lasso.

"Get away from her!" he yelled, letting it go.

The heavy material wrapped itself around Hart, throwing him off balance. He no longer held the knife, but Bree couldn't see where it had gone.

Another strong vibration shuddered. The window rattled in its frame and the door burst open with a thunderous crash. The heat was becoming unbearable. As Bree struggled to her feet, she felt the floor shift as if someone had pulled the rug out from under her, and she grabbed onto Sandy to stop herself from falling.

A churning white fog appeared, furling around them, and Bree felt her boots start to sink.

"The floor! It's disappearing!"

Hart made a little noise, a pained exhalation of breath. He made a dash for the reading booth, where he climbed onto the desk and clung to it.

"Over here!" cried Honey, indicating a clear patch next to aisle 139.

Bree and Sandy waded through the fog until they were standing beside her on solid ground.

A dark hole appeared in the middle of the carpet, and to Bree's horror two hands appeared at the edges. The skin was red and taut, and the fingernails were so long that they curled at the tips.

Algernon Hart had wrapped his arms around his skinny legs and was rocking back and forth saying the same thing over and over again.

"*Go through the veil. Stop them. Before it's too late!*"

Sandy was rooted to the spot. Bree grabbed him, jolting him from his stupor. They darted into the shadows and hid at the back of the aisle. By now the heat was intolerable.

Fear took hold as they heard what was unfolding on the other side of the bookcase. Algernon's screams were so awful, so desperate, that Bree clamped her hands over her ears. In despair she realised there was nothing they could do to save him.

"It's okay," Honey whispered soothingly. "He's a dead man anyway."

Bree closed her eyes and willed the nightmare to be over.

CHAPTER 4
THE BLOOD OF A BORROWER

After a while the noise stopped and the temperature returned to normal, but the air still echoed with Algernon Hart's screams. It was a sound that Bree would never forget.

Huddled in the shadows she dared to open her eyes.

"Do you think it's gone?"

Honey nodded.

Taking a deep breath they stepped out. The carpet was intact but everything that had not been fastened down had simply disappeared.

"My mum is in for a shock when she comes into work on Monday," gulped Bree. "She'll think the library has been burgled."

"I wonder where my coat went," Sandy said, scratching his head.

"The same place as the chairs and tables, I guess," Honey suggested.

"*And* Algernon Hart," added Bree with a grimace.

"At least that thing got what it came for," Sandy said.

Honey sat on the edge of the reading booth, her long legs dangling.

"Did it?" she asked. "Perhaps once it realises Hart didn't have The Book, it'll come back for it."

Bree's hand crept to her throat, feeling for the half-heart locket.

"It doesn't know where it is," she said sharply, her eyes sneaking a quick peek at the top shelf of aisle 142.

"It wouldn't take it long to find out though, would it?" said Honey.

Bree had a flash of those awful hands coming up through the hole in the middle of the floor.

"We need to get out of here," she said, making her way to the door.

"But what about The Book?" Sandy asked.

She stopped in her tracks.

"I say we leave it safely hidden until the morning. It's far too risky to take it at the moment."

"We both have our locket pieces with us. I say we get The Book now," Honey said, as she jumped down from the booth.

Bree tried to think. Once the two halves of the locket had been clicked into the heart-shaped slot on the cover of The Book, there would be no turning back. She didn't feel ready.

"What do you think, Sandy?" she asked, but he didn't reply.

His eyes were fixed on the corner above Honey's head, right at the point where the ceiling met the wall. Bree could see that his hands were shaking.

"We're not alone," he whispered.

A shadow detached itself from high up on one of the bookcases. It slithered down with a grunting, snuffling noise and slid across the floor towards them.

Hardly daring to move, Bree felt for the mobile phone inside her jacket pocket, and swung it in the direction of the sound. The torchlight illuminated a creature the size of a child, with a muscular upper body and a hairless, skull-like head. Bree could already feel the heat coming from its red raw skin. It shielded its face from the beam of light with fingers that were tipped with razor-sharp talons.

As she bolted towards the open door, Honey and Sandy shot past her. With the creature hot on their heels, Bree slammed the door in its face and ran, taking the stairs two at a time without looking back.

When she reached the foyer the others were nowhere to be seen. Feeling the sting of abandonment, Bree wondered where on earth they had gone. Then she heard the frantic whisper of her name coming from behind the trophy cabinet. She ran over and threw herself down beside Sandy and Honey.

"That thing was so hot," said Honey, holding her hand up to show Bree. "Look, the heat even blistered my fingers!"

"Me too," Sandy added, pulling down his turtleneck sweater to reveal a patch of angry red skin on his shoulder.

"Did you lock it in?" asked Honey.

Bree shook her head. "I didn't get the chance."

"We can't stay here forever," said Sandy, shifting uncomfortably. "I'm getting cramp already."

Bree was just about to check if the coast was clear when the temperature soared again. She felt beads of sweat prickle her brow, but she didn't dare move to wipe them away.

Something heavy landed on top of the trophy cabinet and a shadow spread across the floor. Honey was rigid, pressing her lips together so tightly they turned a bloodless white. Bree was sure the thundering of her heart would give them all away.

Time stood still as they waited to come face to face with the creature from the library. *Any minute now! It's going to do to us whatever it did to Algernon Hart,* thought Bree. But as quickly as it appeared, it slithered off, taking the devilish heat with it.

Bree shuffled awkwardly out of the space, glancing nervously at the stairs. Honey followed her, using the edge of the cabinet to pull herself up.

"*Euch!* What is *that*?" she squealed, holding her hand out in front of her.

Sandy stared down at the dark smudge across Honey's fingers.

"Someone is bleeding!" he cried, checking himself over.

"It's okay," said Bree, straightening her jacket. "It's just me."

In the midst of the chaos she had forgotten all about the wound to her hand.

"I landed on Algernon Hart's eyeglass when I fell, it's nothing really."

Honey grabbed her hand and held it up to the dim light.

"It's *not* nothing. I think there's a piece of glass in there. There's blood everywhere!"

She lifted her satchel over her head and tipped it up. The contents spewed out across the floor – Dental Floss, tissues, eyeliner, a nail file, a mirror, and finally – a mousetrap. She rummaged around until she found what she was looking for.

"Let me see that," she said, brandishing a set of tweezers.

Reluctantly, Bree held out her hand.

Honey peered closely at the cut, her tongue poking out in fierce concentration.

"This might hurt a bit," she warned. "But we can't have you walking about with hundred-year-old glass under your skin, can we?"

Bree gritted her teeth as Honey began to scrape the splinter from the tiny hole in her palm.

"Honey – why on earth have you got a mousetrap in your satchel?" asked Sandy.

"Oh, I forgot about that. I hate them, they're cruel. One of the neighbours was complaining about a mouse, and I saw him lay the trap. I decided to save the poor thing. There, offending article removed," said Honey with a satisfied smile. She took a paper tissue from a packet and handed it to Bree, then began to toss things back into her bag.

As Bree watched a blossom of fresh blood seep into the tissue something nagged at the back of her mind.

The power, the cure. It's in our blood.

"I think that creature was frightened away by the blood on the cabinet," she said. "Algernon Hart mentioned something about having a weapon – I think that weapon is blood."

Honey chewed thoughtfully for a moment.

"*'The cut cannot be self-inflicted'*" she said, echoing Hart's words. "The blood must come from another's hand!"

"That's a cheery thought," said Sandy.

"It must be true though," said Bree. "Because I didn't cause this, did I?" She waved her bloodied hand under his nose. "And some of my blood went on the cabinet. It must have been enough to scare it off."

Sandy nodded.

"I think it's time we left," he said.

They walked through the reception area, past the wall filled with photographs, and down a long corridor that led to the dining hall. The air still bore the faint trace of beef olives and treacle sponge. When they reached the door to the drama room Bree whipped around, her senses on heightened alert.

"I heard something," she whispered.

She caught sight of a pair of yellow eyes watching them from the shadows. "Run!" she yelled.

Behind them the corridor echoed with grunting. Bree could feel the creature gaining on them, its hot breath on the back of her neck. With one last burst of speed they threw themselves against the fire exit door and fell out into the playground. Bree scrambled to her feet and slammed it shut just in time.

"*Goodness Gracious* – Bree McCready!"

Bree, Sandy and Honey spun around to find Mrs Matlow, their teacher from last year standing there, her skinny frame lost inside a shapeless cardigan.

"Are you alright?" she asked, her eyes narrowing suspiciously.

Bree snatched some shallow, rasping breaths and tried her best to look innocent.

"Yes, Mrs Matlow, we're fine thank you."

"You seem very out of breath," she said, her cheeks glowing pink from the cold.

"Just trying to stay warm," said Honey, jogging on the spot, as Sandy joined in half-heartedly.

"Good thinking!" she chortled.

"Are you enjoying the funfair?" asked Bree.

"Ooh, yes!" she laughed, a nervous little whinny. "It's lucky I bumped into you, there's someone I'd like you all to meet."

Bree took a last glance back at the fire door, half expecting to see the glint of yellow eyes staring back at her. But there was nothing.

By now the funfair was in full swing, and the flames of the bonfire licked upwards into the sky. The moon had all but disappeared behind some thick clouds, but the stars were clear, and there were flecks of drizzle in the breeze.

"I can't wait for you to meet him!" cooed Mrs Matlow. "There he is!" she squawked, flapping her hands like a demented parrot.

A tall man stood at the Hammer Strike with his hands

clasped behind his back. He was watching a small girl wield a rather large mallet above her head, about to smash it down onto the target.

Mrs Matlow stopped next to him and danced on the spot.

"Tomas! This is the girl I was telling you about. Bree McCready, the prize swimmer!"

He stepped out from the shadows and extended a hand towards Bree. He had messy blonde hair and wore a pair of large glasses with thick lenses that made his eyes appear too small for his face.

"I'm Tomas Deanheart. I'm pleased to meet you, Bree."

"I'm sure you'll have heard the news by now," said Mrs Matlow, hopping from foot to foot with childish excitement.

"What news?" Honey asked.

"Mr Deanheart will be joining the staff at Rockwell High next term – as Head of Physical Education! He was very interested to hear what an exceptional swimmer you are Bree, weren't you, Tomas?"

He nodded, "I went to school with your parents many moons ago. That was such terrible news about your father. I'm so sorry. Tell me, how is your mother?"

"She's fine thank you," Bree replied.

"I'm putting together an under 16's team for the Rockwell swimming gala," he said, his tiny eyes blinking rapidly, "I would very much like it if you joined us."

Everyone stared at Bree expectantly. She opened her mouth to reply, but was interrupted as a large boy smashed the mallet down hard, making the puck strike the bell at the top. His friends cheered and as they began to move away, Bree caught a glimpse of a man coming out of The Hall of Mirrors through a gap in the crowd. Hallux Valgus pulled the hood of his cloak over his bald head before disappearing in the hustle and bustle.

"Bree, Mr Deanhart asked you a question," said Mrs Matlow. "I think it would be polite to answer."

"I...I'm sorry, yes, I'll think about it, Mr Deanhart," she replied, vaguely, her eyes searching the fairground.

"Anyway, it was nice to meet you all," said Mr Deanheart, "but I must go. I have an important meeting." He nodded courteously at Mrs Matlow and strolled off, stopping next to the Waltzers as he remembered something.

"I shall definitely look forward to seeing you swim, Miss McCready. And I'll be in touch soon about the team."

"Great," she replied, although she felt strangely underwhelmed.

Mrs Matlow watched dreamily as Mr Deanheart disappeared behind a blur of flashing lights.

"Off you go and have some fun," said Mrs Matlow, as she realised they were looking at her strangely. "Might I recommend the Nightmare Express, my personal favourite?"

"We've already been on it," sniffed Sandy. "It was pretty boring."

Mrs Matlow looked at him as if he had lost his marbles.

"Boring? I thought it was *marvelous!*" she said, pulling her cardigan tight against the cold. "Let me tell you, that little red creature scared me half to death!"

As Mrs Matlow hurried off towards the roaring fire, Bree saw the realisation creep across Sandy and Honey's faces.

"She saw it too," Honey said quietly. "The creature from the library."

Sandy looked pale and distracted.

"Do you know what I think? It looked like a..." he stopped

and bit his lip to stop the word coming out.

"A what?" urged Honey, giving him an impatient stare.

Sandy sighed reluctantly.

"It looked like a gargoyle."

"A gargoyle," said Honey, rolling the word around her mouth.

Bree nodded. "And not just any old gargoyle. It was one from Castle Zarcalat."

"Yes! It was one of the ones that cling to the columns at the front," said Sandy.

Bree chewed on her thumbnail.

"I'm certain I just saw Hallux Valgus coming out of the Hall of Mirrors, and I'm not imagining things. Maybe it's true, our worlds are colliding!"

A terrible thought entered her mind, one that set her heart racing.

"*Oh, no*. Did we say out loud where The Book was?"

"I don't think so," said Sandy, although he did not look certain.

"I'm pretty sure I never mentioned it," said Honey.

Sandy seemed to read Bree's mind.

"I'm not going back in that library," he said, firmly. "No way."

"It's going to be a long night, but let's leave now and come back first thing in the morning then," Bree suggested.

"Sounds like a good plan," said Sandy. "Although there's a slight problem, my Aunt and Uncle are visiting tomorrow. Gran will want me to be there to welcome them."

"We'll come here straight after they've left," said Bree, glancing up at the shifting clouds.

Honey smiled encouragingly.

"And on the plus side – nothing ever looks as bad in the daylight."

Bree offered a weak smile, but in her heart she knew Honey was probably wrong.

CHAPTER 5
THE GRUESOME TWOSOME

It *was* a long night.

Bree knew she had to sleep, but the harder she tried, the more it slipped from her grasp.

When sleep briefly descended, it was accompanied by visions of Algernon Hart being dragged through the hole in the floor, shouting, "*Go through the veil...stop them...before it's too late!*"

She felt a twinge of hope as the first sign of early dawn light seeped around the curtains. Somewhere in the distance she could hear seagulls too. Surely there would be no birds if the world had ended. She glanced at her alarm clock: 6:53am.

Bree moved her feet slowly so as not to disturb Bustopher, her dippy, cross-eyed cat with a penchant for eating spiders. But he was not at the end of her bed where he usually slept. She dragged herself out from under the duvet and pulled back the curtain.

Under a glowering drape of clouds Rockwell was coming to life, and despite the early hour people were already up and about. The view from the eighth floor was spectacular. On a clear day you could see as far as Keves on Sea, a pretty seaside town, which had once been home to the factory where Bree's dad had worked. The factory was long gone, and had been replaced with holiday homes. Fish and chip shops and plenty of tourist attractions made Keves a popular location for locals desperate to escape the noise and pollution of the city.

She showered quickly and got dressed. Bree's mum, Madeleine, and her partner, Harry, were still sleeping, so she crept through to the kitchen, swigged some orange juice straight from the carton and stuck a slice of bread in the toaster. While she waited she scribbled a quick note to say where she was going, adding – *I love you Mum* – at the bottom. Just in case the world did end today.

The toast popped up, she slathered on some peanut butter and ate it as she made her way to the front door. When she opened it Honey was already waiting, cross-legged on the mat, listening to her iPod.

"You're up early," said Bree, closing the door quietly behind her.

Honey tugged the earphones out.

"I didn't go to bed. My head was spinning with all kinds of weird stuff."

"Me too," said Bree, swallowing the last of her toast. "The sooner we get The Book back the better."

Honey sprung up from the doormat in one graceful motion. The dangling earphones threw out a loud, tinny beat. She folded her arms and several bangles clinked around her wrists.

"We have to get through the visit from Val and Norrie first," she said, shoving the iPod into her satchel.

They made their way downstairs to flat 7B. Bree knocked on the door and a few seconds later Sandy answered it. His hair stuck out at odd angles and it was obvious that he hadn't slept either.

"Come in," he yawned, rubbing his eyes.

They pushed their way past the clutter in the hallway where Bustopher was asleep on top of a pile of clean washing behind the door.

"What are you doing here, Mister?" Bree cooed, rubbing the soft spot above his nose. "I think you've got a thing for clean washing."

Sandy stopped outside his bedroom, yawned again and scratched his chest.

"Plus Gran feeds him treats, I wish she wouldn't he makes me ..."

He let out an enormous sneeze, sending Bustopher scrambling out the front door.

"Spatangalam!" Bree said, grabbing a neatly folded handkerchief from the top of the washing pile.

Sandy stared at it as if it was an unexploded bomb.

"It's all covered in cat hair! Are you trying to kill me?"

"Sorry," she said, stuffing it into her pocket. "I didn't think."

"I'm going to get dressed," he said, swallowing another yawn. "Then I'll be through for a tuna sandwich."

Honey screwed up her face.

"Ew. Tuna? *It's seven thirty in the morning!*"

"I'll stick some cornflakes on it then," he said before disappearing into his room.

When Bree pulled aside the beaded curtain that separated the living room from the kitchen, Annie was leaning over the sink, her hands clutching the draining board for support. Her shoulders pointed sharply through the fabric of her blouse.

"Mrs Hooten, are you alright?"

Annie smiled but she looked pale and drawn, a sketch of her usual self. In recent months she had stopped wearing the make-up which had always brought a touch of glamour to the Rockwell estate. Some days it looked like she had scarcely pulled a comb through her carrot-coloured hair. She straightened up and fiddled with her hearing aid.

"Just a little dizzy, that's all," she said with a feeble smile.

"Are you sure?"

Annie waved her away.

"No need to fuss. Now where's Sandy? There's a lot to be done before Val and Norrie arrive."

"He's getting dressed," said Honey, who had popped her head through to see what was happening.

"In something other than black I hope," said Annie. "It does nothing for his complexion."

Annie seemed unusually anxious and tetchy. She toddled into the living room, as Sandy appeared. She looked pleased to see that he was wearing a dark green hooded top and jeans.

"Be an angel," she said, handing him some loose change. "Nip down to the corner shop and get some chocolate biscuits. And take my skateboard, you'll be quicker."

"No, I'll walk, but thanks for the offer, Gran. I'll be as quick as I can. Back soon."

In honour of Val and Norrie's visit, Annie had unfolded an extra leaf of the dining table. Old photographs and newspaper clippings were scattered over it.

"Any excuse for a walk down memory lane," she smiled.

"Are there any photos of Sandy as a baby?" asked Honey, rubbing her hands together gleefully.

"A few," said Annie. "But these ones are mostly ones of Sandy's mum, Jane, and her big sister, Valley."

"You mean Valerie?" said Honey.

Annie chuckled.

"When Jane was a little girl she couldn't say Valerie, so she called her sister, 'Valley', and somehow it stuck."

Annie held out a photograph of two little girls, one small

and dark, one tall and blonde. She pointed to the older girl.

"That's Auntie Val – dear, cross little Val. When Jane was born it was like a breath of fresh air," said Annie, smiling at the memory. "There was something special about her. I know you're not supposed to have favourites, but it was difficult not to. I always felt guilty about how I felt, but Valerie was such a disagreeable child."

A leather-bound journal, poking out from the pile caught Bree's attention, and she pulled it towards her.

"Keep a diary and one day it will keep you," said Annie, staring fondly at it. "This one was a gift from Jane."

While Honey and Annie looked through some of the photographs, Bree lifted the cracked cover of the diary. She scanned one of the pages near the middle and something caught her eye.

What about Sandy? I fear he's in terrible danger. I'm all he has left in the world

"Are you okay, cookie?" Annie asked, peering over her glasses.

Bree fumbled with the diary and a flimsy piece of material fell out from between the pages.

"Y...yes, I'm fine," she said shakily.

The material may have once been white, but was now it was a brownish yellow, as if it had been soaked in tea. She held it up to the window and admired the delicate, precise needlework. The initials AB had been embroidered into one corner in silk thread.

Annie took it from her and gently traced the threads with her fingertips.

"This little scrap of fabric is as old as me," she said with a wistful smile. "It's one of the only links to my past. When my parents died in 1956, I found this amongst their belongings. There was a poem written for me by my birth mother wrapped inside it."

"I had no idea you were adopted," said Honey. "Does Sandy know?"

"Yes, he has always known."

"Did you ever meet your real mother?" asked Bree.

Annie shook her head.

"All I know is that she was a servant at Sobstoan House in the late 1930's."

"Isn't that the big stately home a couple of miles away?" Honey asked.

"That's right. It feels a little strange knowing that she was somewhere nearby. I found out I was adopted when I was four years old. I overheard my Aunt talking. Secrets always seek an ear. My mother gave me away after being dismissed from her job, and I was raised by the lady and gentleman of the big house, Mary and John Bunsfield."

Bree ran her thumb over the neat stitching.

"The initials must stand for Annie Bunsfield," she said, handing the handkerchief to Honey.

Honey and Annie fussed over it, and while they were distracted, Bree stole another quick look at the diary entry.

...I'm all he has left in the world and it's my duty to protect him. He's so little, so innocent. I know it's dreadful but I don't want Valley anywhere near him. It's terrible to feel afraid of my own daughter but I'm sure she had something to do with Jane and Michael leaving. I have felt this for some time but have felt unable to tell anyone. My psychic abilities go into meltdown whenever she's around. My frequencies muddle and she makes me think dark thoughts. And then there are those awful people she calls her friends... her cold behaviour... those places I fear she goes to. Where does she go? All those 'weekends away' and 'business trips'. Every time she comes home it seems as though another little piece of her has died. I know she was in love with Michael. She has never confessed this to me but I always saw it in her eyes. Thank goodness Janey never knew. I'm so confused and lonely and frightened. And so sad that I may never see my beautiful Jane again. All these emotions! But above all I'm scared. Scared for my Sandy...

Suddenly, the door opened and Auntie Val walked into the living room. Bree quickly closed the diary, sure that she had guilt written all over her face.

"The front door was open," said Val, without a smile. "So I let myself in."

She peered at the gathering suspiciously from behind her steel-framed glasses. Her hair was windswept, and she had sprouted a silver streak through her fringe since Bree had last seen her. She wore a stunning necklace set with a large amber stone; it caught the light, dazzling Bree momentarily. Annie threw her arms open wide.

"Hello stranger," she said, with forced cheeriness. "It's

lovely to see you!"

Val held Annie at arm's length and kissed the air at the side of her cheek.

"HOW ARE YOU MOTHER?"

"No need to shout," smiled Annie, tapping her ear. "I've got my hearing aid in. Where's Norrie, dear?"

"He's just coming," replied Val, pinch-lipped and stern.

"You remember Bree, dear, don't you?"

Bree did her best to smile.

"Hello Auntie Val, I haven't seen you for a long time."

"It's Mrs Van-Lite to you."

She looked down at the diary and then back at Bree. Her gaze was so penetrating Bree wondered if she could read her thoughts.

"And who might you be?" said Val, turning her attention to Honey.

Honey looked up and flashed one of her trademark smiles.

"Honey Pizazz – nice to meet you."

Val looked at her as though she were a new and particularly disgusting species of insect.

"What a perfectly ridiculous name!"

"Please dear, take a seat. You've had a long journey," said Annie, fussing over the cushions.

Now Bree understood why Annie was so on edge. She was frightened.

Val eyed the armchair, considering whether it was clean enough to sit on.

"We'll have a cup of tea soon," said Annie. "Sandy's away getting some biscuits."

Val folded her hands tightly in her lap, her fingers clamped together so hard that the tips turned white. She was showing no signs of warming up. Her face was expressionless but something burned at the back of her eyes, something cold and feral.

"Yoo-hoo." A deep, booming voice drifted through from the landing.

"If that's Sandy then something very weird has happened," giggled Honey.

"Only me!"

A man's face peered around the door. Ginger eyebrows formed a single fuzzy caterpillar, which bristled along the brow of his nose, a clue to the colour of his hair before he became as bald as an egg, and his fleshy cheeks swallowed his beady eyes. He stepped into the room, making the pictures on the wall vibrate, and threw his car keys onto the coffee table.

He was even bigger than Bree remembered, a giant slab of a man whose neck spilled over his collar like expanding dough.

For once Honey was speechless. Her mouth hung open as she took in the sight. Uncle Norrie laughed, revealing a rather haphazard display of teeth.

"Close your mouth love, the flies'll get in!" he roared.

Honey's mouth snapped shut.

"This is Honey," said Val, her lips puckered. "And you must remember Bree."

"How could I forget one so lovely?" he grinned, wiggling his ferocious eyebrows.

Bree swallowed her disgust and smiled back politely.

"Where's that scrap of a lad with the black hair and pipe-cleaner legs?" he boomed, throwing his bulk back into the settee.

On cue, Sandy came through the door a little out of breath, clutching a carrier bag.

Bree noticed that Annie was wringing her hands.

"Say hello to Auntie Val and Uncle Norrie," she smiled encouragingly.

Sandy managed a polite smile.

"Well, my boy!" bellowed Norrie, "you've filled out a bit since the last time I saw you!"

"I hope so," said Sandy. "I was only ten."

"Come and sit down," Val smiled, patting the cushion next to her.

The smile made her look younger, and melted the harsh lines around her mouth. Bree noticed how closely she studied Sandy.

"You *do* look like your father," said Val.

Bree remembered the words from the diary; the words that had revealed Val's feelings for Michael Greenfield.

Annie went into the kitchen to make tea. Bree could see her peering anxiously through the beads as the kettle boiled.

"So how are you getting on at Ramthorpe Junior?" Val asked, changing the subject.

Sandy picked an imaginary piece of fluff from his trousers.

"We're at Rockwell High now."

There was a horrible silence that seemed to go on forever. Sandy shifted awkwardly in his seat, trying to think of something to say.

"Bree's really good at swimming," he blurted. "The new Head of P.E is keen for her to be in the swimming team. His name is Mr Deanheart."

"I'm not interested in what Bree does," she said, sharply.

She noticed the embarrassment on Sandy's face, and quickly composed herself.

Annie came out of the kitchen, the long strings of beads

rattling behind her. Her lips were painted a vivid shade of pink that clashed perfectly with her orange hair, and two circles of rouge added some colour to her cheeks. She was carrying a plastic tray covered with a checked linen napkin, carefully placed, so the corners hung over the edges. She took shuffling steps towards the table, the elegant floral cups tinkling on their saucers.

"Anyone for Lapsang Souchong?"

Val tutted loudly and rolled her eyes.

"I don't know what's wrong with normal tea," she sighed, regarding the tray with disdain.

Annie lit an incense stick. Tendrils of smoke rose lazily to the ceiling and the room was filled with the sweet aroma of vanilla. They drank their tea in silence.

"Anyone for a top-up?" chirped Annie.

Norrie drained his cup in one greedy gulp and burped loudly.

"Don't mind if I do."

He folded his hands over his belly, giant sausage-like fingers with clumps of red hair sprouting above the knuckles.

Bree glanced up at the cuckoo clock on the wall. One minute past nine. The funfair opened at 10am, and she wanted to get inside the school before the crowds arrived. She wondered dismally how long it would take for the gruesome twosome to leave.

CHAPTER 6
THE VISITOR

Honey stood up to pour another cup of tea, creating a welcome distraction.

"You know, Mrs Van-Lite, you remind me of someone."

Auntie Val flattened her hair and sucked in her cheeks.

"A film star perhaps?" she asked, with sudden interest.

Honey stirred the tea and rested the spoon on the saucer. There was a glint in her eye, the kind that usually invited trouble.

"Actually it's someone we go to school with," she replied. "Her name is Alice."

Sandy coughed out a spray of biscuits. Honey picked up the cup and stuck her little finger out in a genteel manner. She took a dainty sip.

Bree stifled a giggle.

At that moment the living room door creaked open and Bustopher sauntered in, his tail held high. Val all but leapt out of her seat, her expression stuck somewhere between terror and disgust.

"Ugh, get that thing away from me!"

Honey tutted loudly.

"He's harmless," she said, putting her cup on the saucer.

"It is NOT harmless, it's smelly and vicious!"

Bustopher made a beeline straight for her, the way he always did when he knew someone didn't like him.

"Shoo, shoo," she flapped hysterically, lifting her feet off the floor.

Bree scooped Bustopher up and hugged him to her chest. "Aw, Bustopher's a big softie," she said, holding him out to Val like a peace-offering. "And he definitely doesn't smell."

"Get – that – furball – away – from – me," spat Val.

Bustopher growled and jumped out of Bree's arms, bolting through the door in a blur of hisses and flying fur. Bree was quite shaken; she had never seen him behave like that before.

"Allergies run in the family but Val gets it worst if she's in contact with cats," Annie explained. "That's why she never liked them."

Bree bit down hard on her bottom lip, not trusting herself to speak.

"They don't seem to like her much either," said Sandy.

"Cats are good judges of character," sniffed Honey, biting into a biscuit.

"Dreadful creatures, nothing but vermin. I think it's time we left, Norrie," said Val, fixing her hair. "It smells like a funeral parlour in here with that dreadful perfumed smoke. I'm getting one of my headaches."

She wafted the smoke away and stood up to leave.

Norrie heaved himself to the edge of the seat and thrust his chubby hand towards Bree. She shook it reluctantly; trying not to focus on the dark, greasy, head-shaped patch he had left on the back of the settee. His hand was sweaty, like it needed wrung out.

"I have a feeling we'll see you again soon," he bellowed.

He gave Sandy a hearty pat on the back and waved over to Honey, who had crammed her mouth full of biscuits so that she wouldn't have to speak to them again. The cuckoo clock hanging on the wall chose that moment to spit out a pair of birds, marking the half hour. They had less than thirty minutes to get to Ramthorpe Junior before the funfair opened its doors.

Val walked across to the table where she looked briefly at the photographs. Her long fingers hovered over the diary and Bree willed her not to open it. Their eyes met for a moment, and then she swiftly slid the diary into her open handbag. Bree could not believe what she was seeing! She opened her mouth to speak but the look on Val's face stopped her.

"Goodbye then," said Val, clutching her handbag close to her chest.

"G...oodbye," stammered Bree.

There was silence for a minute. Then, after checking to see that they were out of earshot, Honey said, "She is the most dreadful person I've ever met."

"And a rotten thief," muttered Bree, still reeling.

"And that awful man," Honey added, stacking the empty cups. "Val had the cheek to say Bustopher was smelly! I hope we *don't* see them again soon."

In her pocket Bree felt her phone begin to buzz. It was a text message from her mum.

Come home. Mr Deanheart is on his way.

An unwelcome image formed in her head – her mother sipping tea and bragging whilst she showed off all Bree's swimming certificates.

"I've got to go," she said. "Mr Deanheart is on his way to see me. We're never going to get to the library at this rate."

"Don't panic," said Honey. "Just get back here as quickly as you can. He must really want you on his team."

"We won't make it before the funfair opens," said Sandy, tapping his watch. "We've only got fifteen minutes."

Honey sat on the arm of the settee and ruffled his hair.

"It'll be fine. We'll stay here with Annie, help her tidy up," she said. "Don't look so worried, Bree. I'm sure Mr Deanheart won't bite."

"It's not him I'm worried about. It's The Book."

As she got up to leave, she spotted car keys on the coffee table and her heart sank.

"Val and Norrie won't get far without those," she said, picking them up, "I'm going out anyway, I'll catch them."

She hurried along the corridor to the landing, where she heard voices drifting up from the level below. She strained to listen, only able to make out the odd word here and there.

"Bree McCready...Must get it back..."

Curious, she leaned over the banister and saw the side of Mr Deanheart's face. He was talking to Uncle Norrie.

"Knows too much...urgent business..."

The keys slipped from Bree's hand and clattered to the ground. The voices stopped and Bree held her breath.

"Who's there?!" bellowed Norrie.

She composed herself.

"It's only me," she said, making her way down the stairs. "You left your keys at Mrs Hooten's."

"Ah, Miss McCready," said Mr Deanheart, his face breaking into a wide smile, "I stopped this kind gentleman to ask for directions to your flat."

Bree handed Norrie the keys. His mouth curled into a gormless grin.

"I'd better get back to Val. She doesn't like to be kept waiting. Women, eh?"

He pressed the 'down' button, and the lift doors juddered open. Norrie stepped inside, the doors closed, and he was gone.

"I live on the top floor," said Bree, "it's only another two flights so we can take the stairs."

Mr Deanheart smiled. "After you."

Bree could feel him watching her every step as she led the way up to her flat.

Who was he? He seemed to know Uncle Norrie, and yet they had acted like strangers when she had appeared. As they passed flat 7B, the words from Annie's diary rang loudly in her head. *Scared for my Sandy...*

When Bree opened her front door she was met by the smell of homemade apple squares. Bustopher was circling restlessly in the hallway.

"Hey there," she whispered, bending to rub his ears. "It's safe to go back to Sandy's, the wicked witch is gone."

"My, my, something smells delicious," said Mr Deanheart as Bree led him up the hallway to the living room.

Madeleine McCready was kneeling beside the coffee table, sorting through some of Bree's swimming certificates. When she saw them, she leapt up.

"Hello sweetheart," she said, her face beaming. "And Tomas! How nice to see you."

Mr Deanheart gave Madeleine's hand a firm shake.

"It's been such a long time," he said, "and you haven't aged a single bit."

Madeleine blushed and he smiled at her, his eyes disappearing almost entirely behind the thick lenses of his spectacles. Bree wondered for a moment how someone so shortsighted could have ended up as a P.E teacher.

"Look what I found," said Madeleine, with a giggle.

She held out an old school photograph and pointed to a boy in the front row with a serious expression. Bree had seen this picture before.

"Mr Deanheart was only at our school for a short time," Madeleine explained, "but I remember him well. He hung around with your Dad for a while."

Mr Deanheart walked over to the mantelpiece and picked up a swimming trophy.

"I'm very impressed with your daughter's achievements. It's no wonder she gets called Flipper."

"That's one of my favourites there," said Bree.

She pointed to a shiny, silver medal the size of a large coin on the coffee table. As Mr Deanheart leaned over to pick it up, his glasses slid off the end of his nose and landed with a plop at his feet. He panicked, trying to conceal his face with one hand whilst grappling for his glasses with the other.

"Let me help you," said Madeleine, reaching for them.

"No, it's quite all right," he laughed, swatting her hand away.

He put his glasses back on and smiled sheepishly.

"I'm as blind as a bat without them," he said.

"I'll make a cuppa, shall I?" asked Madeleine. "Please, take a seat, Tomas."

"That would be lovely," he said, making himself comfortable.

The clock above the mantelpiece read 9:55am. Bree realised he was in no hurry to go – she would have to make her excuses and leave soon.

"Bree! Could you come and give me a hand?" called Madeleine.

On her way to the kitchen her phone beeped with a message from Sandy.

Where R U?!

"Tomas is nothing like I remember from school, I always found him very strange," whispered Madeleine, when Bree joined her. "He's actually quite charming."

"S'pose so," shrugged Bree, glancing up at the clock. "Mum, I won't be able to stay long. I've made plans with Sandy and Honey."

"That's fine," she said vaguely. "Now could you put some biscuits on a plate for me while I take this tea through?"

Bree opened the cupboard and was instantly attacked by an avalanche of biscuits and cakes. She picked up a packet of Custard Creams and crammed the rest back in, slamming the wonky door shut before they could fall out again. She was startled when she turned to see Mr Deanheart watching her from the doorway.

"You gave me a fright, Sir."

A shaft of bright sunlight came through the window. The way it reflected off his glasses made it impossible for Bree to see his eyes. Nevertheless, something in his expression made her scalp come alive.

She picked up the plate of biscuits and smiled at him. His expression slackened and for a fleeting second Bree thought she saw someone she knew. The kitchen ceiling seemed to lower and the walls suddenly felt very close. The sun outside disappeared behind a cloud, casting sinister shadows onto the cupboard doors. Bree could smell something terrible as the kitchen darkened.

For a moment she felt as though she were outside her body looking in. Through the pounding in her ears she could hear Mr Deanheart talking, but it sounded as if he was very far away. The sound of dripping water echoed in her mind, and the kitchen floor felt slimy underfoot. She felt the brush of breath on her ear like a flapping moth, a voice whispery and urgent.

"Where is The Book?"

Her limbs were numb. She tried to shout for her mum, but her voice came out in a strangled croak, and the plate slipped from her grip, landing on the floor with a crash. The noise jolted her back to reality.

Mr Deanheart was staring calmly at her, which she thought was odd considering she was standing in the middle of a pile of Custard Creams.

"Oh dear," he said flatly. "You appear to have dropped the biscuits."

Madeleine came rushing through.

"Bree!" she flapped. "Here, let me give you a hand."

Bree was trembling, but she forced steadiness into her voice.

"No mum, I can manage," she said, avoiding eye contact with Mr Deanheart.

"Tomas, please get your tea before it gets cold," said Madeleine, unhooking the dustpan and brush.

When Madeleine turned her back, Mr Deanheart looked steadily at Bree. Then he ground one of the biscuits into a fine powder with the heel of his shoe. "I'll leave you both to it then," he smiled and disappeared into the hallway.

Bree had to get to the library. There was simply no time to go back for Honey and Sandy.

****

Even in the heart of drab old Rockwell the air was thick with the sharp scents of autumn. Crisp leaves twirled down from the trees and gathered in golden piles along the pavement. A chill lingered, although the sun was now well up in the world and trying its best to push through a low bank of clouds.

Bree took a deep breath, her lungs expanding with the cold air. She tightened her scarf and pulled her hood up. Fuelled by a desperate need to get The Book, she had left the flat in a hurry. Now, as she visualised opening the door to the library, she wondered why she had not stopped for Sandy and Honey, or at the very least brought something to protect herself.

The words in the diary and the incident with Mr Deanheart had put her on edge. With her senses heightened, every tiny noise made her jump.

Making sure she was not being followed, Bree turned into Turret Shore and ducked through a hole in the fence. The shortcut would take her through a tunnel of trees, which would eventually lead to the back of Ramthorpe Junior. In the shady undergrowth the cold made her teeth tingle, and her breath puffed out in white clouds before her. As she followed the muddy path she held the magic key so hard it left an imprint on her palm. When the music grew louder she knew she was nearing the school, and at last she saw the top of the Ferris wheel through the trees. An old, moss-covered wall surrounded Ramthorpe Junior. Bree clambered over a section where some stones had come loose leaving a gap, and dropped down into the playground.

She sidled along the wall and peered around the corner.

To her relief the funfair was still pretty deserted. Workers were setting up their stalls and only a handful of people wandered aimlessly. Bree considered her next move. She looked up and the sky changed from grey to sunny and back again in the blink of an eye, as if the weather could not decide what to do today. She knew the feeling.

She pulled her hood tight and hoped it would be enough to conceal her face from the CCTV. She ran up the steps, pushed the key into the keyhole, and without even having to turn it, the lock clicked and the door swung open.

The reception area was quiet except for the continual hum from the trophy cabinet, and the occasional gurgle of distant plumbing somewhere deep inside the walls. Bree stood at the foot of the stairs and a chill ran through her body. She reached for the banister and immediately pulled her hand back. Thick, frothy goo clung to her and she fought down a feeling of revulsion as she wiped it down her trouser leg.

What if that thing is waiting for me?

She pushed the thought from her head, took a deep breath and grabbed onto the handrail.

"Everything is fine," she muttered to herself. "I'll be home soon."

She repeated this mantra over and over, her resolve strengthening with every step she took. By the time she reached the first floor she felt ready to face anything. She peered cautiously through the glass in the library door and immediately noticed that all the tables and chairs were back in their original positions. Sandy's leather coat was draped over the back of the reading booth chair, the only evidence that they had been here.

She had a quick rummage through the Lost Property box

for some kind of protection, and pulled out a tatty umbrella, flimsy, but better than nothing. Somewhere, in some part of her brain, a tiny voice was screaming about what a bad idea this was. But she had no choice. She opened the door.

CHAPTER 7
A WOOZY EPISODE

Brandishing the umbrella, she flicked the switch on the wall. The fluorescent lights flared once, and then died. With her imagination in overdrive, strange shapes seemed to loom up at her from every shadowy corner.

Bree looked down into the playground. Some of the rides had opened for business but only a handful of locals had braved the early morning chill; a miserable looking dad trailing a ribbon of small, excited children, and a young woman with a dog that was barking at a paper bag flapping across the ground. The funfair did not look half as exciting in the daylight.

"This place gives me the heebie-jeebies," she muttered, as she threw the umbrella down onto a table. The lights suddenly flickered back on, but strained against the storm clouds that were gathering outside.

Bree rolled the rusty stepladder across the floor and lined it up with the middle of aisle 142. She looked up to see one of the books jutting out over the edge of the top shelf, the only clue that there was something hidden up there. She climbed the steps, balancing carefully on the narrow platform at the top and pulled out *Origami: A Beginner's Guide*, sliding the other books along until there was a space big enough for her to put her hand into. She reached in and felt around blindly for the little leather book.

Her first emotion on finding it was relief. She stared down

at the worn cover with the gold spiral spine and glassy screen, and in that moment her pulse started to race.

The Book was all that separated light from dark – and it was in *her* hands. The weight of her promise to keep it safe settled around her shoulders like chains. Only the thought of Sandy and Honey eagerly waiting for her stopped her from tossing it away forever. She rearranged the remaining books on the shelf to conceal the gap, and made her way back down the ladder.

Halfway across the room she remembered she had another reason for visiting the library. She found the Local History section and ran her finger along the spines until she came to a book called, *Sobstoan House: Past and Present*. She worked it loose from the row and slid it into one of the deep pockets of Sandy's coat.

A flash of silver on the carpet caught her eye. She felt the blood drain from her face as she recognised Algernon Hart's dagger. Bree forced the image of his last moments out of her head as she picked it up. The ivory felt cold in her sweaty palm. As her fingers tightened around the horn-shaped handle, the top clicked open. The inside had been hollowed out and a thin piece of paper had been wedged inside. She teased it out and carefully unrolled it.

Sketched on parchment as fragile as a dried leaf was a map. In the bottom left hand corner was an eight-point compass, and in the bottom right was a dark rectangle with a zigzag slicing through the top. She noted a signpost, four crudely drawn lines, a humpback bridge and a lot of trees.

A skull and crossbones were marked on a solid black circle to the right. Bree ran her finger over it and a strange shiver tiptoed up her spine.

She let go of one end and the map rolled back into a tight

cylinder. She put it in her pocket next to The Book, closed the lid of the dagger and hid it in Sandy's coat pocket.

****

As she stepped out into the playground the sunlight faltered. The wind was blowing everything sideways in angry gusts, and a bank of dark storm clouds was sailing in from the west. Walking quickly, nobody noticed her coming down the front steps, and soon she blended in with the rest of the crowd. Just as she reached the school gates the skies opened to release a downpour that turned the tarmac black. Using Sandy's coat as a cover, Bree sprinted through rain that fell so hard it looked like everything was melting away.

When she reached the corner of the road she saw something that stopped her in her tracks. An old woman was standing alone on the opposite pavement, staring blankly in front of her. She was ankle deep in a puddle and soaked to the skin, her long hair resembling rat's tails. As the wind flurried her hair across her face in an ever-shifting veil, her lips parted, and to Bree's horror a large black spider emerged from her black, gummy mouth.

Suddenly, a truck appeared on the road between them and when it passed, she was gone. Bree looked everywhere for her, but she had simply disappeared. The old woman had come straight from a nightmare.

Bree turned and ran with her head down, jumping over puddles that had gathered in the crumbling tarmac. She did not stop until she reached Rockwell Tower Block, where she pushed open the main door and threw herself inside. A bucketful of rain whipped through the opening behind her. She slammed the door closed and leaned against it, struggling to catch her breath.

The lift was out of order – probably a result of Norrie's considerable bulk – so she climbed the seven flights of stairs until she reached Sandy's front door. Shaking the water from his trench coat, she hung it on the stand in the hall, and made her way to the living room.

Honey stood looking out of the window as the rain lashed against the glass in waves. Sandy was on the edge of a chair, his expression tense and anxious. He leapt up when he saw Bree.

"You said you wouldn't be long!" he said, his voice tight and peevish. "Where the heck have you been?"

Honey turned, "Swimming, by the look of her!"

"Look what I've got," said Bree, pulling The Book from her pocket.

Honey's eyes shot open.

"You've got it!"

"That's not all I've got."

"Tell us then!" Sandy said.

"Your coat for starters. And, I'll tell you something else – all the tables and chairs were back in their correct positions in the library. It was as if nothing had happened."

"Wow, weird," he said, pushing his glasses up his nose.

"Your coat is hanging in the hall by the way," said Bree, pulling the map from her pocket.

"What's that?"

She handed it to him and he unrolled it carefully, holding the parchment out in front of them.

"It's a map."

"I think Algernon Hart meant to leave it behind," Bree said.

"Like a clue or something, it was tucked inside his dagger."

Sandy's mouth fell open.

"You found his dagger?"

Bree nodded, "It was just lying on the floor."

"Where is it now?" Honey asked.

"I hid it in Sandy's coat pocket."

Sandy looked horrified. "Have you any idea how much trouble you would have been in if someone had caught you with it?"

"I know, but I couldn't just leave it in the library, could I?"

"I don't suppose so."

"It might come in handy at some point," Honey suggested tentatively.

"There is no *way* I am carrying a knife!" snapped Sandy, letting the map roll back into a cylinder.

"Fine," said Bree, snatching it from him. "We'll leave it here then. Subject closed."

There was an awkward silence filled only by Annie clattering around in the kitchen. Bree flopped down into the settee and waited for the tension to ease.

She cleared her throat. "Something strange happened earlier."

"What kind of strange?" Sandy asked.

"I saw your Uncle Norrie and Mr Deanheart talking to one another."

Sandy shrugged.

"So?"

"Well, it looked like they knew each other but when they saw me they pretended they had never met. Then I was left alone with Mr Deanheart in my kitchen and he changed. I saw something...evil in him."

"What?" said Honey, arching her eyebrow.

"He seemed cruel, and then for a moment it felt like I had left the kitchen even though I was still there. I was somewhere dark and frightening. The floor was sticky and the smell..." Bree shuddered at the memory.

"That sounds familiar," said Sandy. "Like...Castle Zarcalat..."

"*Yes!* That's what I thought!" yelped Bree, relieved that she was not going crazy after all. "Then I remembered something Mr Deanheart said just after I saw Hallux Valgus coming out of the Hall of Mirrors. He said he had an important appointment to go to. What if that appointment was with Valgus?"

They took a moment to digest this suggestion.

"These can't all just be coincidences," said Honey. "Did you leave your mum up there alone with Mr Deanheart?"

Bree swallowed and nodded.

"I figured it would be alright. Harry was due home."

"Have you heard from her?"

A knot of fear threatened to choke Bree.

"No."

She sent a quick text message and they stared at the screen, waiting for a reply.

"Perhaps we should go up," said Sandy.

The phone beeped.

Mr Deanheart just left. See you later.
Mum X

"Thank goodness for that," said Bree.

"So, what do we do now?" Honey asked.

"I've got an idea," said Sandy.

****

Annie was up to her elbows in sudsy water, humming happily to herself as she ploughed through a mound of dirty dishes. She jumped with surprise when Bree appeared in the doorway.

"Don't creep up on me honeybun," she said sternly. "I've not got my ears switched on."

She fiddled with her hearing aid and her eyes narrowed as she looked at Bree.

"There's that look again," she said. "What do you want?"

"Oh, nothing, Mrs Hooten," she said, innocently. "I just wondered if you could use your psychic powers to help us with a school project?"

"Well, that depends," said Annie, drying her hands on a tea towel.

"It's this old map," said Bree, handing Annie the rolled up parchment. "I was hoping you could tell us something about it."

Annie carefully unfurled the paper and tilted her head.

"My, this is old," she said, holding it to her nose and inhaling slowly. "I can't say where it came from, the only way I could tell you more is if I had one of my woozy episodes. But I'm ever so tired and I think that might just finish me off."

"I understand," Bree said.

She reached for the map, but Annie snatched it back and held it close to her chest. "Maybe just this once," she said, with an impish grin.

"Thank you, Mrs Hooten. You're the best ever."

Bree, Honey and Sandy followed Annie to her bedroom.

On the bedside cabinet next to a lamp and a pair of reading glasses, was a tray covered with Scrabble pieces.

"Who were you playing Scrabble with?" asked Sandy.

"Sometimes I like to play alone," Annie chuckled. "That way I always win."

Outside the rain had stopped but the sky was tight with swollen clouds moving fast across it. Annie set a glass of water down and lay on the bed.

Sandy sat at the foot of the bed and laid his hand on one of her slippers.

"Remember, you don't have to do anything you don't want to," he said.

"I know pumpkin. But I feel drawn to this map, as if someone close to me has touched it."

"That would be me," smiled Bree, sitting down opposite Sandy.

"There are no guarantees that this will work," said Annie. "The more tired I am the more the frequencies muddle."

She propped herself up with some pillows and lifted the tray onto her lap. She pushed the Scrabble pieces up into the corner, unrolled the map, and anchored the curling edges with a candle and the glass of water. "I'm ready," she said.

Honey opened the window, then settled into the rocking chair with her legs crossed.

"I'll take some notes," she said, pulling a small notepad from her satchel.

With her pale, thin hands folded limply in front of her, Annie closed her eyes.

She began to breathe slowly at first, then rapidly. Bree started to feel very anxious. "It's happening quickly this time," she whispered, but Sandy silenced her with a finger on his lips.

Annie trembled all over, and began to speak...

> "Near our street a flimsy veil,
> Pass through onto a forest trail.
> A place where twice before you've been,
> Beneath your feet a sea of green,
> A world of beauty but beware,
> Hidden dangers lurk in there.
> Before the map fades you must flee,
> Or lost souls you'll forever be."

Honey wrote the riddle on a blank page, the ink glittery and smelling of strawberry. Annie started moving the Scrabble tiles around the tray in a methodical manner separating out the vowels until she had a neat row of letter a's.

"Strange time to start playing Scrabble again," whispered Honey, closing the notebook and putting it back into her satchel.

"Look," whispered Sandy, his voice taut with alarm. "Look at what she spelled out."

Along the bottom of the map, underneath the dark rectangle with the zigzag through it, Annie had laid out eight Scrabble tiles.

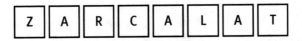

Chilly air blew in through the window and swirled around the room, moaning lightly in the corner.

"Castle Zarcalat," said Sandy, staring glumly at the map, "That must be where we're going."

"No surprise there then," said Honey.

"The riddle is telling us to go through the veil," said Bree. "Algernon Hart said the same thing before he got dragged through the floor... *Go through the veil. Stop them, before it's too late."*

"But why?" said Sandy. "*Why* would we put ourselves in such danger?"

There was a moment of silence. Nobody could think of an answer.

"We can't ignore it," said Bree, "None of us want to go back to Castle Zarcalat, but this *must* have something to do with The Book and the veil weakening. Algernon Hart seemed sure we could stop the two worlds colliding."

"And Gran's riddles are never wrong," Sandy added.

At the mention of her name, Annie's eyelids quivered ever so slightly then flickered open. Dazed, she looked around the room as though she had never seen it before.

"Welcome back, Gran," Sandy said softly.

Annie stared at him, confused.

"I'm so cold," she shivered, her voice nothing more than a dry, rattling whisper.

"Close the window!" ordered Sandy, pulling a blanket up over her.

"Sandy, I'm scared," whispered Bree. "I've never seen her this bad before."

He held the glass of water up to Annie's cracked lips, but she groaned and pushed him away.

"I'm afraid I don't feel very well," she croaked.

"That's it," said Sandy, "I'm calling the doctor."

****

Doctor Brown unfastened the Velcro band from Annie's arm and peered at her sternly.

"You have very high blood pressure, Mrs Hooten. I don't know what you've been doing, but I suggest complete bedrest for a few days."

Annie rolled her sleeve down and fastened the button.

"So no skateboarding then," she said, throwing Honey a cheeky wink.

"You've to do absolutely nothing, I'll come back in a few days to check on you."

"I suppose my hang-gliding lesson is out of the question," said Annie.

"I think it's time Super Granny Annie retired, don't you? Look after your Gran, son," he said to Sandy.

"I sure will," he said.

Annie smiled at him through half-lidded eyes as Sandy saw Doctor Brown to the front door.

"I'll go and put the kettle on," said Honey, putting a comforting hand on Bree's shoulder. "Will you be okay on your own with Annie?"

Bree nodded.

Annie had fallen back into a deep sleep. Bree watched her chest rise and fall steadily. Her eyes were motionless under lids dusted with mauve. The thought of leaving Annie alone made Bree feel dreadful, but The Book in her pocket was a reminder that there were more pressing matters to deal with.

She sent her mum a text message:

Mrs Hooten not well.
Please check on her l8r -

She put her phone on Annie's bedside table and nipped out to the hall to get the book about Sobstoan House. She hoped

Annie would feel up to a spot of reading when she felt better. Sandy and Honey followed her back into the bedroom, dressed for the outdoors.

"We need to go *now*," said Sandy, winding a long scarf around his neck.

Honey sat on the edge of the bed and pulled the blanket up over Annie's arms.

"Let's hope the riddle will help," she said, patting her satchel.

Bree sat down beside her.

"It mentioned the veil being near our street but there wasn't much else."

She pulled The Book from her pocket and rested it on her knees.

"I think it's time."

Slowly, Honey unclasped the chain that held her half of the locket from around her neck. She let it swing for a moment, then slid the half-heart off the end. Bree took hers from its chain, and snapped the pieces together.

She felt a prickle of excitement as she held the locket over the heart-shaped indentation in the cover of The Book. She pressed it into the slot and there was a little click. There was a moment of stillness – no sound, no thoughts, no breath – then the locket lit up.

There was no turning back.

CHAPTER 8
THE CHASE

The locket darkened with each rhythmic throb until it flared a bright, incandescent red. The screen filled with a milky swirl of blue mist. Bree felt a sudden urge to run, but curiosity chained her to the bed. Random letters eventually organised themselves into six neat rows. Bree read the words aloud...

> **Trust in me, do not dismay,**
> **Hold me tight I'll lead the way.**
> **Start off at the railway track,**
> **And very soon you'll travel back**
> **To find a cross of coloured glass,**
> **And then a clue engraved in brass.**

"It doesn't really give us much to go on," said Honey.

"At least we have a starting point," replied Bree, as she watched the letters fade. Sandy sighed and ran his fingers through his hair.

"We could just ignore it," he ventured.

"Eh, how exactly?" asked Honey.

"Remember the first time? Agora Burton said if we couldn't accept all seven wishes we should ignore the first and forget The Book ever existed."

"How can you even suggest that?" shrieked Bree, scarlet with outrage.

Sandy held her gaze, his eyes burning.

"Maybe I don't want to go through it all again! Maybe I don't want to die! Maybe I'm *scared!*"

Bree softened.

"We're *all* scared," she said. "But the Scrabble tiles have spelled it out for us loud and clear. Castle Zarcalat is where we need to go. Something terrible is happening, and we're the only ones who can stop it. So, we start off at the railway track and look for a glass cross like the wish says."

"Who would have guessed it?" Sandy snorted. "A shy swat, a psycho rebel and a lanky nerd saving the world for the third time."

"Looks can be deceiving," said Honey, with a smile. "We're special, just accept it. Let's leave the everyday stuff to dull people like airhead Renshaw."

The book throbbed insistently in Bree's hand. She peered closely at the fading words, trying to absorb them before they disappeared altogether.

"This wish looks quite straightforward."

"Bree, you ought to know by now, that book is never straightforward," said Sandy in exasperation.

He was right, but there was nothing to do now but get on with it.

"I've asked my mum to keep an eye on your Gran," she said, with more assurance than she felt. "Come on, let's go."

****

The lift arrived with a creak and a groan. The doors opened and Bree stepped inside. It smelled stale, and there was an empty crisp packet and a discarded dummy in the corner. Bree pushed the 'down' arrow button but nothing happened.

"Hurry up," groaned Honey, pulling her jumper over her mouth. "It stinks in here!"

"I'm doing my best," said Bree, jabbing the button. "This lift is so temperamental!"

Finally the doors rumbled shut, and with a loud, rasping squeak the lift lurched into action and started its slow descent.

When they reached the ground floor there was a ping and the doors shuddered open. Honey leapt out and gave herself a hefty squirt of *Raspberry Rebel* perfume.

Sandy rubbed his eyes and sneezed.

"Sorry, Sandy, but that was the grimmest ride of my life."

"Okay, Okay!" barked Bree. "I live in a complete hellhole! We can't *all* live on the sunny side of the street."

She hadn't meant to sound so tetchy but Honey had hit a raw nerve. Honey lived in a clean, green world decorated with hanging baskets and neatly trimmed lawns – a world where children took riding lessons and travelled to school in fancy cars. The only decoration in Rockwell came from spray paint, and the only mode of transport came in the form of an unpredictable lift that smelled like a public toilet.

"Can I have my head back please?" asked Honey, looking wounded.

"What do you mean?" growled Bree.

"Well, you bit it off."

Bree instantly regretted snapping at her. That was the thing with Honey; it was impossible to stay mad at her for long.

Outside the rain had stopped, but the air was still damp and the pavement was slick and gleaming.

They walked past the old memorial clock and the funfair, which was busier now. A short cut through Gillespie Gardens took them past the allotments on Turret Shore. After a while they stopped opposite a deserted play park.

"There's the track down there," said Bree, clutching The Book tightly.

All of a sudden a large, threatening cloud moved slowly across the sky, and the moon appeared from behind it. In a few hours it would be out in full.

"Looks like it's going to rain again," said Sandy, but Bree's attention had been drawn to the play park, and the big tyre swing with the bark chippings strewn underneath.

A lone man sat swinging slowly back and forward as he watched them.

"Who's that?" she asked, her grip on The Book tightening.

"Dunno," replied Honey. "But I reckon he's a bit old for swings."

"I was thinking the same thing."

The man stood up and walked towards the gate, his heavy steps crunching on the bark. He was tall and muscular with long hair that covered his eyes. A grizzle of grey whiskers shadowed his face.

"He is giving me the creeps big time," Sandy said, out the side of his mouth.

"I think we should go," Honey said, her voice low.

As the man moved onto the pavement, Bree realised with horror that he had a crossbow in his hand. He reached behind his shoulder and pulled an arrow from a bag. Bree swiveled round and grabbed Honey and Sandy.

"RUN! RUN!" she screamed, against the snarling wind.

The arrow made a hot, buzzing sound as it travelled through the air. Bree barely had time to duck before it flew past her ear. She ran as fast as she could, Sandy beside her, long legs striding out, arms pumping.

"He's right behind us!" wailed Honey.

Bree stole a quick glance over her shoulder and saw the man sprinting effortlessly, his eyes focused on them while he reloaded his weapon with ease.

They ran blindly at first, but soon The Book took on a life of its own. It tugged in Bree's hand, the energy almost dragging her off her feet. She grabbed onto it with both hands, the wish now controlling her. It yanked her sharply to the left.

"This way!"

After a few twists and turns they scrambled down a steep embankment that led into a narrow, graffiti covered underpass, lit only by a row of evenly spaced lights. Halfway through, the lights came to an abrupt end, plunging them into complete darkness.

"I can't see a thing!" cried Sandy.

Bree held The Book above her head.

"Follow the glow from the locket!"

She looked back to see the man silhouetted against the arch of the underpass. Just as they reached a curve in the tunnel another arrow fell to the ground behind them.

They ran for what seemed like miles, until at last they burst out into open air, hurling themselves down a grassy slope and landing in a heap at the bottom. Bree stuffed The Book into her pocket and clambered to her feet. She peered over the top of the embankment for any sign of the man with the crossbow.

Sandy sat up, his glasses dangling from one ear and a smudge of dirt across his cheek.

Bree straightened and scanned the area. The canal stretched out ahead, a mottled quilt of sunlight and shifting shadows. Two ducks paddled side-by-side leaving a little triangle in their wake. In the distance a woman and a small child threw bread from a bridge. There were two houseboats moored to the bank but no sign of life onboard. The adrenaline rush was draining away, leaving Bree hollow with exhaustion. She leaned heavily against a tree.

The arrow came from nowhere, slamming into the bark an inch from her head. The ducks took off, their panicked wings beating the air. Paralysed by shock, Bree could only stare as the feather fletching vibrated with the force. Honey pulled her down just as another arrow sliced the air in two.

"Stay down!"

Hiding amongst the bushes, Bree could hear the thrum of the bowstring and the thud of arrows – one after the other – meeting wood or splashing into the water near them. She pulled The Book from her pocket and willed it to do something. The words on the screen were almost gone but power still surged through the cover. The wish was far from over.

The arrows stopped as suddenly as they had started, plunging them into an eerie stillness.

"He must've run out of ammunition," whispered Honey.

Sandy struggled halfway into a sitting position; fear pulsed from his face. Bree listened hard, every bit of her ready to run. All she could hear was the distant caw of a crow and the empty branches knocking overhead.

"We need to be somewhere busy," she said. "Safety in numbers."

"What about the High Street?" suggested Sandy. "He's not going to kill us in front of loads of people."

Bree was not so sure, but she nodded anyway.

She crept forward on her hands and knees and peered out cautiously from between the leaves. The man was on the other side of the canal, his yellow eyes sweeping around like searchlights.

"He's still there!" she hissed, crouching low. "We're going to have to crawl."

Suddenly The Book started twitching again, tugging at Bree's hands like an impatient child.

"It's pulling me this way," she said. "It's never done this before."

"But that's the wrong way," said Sandy, confusion clouding his eyes. "The High Street is over *there!*"

"The wish said we're going to travel back," Bree said. "I can't control it, we're just going to have to trust it, we have to go in that direction." She shoved The Book deep inside her pocket and began to crawl. Honey and Sandy followed.

They scuttled on all fours along ground choked with fallen leaves, ivy and rotten branches. Eventually they came to a fence with a stile. As Bree clambered over it she felt exposed, aware of the soft space between her shoulder blades – the perfect spot for an arrow to sink into.

"I can see signs of life up ahead," said Sandy, his face breaking into a wide smile.

Sure enough, through the shifting veil of leaves, Bree could see a cluster of shops and houses, and a few ragged columns of chimney smoke.

"I don't recognise it," she said, frowning. "We must be further away from Rockwell than I thought."

"I don't care where we are," said Honey. "Houses mean people and people mean safety."

They ducked into a side alley between two buildings and came out into a cobbled street. It was quaint and old-fashioned, the kind of place you rarely saw these days. Bree looked around and noticed a sign, which read: *Puddock Square.*

It was completely deserted except for a handful of pigeons scrabbling around for crumbs.

"So much for safety in numbers," said Sandy. "Where is everyone? It's Saturday! You'd think people would be out and about, we haven't seen a soul all morning."

"What's The Book doing?" asked Honey.

Bree pulled the The Book from her pocket, but the locket was a weak colour and the throb was faint.

"We must be close," she said.

"Let's look for a cross made from glass," said Sandy. "That's what the wish said we should do."

"Or something brass with an engraving on it," Honey added.

A splinter of sunlight pierced the clouds and slanted straight towards a tiny shop front. Above the front door, a rectangle of vibrant blue glass was lit in the middle with a diagonal white cross.

"Look! Over there," squealed Honey. "I think we've found it."

They walked across the cobbles until they reached number 9, Puddock Square. The shop looked as if it was holding its breath, squeezed between a grotty launderette and a hairdressers with a red and white awning outside. The locket stopped throbbing, signaling the end of the first wish. "This must be our destination," said Bree, slipping The Book back into her pocket.

"It's open for business," said Honey.

A rusty sign swung in the breeze. Bree peered at the faded lettering.

"The shop is called, 'Hart and Soul'."

"It looks ancient," said Sandy.

Bree studied the row of shops.

"They all do," she said. "I mean check out the hairdresser next door."

Honey made a sound, somewhere between a sputter and a groan.

"It looks like they specialise in granny perms and lavender rinses."

The hairdresser's door opened and a young girl came out, dressed in electric blue leggings and a vest. Music drifted above, something about getting into the groove. She stopped to admire her new style in the window; heavily hair-sprayed streaks that resembled a pile of dry sticks. But the girl seemed satisfied. She pulled on a pair of fingerless gloves and strutted past, the smell of her perfume mixing with the whiff of setting-lotion and cigarette smoke.

"Eighties alert!" said Honey, "If they did my hair like that I'd want a refund."

"My mum reckons the 1980's are coming back into fashion," Bree giggled.

There was a distant rumble of thunder, an ominous reminder that danger was not far away.

"Let's go in," she said.

The shop was warm after the chilling damp outside. There was a strong smell of stale tobacco smoke and mouldy paper.

"Hello?" Honey shouted, but nobody answered.

Bree closed the door behind them.

"This entire place is like a ghost town," said Sandy, as he squeezed past a rail of vintage clothing.

The shop was bulging at the seams. Every available space was filled. On one wall, floor-to-ceiling drawers were crammed full. Old books, the sort with marbled paper and gold edges, were piled in all directions, on the floor and up every wall. Some were piled so high it looked as if they might curl over and crawl down the opposite wall like ivy. One bookcase was filled with a variety of dolls with eggshell eyelids that closed when you laid them flat. Above them hung a stuffed seagull, hovering in the new breath of air. Sandy tripped over a tartan bag with black pipes sticking out of it.

"Where is the owner? I mean anyone could just walk in here and take what they liked without paying."

Honey looked at him like he had lost his mind.

"Who is going to want *anything* from this shop?" she said, running her finger along a dusty ledge.

When she came face to face with a stuffed cat, Honey nearly jumped out of her skin. It was glued to a wooden plinth and the brass plaque read: LUCKY: SADLY MISSED.

"You don't look very lucky to me," she said.

"Is that a brass engraving?" asked Bree. "It could be our next clue."

Sandy picked up a Rubik's cube from a dusty shelf next to a pile of neatly stacked comics. His eyes lit up as they settled on the front page.

"Now *this* is more like it," he grinned, flicking through the pages. "Issue one of *Hoot* from 1985."

Honey looked at it, unimpressed.

"How can you get enthusiastic about a stupid comic?"

Sandy held it up to her face and shook it.

"It's like, brand new. You'd think it had been bought yesterday. Look! It's even got the free pencil topper still inside."

Honey shrugged and turned her attention to a row of glass bottles, lined up neatly along a high shelf. She blew on them, sending up a small cloud of dust, and then tilted her head to read the labels.

"Aloe, frankincense, sandalwood...Mort and Saffron would love this place."

She pulled out a little bottle, removed the stopper and sniffed the top.

"Valerian," she nodded. She read the label on the back.

"Soothing, calming, gives hope and freedom from grief."

Bree glanced around nervously.

"I don't think we should be touching anything."

Honey replaced the stopper.

"Judging by the dust it doesn't look like anyone has bothered with this shop for some time."

Bree nodded towards a wall display of various sized knives, some with heavy handles of dark wood, others with angry, serrated blades.

"I wouldn't want to mess with the owner."

Honey's eyes lit up as she studied a lethal-looking cleaver.

"Wow," she breathed, her eyes glinting dangerously.

Bree shook her head: it was typical of Honey to be totally fearless. Something pinned to the wall caught her eye – a head and shoulders sketch of a young boy, his face composed of swiftly drawn lines. There was a haunted quality to his expression as though whoever had drawn this had known something about his past, or foreseen some tragic future.

"Check this out!" squealed Sandy, picking up the receiver of an old fashioned phone and holding it to his ear. "A genuine antique."

"Who still uses them?" said Honey, pushing her finger into a hole and turning the dial as far as it would go.

It whirred loudly as it returned to the start.

"Someone does," said Sandy, looking impressed. "This one

actually works."

He replaced the receiver with a heavy clunk.

"I told you the eighties were coming back," smiled Bree.

She picked up a leather-bound journal. When she opened it, she saw that the pages were blank, except for one short entry, written in black ink that had faded to grey.

> June 29th 1937.
> Rained all day. Nothing much happens around here.
> I miss home.

She was interrupted by a loud cough. She spun round, slamming the book shut with a puff of dust.

CHAPTER 9
WRITTEN IN THE STARS

"Are you always such a wee neb?" asked a man with a soft, Scottish accent.

Bree felt her cheeks sizzle.

"I'm s...sorry," she stammered, her voice coming out in a croak. "I..."

He stepped forward with a theatrical flourish.

"Och, everything in that diary happened many moons ago."

His white hair, although long, had receded from his forehead and the fleshy bags under his eyes sagged loosely as if his skin was one size too big for him. He had a goatee beard and wore a silver earring in the shape of a teardrop.

"Keep a diary and one day it will keep you," he said, as he took it from Bree, and placed it back on the pile.

Honey stretched out her hand and her bangles jangled musically.

"I'm Honey, and this is Bree, and Sandy. I hope you don't mind us coming into your shop."

The man shook her hand firmly and laughed.

"Not in the slightest. I was just footering aboot in the back room, so I didnae hear you come in. My name is William Hart. Nice tae meet you all."

"You have some...*interesting* collections," said Bree.

"Aye," William nodded. "I like tae collect things when I travel. The shop's a bit of a guddle at the moment. Everything's tapsalteerie."

Bree, Sandy and Honey exchanged puzzled glances.

"You would get on well with my Gran," said Sandy. "Her house looks a bit like this."

"She even has a diary like yours," added Bree.

William smiled and gestured for them to follow him over to the bay window where there were four mismatched chairs, and a glass-topped table with bowed legs. On the tabletop there was a pipe in an ashtray, a plate of golden nut brittle, and a half-finished cup of tea. He peered out the window at the empty square.

"It's deid out there," he said sadly. "Used to be hoatching on a Saturday morning. It's a bit dreich today, mind."

Honey tossed her satchel on the floor and settled into an armchair. William sat next to her, and put his feet up on the table. He caught Bree staring at his worn tartan slippers.

"S'cuse my auld baffies," he smiled. "I pretty much live in these."

Bree sat down, but leapt up as her hand encountered something furry and alive.

"A rat!" screeched Sandy, throwing himself into a chair, and lifting his feet off the floor.

William laughed as he reached over and lifted the pipe out of the ashtray.

"Dinnae mind Douglas, he's just a nosey wee rascal."

Bree picked up the small black and white rat and his wormy tail coiled around her fingers.

"He's your pet?" she said, admiring the little black-button eyes and whiskery nose.

"Aye," William said fondly. "He likes to coorie in."

"He's very cute," said Bree, tickling Douglas's chin.

He squirmed free and leapt to the floor, disappearing under William's chair.

"Rats are the royalty of the rodent world," he said, striking a match. "They're much cleaner wee beasties than people give them credit for. They make braw pets."

"If you say so," muttered Sandy.

There was a sizzle as William lit his pipe. Wrapped inside a cloud of thick, bluish smoke he disappeared for a moment.

"Do you have to do that?" Sandy groaned. "The dust and rat fur is already playing havoc with my chest."

"Dinnae get yersel in a fankle, laddie," he said, setting his pipe down in the ashtray.

Smoke curled out of the bowl and teased Sandy's nostrils.

"You're not supposed to smoke in buildings anymore," he said.

"Since when?" asked William. "Jings, it's my only pleasure in life. What's the world coming to?"

"Smoking is bad for your health," protested Sandy, wafting his hands to clear the air.

"My boy, I'll be sixty-one in a couple of months, why on earth would that worry me?"

"Well, because you won't see sixty-two at this rate."

William narrowed his eyes and drew on his pipe.

"Are you always so crabbit?" he asked, his warm smile taking the edge off the insult.

"Crabbit?"

"Bad tempered! Here, have some peanut brittle," he said, nodding towards the plate of cakes in the middle of the table.

"Are you actually trying to kill me?" Sandy said. "I'm allergic to nuts."

"You'd better stay away fae me then!" chuckled William.

"He's being serious," said Honey, pushing the plate away. "One whiff of those and he'll blow up like a pufferfish."

"Crivvens. I've heard everything now," muttered William.

"It's one of the most common allergies actually," Sandy sniffed.

William placed his pipe in the ashtray and sat back so his hair stuck up over the top of the chair. Bree watched the smoke rise lazily all the way up to the domed ceiling, where her gaze settled on a spectacular mural of a night sky complete with an astrologer's wheel, showing the twelve signs of the zodiac revolving around Earth. At the centre was a large circular diagram with a smaller circle inside. There were lots of numbers around the outside and something that looked like a spider's web in the middle. William leaned over the side of his chair and flicked a switch. The ceiling came alive with tiny twinkling lights, which showed the various constellations.

"You're looking at my natal chart," explained William. "It's a map showing the positions of the planets at the exact date and time of my birth."

"It's amazing," Bree sighed, studying the intricate detail. "I feel like I'm floating in space."

"It's not quite the Sistine Chapel, but I'm very proud of it."

"It's awesome," said Honey, crossing her legs. "What are those?"

She pointed to where ten symbols had been carefully painted in silver against the dark blue background.

"Those are astronomical symbols," said William. "Each one represents a planet in our solar system. Earth is the circle with the cross at the centre."

"I've seen these before, I'm really interested in the solar system."

"Aye? Well you must share my interest in astrology then," said William. "I'm a Capricorn, hard-working and reliable, but also a bit of a stubborn old goat."

"I'm a Pisces," said Honey. "Dreamy, funny and honest. My moon is in Virgo so I have the ability to act and take initiative."

William looked at her, impressed.

"What is a typical Pisces like then?" Bree asked, staring up at the ceiling.

"They're gallus souls," he replied. "Trying to grasp the Pisces spirit is like trying to hold water in your hands. Pisceans like to be free to follow their own rules."

"You can say *that* again," giggled Bree, dodging a playful cuff from Honey.

"They make braw pals though," William added. "Friendly, imaginative and intuitive."

Sandy couldn't control himself a moment longer.

"*Surely* you don't believe all this mumbo-jumbo," he scoffed.

"I believe in fate, like our destinies are written in the stars. Perhaps there is a purpose to you being here that we dinnae yet ken aboot," William replied.

"I just don't like the idea of our life being mapped out for us," Sandy said coolly. "Like no matter what we do we'll end up the same at the end of it all. I prefer to think I can shape my future."

William considered this carefully.

"I ken what sign you are," he said.

Sandy folded his arms across his chest and jutted his chin out.

"Go on then," he dared.

William's eyes narrowed as he studied Sandy's face.

"Let's see," he began. "Nervous gestures, a taste for the dramatic, displays of moody behaviour, at times cynical and pessimistic..."

Sandy fidgeted awkwardly in his chair.

" ...and an inability tae sit on yer bahookie for more than five seconds!"

Sandy frowned grumpily.

"You're a Gemini!" William blurted.

"Spot on!" said Honey, clapping her hands eagerly. "June the ninth."

William puffed out his chest proudly and turned to Bree.

"When were you born, lassie?"

"July the seventh."

"Ah, a Cancerian. You are emotionally intense, secretive and sensitive. There is no end to the heroic sacrifice you'll show towards the folk you love."

From his top pocket he pulled out a fob watch and released a catch. The lid sprung open and he squinted to read the Roman numerals.

"You look familiar to me," he said to Bree. "An uncanny likeness to my niece, Mel. If you hang aboot for another wee while you'll get to meet her laddie. He's popping in for his dinner. Aboot your age I reckon."

As he snapped the lid shut, Bree saw that there was an inscription engraved around the outer rim, and she remembered instantly where she had seen it before.

"We met a man called Algernon Hart," she blurted.

William choked on a mouthful of smoke. He plucked the pipe from his mouth.

"Whit made you say that, lassie?" he asked, his eyes wide with surprise.

"Your surname," replied Bree. "And that watch. He had one just like it."

"Exactly *when* did you meet him?"

"Last night," said Honey. "In the library of our school."

"Are you related to him?" asked Sandy.

William put his pipe in the ashtray and sat back in his chair.

"I did have a very distant relative called Algernon Hart. But it cannae have been the same man you met."

"Why not?" Bree asked.

"Well ya doolie!" roared William. "Not unless he was aboot two hundred years old."

"A hundred and two to be precise," said Bree. "But if you count the years he's been dead I guess that would make him around two hundred."

William's whole face changed, joviality replaced by confusion and fear.

"Whit did you just say?"

"The man we met was a ghost," said Bree.

William's eyes slid from Bree to Honey and then to Sandy. Their expressions stayed deadpan.

"You must think I'm doolally!" he said.

"I know what that engraving says," said Bree. "If I tell you will you believe me then?"

William nodded.

She took a deep breath.

"What really determines our futures are the actions of those who came before."

William clutched his chest, letting the watch fall to the floor.

"I told you..." Bree said calmly, "...we met the ghost of Algernon Hart. And he had that watch."

There was a long silence. Sandy picked up the watch and

inspected the engraving, fiddling with the catch. The chime of a Grandfather clock broke the silence.

"There's no point in ficherin aboot with it, it'll no open."

Sandy laid it down on the table, and William muttered grumpily to himself.

"Whit did he say to you, this Algernon Hart?"

"Mostly stuff about the lunar eclipse," replied Bree.

"I dinnae ken anything about a lunar eclipse."

"Oh come on, it's been all over the news," said Sandy. "It only happens once every two centuries. It's a big deal."

"I dinnae ken aboot it. All I ken is Algernon Hart was mad. He lost his entire family and died a bitter old man."

His eyes swiveled back to Bree. She felt a sudden and overpowering urge to unburden the weight of their secret onto him.

"And do you know *why* he was bitter?" she asked, reaching inside her pocket.

"No, Bree!" gasped Honey, grabbing her hand. "We don't know if we can trust him."

"I think he knows something. The wish led us here and he has Algernon Hart's watch."

Honey slumped in her seat with a resigned sigh. Sandy glowered at Bree, but she pulled The Book from her pocket and laid it on the table in front of William. He seemed lost for words, but quickly found his voice.

"You've no idea whit that book can do," he spluttered, recoiling from it as if it might explode.

"This isn't the first time we've seen it," said Bree. "We know perfectly well what it can do."

Outside the sun disappeared behind a cloud, sucking the colour from everything in the shop.

"Something tells me this isn't the first time you've seen this book either," Honey said.

"Ma heid's birlin," he muttered, "I cannae think straight."

"Well, we're not leaving until you tell us what you know," said Bree.

"You must be careful who you tell," he said, his voice dropping to a whisper. "Anyone who kens aboot this book will be in great danger."

"Trust me," she said. "I'm the Queen of Secrets."

William knitted his fingers together. He did not take his eyes off The Book for a moment.

"If you listen carefully, you can hear the whispers of your ancestors breathing from the pages. This book can take you by surprise," he said.

His words hung in the smoky haze. He had a faraway look in his eyes as if he was remembering something from a very long time ago. Not an entirely pleasant memory judging by his expression. Bree waited for him to continue, but he stayed silent.

"Tell us what you know about it," she probed.

A faint smile settled on his lips. He paused, his face relaxing a little as he slipped into a nicer memory.

"I was twelve years old and she was the bonniest thing I had ever seen. A red-haired angel standing on my doorstep. But she was beelin. Absolutely *furious!*"

"*Who* was?" asked Bree, leaning forwards in her chair.

"And *why*?" added Sandy.

"My family had taken her home from under her nose," William explained. "The law in those days meant a father couldnae leave property to his daughter. So my father inherited the little cottage from a distant cousin he had never even met."

"No wonder she was furious," Honey scowled.

Behind a cloud of smoke William's eyes narrowed.

"She visited me often but I had to keep her a secret, which was hard because her wee sister Charlotte – *Lottie* – liked tae blether."

"What does all this have to do with The Book?" Bree asked impatiently.

William puffed on his pipe.

"After a while she asked me if I could keep a very special secret. I told her she could trust me. She showed me a hiding place in the bedroom, a loose floorboard. Underneath it was *that* book."

He took a moment to compose himself before continuing.

"It was covered in stoor like it had been hidden there for years and years. Oh, and the pages wouldnae open. I remember thinking, *Whit use is a book that disnae open?*"

"And the heart locket?" Bree asked hungrily.

William's fingers tapped a thinking rhythm on the arm of the chair.

"*She* had the locket. Her father gave it to her before he died."

Bree's thoughts were flying around her head. William and the mystery girl had been in possession of The Book and the locket at the same time.

"So you know exactly what this book can do," she said, swallowing hard.

A memory seemed to weigh heavy on his mind.

"She was fifteen, I was twelve. We were just bairns! It seemed like the biggest adventure. How could we have known what was going to happen?"

"Her name," said Bree. "What was her name?"

William took a deep breath, as if saying her name was going to conjure up something that he was not willing to face again.

"Agora Burton," he finally said, "but I called her Aggie."

****

There was another rumble of thunder, closer than the last one and accompanied by a flash of lightning, which lit every dark corner of the shop.

"Were you followed here?" asked William, his eyes filled with terror.

"No. Maybe. I don't know!" Bree answered, grabbing The Book. "I thought we'd lost him."

"You have to leave," cried William, pulling himself out of his chair.

A whiplash of light flickered across the room, and he ran to the door, locked it, and turned the 'open' sign to 'closed'.

"Oh, this is very bad," he said, tugging on a cord at the window.

A dusty roller blind rattled down, closing out the last of the light.

"What's happening?" cried Honey, grabbing her satchel.

Outside, something heavy hit the door and the stained glass window exploded inwards in a shower of blue and white shards. The shop bell tinkled hysterically as a hot wind whipped through the shop, stealing their breath and scorching their skin.

"It's happening all over again!" Sandy wailed.

Something nagged at the back of Bree's mind, and she remembered being in Agora Burton's cottage when the same gust of hot air surged through the living room.

Suddenly, the knives broke loose from the wall display and flew past their heads. The seagull flapped and squawked, breaking free from the string and bashing off the walls in panic, and the stuffed cat, still glued to its plinth, swiped its free paw at it every time it got close. The dolls blinked with their half-moon eyelids crying, "Mama" over and over again. The tiny shop was alive with noise.

"How do we get out of here?" shouted Bree, dodging a large cleaver as it spun past her head and buried itself into the door frame.

William struggled against the force of the wind. "This way!" He stopped in front of a tall bookcase.

"What are you doing?" shrieked Sandy. *"Get us out of here."*

William ran a bony finger along the row of books until he reached one with a gold spine. He slid it out to reveal a hidden dial, which he turned this way and that with trembling fingers – five –eight –back to two –round to five – then all the way to nine.

"The combination corresponds to the letters on the phone dial," he explained hurriedly. "58259 spells out, Lucky, the name of my old cat."

A whirring noise sounded from inside the bookcase.

"Stand back," he ordered.

It swung outwards from the wall to reveal a dark space. The shop door handle started rattling, and a shadow spread out like a dark stain across the floor.

"Hurry!" he urged, pushing them inside. He thrust a box of matches into Sandy's hand.

"There's a paraffin lamp in the corner. That'll help light the way. You don't have far to go, but dinnae dawdle."

Sandy and Honey melted into the shadows.

"Where does this lead?" Bree asked.

"There's no time to explain," William wheezed. "Just follow the draught."

"What about you?"

"I'll be fine, just go."

Bree could smell stale tobacco and fear on his breath.

"I'm scared," she said, fighting back the hot sting of tears.

William held her face and smiled.

"I ken yer feart," he said, softly. "But dinnae greet. You're a Cancer child, resourceful and shrewd. You'll always be able to muster up bravery when someone close needs you to be strong."

She turned to go but William pulled her back.

"You'll need this," he said, thrusting the fob watch into her hand. "It'll help you…"

He fumbled around inside his cardigan pocket and pulled out a little black stone.

"This will help too."

"What is it?"

"It's my wee chuckie," said William. "But it's not any auld chuckie. When you give it a shoogle, you'll see what I mean."

Bree had just put it safely into her pocket, when a loud thump was followed by the sound of more breaking glass. William looked to the side and his grey face collapsed in despair.

"Keep a firm hold of that watch," he warned. "Goodbye."

And with that the bookcase closed and she was thrown into darkness.

CHAPTER 10
A HELPING HAND

Bree slid the fob watch into her jacket and fumbled around on the floor in the rough direction of the paraffin lamp. Something cold and speedy scuttled across the back of her hand and she let out a strangled squeal.

At last she found the lamp, picked it up and gave it a gentle shake. There was a sloshing sound.

"Good," she said. "It's full."

She removed the glass top, while Sandy lit a match and held the flame to the wick – it caught immediately, sending flickering, yellow light before them. They were at the beginning of a long, thin passageway with low brick arches spaced evenly along the way to support the ceiling. The ground was a dirt path, uneven and stony.

"Why on earth would William have a secret passageway in his shop?" asked Sandy, the feeble lamplight cloaking him in shadows.

"It's as if he knew he might need to escape from something," said Honey.

"Well, he hasn't, has he?" said Sandy, glancing back.

They were silenced by a muffled howl; a terrible sound that crawled under the sliver of space at the bottom of the bookcase.

Cold despair spread through Bree's veins. Part of her wanted to go back to save William, the other part – the part that won – told her to run. She pushed past Sandy, who was staring in horror at the shadow that was spreading up the thin strip of light around the bookcase.

"Follow me!"

"It's like a Pharaoh's tomb in here," whispered Sandy.

Honey pulled aside a large cobweb like a net curtain. "I don't think anyone has been along here for a very long time."

A gust of damp wind signaled that somewhere up ahead there was a way out.

"Come on, I think we're nearly there," said Bree, holding out the lamp and peering through the darkness.

She took another step and Sandy grabbed her arm.

"A brick wall," he said, pointing ahead. "It's a dead end, there's no way out!"

Bree tried to stay calm.

"William told us to follow the draught," she said evenly. "So there must be a door in here somewhere."

She ran her hand over the moss, feeling for a draught, anything that might indicate a loose brick or a secret door. But there was nothing.

"What now?" asked Honey. "We can't go back to the shop."

Suddenly a ghostly moan echoed around them. Sandy spun around, "Who's there?" he whimpered, putting his fists up, ready to fight.

"I don't think you'll get an answer," said Honey. "That was a pigeon."

Another coo floated down from above.

"If a pigeon can get *in* then we can get *out*," said Bree, swinging the lamp in a wide arc.

"But where's it coming from?" asked Sandy.

Bree spotted something on one of the walls, a large rectangle that stood out a shade darker than the brickwork. At first it looked like a damp patch but when she held the lamp closer she saw it was a fireplace. Feathers drifted down from high inside it.

"Over here! I think I've found our way out."

A metal grating blocked the wide fireplace, the bars thickly coated with rust. Bree thrust the lamp through them and yellow light spilled over onto the back wall.

"We need to pull this grate away," said Honey.

She started tugging on the bars, her face a knot of determination.

"Give me a hand!" she puffed.

Together they pulled until, with a shriek of metal on stone, it came away.

Bree brushed a wisp of spider web aside, ducked and took a step forward, but Sandy grabbed her hood and yanked her back.

"Ow. What are you doing?"

He dangled the lamp inside the chimney, and Bree saw that there was a long drop down into pitch darkness.

"Did your mother never tell you to look before you leap?" Sandy asked.

"I guess not," she gulped, stuffing her hands into her pockets. "Thanks."

She let out a yelp.

"What is it?!"

Honey laughed as a whiskery nose appeared from Bree's pocket. Douglas squirmed out, scampered up her sleeve and sat on her shoulder to give his ears a clean.

"Looks like we have a furry friend," she giggled.

"Just as well he didn't go in your satchel," said Sandy, putting the lamp on the ground, "what with the mousetrap in there."

He picked up some loose stones and tossed them into the fireplace. There was a long silence followed by some muffled plops.

"That sure is a long way down," Honey said, pulling a mirror from her satchel.

She leaned carefully inside the chimney and tilted it upwards.

"I can see light but it's a long way up."

Suddenly there was a commotion inside the chimney. Douglas shot down Bree's sleeve and wriggled inside her top pocket. Honey leapt back just as a pigeon burst out of the darkness. In its panic to escape, it knocked the lamp over. With a whoosh the paraffin caught light. An orange flame travelled along the ground like running water, blocking the passageway.

"We're trapped!" Honey cried.

Bree felt The Book spring to life. She pulled it from her pocket and stared down at the throbbing locket.

Three words had appeared in bold letters across the screen.

PLEASE OPEN ME.

Quickly, she lifted the front cover, and flattened the first page.

"Can you see anything yet?" asked Honey, holding up her satchel to shield them from the wall of heat.

"It usually takes a minute," answered Bree.

"We haven't got a minute!" said Sandy. "The fire is spreading."

Bree slid her hand underneath the page and through the churning mist at the centre, some words appeared.

Six wings doth this wish supply,
Soon like Hermes you will fly.
Use your thumb and fingers four
To change the speed at which you soar.
With feet back down on solid land,
The watch will lend a helping hand.

"Wings!" said Honey, twisting around to see her back. "It's a flying wish."

Bree closed The Book and put it back into her pocket. She felt desperately for the wings at her shoulders.

"I don't have any!"

"Hermes!" said Sandy. "The Greek God with winged sandals. Look at your feet!"

Bree stared down at her boots and watched as two buds appeared on the outside of either ankle, slowly unfurling into tiny wings.

"These are *never* going to be able to lift me up!" she said, her throat tightening against the smoke.

Sandy left the ground with an ungraceful wobble, ducking and diving, until he managed to straighten up and hover.

"Use your fingers!" he ordered. "Like this."

He squeezed his thumb and forefinger together until he had mastered the technique enough not to crash into the wall. The wings on his boots were flapping so fast they were a blur. Honey copied him, slowly rising off the ground. Each time she changed fingers she climbed higher. She pressed her little finger and thumb together and rocketed towards the ceiling, narrowly avoiding bumping her head.

"I've got it!" she said, swooping back down. "Fingers for

speed, body for steering!"

She peered up inside the chimneybreast, tilted her upper half to the right, and with a minor adjustment to her fingers she disappeared.

"Come on, Bree!" said Sandy, "You'll have to try."

He jumped off the edge and shot upwards, leaving Bree alone in the intense heat and choking black smoke. She closed her eyes, pressed her thumb and middle finger together and stepped backwards into the fireplace.

For a terrifying moment she was not sure whether she was falling or rising. She bounced painfully off the soot-covered sides of the flue a few times, before she popped out the top of the chimney like a cork. Honey grabbed her ankles to stop her from soaring too high, and Bree let her fingers hang loose, immediately plummeting towards a flat section of roof and landing on her bottom with a bump.

"That was fun!" laughed Honey, her face bright with excitement.

Bree rubbed her backside, and looked down at her feet to see the wings shrivel and disappear. Inside her pocket The Book stopped throbbing.

"How are we supposed to get down?" she said.

Chimney pots and a couple of old-fashioned TV aerials were spaced out intermittently, and on either side of them, the roof sloped down towards the pavement.

"Follow me," said Honey. A few slates were loose and the moss made walking slippery, so they moved carefully. From somewhere in the distance they heard sirens, and as the sound grew nearer, Bree glanced back and saw thick black smoke billowing from the chimney.

"Oh no. We don't stand a chance!"

Honey turned to look, but lost her footing, and rolled down the roof. She made a last desperate grab at the gutter, before disappearing from view.

Bree and Sandy were struck dumb. For what felt like hours, they stood perfectly still, until Sandy lay on his stomach and moved slowly to the edge.

Bree did the same, and forced herself to look down. Honey was inside the red and white awning over the hairdressers, a tangle of long limbs and blonde hair.

Suddenly, to their immense relief, she waved up to them and then slid to the ground in one lithe movement.

"The shop is well and truly alight!" she called up to them, tying back her hair with a red ribbon that she'd plucked from her pocket. "We should leave before the fire engines arrive!"

"Any sign of ladders?" Sandy shouted.

Honey shook her head.

"No! You're going to have to jump!"

"I'm heavier than Honey," said Sandy. "What if the awning rips?"

Bree chewed her thumbnail as she considered their options. They were going to be in big trouble if they got caught. Nobody would believe their story about how the fire started.

"Give me your scarf," she said.

Sandy unwound it from around his neck and handed it to her. She tied one end firmly around a chimney pot and threw the other end over the edge of the sloping roof.

"Hold on to this and walk down the roof, then dangle as far as you can," she instructed. "The awning should break your fall."

Sandy nodded, and then grabbed the scarf, giving it a quick tug to test how secure it was.

"See you on the ground," he said.

He leaned back and walked down the roof tiles. When he reached the guttering he dropped over and hung from the end of the scarf. His feet were almost touching the awning.

"Atta boy!" cheered Honey, punching the air. "Now let go. It's just like a big hammock."

Sandy fell the short distance, landing safely inside the canopy. The roof rumbled beneath Bree's feet, and she looked back to see a great tongue of crimson fire shoot out of the chimney. The smoke was beginning to choke her. She grabbed the scarf and lowered herself over the edge. The sirens were getting closer and people had started gathering nearby to see what was going on. They didn't seem to notice her dangling helplessly.

"Hurry up!" Honey shouted, as the fire engines turned the corner into Puddock Square.

Bree let go and fell backwards. She landed inside the canopy, bounced and rolled straight out again, landing in a heap at Sandy's feet. There was an explosion of breaking glass and a collective gasp of horror from the growing crowd, as flames spewed from the shattered window of 'Hart and Soul', filling the street with sparks and clouds of smoke. Honey pulled her up, and they took to their heels.

They ran until they stopped to catch their breath at the stile.

"Douglas! We'll have to let him go," said Bree, reaching inside her top pocket to lift him out. She gasped in horror when her fingers found a tiny pile of stick-dry bones.

Honey threw her hands to her mouth.

"Oh, poor little thing!"

"It must have been the heat of the fire, or the fall," said Sandy.

"It can't have been either," said Bree. "I mean my pocket is still intact and even if he had been burned, there would still be some fur and skin left. It's like he's been dead for years."

"Weird," said Sandy.

They buried the bones under a willow tree and left a little pile of wild flowers on top.

"What now?" Honey asked.

Bree pulled the fob watch from her jacket pocket.

"The wish said this would offer us a helping hand."

She lifted the catch and the lid sprung open. Tilting the face to the light she studied the hands carefully.

"I can't see anything obvious," she said, handing it to Sandy.

"It's keeping the right time," he said. "Which is amazing considering how old it is."

He turned it over carefully.

"Hmm, no hidden compartments, no secret messages."

"What about the engraving on the rim?" said Honey. "Remember the first wish said there was a clue engraved in brass? Maybe it wasn't Lucky the cat after all."

Sandy angled it so that it caught the light. The inscription looked brighter than before.

"What do you make of this?" he said.

Bree peered closely.

What really determines our futures are the actions of those who came before.

"Some of the letters are glowing," she said. "It looks like someone has given the watch a polish but forgotten to buff all of the letters."

Suddenly the watch burst into life with a whirr of rusty cogs. They watched as both hands moved slowly together until they became a single arrow at 12 o'clock.

"I think this might be our helping hand," Bree said.

The arrow moved erratically around the face in an anti-clockwise direction, ending up back at the XII before starting through the entire, jerky process again.

"Perhaps it's a compass," Honey suggested.

Sandy scratched his head dubiously.

"It's too random," he said. "The movements have no meaning."

He tilted the watch, and Bree could see that the arrow was stopping at one glowing letter before moving onto the next.

"The arrow starts at 12 where the letter H is engraved," she said.

Honey pulled the notepad and pen from her satchel and wrote down the letter H.

The arrow stopped for a moment at the top of the face before moving round to the numeral XI.

"Next are the letters E and A," said Sandy and Honey scribbled them down. "Then D."

They carried on like this until the arrow had moved full circle around the perimeter of the watch. Honey jotted down the last three letters – ORE – that were beside the Roman numeral I. She glanced down at her scribbled note and smiled broadly.

"So there *was* a secret message after all," she grinned, holding up the notepad.

"Head to Turret Shore," said Bree.

CHAPTER 11
THE SLOPING OAKS

They walked back the way they had come, stopping next to the allotments on Turret Shore. The autumn sun had burnt away the clouds leaving the sky sharp and blue. On a day like this it was difficult to imagine that the world might come to an end.

"Well here we are," said Sandy.

Nothing was out of the ordinary. Sycamore leaves danced across the pavement, trying to escape from a man wielding a leaf blower, who was trying his best to steer them into one big pile. A rubbish truck churned at the end of the road, and in the allotments an old man was digging over his patch of soil.

"Do we just wait here for something to happen?" asked Honey.

"I suppose so," said Bree.

"Are you sure we're in the right place?" said Sandy, sounding uncertain. "I mean there isn't another Turret Shore somewhere else?"

Bree stared at the street sign, which had been screwed to the wall. For a moment she thought she was seeing things. The thick black letters that made up the words TURRET SHORE were twitching like iron filings under a magnet. She blinked hard and looked again. The letters started moving, shuffling around the white background. The two R's at the centre of TURRET overlapped while the rest of the letters came together in a regimental fashion.

"Look," said Bree. "Look at the sign!"

They watched in slack-jawed amazement as the letters rearranged themselves into a neat row that read HOUR STREET.

Honey pulled the notepad through the toothy gap in the zip of her satchel.

"Hour Street!" she exclaimed, tapping the page where she had scribbled Annie's riddle. "Near our street a flimsy veil. It's spelled differently."

She stuffed the notepad back into her bag.

"I know where it is," she said.

They ran all the way, only stopping when they reached the sign on the corner of HOUR STREET.

"According to Annie's riddle, the veil must be nearby," said Bree.

Suddenly the letters began twitching again. This time, the two R's joined together to make a single letter, while the rest organised themselves into the words:

SOUTH TREE.

"South Tree Drive," said Sandy, who was still trying to catch his breath. "I know it."

"It's at the top of this hill!" said Honey, her face bright with the thrill of the adventure. "Come on."

The sign for SOUTH TREE DRIVE was, rather fittingly, screwed to a tree trunk. Sandy arrived in time to see the letters re-arrange to spell out an instruction:

TO THE RIVER.

The surplus letters – USED – dropped directly into another

sign below which now read:

USED NO PATH TO SEATHORN LAKE.

"This is so much fun," Honey chuckled, tucking the stray strands of her ponytail behind her ears. "Like a treasure hunt."

"More like a wild goose chase. It doesn't make sense. I mean – Used No Path To Seathorn Lake – I don't get it," muttered Sandy.

The letters started to jumble and spin once again, repositioning to form another clear instruction -

UNDERNEATH OAKS THAT SLOPE.

"I've got it!" Honey clapped, making her ponytail kick. "We go to the river and find some wonky trees."

Sandy puffed out his cheeks.

"Why on earth couldn't the engraving have spelled that out in the first place?"

****

The riverbank was lined with trees – orange, yellow and rusty red, all the colours of fire. Patches of bright autumn sky sparkled through their branches. An earth embankment shelved steeply down to the river, a foaming torrent that seemed to bubble and boil with rage. The roar of it rose up through the soles of their feet.

Sandy had found a long stick and was using it to hack away at the weeds and nettles.

Bree shivered and pulled her jacket closer around her. She

glanced up at the canopy overhead.

"I'm not sure what an oak tree looks like," she said, her breath misting the chilled air.

Sandy stopped and pushed his glasses up his nose.

"The bark of an oak tree is grey with knobbly ridges," he said, making wiggly lines in the air with his finger. "And the leaves have deep lobes and smooth edges. Most of them will have fallen off the branches by now, though."

"I'm sorry Sandy, but they all look pretty much the same to me. It's going to be like looking for a white cat in a snowstorm."

Sandy sighed. "Trees are as individual as people. Look, there. The trunk of that Elm is grey with brown ridges and that Horse Chestnut has an almost pink tinge to its bark."

Bree tried her best to look interested.

"Horse chestnuts," she sniffed. "That's where conkers come from, right?"

"I love conkers!" squealed Honey. "Help me find some."

Before long they were throwing armfuls of soggy leaves and knobbly fir cones at one another, until Sandy stopped and picked something up off the ground.

"Aha," he beamed, holding up a small brown nut with a tough, leathery shell, "look what I've found."

"That's not a conker, silly!" teased Honey as she pulled a leaf from her hair.

"Well, duh, I know that. This is an acorn."

Bree and Honey stared at him blankly.

"The seed of an *oak* tree... an acorn never falls far from the tree."

He pointed at something on the opposite side of the river.

Bree followed the line of his finger and made out two strangely shaped trees. Even from this distance she could see that they grew out of the soil at such an angle that they intertwined at the top, forming an almost perfect triangle in the space between them.

"Now *that's* what I call sloping!" she grinned, scrambling down the embankment towards the river's edge.

Small rocks tumbled as Sandy and Honey followed. Standing where a bank of pebbles and grit shelved into the mouth of the river, they stared out at the wide stretch of foaming water that lay between them and the sloping oaks. Icy spray rose up in a haze of droplets around them.

"There's no way across," Honey shouted over the thunderous roar.

Sandy picked up a pebble and threw it as hard as he could. It reached as far as the middle of the river, where it dropped and was swallowed instantly by the swirls of rapids.

"Way too deep and fast to wade across. We can't go in there. The cold will kill us if we don't drown first. There's a bridge at the other side of Auriel Forest but it'll take us ages to get there," he said.

He looked upriver, shielding his eyes from the slanting rods of sunlight that bounced off the water.

"There!" he said, pointing towards a small waterfall which somersaulted over a cluster of mossy rocks. "There's a fallen tree that goes right across to the other side."

"It's risky," Bree said anxiously, "but I don't suppose we have much choice."

They followed the stony path that twisted around the contours of the river, stopping where it took a swing to the right, and began to climb up a long, mossy slope. To their left, resting on the riverbank was the base of the fallen tree, its end splintered and cracked.

It stretched across the width of the river, ending in a tangle of broken branches that splayed out over the opposite side of the bank. They could see that the entire length of the trunk was coated with slimy moss. The angry waterfall bashed and bubbled between the black teeth of the rocks below.

"Who wants to go first?" asked Sandy.

Honey pulled a lip-gloss from her pocket and removed the lid.

"You've got to be kidding!" said Sandy.

She applied a thick layer of fuchsia gloss to her lips, and then pressed them together firmly.

"If I'm going to die I want to look my best," she said, sliding the tube back into her pocket.

Sandy shook his head and stepped up onto the trunk. He took a couple of cautious sidesteps, then jumped up and down to test how secure it was.

"Solid as a rock," he smiled, holding his hand out to Bree.

She grabbed it and he helped her up. She wobbled for a moment then caught her balance. Gingerly she shuffled along to make room for Honey.

"Okay, follow my *exact* footsteps," instructed Sandy, wiping the spray from his glasses. "And don't look down."

"How will I see where your exact footsteps are if I don't look down?!"

But Sandy had already begun the perilous walk across the log. He stopped in the middle and shouted back, but his words were whipped away by the deafening roar of the water. Bree took her first steps, not allowing time for her resolve to weaken.

When she reached the halfway point she watched Sandy clamber down to safety on the other side. If she kept her cool she would be on dry land in no time.

Out of the corner of her eye she could see Honey a few steps behind her. Bree did not notice the branch that stuck up from the trunk until it was too late. She tripped over it and her arms shot out, fingers grabbing desperately at fresh air. Honey grabbed her jacket just in time to stop her falling head first into the furious, gurgling froth. She did not take another breath until she reached the section of trunk that was suspended over the shore. They scrambled over the boughs of the fallen tree, the skinnier branches bending under their weight.

"I thought you were going in for a swim back there," said Honey, yanking a wet tail of hair from her mouth.

"Thanks! That was close," said Bree, puffing out her cheeks. "Come on! The sloping oaks are this way."

The forest trail eventually led them into a glade, dark beneath overhanging trees. Suddenly Honey began to run, ploughing through the thick undergrowth, her ponytail swinging from side to side.

"Up here!"

They fought their way through until they reached the sloping oaks. The two trees leaned so far over that it looked as if a single push would topple them. Sandy circled them warily, as though they might spring to life at any moment and gobble them up.

"They look pretty ordinary," he said, examining them.

They were set a few metres apart, but had grown at such an angle that the highest branches intertwined to form a leafy archway. Bree climbed onto fat roots that snaked through the shallow soil around the base of the trees. She slipped on the damp wood, and landed with a thump in a pile of spiky conkers. The motion left behind an eerie ripple of energy in the space between the trees.

"Did you see that?" she whispered, getting up. "it looked

like a heat shimmer."

Honey nodded. She stamped her foot hard and the very same thing happened.

"I think we've found our flimsy veil," she said.

Sandy lifted his glasses and peered closely.

"We should be careful, we don't know what's on the other side."

For a moment Bree's fear was brushed aside by a pinch of curiosity. She reached towards the shimmering air.

"It feels lovely," she said dreamily.

Honey took a deep breath and poked her head through. Sandy threw himself at her, circling her waist and pulling her back. Her hair and eyelashes were sparkling with water. She looked at him and smiled devilishly. "You only need to ask if you want a cuddle."

"What did you see?" he mumbled.

"A forest. A bit like this one except the sky is a totally different colour and it's raining."

"Raining?" asked Sandy. "Are you sure, Honey?"

"Let's go through – Annie's riddle said we should. Then you can see for yourself."

Bree reached out and swept aside the invisible fabric.

The scene before her stole her breath. Rain poured from clouds that covered the sky and a cold, harsh wind blew between skeletal branches. In the black forks of the trees crows folded tightly into themselves, and watched them with beady eyes. A rush of scouring, overwhelming misery washed over her.

"It's *horrible*," groaned Honey.

Bree stared at the stretch of forest, gripped by the same chilly unease she had felt when Mr Deanheart had cornered her in the kitchen. She recognised this place.

"It's not only horrible," she said, "it's familiar."

"Let's go," said Honey.

Sandy followed her into the rain, pulling on Bree's sleeve so she had no choice but to go with him.

She scanned the forest, her eyes resting on a tree that seemed to throw up its bony arms in desolation. The sharp, earthy smells of Auriel Forest had been replaced by the rank odour of stale smoke and dead things rotting. Nothing about this place felt welcoming.

"I think we're back in Calvaria," Bree said quietly, "Dunubas brought us here the last time."

Sandy blinked, rain running off his eyelashes. He stared out at the wasteland.

"This is not Calvaria," he said, a frown of alarm etched across his face.

"Where is it then smarty pants?" she said.

"This is Swarnbideah."

"It can't possibly be!" Bree cried. "We never crossed the border of Strangledoor."

"We didn't need to," said Sandy, "Gran's riddle brought us straight here."

A terrible understanding started to buzz around Bree's brain. The last time they were here they had barely managed to escape. And that had been with the guidance and protection of their friend, Dunubas. Now they were alone in a world of danger.

Her imagination conjured up the ghost of Dunubas. He looked straight at her and whispered,

"A boundary which should never be crossed...Anyone who tries risks being killed."

"I remember the last time we were here," she said.

"Me too," said Honey, wrapping her arms protectively around herself. "We saw some terrible things."

"On a positive note," said Sandy, "I remember that Swarnbideah is not far from Castle Zarcalat."

Honey looked at him like he was mad.

"*That's* the positive note?"

"Well, there's no point in delaying the inevitable," he said. "We all know that's where we're heading. Remember the Scrabble tiles?"

Bree took a deep breath.

"Right then. What are we waiting for?"

"Wait," Honey said, "I want to do something first."

She untied the red ribbon that held her ponytail in place, and tied it in a tight knot around a gnarled branch that poked from one of the sloping oaks.

"Now we'll know which tree to look for on our way back."

She pulled out her bottle of *Raspberry Rebel* perfume and gave it a generous squirt.

Sandy coughed and sneezed at the same time. "You *know* I'm allergic to that."

Honey replaced the lid and shoved the bottle back into her satchel.

"It's better than bouquet of rotten eggs and dead fish. This place stinks."

They started walking, unsure of where the trail would lead them. The forest was eerily quiet.

"The smell is getting worse," said Sandy, pulling his jacket up over his nose. His eyes slid down to Bree's pocket, and he pointed to where a patch of bright light seeped through the material. "The book!"

"It can't be," said Bree, "I don't feel it throbbing."

She pushed her hand deep inside the pocket, until her fingertips found the polished pebble that William had given her. She pulled it out, holding it up in front of her.

"It's so bright," said Honey, shielding her face from the light. "What is it?"

"It's the stone William gave me," replied Bree, examining it curiously. "He called it his chuckie. I had no idea it could do this."

It slipped from her fingers and singed her trousers, leaving a small hole in the fabric, yet when she picked it up it felt as cold as marble.

"Let me see that," said Honey, grabbing it from her.

She immediately dropped the stone and sucked on the small burn it had left.

"Looks like I'm the only one who gets to hold it," said Bree, picking it up.

As they continued their journey the stone melted the darkness with its warm, reassuring glow. Soon they arrived at a narrow muddy stream that ran through the rotten earth. The light from the chuckie died in the blink of an eye. Bree put it back into her pocket and stared down at the water. Scum was dotted over the surface, and a rotten log lay across it, dark green and slimy.

They carried on through a heavy curtain of drizzle until the rain got so heavy it hissed in the foliage. Distant jags of lightning sliced at the sky, and the air shook with a low rumble. Bree stopped and stared ahead.

"We're near Castle Zarcalat."

Sandy and Honey exchanged glances.

"How do you know?"

"I can *taste* it."

The taste terrified her. Bitter and sulphuric, she knew what it meant. They fought their way through a dense mesh of branches and weeds, until eventually they broke out onto the threshold of a steep stretch of hillside that dropped down into a deep gorge. Charred and limbless trunks stretched away on either side of them.

They had stood in this exact spot once before.

"I can't see much," said Honey, edging closer to the verge, "it's very misty down there."

A gust of wind blew the curtain of mist apart giving them a view down over a dark sweep of trees – an entire palette of greens that surrounded the base of the mountain. Thrusting up from the depths like a giant shark fin was the rock upon which sat Castle Zarcalat.

PART TWO
THE REALM OF
THE LOST

CHAPTER 12
THE BRIDGE OF EYES

Bree remembered the last time they had seen the castle – the heat, the smoke, and the flames that licked at the heavy sky as they ran across the bridge.

Metallic rain ran through her hair and trickled from her chin. She wiped away the drips that clung to her lips and turned to Sandy.

"I so badly do not want to go back in there," he shivered.

"You took the words right out of my mouth. But we have to stop Valgus and Theramonde. We can't turn back now."

"What if they're still in Rockwell?" Sandy asked.

Bree shook her head.

"They're here. I can *feel* it."

She gazed at the vast forest below where vibrant greens stood out against the cruel, jagged base of the rock. The trees were so closely knitted together that she could not see what lay beneath them, but she recalled the warning in Annie's riddle – *Beware, hidden dangers lurk in there*. She suddenly remembered something else.

"The Realm of the Lost! That's what Dunubas called it."

"The lost *what* I wonder?" Sandy said.

Through the shifting wreaths of mist Bree caught sight of something that turned her blood to ice. Out of nowhere, an army, in red hooded cloaks was marching across the cobbled courtyard. They moved with a single-minded determination, accompanied by a pack of ferocious Cleptathorns, the guard dogs of Castle Zarcalat. These ones were particularly vicious looking, tied together with rusty chains and frothing at the mouth.

"We've got company," she said.

Sandy jumped back into the undergrowth. "How did they know we were here?"

"I don't think they did," replied Bree. "Perhaps they won't see us."

"But they're making their way across the drawbridge!" Honey cried, her bottom lip trembling, "and there's nowhere to hide."

Even the thunder could not drown out the bloodthirsty barks. The baying chants from the approaching army were getting louder. Suddenly, Bree felt The Book spring to life inside her pocket. She pulled it out and quickly lifted the cover. The second page had already begun its transition from paper to glass and a white fog churned at the centre. Sandy ventured out of the bushes and peered hopefully at the emerging words.

"Hurry!" he urged.

At last the third wish materialized. Bree squinted through the driving rain to read it aloud.

> Danger nears! You must take flight,
> But first some help you should invite.
> Normal rules do not apply
> To these great beauties of the sky.
> They'll take you down in swerves and dips
> but first a sound must leave your lips,
> A whistle loud enough to bring
> A winged insect Queen and King.

Without hesitation Sandy rammed his fingers in his mouth and blew out something resembling a strangled raspberry. Honey pushed him aside, cupping her hands around her mouth and blew a long, low whistle that was immediately snatched away by the wind.

"It's no use!" she cried. "No-one will *ever* hear that."

The faceless army ground to a sudden halt.

"INTRUDERS!" someone yelled, followed by a triumphant roar as the army charged forwards in one seething mass of fur and fury.

Bree closed The Book and stared down at the throbbing locket in despair. "Well, *they* heard it! We're doomed."

For a moment nothing happened. Then a rush of warm air quickly grew in intensity, blowing Bree's bedraggled hair back from her face. Sandy held onto his glasses, as the wind grew so strong it bent the trees.

"What the ..."

His words caught in his throat as two giant butterflies crested the verge and hovered in front of them, their wings flapping like huge silken sails.

Sandy stared in amazement.

"They're wearing reins," he said.

"Wowzers," smiled Honey, "I guess that means we can ride them."

Bree gnawed her bottom lip.

"I'm not sure," she said.

"Are you *kidding* me?" said Honey, staring at her as if she was mad. "What part of riding on a giant butterfly is not super cool? Besides, we don't have a choice."

Bree put The Book into her pocket, and climbed warily onto the nearest butterfly, grabbing the reins tightly.

The butterfly turned in a graceful swoop, and then plummeted with sickening speed towards the sea of green below. Bree choked on the freezing air and her teeth tingled, until they leveled out and began to soar in a wide loop with the ease of a glider. She looked up to see the other butterfly directly above her, Honey at the front with Sandy behind, his arms wrapped tightly around her waist.

There was hardly any noise in the void between grey and green – nothing except Honey's excited whoops, the rush of air and a quiet beating of wings. The sinister atmosphere that surrounded Castle Zarcalat lifted and the air turned warm.

They descended through a gap in the trees, and landed gracefully in a clearing. The moment Bree's feet touched the soft soil the locket stopped pulsing. Wish three had come to an end.

"Wow! That made the Scare-O-Planes feel like a ride in a shopping trolley," giggled Honey as she dismounted, her cheeks flushed with pleasure.

Bree pushed her hair out of her eyes and took in their surroundings. This was nothing like Auriel forest. More like a rainforest. A jungle. The trees had smooth trunks and waxy leaves and the soil was dark and moist, covered with vines. The chaotic noise of animal life — croaking frogs, chirruping insects and exotic birds — filled the ripe air, which was heavy with moisture. The butterflies hovered for a brief moment, then fluttered gently upwards until they were out of sight.

"I've just remembered something else Dunubas said about this place," said Bree.

"What?" asked Sandy.

"He said no-one ever comes back."

****

They pushed on through drooping ferns and twisted roots. Funnels of muddy green light filtered down through the thick treetops, penetrating the gloom. Droplets of sweat trickled down the ridges of Bree's spine.

"I'm boiling," she gasped, rubbing a clammy hand down the back pocket of her jeans, "I need a drink so badly."

Sandy tied his jacket around his waist. Crescents of sweat were forming under his armpits.

"It's a nightmare," he said, wiping the steam from his glasses, "like being fully dressed in a sauna."

Honey tugged on the stubborn zip of her satchel and rummaged around inside. She pulled out her notepad and flicked through the pages, which were damp and wrinkled from the humidity.

"I've just remembered something," she said, "something Annie said about the map."

"What? That old scribble?" said Bree.

Honey flattened the page where her glittery pen had scrawled Annie's riddle, and read the words out slowly.

"Before the map fades you must flee or – darn it – some of the letters are smudged."

Sandy peered over her shoulder.

"Or lost souls you'll forever be."

Bree nodded.

"Yes, I remember now," she said, taking the map out of her pocket.

She unfurled it carefully. Where once there had been nothing but a charcoal sketch, there was now a beautifully illustrated map.

"I don't believe it. It's…it's *amazing!*"

"Look, there's a waterfall," said Sandy, stabbing his finger where the original crudely drawn lines had been replaced by a turquoise cascade, complete with parrots circling above.

"It's called Orchid Falls," said Bree, running her finger along the name written beneath it in elaborate calligraphy. "It looks lovely."

Honey pointed to an arched bridge. "The Bridge of Eyes," she read. "It's not far. Look, we're here…" she pointed to some giant trumpet-shaped flowers and then back to the map.

Bree moved her thumb and saw the dark, ominous outline of Castle Zarcalat in the bottom corner. All the tiny details were there, including the rickety bridge and the roiling thunderclouds.

"We're some distance away from Castle Zarcalat. We're going to have to find our way there as quickly as possible."

"Definitely before the map fades," said Sandy.

Honey pointed to the top left of the map, where a cluster of tipis was surrounded by a high, stone wall.

"It looks like a village," she said, "maybe we should steer clear." The others nodded their agreement.

It did not take them long to reach the Bridge of Eyes, which had been constructed from hundreds of tightly packed stones, and spanned the width of a long stretch of crystal clear water.

"Should we cross it?" Sandy asked.

"I suppose so," said Bree.

Just then a huffing, shuffling noise came from behind a large boulder. A little man with a sleepy expression crept out from behind it. His complexion was as tanned as leather, and his wiry eyebrows resembled an untidy hedge. A lump on his back had bent his spine into an unyielding curve. He scuttled forwards, acknowledging their presence with a jerk of his chin.

"He looks harmless enough," Bree said.

"Like Rumpelstiltskin," Honey muttered.

The man scratched his head and yawned rudely, revealing a mouth full of crooked, yellow teeth.

"I'm Eed," he growled, his nostrils flaring angrily, "whaddya want?"

Bree smiled politely and bent down so she was face to face with him.

"Oh, we don't want anything from you," she said, "we only want to cross this river."

Eed's face crinkled like a used teabag.

"If that would be alright?" she added quickly.

He rubbed his chin.

"Might as well," he sniffed. "But I must warn you. At least one of you must outsmart me or you'll all be very sorry. You can ask me any question," he added, eyeing Honey. "Her first."

"O...okay, let me think..." Honey swallowed nervously. "The person who makes it sells it. The person who buys it doesn't use it, and the person who uses it doesn't know he's using it. What is it?"

She glanced sideways at Bree and winked confidently. Eed pursed his lips, taking his time before answering.

"A coffin," he said finally, with a smug grin.

"Oh," said Honey, her voice flat with disappointment.

Bree gnawed her bottom lip. Her question would have to be good.

"How long is a piece of string?" she asked nervously.

"Twice as long as from the middle to the end," he answered without hesitation.

Honey's mouth hung open in quiet disbelief. Eed had said

if they failed they would all be very sorry. All eyes swung to Sandy. He was their only hope of getting over the bridge and avoiding a terrible forfeit.

"So, boy," Eed said tiredly, "Do you have a question for me?"

Sandy stepped forward and nodded.

"Go on then, I haven't got all day," snapped Eed.

"Okay," said Sandy. "What is the question I am thinking of asking you?"

Eed's face became a picture of bewilderment, his lips pursed and his eyebrows twitched. Slowly his cheeks reddened with a mixture of rage and frustration until eventually he stamped his foot.

"I'M A GENIUS!" he roared. "NOT A MIND READER!"

A slight smile of satisfaction lifted the corner of Sandy's mouth.

"You said any question. That's mine."

Eed's face grew redder and redder.

"Fine!" he snarled. "You win."

He stepped aside with a grumble, and gestured towards the Bridge of Eyes.

"Go on then. What are you waiting for? You will find my son, Theb somewhere in there," he huffed, stabbing a thumb in the direction of the trees. "He is a good boy."

"He must have taken that from his mother's side," Sandy muttered as he followed Bree and Honey onto the bridge.

When they reached the middle, Sandy stopped and stared in horror.

"We're being watched!"

An eye had appeared in every stone, each one a different shape and colour, watching every step they took.

"Keep walking," whispered Bree. "They're only eyes."

"Creepy eyes," said Honey.

When they reached the other side, the eyelids closed one after the other, merging back into the stonework until they had disappeared altogether.

"It's as if we woke them up from a deep sleep," Sandy said.

"We might be the only people who have ever made it across, thanks to our super hero!" Honey said, as she threw her arms around Sandy's neck and planted a wet kiss on his cheek.

"Yuk," he said, wiping his hand down his face.

They trekked on through more dense jungle, following the curve of the river. After a while they stopped and rested against a tree root.

"What I would do for some of Mrs M's homemade lemonade right now," said Sandy, wiping his brow.

"With ice and a slice," drooled Honey.

"We should keep moving," said Bree.

****

They walked in single file. Sweat pooled between their shoulder blades, branches scraped their arms and strangler figs tripped them up. The humidity was relentless and they felt the shadowy presence of Castle Zarcalat through the treetops.

Bree smiled as she noticed a tiny bird with pink and yellow feathers tweeting merrily from a branch. She clicked her tongue and spoke to it with a gentle lilt. The bird tipped its head at a quizzical angle and mimicked her.

"It's talking to me," said Bree. "How sweet."

Just then, something large swooped down in a flurry of leaves and twigs. Bree shielded her face and when she looked back the little bird was gone. A single pink feather floated down and came to rest on the ground. Sandy and Honey's expressions darkened. Slowly, Bree crept backwards, her terrified eyes sweeping the trees. She opened her mouth, hardly daring to speak.

"We need to…"

Suddenly, with a crashing and rending, a huge bat tore through the leaves. It landed directly in front of Bree and split the air with a shocking screech.

"RUN!!"

All around, the air was filled with noise – birds screeching and branches snapping. Everywhere, animals ran from the giant bat as it gained ground in a crawling mass of claws and fangs.

They didn't stop running until they reached a waterfall where plumes of sparkling water crashed into a wide pool. Bree glanced back nervously as she tried to catch her breath. The terrible noise had stopped and the air was still.

"I think we lost it."

Sandy bent over and gulped in a lungful of air.

"I thought Vampire bats were nocturnal."

Honey straightened up, adjusting her satchel.

"And I thought butterflies were small enough to fit in the palm of your hand. You heard what the last wish said. Normal rules do *not* apply."

Bree looked up at the waterfall but it was so high she could not see where it began.

Sandy ran his tongue along his parched lips.

"Do you think it's safe to drink?"

"I'm not sure," Bree said, although the thought was tempting.

Nearby, something crashed through the undergrowth.

"No time for refreshments," she said.

CHAPTER 13
A SMALL SURPRISE

They climbed quickly up a steep path littered with tiny rocks. The higher they went the more treacherous the path became, snaking all the way round to a narrow shelf that ran behind the waterfall.

"We can hide in here," Bree shouted above the roar of water.

One by one they stepped onto it, forced to flatten their bodies against the sheer face of rock, and shuffle sideways until they reached the middle. Water slicked down, pooling in the crevices and making it perilously slippery underfoot. With her back pinned to the wall, Bree was too frightened to move. Sandy stood beside her, his features mottled in the eerie half-light.

"Tell me it's gone, Sandy. *Please.*"

"I don't know. But we should..." he broke off as a huge shadow flew past, its outline warped, on the other side of the falling water. Bree squeezed her eyes closed. The sound of the waterfall dissolved to nothing and all she could hear was the blood coursing in her ears. After what seemed like an eternity Sandy squeezed her hand.

"I think it's gone," he whispered.

"Let's get out of here while we still can."

Suddenly the water parted as the giant bat broke through, and Bree found herself face to face with it. Her foot slipped on the rock and she landed awkwardly, feeling herself sliding down. Sandy grabbed her collar and hauled her back up. With deafening shrieks the bat lunged at them. Sandy kicked it hard between the eyes and for a second it looked stunned.

"Get out of here!" Honey screamed, pulling a metal nail file from her satchel. "I've got this covered!"

Sandy and Bree scrambled along to the ledge and jumped down onto spongy soil. They turned in time to see the bat clamp its jaws around Honey's wrist. She struggled wildly, clutching her nail file so tightly her knuckles turned white.

"It's going to drag her off the ledge!" cried Bree.

She ran towards the waterfall but Sandy pulled her back.

"It's too dangerous!"

Somehow Honey mustered enough strength to raise the nail file so it was level with the bat's nose. She squirmed awkwardly, and then pulled back the pointed tip until it looked like it might snap. She let it go and there was a loud *thwap*. Shocked, the bat released her and drew back through the waterfall with a long, drawn out *eeeek*.

Honey dropped the file and clambered across the ledge, tripping and sliding in her haste to escape. Sandy caught her as she jumped off the end.

"It's gone. You're safe now," he said.

Without stopping to recover from the shock, they made their way into the dense undergrowth, where the fine spray from the waterfall stuttered onto thick leaves.

"Look!" Honey whispered, pointing at an overhanging branch.

A tiny frog, bright yellow with waxy skin and large black eyes regarded them indifferently, then licked its eye with a long, pink tongue.

"It's so sweet," Honey gushed, reaching out to touch it.

Sandy grabbed her hand.

"Don't touch!"

"It's only little, I hardly think it'll bite my hand off."

Sandy peered closely at the frog.

"If I'm not mistaken, that is Phyllobates Terribilis. Otherwise known as the Golden Poison Frog. Don't let the small size and pretty colour fool you."

"It doesn't seem to be scared of us," said Bree.

"It has no need to be," said Sandy. "That sweet little frog has enough lethal toxin on its skin to kill twenty adult males."

A sudden downpour spilled through the leaves, and Bree shivered with pleasure as the cool liquid streamed down her neck. She tipped back her head and opened her mouth wide, letting the water fill her mouth and run down her throat.

Honey danced in circles, catching as much water in her mouth as she could.

"I didn't think I could get any wetter, but this feels great!"

They ran for shelter, laughing as they did. Crouching under a large, umbrella-shaped leaf, they watched as the rain hit the ground, hissing and spitting as it evaporated into steam. The jungle was quiet except for the calming sound of twittering insects, and the tapping of rain dripping from one leaf down to another. The downpour ceased as suddenly as it had begun.

Bree wondered if they were any nearer to Castle Zarcalat. She tucked a wet strand of hair behind her ear and pulled the damp map from her pocket. When she unfurled it something immediately caught her eye.

"I wonder what those red lights are?" she said, her brow following. "They weren't there before."

On the map three small, red circles seemed to hover alongside the waterfall – in exactly the same spot they were standing. Bree looked around, but there was nothing that resembled three red objects.

"That *is* strange," she muttered.

Sandy shifted uneasily.

"I'm starting to think there might be another nasty surprise heading our way," he said.

"Me too," said Bree, her eyes sweeping the undergrowth.

Honey turned and skipped away, her long hair flicking behind her.

"Wait there a minute," she called back to them.

"Where are you going?" Bree shouted, but Honey was already too far away to hear her.

She stopped short of entering the thick undergrowth, turned back to face them, and began waving both arms above her head.

"What is she up to now, Bree?" said Sandy.

"I have absolutely no idea."

She glanced down at the map, and to her surprise there were now only two red dots beside the waterfall. The third had moved to the left – exactly where Honey now stood.

"I don't believe it," laughed Bree. "Those dots. They're... *us!*"

She held the map up for Sandy to see. As Honey ran back over, the dot moved in time with her. She stopped beside them, her face flushed with excitement.

"Well..." she asked expectantly, "...was I right?"

Bree smiled.

"You were. Those tiny red dots are *us*."

Honey slapped her thigh.

"Genius!" she roared, looking to Sandy.

But he was looking closely at something else on the map,

and his expression had darkened.

"What is it, Sandy?"

"If those red dots are *us*," he said slowly, pointing at a fourth red circle moving across the paper, "then who is *that?*"

There was a rustle of leaves as something struggled to break through the undergrowth.

They were searching frantically for something, anything, to use as a weapon, when the bushes finally parted and a tiny man appeared holding a bow and arrow. Most of his face was shrouded in a mop of hair that looked like matted straw.

"Follow me!" he said, his weapon poised for action.

They stayed rooted to the spot. The man pushed aside his fringe and smiled.

"You can trust me," he said. "My name is Theb. I am Eed's son. I know the way out of here, come on."

"If he's anything like his father, I don't think we *should* trust him," Honey whispered to Bree.

"I don't think we've any choice, time is running out and the map will fade, we need to take the chance," Bree answered.

They followed him through dense foliage that reached their waists, but which completely buried him. At one point he disappeared altogether only to re-emerge seconds later brandishing a machete, which he used to cut a pathway.

When they stopped to rest, Bree studied him carefully. Apart from his tiny stature, it was hard to believe this boy was related to the nasty little man at the bridge.

"You must have outwitted my Father," he said.

He looked cross, but then a satisfied grin split his face in two.

"I'm impressed," he nodded approvingly. "Most people who try to cross the Bridge of Eyes end up in Eed's prison. Left in there long enough a person dies."

"It was Sandy who managed to trick him," Honey said quickly. "Bree and I had an epic fail."

She lowered her hand for him to shake.

"I'm Honey."

He took her hand and kissed the back of it. She blushed and giggled.

"What brings you here?" he asked.

"We sort of ended up here by accident," replied Bree.

Theb considered this for a moment.

"*Nobody* ends up here by accident."

"*We* did. We really want to be up there..." said Honey, pointing through the treetops and lowering her voice to a whisper, "...in Castle Zarcalat."

"Why?" he gasped.

"Unfinished business," replied Bree.

"It's a long story," Honey added.

"But you'll *never* get out alive," he said.

"We've managed twice before," Bree said. "We're hoping it's a case of third time lucky."

"*You've been in the castle before?*"

Sandy, Bree and Honey nodded in unison.

"Well, I can *try* and help you get there, but my advice would be to go home while you still can."

"I wish it were that easy," Sandy said, glumly.

"What could be easier than going home?"

"At this point, pretty much everything."

"Why don't I find you something to eat?" said Theb. "You must be famished."

Sandy's stomach growled.

"You could say that."

"And I'm totally parched," Bree said, licking her lips.

"I know just the thing," said Theb. "Follow me."

They walked a short distance through a patch of spongy ground, where thick vines hung like ropes from the trees. Theb led them to a row of tall plants with black stems, red flowers, and curling leaves.

"These are Acoomathids," he said, as he jumped up and pulled on one of the flower heads until it bowed over. Clear, fresh water poured from the petals, and he opened his mouth wide to catch it.

"Help yourselves," he said, wiping the drips from his mouth, "it's delicious."

"What are those?" asked Honey, pointing to the plump, black fruits which hung from the stalks.

"For goodness sake don't knock those off," Theb warned. "If they hit the ground with enough force…BOOM!"

Sandy took a step backwards.

"Don't worry, I'll be careful," Theb chuckled and he twisted one of them until it broke free.

He handed the fruit to Sandy who inspected it thoroughly over the top of his glasses.

Once Bree had satisfied her thirst, she noticed that the area widened into a boggy marsh bordered by ferns with graceful, drooping fronds. She was too busy studying the plants to notice her feet sinking into the moist ground. By the time she realised what was happening she was already ankle deep.

CHAPTER 14
TRAPPED

Bree panicked, and struggled to pull herself free. To her relief her right foot emerged with a loud slurp. Dirty water oozed into the print she had left behind. Hastily she pulled her other foot free and squelched back to the others.

"Is it supposed to be this muddy?" she asked, treading the surface so she would not sink again.

Theb looked down at his feet, which were disappearing at an alarming rate. His forehead wrinkled into an anxious frown.

"Acoomathids attract water, although I don't recall it ever being quite this bad before. We need to get to the other side," he said, freeing his feet only for them to sink again almost immediately.

"I'm having a strange sense of Déjà vu here," said Sandy, staring down anxiously as a quiver of tiny ripples disturbed the surface of the mud, where his feet had all but disappeared.

"Me too," said Bree, feeling for The Book in her pocket, "I remember one of the wishes helped us across quicksand before. Maybe it'll do the same this time."

Honey and Sandy's horrified glares told her that she had let the cat out the bag. Appalled at her stupidity she slapped a hand over her mouth.

"Don't look so worried," Theb said, flicking a glance at her pocket, "I know all about The Book."

"You do?" asked Honey.

He leaned in and whispered.

"*Everyone* here knows about it."

"You mean there are people here?" asked Bree.

Theb nodded.

"Good *and* bad. Some were banished here because knowledge of The Book is a very dangerous thing to possess. The dark forces at Castle Zarcalat will not rest until they have it."

"There's a little village," said Honey. "Do people live there?"

"Some do. Others roam. Most hide."

"I'm glad we met you, Theb," said Bree. "I know we can trust you."

"You certainly can. But in future you must be careful whom you tell your secret to. There are many people who would gladly take that book from you."

His gaze dropped back down to her pocket.

"I have to give it willingly though," Bree said fiercely, "and I'm in no hurry to do that."

"Let's say no more about it," said Theb with a broad smile, which slipped when he realised he was now waist deep in mud.

"Oh my goodness," he chuckled.

Bree tried to pull herself out of the mud using a branch but it bowed under her weight.

"I'm up to my knees!"

"Don't panic," said Theb.

"You're the one who should be panicking!" shrieked Sandy, "It's going to reach *your* head before it reaches *ours!*"

"I'll get us out of here in a jiffy," Theb smiled.

Honey looked at the rising mud.

"How exactly?"

"Well, if you can't go forwards you must go up. Watch and

learn my dears."

He took a deep breath and then, at the top of his lungs he shouted,

"Arise weedy!"

The hanging vines began to twitch, and Theb lifted his arms out to the side.

Sandy watched dubiously as the vines wound around Theb's wrists.

"Are you sure these things are friendly?"

Theb winked.

"Trust me."

The vines travelled down his body until they were wrapped securely around his middle. They lifted him gently out of the mud and over to the other side of the swamp.

"See!" he exclaimed. "They're on our side. Now you need to be on my side! Arise weedy!"

The vines crept up their arms.

"They tickle!" Honey giggled.

Bree felt the creepers tighten until they had her in a firm grip. The mud tried to suck her back down, but it was no match for them. She was lifted safely to the other side. When everyone was across, Theb clapped his hands loudly and the vines shriveled to dust.

"They die when you clap," he said, "but there's plenty more where they came from."

"Are these vines all over the jungle?" Honey asked.

Theb nodded.

"Yes. You just have to know what to look for."

"Theb, are we near Castle Zarcalat yet?" asked Bree. "We really need to –"

Theb held up his hand as a signal for silence. There was a

movement in the bushes.

"What is it?" hissed Sandy, raising his fists.

Theb silenced him with a warning glare. His eyes narrowed and slid from side to side, as he tried to locate the sound.

The leaves rustled and they heard a growl and the rhythm of heavy paws.

Slowly, Theb raised his machete. Behind Bree the bushes shifted and moved. She looked at Theb and when his eyes swung back to hers she immediately knew what he was going to say...

"RUN!"

She ran for her life. The trees grew so thickly that she couldn't see in front of her. Her legs pumped harder, muscles burning. Stealing a quick glance over her shoulder, there was no sign of Honey or Sandy. She hurdled a fallen tree, bursting into a clearing, and only then did she stop to catch her breath.

A bird screeched somewhere above her and she flinched. Exposed and vulnerable, she scanned the shadows, listening and watching for any flicker of movement. Somewhere she could hear distant shouts.

"Bree! Where are you?!"

She turned and began to answer, but her words were swallowed up by the crash of breaking branches as the ground gave way beneath her. She flung out her hands and tried desperately to grab onto something, but she was swallowed by darkness. A surge of pain exploded as she landed heavily on her back.

When she gathered her senses, a circle of light above told her that she was lying at the bottom of a pit. The earthy walls were coated with a thick oily substance that would make climbing out impossible.

She hauled herself onto her side and pulled William's chuckie out of her pocket, holding it between her thumb and forefinger. She gave it a shake and it lit up immediately, sending a pool of white onto the walls. Bree glimpsed a square of brown material and then, to her horror, a skeletal face with leathery skin, which stared back at her from empty eye sockets. The jaw hung loosely in a silent scream. She passed the beam slowly down the length of the body. Strips of damp material had rotted and fallen away to reveal broken ribs, and a claw hand. Her mind reeled with a single, gut-wrenching thought. *I'm never going to get out of here.*

She struggled to her feet. The space was small and appeared to have been carefully concealed with branches and leaves. She screamed upwards at the top of her lungs.

"SANDY! HONEY! I'M IN HERE!"

In answer, she heard nothing but a slow, steady drip. Her heart sank. No one would ever find her down here. She would spend her last hours with only a dead person for company. Suddenly the drip got faster, more insistent, until it was a definite trickle. She swept the small light around the perimeter. The trickle became a gush. Her heart hammered as she imagined the pit filling with water and drowning her.

"HELP! I'M DOWN HERE!" she cried, but there was no answer.

Bree watched in horror as a dark puddle expanded and oozed across the floor, creeping up over the mummified body. A black mist rose upwards from it, coiling around her legs. She closed her hand tightly around the chuckie, the light still seeping out through her fingers, and pounded her fists on the sticky walls until she could no longer feel her hands. Soon she was too exhausted to move. Above her the circle of light closed as the mist formed a thick skin across the pit opening. Soon the chuckie flickered and died, plunging Bree into total darkness.

Her brain felt hazy and frayed, as if it was slowly rotting. Hopelessness seeped into her like ink into blotting paper. Her head was too heavy to lift, her limbs as feeble as leaves. She was trapped in this foul, open grave.

Bree closed her eyes. Soon her head was unclouded by thoughts and she was nothing.

CHAPTER 15
FINDERS KEEPERS

"Where *is* she, Sandy?!"

Sandy tried to quell his rising panic.

"She can't have gone far."

"Maybe she's with Theb," said Honey, her eyes wide with hope. "He'll look after her."

Sandy wasn't convinced.

"We should never have split up," he said. "We *always* stick together. That's the rule."

"We need to find her. Which way should we go?"

"I have absolutely no idea. Bree has the map."

They wandered for a while, shouting her name the entire time. Eventually, they stumbled across a dirt path, which abruptly forked in two. One half curved to the left, and led into an overgrown track where the bushes grew so thickly it looked impossible to find a way through. The other path dipped slightly into a tunnel of trees. Two signs had been nailed to a dilapidated wooden post. The one that pointed at the overgrown track read: A MOODYHEART WYND, in letters a shade darker than the damp, moss-covered wood. The other read: LITTLE FERNRUSH ROAD.

An unpleasant memory prickled Honey's skin. "Do you remember when we visited Gypsy Sue?"

"How could I forget?"

"She said something about following the wrong path, and

dying before your time is due, didn't she?"

Sandy looked in the direction of the wild track.

"Looks pretty rough in there," he said, a little uncertainly.

Honey nodded in agreement.

"Little Fernrush Road sounds a bit nicer, don't you think?" she said.

Gypsy Sue's warning echoed in Sandy's head. He stared miserably at the sharp thorns that encircled the track like loops of barbed wire.

"We'll get torn to shreds trying to get through there," he muttered, as he weighed up their options.

"Little Fernrush Road it is then!" said Honey, striding purposefully ahead.

After a short while they reached a clearing where the air was cooler, and rich, dark soil softened their footsteps.

"I'm beginning to think we chose the wrong path," said Sandy, "I feel like we're moving further away from Bree."

Honey stopped in her tracks and threw up her hands.

"We made a choice, Greenfield," she said crossly. "We have to stick with it now, okay?"

"I'm just saying. Am I not allowed an opinion?"

"Ssh!" she hissed, breaking up their spat. "*Can you hear that?*"

They stopped arguing and listened. Dark, angry voices drifted through the trees. Suddenly, the figures of men on horseback were silhouetted against a background of greenery.

"Who are they?" said Honey, backing into the cover of the bushes.

She did not hear the snap of a twig or realise there was someone behind her, until a rough hand clamped over her mouth and strong arms lifted her off her feet.

She fought, trying to break free, but it was hopeless. Twisting round, she saw a dark-skinned man, with piercing green eyes and close-cropped hair. From somewhere above, Sandy landed on the man's back, pummelling him with his fists.

"Let her go!"

The man cursed under his breath and swatted him away. "Shut up and get down on the ground! Unless you want to die!"

Honey and Sandy dropped down and lay on their fronts with their hands covering their heads.

"I'm not going to hurt you," he said in a whisper, that was drowned by a wave of thundering hooves.

He pulled them into a hollow which was partially concealed by some thick bushes.

"My name is Anando. You can trust me."

Nearby, a group of cloaked figures on horseback ground to a halt. Peering through a gap in the bushes, Honey glimpsed a red horse with a serpent tail. Sitting astride it was a huge man with a bald head and a ginger beard. She gasped when she realised she had seen him before. Anando slapped his hand over her mouth but it was too late. The man spun around in their direction and pulled a sword from its scabbard. His eyes narrowed beneath shaggy brows as he scoured the undergrowth.

"He told me they'd come this way!" he bellowed, his cheeks flushing scarlet.

"Reinor, they could be anywhere by now," said a woman. Her dark cloak and long skirt stood out against her white horse. Her hood was trimmed with fur that hid all but the curve of her cheek.

"THAT'S NOT GOOD ENOUGH!!" he roared. "WE HAVE TO STOP 'EM BEFORE THEY GET TO THE CASTLE!"

The horse pranced under the weight of his anger. Twisting, yellow flames which were at the centre of its blue breastplate came alive, and the serpent tail flicked from side to side, its tongue tasting the air.

"Stand STILL you stupid creature!"

The horse whinnied and reared defiantly, its hooves crashing down inches from Honey's head. Reinor cursed and tossed his sword through the air, and she felt it hurtle past her ear.

"I WANT THE IDIOT WHO SENT US ON THIS WILD GOOSE CHASE KILLED! *DEAD! GONE! AND IN THE MOST HORRIBLE MANNER IMAGINABLE!*"

Reinor yanked hard on the reins. His horse let out an angry snort then turned and fled, throwing up clumps of dark soil.

Anando sagged with relief and peeled his hand away from Honey's mouth. "That was close."

A scar, white against his brown skin flashed along his chin. He scrambled across the ground to get Reinor's sword. He lifted it and twisted it towards the light, admiring the jewel encrusted hilt.

"Finders Keepers," he said with a wink.

Brushing the dirt from his clothes, he slid the sword into his belt and thrust his hand out towards Honey.

"I'm sorry if I scared you," he said, helping her up.

"Only a little bit," she said coolly. "Thank you. You saved our lives.

"Why are you here?" he asked. "You *must* realise this is a very dangerous place."

"We're getting that message loud and clear," said Sandy, straightening his glasses, "but we can't leave until we find our friend."

"I recognised the man on the red horse, I'm *sure* we've seen him somewhere," said Honey.

"We had the pleasure of his company before," Sandy reminded her. "Except the last time we were hiding behind some boulders with Mimi. He had Bree by the hair! Do you remember?"

Anando stared, open mouthed.

"Are you telling me Reinor had a hold of you and you lived to tell the tale? He is not the kind of man to suffer defeat gracefully. You're lucky he didn't bring the HeatSeekers with him, they'd have found us in seconds."

"*HeatSeekers?*" queried Sandy, his face draining.

Anando nodded.

"They hunt people down by homing in on body heat."

"So it would be impossible to hide from them?" Sandy asked.

"Unless you're made of ice."

"But what about Bree?" Honey cried. "They're sure to find her."

"Who are you talking about?" asked Anando.

"Our friend." Honey explained. "We lost her and now she's out there all alone with goodness knows what and…"

"Try and remain calm," Anando said gently. "Let me take you somewhere safe. Somewhere you can eat and clean up ."

"We're in a hurry," said Honey, "we need to find Bree and get to Castle Zarcalat before it's too late."

Anando's expression darkened.

"Reinor knows you are going there, I heard him. You seem very sure of what you are doing, but I must warn you against it."

Honey folded her arms across her chest.

"We're going to Castle Zarcalat and that's that."

Sandy looked at her with a pleading expression.

"We'll be no use to Bree if we're hungry and tired," he said.

"Okay," Honey said reluctantly, "but we'll have to be quick. How far away is it?"

"A couple of miles that way," said Anando, pointing in a westerly direction.

Sandy groaned.

"A couple of miles? It'll take us ages to walk."

Anando's eyes glinted and his face broke into a broad grin.

"Who said anything about walking?"

He let out a short, sharp whistle that ricocheted off the trees. Suddenly the ground beneath them rumbled with the sound of heavy hooves.

"They're coming back!" cried Sandy.

There was no time to run. A huge, black horse burst through the bushes and reared up in front of them before crashing back down with a loud whinny. To Sandy's relief the saddle was empty. Loose stirrups flopped at its sides and the reins dangled. His eyes swept the bushes, waiting for Reinor and the rest of his army to follow.

Anando stepped forward and grabbed the reins.

"Ah Perignod, my faithful stallion," he laughed and slapped the horse's neck. "Always there when I need you."

The horse snorted and nudged him lovingly.

"This is *your* horse?" said Honey.

"Yes. And not a serpent tail in sight."

Perignod was completely black, except for a distinctive white diamond blaze in the space between his ears. His coat was glossy and his muscular withers rippled with power.

"He's *very* handsome," Honey gushed, stepping forward to pat him.

"I suppose *this* will be our mode of transport?" Sandy asked dubiously.

"Yes it will. Have you been on a horse before?"

"Yes. And I can't say it was the highlight of my life," Sandy said uneasily.

Anando lifted his foot into the stirrup and swung himself up onto Perignod with the ease of an accomplished horseman.

"Perhaps this time will be more fun," he said, settling into the saddle.

Honey nuzzled her face into the side of Perignod's neck, and he returned her gesture with a gentle nudge. She looked up at Anando.

"So, what's the plan?"

Anando adjusted the stirrups.

"I'm afraid it'll have to be one at a time," he said. "Who wants to go first?"

Sandy took a step backwards.

"I'm allergic to horses."

"Well you're welcome to walk," said Anando. "It shouldn't take you too long if you avoid all the danger spots."

Sandy's face drained.

"In that case, I accept, but I'll be sneezing the whole way."

Perignod stamped his hooves and thrust his nose skywards.

"Looks like someone is eager to get going," said Honey.

Anando offered her his hand.

"Hop up then."

"I can ride," said Honey. "I'm used to being up front. Are you okay with me going first, Sandy?"

"Sure. I mean what could *possibly* happen to me while you're away?"

Anando lifted Honey up into the saddle with one effortless

movement. He wrapped his arms around her and grabbed the reins.

"See you soon, Greenfield," Honey said.

"I hope so."

She dug her heels into the horse's sides, and the jungle became a blur as Perignod broke into a fast gallop, kicking up the soft earth as his strides lengthened. Honey ducked and dodged as branches whipped past her head.

Up ahead she spotted a mound of earth partly concealed by moss and lichen. Something lay on the ground beside it, fluttering gently.

"Whoa!" She tugged on the reins and Perignod ground to a sudden halt.

"What are you doing?" snapped Anando. "I nearly fell off!"

Honey leapt out of the saddle.

"It's the map!" she squealed. "Bree must have dropped it!"

Anando looked baffled.

"Why is it so important?"

Honey held it up to him and pointed to the bright red dot next to the skull and crossbones.

"*That's* why," she grinned.

CHAPTER 16
RESCUED

Dirty, black petals fell around Bree and golden sunlight streamed through the murk, so strong and bright it was difficult to look at. She sucked in air like someone coming up from the dark depths of the ocean. Forging strength out of nothing she looked up and saw the vague outline of Honey, brandishing a branch.

"SHE'S DOWN HERE!"

Bree tried to stand but fell backwards on wobbly legs.

"Don't move!" Honey shouted down. "I'm coming to get you!"

There was lots of swishing and rustling and then suddenly, wonderfully, Honey was right there. She slid a hand under Bree's head.

"Drink this," she instructed softly. "It'll make you feel better."

She tilted a small bottle to Bree's lips and warm liquid trickled into her mouth. The warmth spread to her limbs and soon she was able to sit up without help.

"Better?" Honey asked.

Bree nodded as she slipped the chuckie back into her pocket.

"SHE'S OKAY!" Honey shouted up to the pale oval that was Anando's face.

Bree's vision cleared and she saw that a thick bough

stretched all the way from the foot of the pit up through the circle of light.

"So *that's* how you got down here," she croaked.

Honey smiled.

"Here, finish this."

Bree took the bottle and tipped it so the last drops splatted onto her tongue.

"What *is* this stuff?" she asked.

"I took the Valerian from William's shop," Honey replied. "I thought its calming properties might be useful."

Her eyes swung to the mummified body.

"Looks like he could have done with some too," she said with a shudder.

"How did you find me?"

"You dropped the map. I could see the red dot...*you*...at the bottom of this pit."

Bree glanced around at the earthy walls.

"Where am I?" she asked, baffled.

Honey leaned in closer and whispered.

"Eed's prison. Remember, Theb told us that most people who tried crossing his bridge ended up in here."

Bree clambered to her feet. "We need to get out!"

"You go up first," said Honey, "I can catch you if you slip."

Bree tested her weight on the bottom bough then used the branches like a ladder.

"Bree, please tell me you still have The Book," said Honey.

Bree pulled it from her pocket and tilted it so the locket caught a shaft of green light.

"You don't think it's broken do you?" she asked. "I mean perhaps it got damaged in the fall."

"Don't be silly," said Honey. "That book has been through

fires and floods and goodness knows what else! I hardly think a little fall is going to hurt it."

When Bree reached the top she almost fell backwards with the shock of seeing Anando.

"It's okay, Bree," Honey explained quickly. "His name is Anando. He's a friend, let him help you."

Bree allowed Anando to take her hand and help her out.

"He saved us from Reinor," said Honey, pulling herself out of the pit.

"Reinor?" gasped Bree.

Honey nodded.

"And his army. They're looking for us. And they know we're heading for the castle."

"Where's Sandy?" Bree asked.

"He's waiting for me to return," said Anando, glancing back at Perignod. "I'm taking you all somewhere safe, but I can only do that one at a time."

"And Theb. Where's Theb?"

"We lost him," said Honey. "We ran after you and when we looked back he was gone. But he knows this jungle like the back of his hand, *and* he's got his machete."

Bree did not have the strength to argue. She glanced down into Eed's prison and a shiver crawled across her skin.

Honey pulled the map from her satchel.

"I'm so glad you dropped this or we might never have found you," she said, slowly unfurling it.

She uttered a horrified sound and dropped it.

"What's the matter?" said Bree, picking it up.

Most of the trees around the bottom of the map had disappeared and the Bridge of Eyes was nothing more than a ghostly sketch, fading fast.

Bree rolled it up and shoved it into her back pocket.

"Right," she said bluntly. "Let's not waste any more time."

Anando ducked under Perignod's neck.

"Who wants to go first this time?" he asked, smiling.

"You go, Bree," said Honey. "I don't mind waiting here."

Anando pulled himself into the saddle, reached down and lifted Bree. She wrapped her arms around his waist and pressed her cheek flat against his back.

"Don't disappear," said Honey, with a weak smile. "I only just got you back."

Bree opened her mouth to answer but Perignod took off in one graceful leap, his hooves drumming a swift rhythm in the soil. As they moved deeper into the jungle Anando pulled out Reinor's sword and held it aloft.

"Hold tight!" he shouted back to her.

He waved the sword above his head, the blade slicing through the overhanging branches. Bree ducked as leaves rained down around her.

After a while they emerged into a clearing where Perignod slowed to a trot as Anando steered him around the outside of a high, circular wall. It stood in isolation and was surrounded by dense vegetation. There was no gap or door in the stonework.

They came to a halt beside two large boulders, and Anando slid the sword through his belt and helped Bree dismount.

"Where are we?" Bree asked.

Anando looked down at her and smiled.

"Somewhere safe. Nothing will harm you here."

Bree glanced around. She strained to hear something – anything – but for now the forest was still.

"Wait here," said Anando. "You will need me to get inside."

"What's on the other side?" Bree asked, puzzled.

"You'll find out soon enough. But now I must return for your friends."

"Please hurry, I'm not feeling very brave."

He smiled, "I think you are very brave...putting your trust in a complete stranger."

"Well, you're not a complete stranger," she blurted.

Anando looked baffled.

"I don't think Honey remembers," said Bree. "But I do. Dunubas told us about you."

He recoiled as though he had taken a physical blow.

"You *saw* Dunubas?"

She nodded.

"We met him the last time. In Calvaria. He told us about your great-grandmother's prophecy and about your friendship and how much you loved his sister..."

"My beautiful Nevidas."

He dismounted.

"What else?" he asked.

"You have a daughter," Bree said softly.

He tried to steady himself, lost for words.

"She's beautiful," said Bree. "Her name is Pamela and she looks just like you."

"Pamela," he muttered, rolling her name around his mouth like a delicious treat.

His smile slipped and the muscles in his jaw tightened.

"A daughter I've never seen. The worst thing is not knowing whether they are alive or dead." His eyes searched Bree's for an answer.

Bree looked down, not able to stand his stare a moment longer. Burdened with a horrible truth, she did not know how to respond. Eventually her eyes lifted to meet his.

"Will you ever get out of here?" she asked.

"Never."

He took hold of the reins and swung himself back into the saddle.

"How did you end up in the Realm of the Lost?" asked Bree.

Anando shook his head wearily. "We wanted everything to return to how it had been before the Flame of Irenus tore it all apart. We attempted to infiltrate Castle Zarcalat, but we were outnumbered ten to one. The lucky ones died and the rest of us ended up here."

He allowed a moment for his words to sink in.

"Why weren't *you* killed?" asked Bree.

"I was offered a cruel choice. To join my enemies or to live here for an eternity."

"You made a brave and honourable decision."

"Perhaps. But I have paid the price for it. I lost everyone I loved."

His expression hardened.

"I should get back to the others," he said, gathering the reins. "They'll be wondering why I'm taking so long."

Bree felt a sudden surge of panic at the thought of being left alone.

"Shouldn't I have a weapon or something?" she spluttered.

"The best weapon you'll ever carry is between your ears," said Anando, tapping the side of his head. "Now do *not* move from this spot, I'll be back soon."

He smacked Perignod's rear end with a flat hand and they disappeared into the jungle. Bree hugged herself and looked up at the high wall. It was covered with patches of green moss and wispy cobwebs. In the nooks and crannies, where the mortar had flaked off, scorpions and spiders hid from the heat.

She sat down on one of the huge boulders and noticed that the other one was topped by a flat rock with a whorl pattern carved into it. When she ran her hand over it, it tipped like a seesaw.

She remembered seeing something like it on the original charcoal sketch of the map. She pulled it out of her pocket and carefully unfurled it. The first thing she noticed was that Eed's prison had now disappeared. There was no doubt the map was fading fast. Two glowing dots indicated where Sandy and Honey were waiting, and another moved steadily across the page in Sandy's direction. *Anando*. In the top left, the third red dot shone brightly alongside the cluster of tipis. Now Bree knew where she was.

She shoved the map back into her pocket and waited. Soon her thoughts turned to home and before she knew it she was imagining the worst – Annie getting ill, Adam moving away, being trapped here forever. Tears began streaming down her face. As she leaned forwards a single teardrop landed on the flat rock, and trickled into the groove. The rock tilted and Bree jumped with surprise. She wiped her eyes and watched the tear travel round the spiral until it reached the middle, where it disappeared through a hole. A loose stone in the wall scraped aside to reveal a small, dark space.

Bree peered inside and saw a lever. She stuck her hand through the gap, and pulled the lever forwards. At first nothing happened, until a join in the wall broke open with a spray of moss and mortar dust. She looked through and saw a winding path, bordered with flowers. Tentatively she stepped on to it, and the wall closed behind her seamlessly like a zip. She tried to focus on Anando's words, *nothing will harm you here*.

A little blue bird swooped up and down above her head,

cheeping excitedly. It climbed and dropped in strange, random zigzags, its wings moving so fast they looked fuzzy.

"Hello, you're a friendly chap," said Bree.

The bird was nothing but a blur as it flew around in jerky loops. It was as if it was telling her something, beckoning her. She followed it around the curve of the wall until the path opened up into a wider area filled with tipis. She noticed the smoke first, and as it parted she saw a crowd of people laughing and chatting around a large pot, which hung over an open fire. They were too far away for her to hear what they were saying, but something about them told her she had nothing to fear.

Bree locked eyes with a tall man with black hair who was looking at her with interest. She held his gaze until the bird fluttered in front of her face again, and when she looked back, he was gone.

The bird led her through a maze of tipis until it darted ahead and swooped under a blanket that was hung over a washing line.

"Wait!" she cried, jogging to catch up with it.

She ducked under the blanket and on the other side came face to face with a woman who seemed to have appeared from nowhere.

"Oh I'm s..sorry," gasped Bree.

The woman smiled, her eyes crinkling at the corners. She had a long, elegant face, bright eyes and dark hair.

"My goodness, we haven't had a young person here for some time," she said. "Most of us had to leave our families behind. Would you like something to eat or drink? I hope you don't mind me saying, you look a little worn out."

"I...I suppose a drink would be nice," said Bree.

The woman turned and gestured for her to follow. They made their way to a tipi with a goat tied up outside. It ignored them, preferring instead to tug on the leaves of a bush. Bree followed the woman into the tent. It was small inside and she was forced to stoop. It smelled of lush greenery and stale smoke, and the cool shadows offered a welcome release from the oppressive heat of the jungle. The woman pointed to a low bed covered with furs.

"Please, have a seat," she said, collecting a pile of sticks that had been stacked near the door. "I'll boil some water."

Bree crawled over a dirt floor strewn with woven rugs and sat on the edge of the bed. She stole a quick glance at her surroundings. Long wooden poles stretched upwards in a cone shape, tapering at the top where they poked out through an opening. In the centre of the floor there was a ring of stones filled with a pile of ash. Beside the bed was a table carved from wood.

"Nettle tea should sort you out," smiled the woman. "Don't be afraid, I don't bite!"

Bree shifted awkwardly.

"I'm sorry, it's just that you didn't seem surprised to see me. Nobody did. I think that's a bit odd."

The woman started arranging the firewood inside the stone circle.

"Well, you must be one of us. Otherwise you couldn't have come through the wall."

She sat down cross-legged on the floor opposite Bree, and rummaged inside a large pocket at the front of her dress. She pulled out a pointed stick and a long piece of wood with a groove cut down its length, then rubbed them together in a rapid sawing motion. After a few moments a thin stream of smoke curled upwards, and she blew gently until a red glow appeared. Then, very carefully she tucked the stick under the woodpile, crouched low and blew into it. The firewood caught light and started to crackle and smoke.

"You made that look easy," Bree smiled.

The woman added kindling to the fire and the wet wood hissed and spat.

"In The Realm of the Lost it's best to learn things fast," she said. "How did you come to be here?"

"It all happened very quickly," replied Bree.

"Did you *choose* to come?"

Bree thought about this for a moment.

"I suppose so. Is that a good thing?"

Behind a rising cloud of smoke the woman leaned back and wrapped her arms around her knees.

"If you came here of your own free will, that changes things slightly in your favour," she explained. "It means that you might be able to leave. Unlike me."

"How did *you* end up here?" Bree asked.

The fire spat tiny embers onto the stone surround. The woman stared ahead at the twisting flames, as though her mind was back in some other place and time.

"It all started when we went to a little cottage and – *he* – was there."

"Who?"

The woman's face crumpled and she hugged her knees and began rocking from side to side.

"The stealer of hope, the source of all nightmares."

"Who?" said Bree, impatient now.

The woman flicked her a haunted look.

"The Evil One."

CHAPTER 17
SECRETS

The woman stared into the fire, reliving the terror.

"It was as if he *knew* we were going to be there," she said, her voice low. "He was lying in wait for us."

Fear coursed through Bree as she started to make the connection.

"Do you mean…*Thalofedril?*"

The woman gasped.

"But h…how would you *know* that?"

Bree swallowed hard.

"I think I know the cottage you're talking about," she explained. "Were there lots of cats?"

"Yes! That's why we didn't go inside. I'm allergic you see."

Bree pulled her knees up to her chest.

"His intention was to kill the old lady who lived there," she said. "Her name was Agora Burton, did you see her?"

The firewood shifted, sending sparks into the air.

"We tried to find her, but we didn't see anyone. I only wish we had never gone anywhere near that cottage."

Bree leaned forwards.

"But don't you see? You being there that night. You saved that old lady's life."

"I don't *care* about some old lady! I never saw my son again because of her and her stupid book!"

Bree turned cold.

"*Book?*"

"Thalofedril kept saying, *The Book...The Book...*over and over. We told him we didn't know where it was. We pleaded with him, told him we had a child but he laughed and –"

"What?"

The woman's shoulders slumped.

"I don't remember."

Her face looked pale and tortured in the flickering light.

"I've *tried* and *tried* but it's as if I've blocked everything out. I only remember waking up in the Realm of the Lost. We had nothing with us, only the clothes we were wearing. I thought I was having a nightmare. As the days passed my husband told me that we would never return home. We would *never* see our precious boy again. I didn't even say goodbye."

Her voice cracked and she buried her head in her hands. She cried silently, small muffled sobs hidden by the crackling of the fire. After a few moments she lifted her head.

"He must have wondered where we were, and all because of a book we never even saw."

She grabbed a stick and tossed it into the fire. There was an explosion of sparks followed by a heavy silence. She rested her chin on her knees, a deep, angry furrow creasing her brow.

"Would you like to see it?" Bree asked tentatively.

The woman sat bolt upright.

"*You have it?*"

"Yes," replied Bree, ever so quietly.

After a long moment the woman gave the slightest nod, then watched eagerly as Bree dug her hand inside her pocket and produced The Book.

"That's it? *That* is the thing that ruined my life?"

Bree looked at the little volume in her hand. It did look

rather pathetic. She held it out, the flames lighting up the locket, making it look as if it had come alive.

"This book is more powerful than you could *ever* imagine," she said, "I've seen first-hand what it can do."

"I've seen enough. Please put it away."

Bree slid it back inside her pocket.

The woman stoked the fire with a long stick.

"I don't know why you have it, how you found it," she said, "but you must be careful. Thalofedril will destroy everything in his path to get it."

"Don't worry," said Bree. "He's dead. Gone."

The woman shook her head vehemently.

"*No.* I don't believe you!"

"We saw it with our own eyes," Bree explained. "He's dead."

"No. He is the dark shadow that passes your window. He is what nightmares are made of. He is the stealer of hope, the giver of misery – "

"He's *gone!*" snapped Bree.

The woman jolted out of her trance with the look of a child waking from a nightmare.

"I want to show you something," she said, stretching over and sliding her hand under the furs.

She pulled out a crumpled photograph.

"I have slept with this under my head every night for the last eleven years," she said, gently smoothing a crease. "It's all I have left of him, my most treasured possession. I am glad I had it in my pocket that night or I would have had nothing to give me strength all these years."

She handed Bree the photograph, carefully, like it was the most precious thing on earth.

"I have to live with my grief and guilt," the woman added.

"And there is *nothing* worse than a mother's guilt."

Bree tilted the picture to the flames to get a better look. A serious looking toddler with black hair and questioning eyes stared out at her.

Just then the man she had seen in the crowd earlier appeared in the entrance. His hair was the blackest black imaginable, and stuck up at the crown. His jaw was strong and square, and his eyebrows ran in two bushy curves that gave him a slightly startled expression.

He crawled across the floor and sat beside the woman, planting a kiss on her cheek.

"I see we have a visitor," he said.

"Goodness, how rude of me!" gasped the woman. "I haven't introduced myself. Jane. And this is my husband, Michael."

The ground seemed to tilt beneath Bree.

Sandy's parents! The parents everyone thought had died eleven years ago. Bree's mouth opened, but no sound came out.

"Are you alright?" asked Michael.

"I thought I recognised you earlier," she croaked. "You look just like Sandy."

She held the photograph out and the man stiffened.

"What do you...Who *are* you?"

"Bree. Bree McCready."

Jane's expression changed – surprise, fear, sadness – Bree could not tell which. It might have been all of them at once.

"What happened to him?" she asked. "I've always wondered."

"Annie stepped in," replied Bree. "Lovely, kind Annie."

A sad smile spread across Jane's face.

"Did he miss us?" Michael asked expectantly.

"Of course. I think he always knew you weren't dead, which in some ways was worse for him."

Jane put both hands over her chest as though she were trying to stop her heart from breaking. It suddenly felt as if there was not enough oxygen inside the tent.

"Bree, could you give us a moment alone, please?" said Michael.

"Yes," said Bree, sensing an uneasy shift in the atmosphere. "I'll wait outside."

She ducked out of the tipi, and paced anxiously, wondering why Sandy and Honey were taking so long. Michael was the first to come out and he looked angry. When Jane emerged it was clear she had been crying. Michael folded his arms, took a deep breath and stared right at Bree.

"Sandy must never know about us," he said firmly.

"So I'm supposed to leave here and pretend I've never seen you?"

Jane took a very deep breath. "Yes."

"But if he ever finds out that I knew where you were and didn't tell him he'd...*he'd*..."

"That is *why* you can never tell him. Imagine what it would it be like for him having that knowledge? It would be unbearable for him," said Jane.

"Could it be worse than thinking his parents abandoned him?" said Bree, wiping her tears away angrily. "That they didn't care what happened to him?"

Michael glared at Bree. His lip curled angrily. "You must never speak of this to him and that is the end of the matter."

"And I *do* care – He's my son. I...love him..." Jane said absently, looking past Bree.

Bree turned. Sandy stood there wide-eyed with shock. He

looked at her, his mouth forming a question.

"Sandy! I would have told you. Honest! This is as much a shock for me as it is for you!"

But he was not listening. His eyes were fixed firmly on his mother.

"Sandy. Darling," Jane said tentatively, holding out her hands to him.

His eyes filled with tears. "You...you're *alive!*"

"Yes, darling. Isn't it wonderful?"

Sandy backed away.

"No! No it's not! Where have you been for the last eleven years?"

"Here," said Jane. "We've been here."

"We had no choice, son," said Michael, with a look of fatherly concern. "We would never have left you willingly."

Bree reached out to Sandy, her fingers brushing his sleeve. He whipped around, suddenly remembering she was there.

"Their disappearance had something to do with The Book," she said.

Sandy laughed mirthlessly. "Why is *that* not a surprise?"

"Come inside," Jane said. "We can explain everything to you."

Sandy pulled himself together. "We have to be going. Our friend is waiting for us."

He lifted his glasses and rubbed a bloodshot eye.

"Have you been crying?" asked Jane.

"No... horse... allergic," he managed to say.

Jane nodded, remembering.

Sandy looked at Michael, and his scowl melted a little.

"I remember you," he said. "A car, ice-cream, an itchy blanket."

"Yes, son. We were on holiday. There isn't a day that passes when we don't miss you. *Please*, come inside and we will tell you everything you want to know."

Sandy put one foot forward, and Bree realised things were never going to be the same after this. It was as if some big, ugly monster had burst out of a box and would never fit back in again.

He turned back to Bree and she smiled awkwardly.

"I won't be long," he said.

Bree felt a stab of jealousy as she watched them huddle together, weeping and laughing all at once. She was invisible now.

Time passed: half an hour, five minutes, it was difficult to tell. When Sandy finally emerged he looked like the same boy but he wouldn't – *couldn't* – catch her eye.

"Let's go for a walk," he said.

Bree followed him back the way they had come. Everything was green and dripping from a recent rainfall. They stopped away from the encampment, near the gap in the wall.

"Honey must be wondering where we are," said Bree, breaking the silence.

Sandy kicked the ground with the toe of his boot and shrugged his shoulders.

"She's with Anando," he said. "She'll be fine."

"It must have been really difficult saying goodbye to your mum and dad," said Bree. "I feel like this is all *my* fault."

He bit his lip hard.

"Oh Sandy, *please* tell me you don't think this is my fault!"

He shifted awkwardly then threw his hands in the air.

"It's The Book! It's ruined *everything!*"

The anger deserted him and his shoulders slumped.

"It's all so much to take in," he said, holding his head.

Bree reached out, her fingertips skimming his sleeve.

"I know your mum and dad went to Agora's cottage the night they disappeared," she said gently. "But why? What were they doing there?"

Sandy swept a hand through his unruly hair.

"They were good friends," he said, "your parents and my parents."

Bree nodded.

"I know. But what does that have to do with anything?"

"Good friends share deep, dark secrets with one another."

Bree's stomach clenched with dread.

"My dad wouldn't have told them about The Book."

"Bree, he told them *everything*," Sandy replied wearily. "Everything except for where it was hidden. Of course, he quickly denied it all but it was too late. He'd already put them in danger. He begged them not to tell your mum. They never did."

"What *did* they do?" asked Bree.

"Nothing. Not until three years after he died."

"Why then? What happened?"

Sandy puffed out a long, slow breath.

"It was the day of your third birthday. When the party was over, Mrs M broke down in tears in front of my parents. She was barely coping. Mrs M told them her heart was broken just like the one around her neck. When they saw the half-heart locket it brought back what your Dad had told them three years earlier."

"Is that when they decided to investigate the cottage in the woods?" Bree asked, quietly.

Sandy nodded.

"They hoped Agora Burton would be able to shed some light

on things, put their minds at rest. So that evening, while my Auntie Val looked after me, they drove to Auriel Forest."

Bree remembered the words Annie had written in her diary. *I'm sure she had something to do with Jane and Michael leaving...*

She touched Sandy's arm but he pulled away from her.

"My parents don't blame your dad for any of this," he said bitterly.

Bree searched his face.

"But *you* do, don't you?" she said.

He gazed miserably at his feet.

"It's not that," he said quietly.

"Well, what then? You've hardly been able to look me in the eye since you stepped out of that tent."

His eyes lifted and she was startled by their fiery intensity. There was a silence in which she heard him draw in a breath, steeling himself.

"I'm staying here, Bree."

CHAPTER 18
LOSING SANDY

"Don't be silly," she laughed.

"Seriously, Bree. I'm staying."

"Why?" she heard herself say.

"I've waited a lifetime to find my parents and now they're right in front of me. That kind of miracle doesn't happen every day."

"But you *can't* stay. It's a ridiculous idea!"

"Why?" Sandy asked, matter-of-factly.

Bree folded her arms across her chest and scowled at him.

"Well for starters you've only just met them. They're complete strangers."

"They're my parents Bree. They're in my blood, I'm in theirs."

"Fine! But what about living here? There'll be no home comforts and I'll bet the food makes school dinners look like top-notch cuisine."

"I'll cope," said Sandy. "Try and imagine how you would feel if it was your dad."

The words struck Bree like a slap.

"That's not fair. I *did* have a chance, but I chose not to turn my back on you."

"We're just different. Perhaps we want different things. I'm not sure what there is for me in Rockwell anymore."

"How can you say that? What about Annie?"

Sandy squeezed his eyes shut.

"I love my Gran more than anything, but she's not going to be around for ever."

"Yes she will!"

"No, Bree. We've all been denying it, but I've seen her struggling to get out her chair and feeling dizzy all the time. She's an old lady and what's left for me when she's gone? Where will I go? Who will care about me?"

"*We* will!" cried Bree, thumping her chest. "Me! Honey! My mum and Harry!"

Sandy sighed wearily. "I know you will but I've thought about this and I'm staying here."

"Oh no, *please* don't say that. We'll never see you again. Besides, we need you! If Reinor knows we're heading for Castle Zarcalat, goodness knows what he'll have in store for us there!"

A heavy silence sagged between them. There was so much to say, so much not to say. After a moment Sandy reached out to her, his fingertips brushing hers.

"What are you thinking?"

"Perhaps I could stay with you," she said half-heartedly.

Sandy shook his head firmly.

"No. You belong in Rockwell. Just think, hot chocolate at Kimbalee's Café, clothes shopping with your mum, double maths on a Thursday morning..."

"You make it sound so appealing," and they laughed, a dry humourless chuckle that quickly petered out.

"Besides, you've got Adam now."

"That's not the same. He could *never* replace you. And he would miss you too," she added, hoping this might make Sandy see sense.

She threw herself at him, knocking the wind from his lungs, sobbing a stream of tear-soaked words.

He gently disentangled himself from her and held her at arm's length.

"Sandy..."

He placed a finger on her lips. His eyes were dark pools in which she could see a future that no longer involved her.

"I've made up my mind. Just imagine that I'm on holiday," he said with an attempt at a smile. "I'll be in another country, that's all."

"Another world more like."

"You are the bravest person I know," he said, his voice cracking painfully. "I'm only doing this because I know you'll cope in the castle without me. You'll get over me."

Bree threw her head back and wailed.

"No! I won't. Don't you see? I'm only brave because of you!"

He planted a kiss amongst her messy mop of hair.

"Thank you, Bree."

"What for?"

"For being you."

"I'll never give up hope that I'll see you again," she said, and Sandy nodded.

Jane was making her way over. Bree's time with Sandy was coming to an end and yet there was still so much more to say.

"Bree, I took a picture of your parents a few days before your dad died," said Jane, as she took Sandy's hand in hers.

She knew the photograph; her mum and dad together, young and in love. Him smiling proudly with his hand on her bump, her beaming with happiness.

"They were happy and carefree," added Jane, "I hope that helps."

Bree stared at the ground and blinked away her tears.

Sandy cleared his throat and squeezed her hand. "See you

later alligator."

"In a while crocodile."

Bree watched them turn and walk away, until at last they disappeared, and with that Sandy Greenfield was out of her life forever. She turned and did not look back. She never knew she could be so brave.

****

The shock of losing Sandy left Bree gasping for air. And she still had to break the news to Honey. Wherever she was.

How could he just leave me like this?

There was a shifting and grinding of stone as the two sections of the wall tore apart. Bree wiped away her tears and stepped back out into the jungle.

"There you are!" cried Honey, "I've been *frantic* with worry. Anando left to look for you, we thought – "

She stopped and her eyes slid to the gap in the wall. She tried to peer through but the two halves moved back together.

"What were you doing in *there*? How did you *get* in there? What's *in* there? *Who's* in there?"

Bree felt too numb to answer; hollow, as if someone had taken a large scoop out of her.

"Forget it," said Honey, "you can tell me later. The main thing is you're safe. I mean when I got here and you and Sandy – "

Her relief was instantly replaced by suspicion.

"Where *is* Sandy?"

"Gone," Bree said flatly.

Honey laughed nervously.

"Gone? What do you mean *gone?*"

"He's with his parents."

"His parents? But I...I thought they were..."

"Dead?" said Bree. "Yeah, me too. Well *everyone* did. They were here all along. I mean who would have believed it? Turns out Sandy's mum and dad knew all about The Book. They were captured and brought here eleven years ago..."

She waved her hand flippantly.

"...Anyway, to cut a long story short, Sandy has decided to stay here with them."

"*What?* Stay here? And never see us again? Or Annie? What about school?"

"It seems none of that matters to him," Bree said.

Honey flopped down onto the boulder. She looked so upset that Bree felt a rush of sympathy. Then she remembered. Anger was her refuge.

"Come on," she said coldly. "We can't stay here all day. We've got things to do."

"We should wait for Anando, he'll be back soon and he can help us," Honey said, wiping her nose along her sleeve.

"I'm *sick* of relying on other people!" barked Bree. "It only brings trouble. Besides..." she pulled out the map and waved it in front of Honey, "...we don't have *time* to wait."

The map was almost blank, except for the fading image of a ridged cliff along the top.

"*It's all gone...everything...*" whispered Honey.

Bree shoved the map carelessly back into her pocket.

"Not everything. If we hurry we can still get out of this awful place."

"Without Sandy?" Honey sniffed.

"Well it looks that way, doesn't it!" Bree turned and strode purposefully ahead, leaving Honey with no option but to follow.

They walked in silence, following the natural curve of the silver stream. Tall trees shot upwards and met at the top in a matted roof of green through which only the most stubborn rays of light could penetrate.

Bree gazed around at the dark shadows that surrounded them. Even if they got out of here alive she knew the next leg of their journey would take them to Castle Zarcalat. She didn't know if she had the courage to face what lay ahead. Not without Sandy.

Eventually they came to a wide pond bordered by weeds and tall rushes. Floating in the centre were lily pads as large as umbrellas.

"Typical," spat Bree throwing her hands up in the air. "Like we *really* needed this."

"Remember what your mum always says?" chirped Honey. "Every path has its puddle."

Bree scowled.

"This is hardly a puddle, more like a flippin' ocean."

Honey picked up a rock and tossed it. It landed with a plop and sent ripples across the surface.

"Maybe we could use the lily pads as stepping stones?"

Bree made a face.

"They're too far away, we'll have to swim."

Glimpsing strange shapes looming up from the depths she tried not to imagine what lurked beneath the lid of dark water.

Honey gave her a playful shove.

"It should be simple, they don't call you Flipper for nothing."

"Only Sandy calls me that," muttered Bree, squatting down to sink her hand into the water.

"It's freezing."

"That's strange," said Honey. "We're in a tropical rainforest after all."

Bree shrugged sullenly.

They stood for a moment staring down at the twisting shadows of fishes and weeds. Honey made a little noise, and Bree saw that she was crying.

"What is it now, Honey?" she asked a little more impatiently than she had intended.

Honey sniffed.

"I keep thinking, *what would Sandy do?*"

Bree dug her nails into the palm of her hand at the mention of his name.

"I know you must think I've got no right to be this upset," Honey said cautiously. "I mean, you've known him all your life and I've only known him for five minutes."

Bree bit down hard on her bottom lip.

"But it felt like a lifetime to me! And now I'll never get a chance to tell him how I feel!"

She wiped her snotty nose and took another juddering breath.

"Are you alright, Bree?" she asked.

"I'm fine."

"You don't seem fine. In fact you're acting like nothing has happened."

Bree spun around and glared at her.

"I can't talk about it just now. If I talk about it I'll fall to pieces. Do you want me to be a complete and utter basket case?"

Honey shook her head and bit her bottom lip until it turned white.

"Well *shut up* about Sandy," said Bree. "When this is all over – when The Book is safe and we're back in Rockwell – *then* we can fall apart. But not now okay?"

Honey nodded and silence piled up around them.

After a few moments, Bree turned to Honey.

"I know how you feel about Sandy," she said softly.

"You do?"

"It's pretty obvious you like him."

For a moment, the words hung in the air between them.

"He doesn't like me back. Not the way I want him to."

They were interrupted as the ground began to quiver beneath their feet. Bree strained to listen, hearing a rumble, like distant thunder. Honey's face lit up.

"It's Anando! *He'll* know what to do."

The rumble got louder, closer.

"That's not Anando," said Bree, "there are too many of them."

Honey's eyes fixed on her. "They're heading this way."

Bree slipped feet first into the water. The coldness snatched her breath, but she forced herself under until only her head and shoulders were above the surface.

"Come on. Get in! There's no time to find anywhere else."

Honey stared down at her, terror flashing in her eyes. Hammering hooves and angry shouts echoed through the trees.

"I'm scared," she said.

"I know. Me too," said Bree. "How long can you hold your breath?"

"Not long, a minute or two?"

"You'll have to do better than that," said Bree, "or they'll find us."

Honey swung her satchel over her head and dug around inside. She pulled out her glittery, strawberry-scented pen and bit down on the end, pulling the ink wand out with her teeth.

"We can breathe through this," she said holding up the plastic cylinder.

"Hide The Book first, Honey. Here, take it. Quickly!" Bree ordered.

Honey shoved The Book inside the satchel and hid it under a clump of ferns and rushes.

As she slipped into the icy water her face creased in anguish.

"Think of a warm bath," said Bree, her teeth chattering, "it helps a little."

An angry voice boomed somewhere close. Bree instantly recognised it as Reinor's.

"THEY MUST BE HERE!"

She felt her whole body start to shake with fear and the cold.

Bree felt for Honey's hand and pulled her towards a thick patch of reeds near the edge of the pond. Together they took a deep breath and sunk under the surface, into the murky depths below. The shifting shadows tested the limits of Bree's bravery.

Two figures on horseback appeared at the water's edge. One of the horses was red, the other white. Bree watched as the distorted figures dismounted and stood in muffled conversation, pointing this way and that. She could see Reinor's unmistakable outline. Next to him stood a woman; Bree noted the detail of her fur cloak and her head of silver hair. Blood red lips stood out against the white of her face. Her voice sounded like a warbled echo through the water.

"They'll have to come up for air at some point."

"Aye, or they'll drown like rats!"

"Not if the cold kills them first."

Bree turned to Honey. Tiny air bubbles stuck to her face, her cheeks were puffed out, and her eyes were wide and filled with panic. Slowly, silently she pushed the plastic cylinder up through the surface and sealed her lips around the end. She stayed like this for a few seconds, her long hair billowing out around her like seaweed. Then she signaled for Bree to take a turn. Bree sucked as hard as she could at the tiny opening and drank in the air with huge, heaving gulps. Even with a supply of oxygen she knew they would not be able to stay in the water for long. Already the cold had seeped into her bones, chilling her to the core. But Reinor and the woman were not in a hurry to leave. This had become a waiting game.

All of a sudden a commotion broke out above the water. Men started shouting to one another in panicked, frantic tones. Reinor disappeared from view and was replaced by the watery outlines of horses rearing and thrashing. Honey tugged on Bree's sleeve and gave her a look that said, *What's going on?* Still hiding amongst the rushes Bree poked her head out of the water. A wild wind rushed past her ears, scouring her cheeks and instantly freezing the drops on her eyelashes. There was chaos all around, men running in every direction, horses wide-eyed and frothy with terror. Trees snapped in the wind and ice crystals bloomed on everything.

"ICE TORNADO!" screamed Reinor. "RETREAT! *RETREAT!*"

Lily pads hurtled past Bree's head. Shooting through the surface, Honey gasped, gulped in air and tossed her wet hair out of her eyes. Feathery ice particles immediately started to form on her eyelashes.

"What the – "

A twisting cone of white cloud crashed through the trees, turning everything it touched to ice, including the remaining men and their horses.

"Get back under!" Bree screeched, ducking below the

surface.

The cone of churning air passed over them, turning the surface of the water to solid ice. Trapped beneath a transparent ceiling, the water reached a new level of coldness. It flared on Bree's skin and scorched her with a sudden, unbearable pain. They clawed and punched at the underside of the ice, but it was as solid as a slab of concrete. Honey grabbed hold of Bree, her eyes frantic. Bree's body was numb. She no longer had the strength to fight. Honey let her go and started hammering at the ice again. The undertow pulled at Bree's legs, and she felt herself slip down into the depths. Voices swooped in and out of her head, distant whispers, laughter, a lullaby she had once heard. The sweet song echoed in her mind as she sank further, and the light inside her head went out.

Somebody was groping around inside her pocket. She struggled and kicked wildly, fighting the urge to gasp for oxygen, when she saw it was Honey. She was holding something up to her face and signaling upwards.

The chuckie.

Bree grabbed the little stone and it immediately lit up, cutting a path through the darkness. Mustering the last of her strength she struck out, forcing her arms and legs into long, powerful strokes. When she reached the ice ceiling she wasted no time. The chuckie melted through the ice like a hot knife through butter. She cut a large circle and punched it out, dropping the chuckie in the process. It sank into the murky depths, leaving a streak of light in its wake.

They broke through the water at the same time, their frantic gasps echoing across the frozen silence. To her relief, Bree could see the purple material of Honey's satchel sticking out from the ice-dusted reeds. She wriggled desperately upwards, kicking with her legs and pulling with her arms until at last she was out of the water, and lying breathlessly on the ice. She struggled to help Honey out, and they sat, the cold nipping their cheeks, turning their breaths into ragged white clouds.

The jungle was unrecognisable. Everything that had once been green was now white. Broken trees lay all around and the ground was dusted with powdery snow. Icicles hung from branches and frost lit everything with the hard sparkle of diamonds. The frozen bodies of men and their horses were scattered around like debris.

The cold sliced through Bree's wet clothes and froze her skin.

"I dropped the chuckie," she said through chattering teeth.

"That little stone saved our lives," said Honey.

Bree took Honey's hand.

"*You* saved our lives," she said.

Honey's hands, blue and useless, fumbled with the zip on Bree's jacket.

"Try and keep as warm as possible," she shivered.

Bree nodded.

"What I would do for some hot chocolate now."

"I promise you we'll live to see another hot chocolate," said Honey, huffing out a plume of white breath.

She started to get up but Bree pulled her back down.

"*Sssh!*"

Honey looked questioningly at her and was about to speak when all of a sudden the bushes moved, spilling their dusting of snow. Two spiders, the size of large dogs emerged, their red eyes shining like spotlights. They crawled over the mounds of frozen bodies and stopped near the pond, prodding the solid ground with their jerky limbs.

"*Heatseekers!*" whispered Honey. "*Anando told us about them.*"

They watched in horror as the spiders cautiously approached the edge and peered over, hesitating for a moment before click-clicking their way onto the ice. Bree and Honey sat completely still and silent as the creatures stopped centimetres from them.

The HeatSeekers communicated with one another in a series of loud clicks and squeaks for a few moments before scuttling away. Honey let out the breath she had been holding, and one whipped around, its eyes narrowing to a mere slit of light. Rigid with terror, Bree watched as a beam of red light swept past her, just missing the toe of her boot. The smaller of the two creatures turned and scurried over to where the satchel and The Book were hidden. With a long, angular leg, it lifted the strap and inspected it closely – poking it – scanning it with its red beam. Then it dropped it and darted away, closely followed by the other one.

"Do you think they saw us?" said Bree, when she was sure they were gone.

"If they had they would've killed us," said Honey. "Let's get out of here while we still can."

She stood up and a loud snapping sound tore through the air, sending a thousand invisible cracks spidering across the ice.

"Get to the other side!" yelled Honey, running in the opposite direction. "I'll get my satchel."

Bree started to slip and slide in her haste to reach the icy banks. She climbed onto solid ground and turned to see Honey clambering towards her followed by a spreading crack shaped like a lightning bolt. The crack started to split apart, water oozing out.

"HURRY!"

Honey threw herself onto the embankment at the exact moment the surface broke into a hundred jagged ice islands.

"Phew," she breathed. "Talk about a close shave."

A deep rumble stopped them in their tracks, and Bree grabbed onto a branch as the ground shook beneath them yet again.

"*What now!*" she wailed in despair. "Will this ever stop?"

CHAPTER 19
AN OLD FLAME

They turned to see a whirlpool swirling at the centre of the pond. It built in speed, sucking down the ice and the lily pads, as if a plug had been pulled. A sudden swell spilled over the embankment rushing towards them.

"Quick! Climb a tree!" screamed Honey.

Bree glanced back to see a tidal wave smashing everything in its path. She grabbed Honey's hand, but as they started to run the water engulfed them. They rose and sank, choking and grabbing at branches. The surge carried them through the jungle at breakneck speed, closing over Bree's head and sending her into an icy whirl. She felt Honey's hand slip from hers. Trapped in a chaos of driftwood she was washed downstream like a rag doll. When she resurfaced Honey was nowhere to be seen. She tried to call out, gagging as the water filled her mouth.

Eventually the water receded, and Bree washed up grazed and bruised on the wet soil. Her entire body tingled painfully as it gradually thawed and came back to life. Slowly she sat up and looked around. The wave had carried her far away from the frozen pond and back to a familiar, humid world of greenery and jungle noises – droning insects, squawks and screeches.

There was another noise too – a groaning coming from the bushes. As she watched, Honey emerged, crawling on all fours.

"Honey! Honey! I'm over here!"

Honey pushed her hair out of her eyes, and a broad smile

stretched across her face. She struggled to her feet and staggered over.

"I can't believe we survived," said Bree, as they hugged.

Honey coughed up a lungful of water and wiped her mouth.

"Only just," she wheezed. "I've never been a fan of water flumes."

"Is The Book still in your satchel?" asked Bree.

Honey nodded and glanced around.

"Everything is green again...and warm..."

"I know. And the water brought us here in double quick time. It would have taken us hours to walk. We may still make it to the castle before it's too late."

Honey gave her a withering look and squeezed the water out of her hair.

"I still think I'd rather have walked."

They climbed a fern-covered slope which led them to a gap in the trees. Through a cloud of flying insects they saw a solid rock face straight ahead.

"I think that's the cliff on the map," said Bree.

She pulled the water-logged map from her back pocket but it disintegrated between her fingers.

"Oh," said Honey, staring down at it anxiously.

Bree salvaged a couple of soggy slivers and held them together.

"I can just about make out the cliff. I think we might still make it out of here."

The last remnants of the map fell apart and landed on the soil in a mushy heap. "It's no use to us now anyway," said Bree.

The ground was heaped with loose rocks, making it difficult to clamber up to the base of the cliff. They used the thick vines that grew out of the cracks and dangled down from high above to haul themselves up. The cliff rose to the sky, a great grey wall soaring into the black clouds. Away in the distance Bree could see a green line that fringed the summit.

"How are we going to get up there?" asked Honey.

"Well...I hadn't really thought that far ahead," admitted Bree, "but I'm sure there's a way."

She tugged on a vine. It felt secure but she doubted either of them would have the strength to climb all the way to the top. A cluster of rocks tumbled down as she tried to get a better foothold. Above their heads leaves rustled. Bree jumped back. "Watch out!" she cried as something fell from the branches and landed in a ball at her feet.

"*Theb!*" Honey clambered over the rocks to help him up.

"At your service," he grinned, brushing the dirt off his clothes.

Bree threw herself at him, "You're alive!"

"Of course, and I've been looking everywhere for you. *What happened to you?*" he asked.

"A massive wave," said Honey. "We're in trouble, and we have to get out of here, now."

Theb scratched his head, puzzled.

"What about the boy?"

The words hit Bree like a blow.

"He's gone," she said.

"Oh – that *is* a shame. Never mind, eh? Two out of three ain't bad!"

"Can you help us?" Bree asked.

"You can help yourselves," he replied cryptically.

Honey sighed.

"Well, we don't have wings or springs, so I don't see how."

Theb folded his arms and shook his head in mock

disapproval.

"Have you learned nothing today, my dear girl?"

"What do you mean?"

"Remember, if you can't go *forwards* you must go *up*," he said, jabbing a finger skywards.

Honey's face lit up.

"Of course!"

She ran her hand along the vines.

"Arise weedy!" she commanded, and immediately they began to coil around her wrist.

"Say it too, Bree!" she yelped excitedly.

Bree shouted the command, and to her relief vines began to tighten around her waist.

"Thank you, Theb. I would *never* have remembered that."

"They will take you up there safely," he said. "But I must warn you, when you reach the top you will still be miles away from the castle. If that's where you're still going of course."

"It is," said Bree as the vines lifted them slowly from the ground.

"Take care!" Theb shouted.

"Goodbye Theb! We'll never forget you."

Bree wasn't sure if he'd heard her, already he was nothing more than a tiny spot beneath her. The vines felt tight around her middle, but that did not stop her wild anxiety as the ground dropped away.

"This is fun!" whooped Honey.

Bree smiled nervously. Soon the top of the cliff was in sight.

"Nearly there," she said, not daring to look down.

Suddenly Bree felt the vines loosen. One by one they turned brown and shrivelled up. She screamed, grabbing the one remaining at her waist, but it turned to dust beneath her fingers, and she plummeted towards the ground, the rushing air plucking the breath from her mouth. As she braced herself for a hard landing, she came to a sudden stop on something soft and velvety. When she opened her eyes she saw two purple wings stretched out on either side of her.

Giant butterflies filled the sky in a kaleidoscope of colour. Honey drew up alongside her on a beautiful yellow specimen.

"Talk about perfect timing," she laughed.

As they glided effortlessly over the Realm of the Lost, Castle Zarcalat soared into sight, a black mass atop a jagged rock. The sky grumbled ominously, a prolonged rumble of thunder that felt like a warning.

They were swallowed up by a black cloud, and for a second everything was silent and grey. It was so dark and dense it felt like breathing in ash. Just when Bree thought she would choke, they flew out the other side into pummelling rain.

As they circled down towards the cobbled courtyard of Castle Zarcalat the rain slackened, but it still felt hard and cold, like needles against their skin. Bree turned and saw Honey's butterfly flapping furiously, struggling to stay in the air. Holes had appeared all over its wings. Honey clung on, terrified, as it tilted this way and that in erratic loops.

It was a rough landing, broken only by the soft, cushiony bodies of the butterflies which quickly dissolved on the wet cobblestones. Honey stared down miserably at the watery yellow and purple streaks that merged together before being washed away.

"They...they melted!"

A snapping noise above their heads made them jump. They looked up to see the charred remains of a crimson flag wrapping around the pole. The letter Z stood out at the centre, bold and defiant.

"I had hoped this place would've burned to the ground last time," Honey said.

Bree remembered running towards the drawbridge, away from the hungry, crackling roar of fire. She remembered hot sparks raining down through thick, swirling smoke, and the castle glowing orange through a crown of burning cloud.

Part of the building *had* been destroyed. The stone was charred and cracked where the flames had licked at it, and an entire section of roof had completely caved in. Some of the windows were broken, and exposed rafters stuck up in the air like the ribs of an animal carcass. A thick mist clung to everything and Bree shivered as the wind whipped her hair and pulled at the hem of her coat.

"Let's get some shelter," she said, "we'll have to be extra careful. They're expecting us."

As they scurried across the courtyard the windows seemed to watch them. They hid in the shadows with their backs to the wet stone. Honey looked up, rain sparkling like glitter on her eyelashes, and her expression darkened.

"What is it?" asked Bree.

"Don't you see what's missing?"

Another flash of lightning lit up the glistening walls and stone pillars.

"The gargoyles," Bree muttered, "they're gone."

She exchanged a worried look with Honey.

"The question is: where are they now?"

The rain began to fall again, blowing in gusting waves across the bleak courtyard. Thunder boomed as the sky lit up in a single flash of yellow. It was then that Bree saw him, standing at the drawbridge. Tanas Theramonde. And he was not alone.

The red-skinned creature from the library stood beside him with at least five more, just like it.

"That answers our question about the gargoyles," Honey whispered.

"I *knew* he was back here," Bree said.

Honey signaled for her to stay quiet. The gargoyles appeared to be having a discussion in a language of grunts and sniffs as Theramonde looked on. Much to Bree's relief, they all crossed to the other side of the bridge, disappearing out of sight.

She turned to see the yawning archway with the shield above it.

"Hurry, I remember how we got in before," she said, making her way towards it.

Honey pulled her back.

"This time we're going in the front way."

"Are you crazy?"

"Maybe just a little," said Honey as she crept towards the flight of stone steps.

Crouching low they moved silently up to the arched door, where a giant handle hung in the shape of an upside down heart.

"Here goes," Honey whispered as she slid through the narrow gap.

Bree squeezed in behind her and closed the door as quietly as she could. Burning torches lined a long, dark corridor and a wheel of candles hung from the ceiling. To their right a spiral staircase indicated another level.

"At least there's no welcoming committee," said Honey, shaking off the rain. She turned, the flames casting flickering shadows on her face.

"Which way?"

Bree looked at the staircase as it curved gently, disappearing into darkness.

"Let's try the corridor," she said.

The floors were dark polished wood, and the walls were lined with portraits and tapestries. A gallery of solemn faces seemed to come alive in the shifting light, and haunted eyes followed them as they ventured down the draughty corridor. Bree looked up at a painting with a wisp of spider web stretched across the corner of the frame. Shadows danced across the face of a pale woman with silver hair that was fastened in a coil around her head. Her lips were blood red and she wore a dress made from rich, elaborate fabric. Bree recognised her as the woman who had stood alongside Reinor at the water's edge. A plaque at the bottom of the frame read, *Sister of the Valley*.

"I'm glad she's not *my* sister," muttered Bree, turning to look at the portrait opposite.

A bald man with a ginger beard stared out at her with eyes that were swallowed up by his ruddy cheeks.

"It's Reinor," she gasped, tugging on Honey's sleeve.

As Honey stepped forwards to inspect the painting, a huge spider scuttled across the centre. She shrieked and as she jumped backwards, her hand slammed into the corner of the portrait of the woman. It began to move and rotated into the wall, turning on a central pivot like a revolving door. The torches guttered in a gust of cold air.

"Well whaddaya know!" laughed Honey.

She stuck her head through the hole and pulled it back out immediately.

"Smells weird. And there's a staircase."

Bree peered in and saw a dark, cramped space with a flight of crumbling stone steps that rose up to meet a wooden door.

The smell of wet soil and stale air filled her nostrils with a cloying earthiness.

"Do you think we should check it out?"

Just as Honey was about to answer, the main door opened with a creak.

"Quick! Get in!" she hissed, shoving Bree through the hole and leaping in after her.

Together they pulled the painting closed until they were standing in absolute darkness. Heavy, shuffling footsteps passed on the other side, and then grew fainter as they disappeared down the corridor. Bree sagged with relief.

"I didn't have time to grab a torch," she whispered.

"Don't worry," said Honey, rummaging inside her satchel, "I've got just the thing."

There was a crack, and all of a sudden the darkness was swallowed up by a yellow glow. Bree glanced down to see light leaking out through Honey's cupped fingers.

"A glow-stick!"

"Yip," smiled Honey, "and there are more where this came from. I had a feeling they might come in handy when I bought them."

She held it out in front of her and illuminated the first few broken steps. Slowly, carefully, they climbed them. The door at the top was heavy, and when they pushed against it there was a ripping sound as it freed itself from the frame. A wave of cool air enveloped them along with the smell of burning wax.

Honey pushed the door wide to reveal a small candlelit room.

"Ladies first," she grinned, stepping aside.

Bree stepped through. Standing very still, her eyes raked the shadows. Over on the left wall there was a very narrow window and a red door. In the centre of the floor was a small hole, and tucked in the corner of the room was a set of old-fashioned scales, jugs of varying sizes, and a tap in the wall. Honey closed the door behind her and peered out of the window.

"I can see the courtyard. Mmm, I wonder what's behind that door," she said, moving towards it.

"Be careful!" warned Bree. "You never know what – "

A soft click stopped Honey in her tracks. She turned slowly, her eyes brimming with panic.

"Something moved under my foot."

Cautiously she stepped forwards and nothing happened.

"Phew," she sighed. "Just a loose tile."

Suddenly, the wall to their right broke free and started moving towards them.

"It must have been some kind of trigger," Bree shouted, as she tugged on the door they had come through. "I can't get it open!"

Honey ran over to the red door and pushed and pulled, but it remained firmly shut.

"Quick, give me the magic key."

Bree fumbled inside her pocket and pulled it out. Honey grabbed it and crouched down.

"There's no keyhole in either door."

Plumes of dust rose up as the wall scraped slowly across the floor. Bree searched the room for an escape route, but there was nothing. Honey grabbed her satchel and leapt up, her face filled with hope.

"It's The Book! It's vibrating!"

She pulled it out and the red glow from the locket lit up her face in pulsing waves.

"About time too," she said, thrusting it into Bree's trembling fingers.

Bree quickly opened the cover and flattened the third page. While the wall moved ever closer the paper began to change until, at last, it was transparent. Out of the swirling mist the fourth wish appeared.

> **In order for the walls to stop,**
> **Use the tap - don't spill a drop!**
> **Measure out but be precise,**
> **Exactly four pints will suffice.**
> **The scales and jugs marked three and five,**
> **Are what you need to stay alive.**

Honey searched frantically through the jugs, kicking them aside and throwing them over her shoulder until she found what she was looking for.

"Gotcha!" she said, holding up the one with a number five on it. "Now we can fill this with four pints of water."

"But how will you know when it gets to four pints?" asked Bree, closing The Book and slipping it into her pocket.

"Well it's going to be approximately four fifths of this jug, isn't it?"

"But the wish says *exactly*, not *approximately*."

The wall inched its way across the floor.

"Tell me what to do then!"

"Let me think!"

"There's no TIME to think!"

Honey grabbed the tap.

"Wait!" said Bree. "Fill the five-pint jug all the way to the top."

"But –"

"JUST DO IT!"

Honey turned the tap and it let out a stiff, rusty squeal. Water poured out and started filling the jug.

"Now, using some of the water from that jug," said Bree, "fill the three-pint jug to the brim."

Honey did what she was told, careful not to spill any.

"But that leaves only two pints," she said, waving the five-pint jug so the contents sloshed around inside.

Bree nodded.

"I know. Now pour *all* the water from the three-pint jug down the hole in the floor. We don't need it."

Honey looked baffled but she did what Bree asked. She shook the empty three-pint jug.

"What now?"

"Pour the two pints of water that are in the *five*-pint jug into the *three*-pint jug," said Bree.

"This doesn't make any sense!"

Bree flapped her hands impatiently as she watched the wall edging closer. "You'll have to hurry, Honey!"

Honey worked quickly as the wall moved closer towards them.

"Remember not to spill any," said Bree, "the wish said this has to be precise."

Honey held up the empty five-pint jug and looked like she might cry.

"I'm totally confused," she said.

"We're almost there," said Bree. "We now have two pints of water in the three-pint jug, leaving one pint of empty space at the top. Right?"

Honey nodded.

"Now fill the five-pint jug to the brim again," Bree instructed.

"What the –"

Bree silenced her with a glare.

Honey held the five-pint jug under the tap and the water quickly reached the top. She looked up to see the wall almost upon them.

"Quickly!" said Bree, straining to halt its advance. "Pour enough of the water from the five-pint jug to take the water in the three-pint jug up to the brim. That'll leave exactly four pints in the five-pint jug!"

Honey completed her task, careful not to lose any of the precious water.

When she placed the jug onto the scales there was a horrible moment where nothing happened. All hope trickled away, and then as suddenly as it had started, the wall stopped and began to move back to its original position. Inside Bree's pocket the pulse of the locket grew so faint she could barely feel it.

"Well done Honey, you were amazing," she said.

"I'm still not entirely sure what just happened," said Honey. "I think I had a bit of a blonde moment."

She tugged on the handle of the red door.

"I don't understand. It's still stuck."

"The locket is still throbbing," said Bree. "The wish isn't over yet."

The handle of the other door rattled. Frozen with fear they watched the handle move again, more urgently this time. Honey backed away as a loud thump was followed by a crack of wood.

Bree ran over to the window and looked down at the cobbled courtyard. There was no way they could fit through the narrow slit, and even if they did the fall would kill them. A jagged fist of splinters appeared in the middle of the door and a meaty hand reached through and groped for the handle. A diamond ring flashed on an index finger.

The shattered door flew open with enough force to rip it from its hinges. Bree saw the outline of a heavy man and the gleam of a knife. Hallux Valgus heaved himself over the threshold and shuffled across the floor with shallow, wheezing breaths. He turned, revealing wrecked, purple skin on one side of his face, and the mangled remains of a flame tattoo on his forehead. Honey moaned softly and turned her head away.

"What, can you not bear to look at me?" he growled, stabbing the air with his dagger. "*You* did this to me! *You!* And, so, we meet again. Only this time there appears to be only two of you."

Honey stepped forward, her blue eyes flashing.

"Sandy's coming for us soon. And he won't be alone so you'd better let us go."

Valgus threw back his head and laughed, making the veins in his neck bulge.

"You must think I'm stupid. No-one knows you are here."

Honey swallowed noisily.

"We know what you want..."

Bree threw her a sideways glance. In her pocket the locket still throbbed faintly.

"...But we'll never give it to you," she added, stubbornly.

"Have it your way," said Valgus, his voice a hot ball of venom.

He muttered some dark words under his breath and turned the diamond ring three times. With a rush of horror Bree remembered the swarm of bats and the rising waters that had come the last time Valgus had done this.

"*Wait!* We'll give you what you want."

Slowly she slid her hand into her pocket, her fingertips

brushing the edge of The Book. Honey stepped in front of her.

"*I've* got The Book!" she blurted, tapping her satchel. "It's in here."

"I won't fall for your tricks like the last time."

"Do you *really* think I'm going to trick you when you're holding a dagger?"

She held out her satchel with shaky hands.

"Come on. It's in here if you want it."

Valgus shuffled over the tiles, his eyes glinting greedily. He stopped in front of Honey and ran his tongue over his lips. She slid the zip along slowly. He eyed it suspiciously then stuck his hand through the opening.

SNAP!

He yelped with pain and staggered backwards, trying to flick the mousetrap off his fingers. His dagger fell and skittered across the tiles.

"GET IT OFF ME!" he roared. But Bree and Honey had already disappeared through the red door.

CHAPTER 20
SEVENTEEN DOORS, FIFTEEN KEYS

They burst through a door at the top of a steep staircase and Honey slammed it behind them. Inside an alcove a single torch burned steadily, throwing shadows onto the moss-cloaked stone. The tiny space was so dimly lit it took several blinks for Bree's eyes to adjust. She soon saw that the only way out was through a hole that had been cut into the wall. Honey pressed her ear to the door.

"I don't hear anything," she whispered, dropping to her knees and peering through the keyhole, "but he's sure to come after us."

"At least we know Valgus and Theramonde are not in Rockwell anymore," said Bree. "And we *did* come here looking for trouble."

"I wasn't expecting to find it so soon though," said Honey, "and I didn't think there would only be the two of us."

"We're going to have to find a way of stopping them before the veil disappears during the lunar eclipse," said Bree. "We can't just run away every time we're faced with danger."

"I know," said Honey, "but we have to be completely prepared. We're going to need weapons. Let's see what we can find."

She pulled the torch from its holder and held it out in front of her.

"More steps," she said as she swept aside some cobwebs

and ducked through the hole. "Come on, it's not like we've got any choice."

The flame spat and flickered, throwing an uncertain light onto the worn steps. The space got narrower towards the top, forcing them to sidle up the last few steps. Eventually they came out into a room where lots of doors were spaced out evenly along the walls.

Bree counted seventeen, all of them familiar, each one with a number above it. 8 – Bree's bedroom, 13 – Mr Patel's shop, 27 – her Granny Lissa's front door. There were the beads from Annie's kitchen, and the main entrance to the Rockwell Tower Block too. Bree felt a sudden longing for home.

"Look! It's Kimbalee's café," said Honey, striding towards a door with a glass pane.

Bree pulled her back.

"Stop! It's probably a trick."

"You're right. They knew we were coming. They're sure to have set traps for us."

Bree scratched her head.

"We're going to have to choose one though. Or else we'll be stuck here forever."

"Any ideas?" Honey asked.

Bree shook her head.

"Now would be a good time for wish five," she sighed, sliding The Book from her pocket. She noticed that the faint outline of wish four was still on the screen.

"The last wish hasn't come to an end," she said, as a tiny pulse reawakened beneath her fingers.

"Let me see that," said Honey, staring eagerly at the screen.

They watched a swirling mist fill the screen and devour wish four. The fog cleared and more words emerged. Bree read them aloud.

> How many chances has a cat,
> To wear a suit and bowler hat,
> To spend an hour, a stitch in time,
> Upon this happy cloud he's climbed?

Honey looked at her with a puzzled frown.

"Well that was about as much use as a chocolate teapot."

Bree read the words over and over again while Honey paced the room. Suddenly the answer jumped out at her.

"I've got it!"

In a flash the words on the screen disappeared and the locket stopped throbbing.

"The answer is nine."

"How exactly?"

Bree slipped The Book into her pocket.

"Well, a cat has nine chances because it has nine lives. And if someone is wearing a suit and a hat they would be dressed to the nines..."

A smile spread across Honey's face.

"A stitch in time saves nine and if you're happy you would be on cloud nine."

"Not just a pretty face," Honey laughed, giving Bree a high five.

Door number nine was the front door to *Hart and Soul*. Every detail was there, down to the 'Open' sign and the stained glass cross.

"I know we're not going to see William," said Bree, "but it

would be nice if we did, wouldn't it?"

Honey nodded and pushed down on the handle. A bell tinkled and for a moment Bree thought they were going back into the tiny shop. Instead the door led them to one flight of stairs after another – stone steps, metal steps and creaky wooden stairs. Once Bree and Honey started climbing it felt like they would never stop. They followed the stairs as they spidered off in different directions. Up and up, round and round. It made Bree dizzy.

"I've lost all sense of direction. We must be at the other side of the castle by now."

Honey stopped to catch her breath.

"The amount of stairs we've climbed I wouldn't be surprised if we were on the *moon*."

They followed a narrow corridor, which led eventually into a small room. Natural light peeped through diamond-shaped windowpanes, and velvet curtains were draped around the frames. Glass chandeliers twinkled above their heads. The floor looked like a chessboard, and the only furniture was a window seat – a rectangular box with a padded cushion and a heavy padlock. Fifteen identical keys were hanging from hooks in the wall.

"There's no way out of here except the door we came through," said Bree.

"I hope we're not going to have to climb out the windows," Honey said nervously.

"I daren't look," said Bree. "We must be *miles* up after that climb."

She braced herself and peered through the murky panes.

"I...I don't understand. We're the same height off the ground as we were in the first room."

"That can't be right," said Honey. She stared down to the courtyard, confusion clouding her eyes.

"But...but we climbed and *climbed!*"

Bree slumped wearily onto the window seat. The lid creaked under her weight and she leapt up.

"There's something in here," she said, tugging on the padlock.

"Maybe we'll find some weapons!" said Honey, her face alight.

Bree studied the row of keys along the opposite wall.

"I suppose we could try every key," she suggested, "one of them must fit the padlock."

"I'll bet there's some terrible forfeit if we choose the wrong one," said Honey. "I'll try the magic key first."

She tried to push it into the hole but it would not fit.

"It's too big," she said, handing it to Bree. "It's the first time *that's* happened."

Bree climbed onto the window seat and stretched up, running her hands along the tops of the curtains. They were furred with dust and thick with cobwebs.

"What are you doing?" asked Honey.

"Perhaps there's a clue hidden somewhere. Or another key."

She inspected every crease of the musty fabric, but there was nothing except a thick layer of grime and some dead spiders. She coughed and wafted away the dust.

"Anything?" Honey asked.

"Nope."

A flash of lightning momentarily lit up the floor, and Bree's eyes were drawn to a grid made up of nine tiles with numbers carved into them.

"Come up here," she said. "There's something you might like to see."

Standing shoulder to shoulder they stared down at the mysterious number square.

"I *know* this is a clue," said Bree, "I'm just not sure what we're supposed to do with it."

4	9	2
3	5	7
8	1	6

"It's some kind of wonky phone pad," said Honey. "Or a giant game of Sudoku."

Bree tried to make sense of the random numbers.

"Somewhere in this grid lies the answer to which key we need."

"But the numbers only go up to nine," said Honey. "And there are fifteen keys."

Bree scratched her head.

"It's a code and we have to crack it," she said. "Simple."

"Yeah, simple," muttered Honey. "I wish Sandy was here. He's great with numbers."

"Well," Bree said bluntly, "we'll have to think like Sandy then, won't we."

"Perhaps it's the tile in the middle," Honey suggested, "number five."

"I doubt it. Far too easy."

Honey flicked her hair over her shoulder.

"Well four times nine equals thirty-six," she said slowly. "Multiply that by two and you get seventy-two then add the next line and divide it by – "

"Stop! That's *far* too complicated!"

Honey threw her hands up.

"First it's too simple, now it's too complicated. Make your mind up!

"Stop yelling! I nearly had something there!"

Honey crossed her arms and sulked silently.

"Look," said Bree. "The top row adds up to fifteen and so does the middle row."

Honey's eyes flicked across the grid, following Bree's calculations.

"The bottom row adds up to fifteen too," she said with a sudden, wide smile.

Bree clapped her hands excitedly.

"Whether it's horizontally, vertically or diagonally, each row adds up to the same number!"

They turned to each other and laughed.

"Fifteen!"

Bree jumped down, ran over and grabbed the last key in the row.

"It's this one," she said, thrusting it into the keyhole. The padlock sprung open.

Bree looked at Honey, whose huge eyes sparkled with anticipation.

"Are you ready to see what's inside?" she whispered, and Honey nodded slowly.

The hinges creaked as Bree lifted the lid. Inside, a narrow flight of stone steps plunged down into darkness.

"Not more steps!" said Honey.

"At least it wasn't a nasty surprise," Bree said, climbing inside.

As soon as her foot touched the top step they disappeared, one by one, into the wall.

"AAAAGGGH!"

Bree was tumbling into complete darkness, falling for what seemed like an eternity before landing roughly onto a pile of wet straw. She scrambled to her feet and saw that she was in a room, which was saved from total darkness by a line of burning torches along one wall. Water dripped from a low stone ceiling, and the thick walls were damp and cold. Her eyes were drawn to a row of iron shackles bolted to the wall. *A dungeon!*

Strange shapes loomed up at her as she tiptoed towards a heavy wooden door with a square grille cut out of the centre. Reaching up, she wrapped her fingers around the bars and tugged on them with all her might. The door was stuck.

"Bree! Breeeee! Are you theeeere?!"

Honey's frantic voice wafted out from the mouth of the tunnel. Bree ran over and threw herself at it.

"I'm down here! In some kind of prison cell!"

"Are you hurt?"

"No! But the door is locked. I can't get out!"

There was silence at the other end.

"*HONEY!* Are you still there?"

"Yes! Can you climb up?"

Bree crawled into the hole and tried to clamber up but it was steep and slippery and she slid back down.

"NO!

"I'm going to try and get to you another way!"

Bree leaned back against the cold wall, and as she did she

noticed symbols and words had been scratched into the stone, the pleas of desperate people who had been here before her. Bree paced the chamber, stopping to press her ear to the door. Cautiously she went up on her tiptoes and peered through the bars. She could see a torchlit corridor. A hollow moan echoed out of the depths and cold air brushed her cheek. Footsteps were heading her way. *Honey!* She was on the verge of shouting when she heard grunting breaths. Crouching behind the door she listened. A swishing cloak passed by on the other side. Bree waited and then slowly slid back up the door and peeped through the bars.

A face stared back at her, a mangled mess of melted flesh and an egg yolk eye. Bree ran to the furthest corner of the dungeon and hid in the shadows. The eerie silence was shattered by the jangle of keys. With a creak the door opened and a shadow spread out over the floor. Hallux Valgus lumbered over the floor and stopped. A scream lurked somewhere at the back of Bree's throat. She glanced at the open door and prepared to run. Valgus took a step to the side, blocking her escape route. He slammed the door shut and turned the lock with a key that hung at his hip.

"Where to now my frightened little rabbit?" he said, his mismatched eyes glinting.

"*Please.* I've done nothing wrong."

His lip curled in malicious triumph as he shuffled forwards.

"My heart bleeds."

"Please let me out of here."

Valgus sniffed and casually inspected the ring on his finger.

"You know what you have to do first," he said with a chilling calmness.

Bree put her hand over her pocket.

"I'll never give it to you!"

"I admire your courage, but surely you must have known that by coming back here you were risking The Book?"

"We came back to kill you!" cried Bree.

Valgus laughed humourlessly.

"Not long from now our worlds will collide. Everything that is yours will be ours. There is not a single thing you can do to stop it."

"Yes there is! I think you're forgetting something."

The smile slipped from his mangled face and his mouth settled into a cruel, thin line.

"What?"

"Even if our worlds *do* collide, I'll still be the one who has The Book. And I have to give it willingly. Nobody can take it from me."

Valgus puffed up with annoyance.

"I *will* get it from you," he snarled, his breath rattling in his chest. "One way or another."

"If you kill me you'll *never* get it," she said. "You can't take it from me without my consent. Even if I'm *dead!*"

Valgus's eyes narrowed and his cheek twitched. With an angry curse he stamped his foot down and paced the room, muttering under his breath. He stopped next to the door. As he turned, the torchlight cast ragged shadows across his cheek and for a moment he looked as he had before the fire.

"I can give you anything you want," he said, desperation creeping into his voice.

"Anything?" Bree asked quietly.

He nodded.

"I want my Dad."

Valgus stared at her, his eye twitching.

"See! You can't give me *anything I want!*"

He spun around and pointed his finger at the far corner of the room.

"Tribuo Abbas Vita!" he bellowed, then everything went quiet except for the hollow drip of water on stone.

Valgus stood by the door, but there was another presence; something lurking in the darkness. Bree caught a movement out of the corner of her eye and leapt up as a long shadow poured over the floor.

"Get away from me!" she cried, staggering backwards. "Leave me alone!"

A man appeared before her. His lips curved into a smile.

"Dad?"

Richard McCready's eyes twinkled as she inched cautiously towards him.

"My sweet Bree."

"I knew you'd come back for me!"

"Of course," he said softly. "I love you."

She felt a desperate need to touch him and confirm he was real. Her fingertips brushed his sleeve and he disappeared.

Valgus laughed a cruel laugh.

"He's DEAD you stupid girl! Even magic can't bring him back!"

Bree could not control the roar of murderous hatred that flooded her veins.

"I HATE YOU!" she spat.

His face twisted into an expression of wild fury.

Her blood ran cold as he started chanting under his breath with vicious precision. He turned his ring three times and held his palm upwards. Kneeling down beside her, he thrust his hand in her face. She backed away.

"Look at it," he said calmly.

She squeezed her eyes closed.

"LOOK AT IT!"

Reluctantly she stole a glance and saw, at the centre of his palm, a blurry image. It was Adam. He was laughing and tuning his guitar.

"Don't you *dare* hurt him."

Valgus grinned with cruel satisfaction.

"I have no intention of touching the boy," he said coolly. "But after I'm finished with you, he'll never look at you again."

"What are you going to do?"

He closed his fingers into a fat fist and the image disappeared. He paced up and down the chamber muttering under his breath. All of a sudden he stopped and pointed at her. The diamond flashed in the torchlight.

"Verto Virgo Vetus," he chanted repeatedly, until his mangled tattoo changed from black to red, glowing stronger with each sinister word.

Bree closed her eyes and curled up into a tight ball. Suddenly the chanting stopped and she dared to open one eye. Everything was blurry. She opened both eyes. She could see dark shapes and shadows but nothing more. She blinked rapidly but that only made things worse. She tried to unfurl her limbs but everything creaked and ached. Even the roots of her hair hurt. She felt cold and brittle. Her bones rattled beneath paper skin and her mouth felt dry. She was tired – *exhausted* – even the slightest movement used up all her energy. She tried to sit up but a rattle deep in her chest stopped her.

"What have you done to me?" she said, not recognizing the croak that left her lips.

Valgus squatted beside her.

"Such a shame," he said sadly and pushed the hair from her eyes. "You were so beautiful."

Bree heard him slide the knife from his boot, and she tried to scramble away. Slowly he lifted it to her face and tilted the blade so she could see her blurred reflection. Her mahogany eyes had a milky sheen on them. Her hair had thinned and was streaked with grey, while her face was a mass of savage, deep wrinkles. She brushed her cheek with a liver spotted, wrinkled hand.

"I'm an old woman."

"Old and withered," said Valgus, standing up and sliding the knife back into his boot. "Who could love you now?"

He pulled her up from the floor and she held onto the wall. Her spine was curved and her legs were shaky.

He moved close and whispered in her ear.

"Perhaps if you were my wife we could *share* The Book."

Bree wheezed in a painful breath and nodded.

Valgus stroked her cheek with a clammy finger. "I knew you would see sense."

"But if I am to be your wife I will need a ring," she said softly.

Valgus looked puzzled.

"In my world every bride must have a ring," Bree explained. "It is a symbol of eternal love."

Her chest rattled and she coughed.

"We must hurry though. I don't have much time left."

Valgus forced the diamond ring over his chubby knuckle and pushed it onto her gnarled finger. She felt a shiver of power crawl along her skin.

"We are married now," he grinned, his eyes travelling down to her pocket. "What's yours is mine."

The grin wilted from his face when she pointed a bony

finger in his direction. Words left her lips in a voice that did not belong to her.

"Planto Is Atrox Intereo," she said over and over, in a dark whisper.

Valgus staggered backwards, horrified and then fell to his knees.

"You...you tricked me!"

Bree felt her spine slowly straighten and her vision clear.

"I may be old, but I'm not stupid."

He clutched his forehead and staggered to his feet. He reeled around in circles, screaming and clawing at his head. Bree shielded her eyes against the light that bloomed in the centre of his chest and spread outwards until it reached the tips of his fingers and the toes of his boots. For a moment their eyes met before he turned to dust and was sucked into a wall of light. There was a soundless explosion and the light vanished, leaving Bree alone in the dark confines of the dungeon.

She looked down and saw that her hands had returned to normal. She felt her face and found soft skin beneath her fingertips. The pain and wheezing breaths had vanished. She ran to the door, fumbling for the magic key but to her dismay the keyhole had disappeared.

A cold draught swept along the walls and extinguished some of the torches. Bree held her breath and listened. Someone – *something* – was on the other side of the door. Cautiously she peered out through the bars. The face that stared back at her was an unearthly white with hair that shone jet black.

"Sandy! Is that *really* you?"

"Yes it's me," he laughed as their fingers locked together through the bars.

"And me!"

"You took your time, Honey," Bree laughed.

"I came as fast as I could," said Sandy.

"How on *earth* did you find us? And why the change of heart?"

Sandy sighed.

"I knew that I'd made the wrong decision the minute you left. I guess I was in shock and really confused, but when I imagined never seeing you again I…"

Bree squeezed his hands.

"How did you get out of the Realm of the Lost?"

"It wasn't easy! My Mum and Dad helped me."

"Oh, Sandy, they must've been so sad to see you leave."

"Well…" he cleared his throat. "It was hard, but they understood. *You're* my family now. You, Honey, and Gran. They knew I didn't belong in the Realm; they don't want me to suffer the way they have. All they want is for me to be happy."

Honey's face appeared.

"I know you guys have some catching up to do but now is not the time. We really need to get you out of there."

She stepped aside and Sandy took a run at the door, ramming it with his shoulder.

"It's stuck solid," he said, "is there a key?"

"Valgus took it with him," replied Bree.

"*Valgus!* Hallux Valgus was in there with you?"

Bree nodded.

"I think he's dead."

"Good. That's one less to think about," said Sandy.

"We saw Theramonde at the drawbridge and I think Reinor is here too. There was a portrait of him."

Sandy's expression darkened.

"Do you have the magic key?"

"Yes, but there's no keyhole. What about on your side?"

"None here either. Is The Book okay?"

Bree nodded.

"Stand back and cover your face," said Sandy.

Bree scurried to the corner and stood facing the wall. There was an almighty bang and the sound of splintering wood. She turned slowly and saw, through a reeking pall of smoke, the door hanging from its hinges. Sandy and Honey ran into the chamber and threw themselves at her, knocking the air from her lungs.

"What on earth *was* that?" Bree squeaked.

"It was the fruit from the Acoomathid plant," said Sandy, straightening his glasses. "Theb told us if they hit the ground with enough force...*BOOM!*"

"Well he was certainly right about that," said Bree. "Do you have any more?"

Sandy shook his head.

"I only took one. But I'm glad I did."

Honey threw her hand to her mouth.

"Is that what I think it is?" she gasped, staring down at Bree's hand.

Bree suddenly remembered Valgus's ring was still on her finger.

"Get it off me!"

"Stay still," ordered Honey as she wiggled it from side to side until it slid off and landed on the stone.

"What should we do with it?" asked Sandy.

Honey's eyes flashed.

"I think it might come in handy," she said, picking it up and putting it in her pocket.

Suddenly the sound of heavy footsteps echoed at the other

end of the corridor, and a chorus of angry voices grew louder. Honey peered round what was left of the doorframe. She shrank back against the wall, her eyes filled with fear.

"Guards. And they're heading this way."

CHAPTER 21
THE DREAM

"They're searching all the rooms," said Sandy, peeking out. "That should buy us some time."

Honey jabbed her thumb to the left.

"There's a flight of stairs that way. Let's make a run for it."

They waited until the guards had their backs turned and then crept along the passageway, dodging puddles of slime along the way. The sound of a sword being drawn stopped them in their tracks. Bree turned around to see a man emerging from the shadows. He had a bald head, chalk white skin and red eyelids. Honey pulled the packet of popping candy from her satchel and tipped the contents onto the wet stone. Immediately, the floor fizzled, cracked and popped, and the guard backed away in horror as sparks shot out at him. They ran without looking back.

Halfway along the passageway a cold draught swept through, extinguishing most of the flames in one icy breath.

Bree ran her hand along the wall to discover a wooden surface. After a few moments the darkness rearranged itself into slabs of grey and it was possible to see they had come to a large, studded door. A blade of light shone out from underneath.

She pushed down the handle and damp air whispered across her cheek. One by one they stepped into an empty room where the shadows were brought to life by flickering, amber flames. The air felt dank and chilly, like a tomb. Their footsteps echoed over uneven flagstones. The door closed behind them with a bang. In a panic, Sandy ran back, but he tripped and sprawled across the floor, his glasses askew.

"Are you okay?" asked Honey, helping him up.

"I think so. One of the stones was sticking up."

He looked past Honey to the far wall where there was a bricked-up door.

"Look," he said, straightening his glasses. "I can see some Roman numerals."

When they got closer they saw that CLXXX had been engraved into the archway above what had once been a doorway.

"I wonder why the door was filled in," said Bree, tapping the bricks with her knuckles.

"Maybe to keep people in," said Honey, pulling a packet of gumballs from her satchel and popping one into her mouth.

"Or to keep something out," said Sandy, putting his ear to the wall.

Honey ran her finger around the numeral C.

"Roman numerals are based on seven symbols," she said, chewing wildly. "A single stroke is one, V is five, C is one hundred and X is ten." She scratched her head and frowned. "I've forgotten what L equals."

"L is fifty," said Sandy. "They all add up to one hundred and eighty."

Honey stabbed her tongue into the gum.

"I wonder what it could mean?" she said.

"A semi-circle has 180 degrees in it," suggested Bree, following the line of the arch with her finger.

Sandy paced up and down the room, staring intently at the floor. Suddenly his face lit up.

"This stone I tripped over. It's one of three. Look, there's one beside your foot, Honey, and another one next to the bricked-up door."

Honey and Bree stared blankly at him.

"Each stone is about four metres apart," he explained. "And they form an equilateral triangle..."

"Go on," said Bree, impatient now, "get to the point."

"Well, the angles in a triangle add up to – "

"One hundred and eighty degrees."

"So what do we do with them?" said Bree.

"Well, I hadn't thought that far ahead," confessed Sandy, scratching his head.

Honey gave the stone at her foot a gentle kick. When nothing happened she stepped up onto it.

"There are three of us and three of them," she said, balancing carefully, "I wonder if..."

She dropped down as the stone lowered, stopping when it was level with the floor. She stood as still as a statue, her panicked eyes flicking between Bree and Sandy.

Bree waited for the walls to start moving. But nothing happened.

"What do we do now?" asked Honey.

"Whatever you do *don't* step off the stone," said Sandy.

"I can't stay here for the rest of my life!"

"*I know*. Just let me think."

The torches spluttered in the heavy silence. Eventually Bree turned to Sandy.

"What if *we* stand on the other two?" she said. "Maybe something will happen then?"

"I guess we'll only know if we try," said Sandy, stepping onto the stone.

There was an echo of grinding stone as he lowered to the floor. Honey stared expectantly at Bree.

"Your turn."

Reluctantly she stepped up onto it, balancing there for a few moments before it sunk.

"We've formed a human triangle," said Sandy.

"But nothing's happening," said Bree.

A rumble shook the floor and Honey lost her balance.

"It is now!"

"Don't fall off!" screeched Sandy.

Honey shot him an icy glare.

"I'm trying my best."

There was another rumble, louder this time. The torches flickered and mortar dust puffed out from the cracks in the stone.

Honey's eyes filled with panic.

"We're all going to die!"

Bree waited for the walls to close in on them, for the roof to fall, for some terrible creature to burst through the door and eat them alive. Instead, the bricks inside the door slid aside one by one to reveal a dark passageway.

Honey snorted.

"Well, *that* wasn't very exciting, was it?"

Sandy glared at her.

"Good!"

He pulled out his mobile phone.

"We can use this to light the way," he said, shining the torch into the passageway.

When they were all inside, the bricks closed back over one

by one and the cone of feeble light vanished into the darkness.

"Let's hope it's not too far," said Sandy, "I can hardly see a thing and the battery is dying."

There was a crunch and everything lit up yellow.

"These things are pretty useful," Honey grinned, holding up another of the glow sticks she'd bought at the fair.

"Brilliant!" said Sandy.

Bree spotted a circle of light through the inky darkness.

"I think I can see something," she said, pointing ahead.

Suddenly there was a snuffling noise behind her. She spun around quickly, and then stood perfectly still.

"What is it?" whispered Honey.

Shuffle. Scrape. Grunt.

Bree's scalp crawled.

"Something is in here."

Honey swept the glow stick in an arc and Bree glimpsed a clot of shadow. It moved and she saw it – a gargoyle. It twisted its skull-like head, yellow eyes fixing on her. Honey dropped the fading glow stick and grabbed her.

As they scrambled through the darkness Bree glanced back to see the gargoyle gaining on Sandy. Suddenly he stopped and fumbled inside his pocket. She ran back.

"What are you doing? Run!"

"Keep going," he said, shaking her off, "I've got something."

He lifted a long thick straw to his mouth and puffed hard on the end. Something shot out just as the gargoyle leapt at them. It dropped to the floor clutching its throat. Eyes bulging, mouth frothing, it staggered drunkenly then fell at their feet.

"I hit it!" laughed Sandy. "I actually hit it!"

"What was that?" asked Bree.

"Frog poison," replied Sandy, holding up a blowpipe. "Mum

gave it to me."

Honey's footsteps echoed down the passageway.

"What happened?" she panted. Her eyes slid down to the gargoyle. She shuddered as frothy slime trickled from its mouth. "Is it dead?"

"As a doornail," replied Sandy, shoving the blow dart into his pocket. "My mum said there was enough poison in that to kill ten men."

"Let's get out of here," said Bree, "in case he brought his friends."

As they turned, the sound of grinding stone travelled along the passageway. The ceiling started lowering, a great square of stone rumbling downwards.

The gargoyle heaved a final breath and curled its talons around Sandy's ankle. He fell forwards, striking his head on the wall.

Honey kicked away the dead gargoyle's fingers and shook Sandy's shoulders.

"He's out cold!"

Together they dragged and heaved him across the ground.

"He's too heavy! We're not going to make it."

The ceiling reached halfway, descending on them like a giant flower press.

"Get up Sandy!" screamed Honey. "We can't do this without you!" Her anger was replaced by desperation as the ceiling forced her onto her knees. "Do it for us Sandy. For goodness sake do it for *me!* I love you, I always have!"

Bree pushed her aside and grabbed Sandy's lapels. Mustering her strength she hauled his top half off the ground, her fingers bending painfully under his weight. She forced steadiness into her voice.

"Sandy, listen to me. You *need* to wake up."

She slapped him hard across the face.

"WAKE UP!"

His eyes shot open and he gasped for air. When he saw how close the ceiling was he scrambled to his knees.

They clambered through the passageway until they reached the hole. One by one they wriggled through the tiny gap that was left, into a candlelit room. A banquet table was laid with silver goblets and cutlery, and there were chairs at each end. A tall wooden cabinet stood in the corner of the room.

Honey walked over to the door and locked it with the rusty key that stuck out from the keyhole. She pulled it out and replaced it with the gum from her mouth.

"That trick has worked for us before," she said, looking satisfied.

Suddenly the doorknob rattled. Honey leapt back.

"It's okay, I locked it."

It rattled again and the blob of gum fell out. An eerie silence descended.

"Are they gone?" asked Sandy.

There was a loud thud on the other side. Bree stared at the warped wood, horrified.

"It's going to –"

The door flew open to reveal the silhouette of a tiny figure. "Well hello again, I wasn't expecting to find *you* in here."

Theb stepped into the room.

"You frightened us half to death!" said Sandy.

Theb looked shocked to see him.

"I...I thought you were – "

"We got him back," said Honey. "What are you doing here?"

"Not that we're sorry to see you," Bree quickly added.

"I thought I might be of some assistance," he said.

He made his way over to the cabinet, stood on his tiptoes, and pulled on the handle. The cabinet door sprung open on rusty hinges.

"I know this castle like the back of my hand," he said. "This is not the first time I've been here."

Bree scratched her head.

"I don't remember you telling us that," she said, watching as he pulled out a bottle. "Aren't you worried you'll get caught?"

"Being small has its advantages," he grinned, and closed the cabinet door. "I know all the best places to hide."

Sandy pulled a chair out for him.

"So you can help us then? Find us some weapons?"

Theb hopped up onto the chair and pulled the cork from the bottle.

"I can only help you if you tell me why you're here," he replied, as he filled three goblets with a fizzing liquid. "But first have a drink. You must be ever so thirsty."

"And hungry," said Sandy.

"I'm afraid there's not much in the way of food around here, but this cordial will revive you."

He handed each of them a goblet. Bree focused on her reflection in the silver before swallowing a glorious, citrus sip. The fiery bubbles singed her tongue.

"Ooh, that's lovely," she sighed.

"So, why *are* you here?" asked Theb.

"Tonight, during a lunar eclipse, our worlds will collide," Sandy explained. "It'll be the end of everything as we know it."

"That's why we're here," said Bree, "to stop that from happening. We still have The Book and we've already taken care of Hallux Valgus."

"Next up is Tanas Theramonde," said Honey confidently. She drained her goblet and held it out for more. "Aren't you having any, Theb?"

"I'm not thirsty," he replied, dutifully topping up her glass.

"It's absolutely delicious," said Sandy.

Bree swallowed another large mouthful, and then she began to feel uncomfortable. She ran a finger around her collar.

"Phew, it's really warm in here," she said, feeling her cheek with the back of her hand.

"I feel hot too," said Sandy. "And kind of... *drunk*."

Honey giggled, pink circles springing up on her cheeks.

A heat had started to build under Bree's skin. It spread through her veins, and she wobbled from side to side.

"Let me take that," said Theb, reaching for her goblet.

"I'm sorry," she slurred. "I feel strange."

Honey plopped down into a chair and rested her forehead on the table. Her hair fanned out around her. Sandy clutched onto the back of a chair and his goblet slipped from his grasp, landing with a clatter on the floor.

Theb helped Bree up onto the table. A woozy blanket of sleepiness covered her. Her tongue moved around some words but she could not seem to say them.

"There, there," said Theb, his voice slowing, "just you have a nice rest."

Bree closed her eyes and gave in completely.

****

She knew she was dreaming. A snapshot of the happiest day of her life; her first date with Adam. The first flush of spring meant it had been warm enough to wear T-shirts with no coats.

They had browsed some gift stalls then stopped for a picnic in the city gardens. The thunder had been unexpected and they had had just enough time to pack away the food before the rain came, great drops that made everything look fresh and green. Adam had grabbed her hand and they had run together, splashing through puddles and laughing. They sheltered under the lowest branches of a spreading oak tree where the air had taken on a different quality – solid, warm and real. Adam's fingertips had grazed her hand lightly. When he smiled, something somersaulted in her stomach before dancing up and down her spine. Then something in the dream changed. They were no longer under the oak tree, but in a forest where the sky felt dark and heavy. Bree could smell mouldy earth and she had a terrible feeling that she was searching for something, something she urgently needed to find.

She turned to face Adam and he stared back at her with black, soulless eyes. When he blinked, a thick, dark liquid trickled down his face. Bree tried to run but her feet were stuck. She looked down to see the ground, hot and black, melted tar that sucked at her shoes and stretched in thin bands when she tried to pull them out. She tried to scream but she found that her lips had been sewn shut with rusty wire. She clawed her way to consciousness, bursting through the dream and back into reality with a gasp of air.

CHAPTER 22
SISTER OF THE VALLEY

Bree let the last fragments of her dream tumble away. Her head began to throb. She could not remember where she was.

It was only a dream she repeated to herself until her breathing returned to normal. Opening her eyes took as much effort as swimming through treacle. When she saw the rafters in the ceiling she immediately remembered. She was curled up on top of the banquet table, the empty goblets strewn at her side. She glanced over at the door. It was closed and the rusty key had been replaced. Her eyelids were so heavy she allowed them to close again. Suddenly she was filled with a certainty, a nameless dread, that there was something terrible in the room with her.

A face swam into view; red lips against skin as white as the moon.

"Trick or treat?" whispered a woman, and Bree wondered if she had actually woken up, or if she had simply moved onto one of those dreams where you dream you are awake.

Her gaze dropped to a lump of amber and then travelled back up to eyes that matched. Painfully she hauled herself into a sitting position.

"*Mrs Van-Lite..?*" she croaked. "Is that you?"

Auntie Val ran her cold gaze over Bree, drilling through her skin with the gimlet glare of a hawk.

"In this world I am known as Evelin Alvariet," she said, the hollows of her cheeks exaggerated by the dim light.

Bree tried to focus on the woman standing in front of her. Moss green fabric was draped over her slender form in generous swathes that fell to the floor. Gone were the steel-framed glasses and the silver streak through her fringe. Now her entire head was covered with silver hair that had been crocheted into an elaborate cobweb of knots, held in place with a delicate rope of pearls.

"I saw you at the pond," muttered Bree. "And it was you in the portrait. *Sister of the Valley.*"

In a single instant, vague confusion was replaced by a horrible understanding. She tried to swallow but her mouth felt like sandpaper.

"Mrs Hooten knows who...*what* you are."

Alvariet threw back her head and laughed.

"So you did read her stupid diary! And here was I thinking Mother only ever had eyes for one of her daughters. But she noticed me after all."

The amber jewel at her neck caught the candlelight and glittered like a cat's eye. "Even when my darling sister..." she groped the air for the right word "...*disappeared*, she couldn't bring herself to love me. I always knew she wished it had been me that had vanished instead."

Alvariet glided across the floor and the material of her gown rustled softly with her movements. Bree slowly swung her legs over the side of the table. Everything ached.

"Jane and Michael have no idea who you are," she said. "Jane couldn't understand why Thalofedril knew they would be at the cottage that night but it was you...wasn't it? *You* told him."

Alvariet's yellow eyes glinted.

"I thought they had The Book with them. But I was wrong. They didn't even know where it was hidden. Your father took that information to the grave with him."

"Why didn't Thalofedril take Agora Burton that night too?"

"She wasn't there. She had a lucky escape."

Bree remembered something.

"*You* were looking after Sandy that night. And all that time you knew what was going to happen."

Alvariet held her head high.

"Thalofedril was only supposed to take Jane. I wanted Michael returned to me." Her expression softened. "In time he could have grown to love me like I loved him."

"But that's crazy! He could never have loved you. Jane and Michael are still madly in love with each other, even after all you've put them through."

A thread of annoyance pulled Alvariet's lip into a sneer.

"I can still get to them by using the boy," she hissed.

Fear gripped Bree's heart as she suddenly remembered.

"Where is Sandy? And Honey? What have you done with them?"

Alvariet looked over Bree's shoulder to a dark corner of the room. Bree followed her gaze until it settled on something that stopped the breath in her throat. Sandy and Honey drifted in and out of focus. For a moment she thought they were one and the same – a strange mythological creature with two heads and eight legs. They lay lifelessly in the shadows.

"Are...they...*dead?*"

Alvariet picked up one of the goblets from the table and admired her reflection in it.

"They drank more of the cordial than you did," she said coolly, "they are sleeping it off."

Suddenly, Theb appeared in the doorway. Before Bree reached him, the words were tumbling from her mouth in a garbled rush.

"I knew you would come back for us! We have to get out of here. The cordial was poisoned! I'm so glad you didn't drink – "

He stared up at her with a stony expression and closed the door gently. Alvariet laughed a sudden, mirthless trill.

"*Why* do you think he didn't drink any you stupid girl?"

Bree searched Theb's face but there was no sign of the friendly, trusting man she knew. His features were distorted with hatred and the twisted joy of revenge.

"No. *Please*... not you."

He fixed his hard little eyes on her.

"I could have killed you at any time," he said. "I thought you were done for when I tricked you into running straight into Eed's prison."

"But...but there *was* something in the bushes," Bree said feebly. "We all heard it."

Theb brushed her aside and laughed. "You ran like your life depended on it! You all ran like fwightened widdle piggies."

Bree remembered what Reinor had said when they had been hiding in the bushes with Anando.

He told me they had come this way.

"It was you who informed on us. Have you no conscience?"

"The cliff face," he scoffed. "I tried to kill you back there too."

Bree was confused until he clapped his hands together. She suddenly remembered the vines shriveling up like dried paper.

"You! *You* made us fall."

Alvariet narrowed her eyes. "Theb, go and get Reinor."

"No!" Bree pleaded, running after him. "*Please.*"

"You won't know what's hit you," he said, as he left the room.

She had to think of a way to get out. She pressed her back against the door.

"Are you going to kill me?" she asked.

Alvariet picked up a cutlery knife and tilted it close to her face, studying her reflection carefully.

"Perhaps," she replied with icy calm. "I could extinguish you just like..." she clicked her fingers and one of the candles puffed out, trailing a line of black smoke into the air, "...that."

"I'll never co-operate," said Bree. "I have kept The Book safe since I was twelve years old and my father looked after it before me. It stays with me."

Alvariet's eyes filled with anger – and just a hint of something else. Bree saw an opportunity.

"I know you are a good person underneath all this. Please, let us go. I promise never to speak of this to anybody."

"I watched Agora Burton for many years," Alvariet said quietly. "I was the only one who knew her *real* secret. And I watched Jane's friendship with your mother and father grow stronger by the day, all the time knowing he could tell them about The Book at any time. What he did not realise was that Jane carried the blood of a borrower in her veins. Just like me... and our mother."

Bree stood in a swirl of confusion.

"What are you talking about?"

Alvariet ignored her.

"There were many people from this world watching your father closely. Every move he made, every word he spoke."

A shiver ran up Bree's spine as something dawned on her. Something she had known all along.

"Tomas Deanheart."

"My, my, you are observant. When your father finally confessed to Jane and Michael, a decision was made that they should all be destroyed. But only after they handed over The Book."

"So Sandy's mum and dad were simply disposed of," said Bree.

Alvariet's eyes gleamed with righteous malice.

"They should have been killed. It was only because I asked for leniency that they were spared."

"What I don't understand," said Bree, "is how you've managed to get away with this for so long. I mean you're living a double life. How can you live such a lie?"

Alvariet stroked the piece of amber around her neck.

"I only really had mother to worry about and she seemed happy not to see very much of us."

"*Us*? You mean there are more of *you?*"

The question seemed to hang in the air between them. Alvariet's face twisted into a cruel smile.

Without warning she threw the cutlery knife at Bree. She leapt aside and it embedded itself in the doorframe.

"Consider that a warning!" Alvariet screamed. "If I had wanted to finish you off I would have!"

"You wouldn't dare!"

"And why NOT?"

"Because you can't get what you want if I'm dead."

Alvariet laughed and glared at her, coiled and alive and ready to pounce.

"My dear, I already have what I want," she said. "I was only sparing you for the sake of my nephew."

Bree thrust her hand into her pocket, but there was nothing

there except for the handkerchief she had taken from the pile of clean washing at Annie's. She let it go and it fell to the floor.

"Is this what you're looking for?" asked Alvariet, plucking The Book from a fold in her dress and waving it teasingly in the air.

"Give it back!" Bree cried, grabbing for it.

"Tsk tsk," said Alvariet, waving a long finger, "I think you're forgetting the golden rule. I have to give it to you willingly."

"I didn't give it to you willingly!"

"Yes you did. It's just that *you* were asleep at the time."

Over in the corner Sandy let out a soft moan.

Alvariet glanced over at him and a haunted look crept into her eyes.

"He's your flesh and blood?" croaked Bree. "Are you going to destroy the only thing Annie has left? Are you going to kill me in front of him?"

Bree could see the cover of The Book through her bony fingers. The half-heart locket appeared to throb in the candlelight.

"Please. Think of Sandy, think of your poor mother."

Alvariet cackled.

"She never thought of *me*. Not once!"

"She was frightened of you!" cried Bree. "She was protecting Sandy!"

"Well you're never going to see her again. Not her, not your pathetic mother..." she gave a tight little shiver "...not even that revolting animal."

A vivid memory sprang to Bree's mind. *Allergies run in the family but Val gets it worst with cats.* She snatched up the handkerchief and held it under Alvariet's nose.

"Can you smell him? His hair is all over this."

Horrified, Alvariet began backing away.

"Get it away from me," she spluttered, staring in horror as Bree waved the scrap of material.

"Look!" Bree said gleefully. "Little bits of Bustopher are floating *everywhere*."

Alvariet turned and ran, smashing into one of the chairs. As she fell forwards The Book flew out of her hands and tumbled in a high arc over her head. Bree raced backwards in the direction of its fall, catching it before it landed. She clung to it as if her life depended on it.

Alvariet scrambled to her feet. "It's too late!" she laughed. "I have already used its power."

Bree stared down at the locket and immediately realised it was throbbing. With shaking fingers she prised open the cover and turned to page four. Wish five was faint but she could still read it.

> **What once was dust be whole again,**
> **Flesh and blood and fingers ten,**
> **A heart that stopped will beat once more,**
> **Faster, stronger than before.**
> **A fallen tear, a promise said,**
> **Will raise a lost one from the dead.**

A red stain spread like blood across the page and Bree slammed The Book shut.

"And to think you could have used this wish to bring back your father," Alvariet said with a twisted smile. "What tragic timing."

"What have you done?"

"I made a promise, like the wish asked. Never to let The

Book out of my hands."

She pulled a long chain from inside the front of her dress. A heavy pendant in the shape of a Z slipped out, shiny, silver and terrifyingly familiar.

"I think it's time we gave this back to its rightful owner, don't you?" she said, swinging it like a pendulum.

"That's n...not possible," Bree said.

Alvariet laughed hysterically.

"*Anything* is possible with The Book."

A sudden movement in the far corner of the room caught Bree's eye. Sandy was sitting up, rubbing his eyes. She willed him not to make a noise.

"But *I* have The Book now," she said, trying to keep Alvariet's attention away from him, "so surely you broke your promise."

The smile slid from Alvariet's face.

"I...I..." she stammered, lost for words.

A warm draught sent the candle flames into a flare. Alvariet's eyes darted around the room nervously as though the draught had brought something unwanted with it.

Sandy watched them from the shadows. He looked drowsy and confused.

Alvariet started to tremble. A wind rushed outside, making the keyhole whistle. Alvariet stared in horror at the rattling doorknob. Bree leapt aside just as the door burst open, letting a gust of hot air in. Sandy threw himself on top of Honey as Bree cowered in the corner.

Alvariet clung to the table. Her hands slipped and she was whipped into the centre of the room. She howled and slowly raised her arms skywards. She began to turn around on the spot, her long sleeves streaming behind her, spinning so fast she was nothing but a blur. With a sudden whoosh she burst into flames.

Fire snaked up and down the length of her dress, angry flames twisting and turning. There was a sudden, unbearable wave of heat then Alvariet disappeared in a burst of yellow and red.

Bree ran over and threw herself at Sandy.

"Are *you* alright?" he said. "Who was that? She looked like... like..."

"Auntie Val."

Sandy turned a strange colour.

"*I can't believe it*...What am I going to tell my Gran?"

"We'll think of something. It's not like they were close," said Bree. "Sandy, there simply isn't time to explain everything. We have to get out of here. Reinor is on his way."

"But Honey is still out for the count," he said. "I don't think I can carry her far."

He shook Honey gently and her forehead crinkled.

"It was Theb," said Bree. "*He* poisoned the cordial. There's something else too, something much worse."

"What could possibly be worse than watching my own Auntie fry?"

Bree held up The Book. "Wish five happened when we were asleep."

"I...I don't understand."

"Your Auntie Val...*Evelin Alvariet* had The Book at the time," Bree explained, slipping it into her pocket.

"Do you know what the wish said?"

Bree nodded.

"It was to bring someone back from the dead."

"Who...what...?" Sandy's expression suddenly darkened as the realisation dawned on him. "No! Surely not..."

Bree nodded. Without another word Sandy scooped Honey up and made his way towards the door.

"We can take turns to carry her," said Bree.

He peered cautiously around the doorframe.

"The coast is clear," he whispered, and slipped out into the corridor.

Halfway along, he started struggling. He stopped and gently laid Honey down. She moaned and stirred a little.

"She's coming round," said Bree.

"About time too."

Bree felt the pitter-patter of rain on her head and looked up to see a gaping hole in the rafters through which the wind whistled mournfully.

"We must be at the end of the castle that was ruined in the fire," she said, stepping out of the funnel of rain.

"Well that's good, isn't it?" said Sandy, watching the rain swirl in a faint shaft of light. "It means we're close to the drawbridge and the forest. I think we should get out while we still can."

"But do you think we've done enough to save the world?" asked Bree.

Sandy shrugged.

"I don't know. If I'm honest, all I care about at this point is saving ourselves."

Suddenly there was a movement, high up in the rafters. Debris rained down and with it came a terrible sound that seemed to warp in the confines of the corridor. It sounded like the unfurling of wings.

"HONEY! GET *UP!*"

Honey mumbled something but her eyes stayed shut. Bree glanced back to see Thalofedril descend from the rafters as though on spidersilk, landing on the ground with a heavy thump. He towered head and shoulders above them, his wings folded like leather curtains. The stench of evil rolled over them in waves. Reptilian eyelids closed over then opened again to reveal two crimson eyes.

"Don't look at him! He'll turn you to stone!"

Thud, slide...

Thalofedril stopped and puffed out a hot, fetid breath. Bree fought the temptation to look into his eyes. Suddenly he bellowed a bone-chilling roar, unfurled his wings and shook them. Bree braced herself, but he rose heavily into the air and disappeared through the hole in the roof.

CHAPTER 23
TWISTS AND TURNS

Honey's eyes fluttered open.

"Where am I?" she muttered groggily.

Bree crouched down beside her.

"We're still in the castle. You've been asleep."

Honey yawned and rubbed her eyes.

"But I wasn't even tired," she said, then flinched when she tried to sit up. "I've got a pounding headache though."

"We were *all* asleep," said Sandy, "we were poisoned."

"I'll bet it was the cordial! I thought it tasted dodgy."

"Well that didn't stop you drinking two cups of the stuff!" snapped Bree. "We thought you were *never* going to wake up."

Honey stood up, wobbling drunkenly before finding her balance.

"Did I miss anything?" she asked, straightening her satchel.

Bree and Sandy exchanged glances.

"Nothing much," Bree said.

Honey looked at her suspiciously, then her nose crinkled in distaste.

"What is that *awful* smell? I recognise it."

Bree took a deep breath.

"Thalofedril," she said.

"What? When? Where? *HOW?*"

"Don't panic," said Sandy, nervously, "he's gone."

"That is what's worrying me," said Bree. "I mean why would

he confront us like that and then leave?"

Sandy stared up at the hole in the roof.

"Perhaps we're not that important to him anymore."

Bree shook her head.

"We're still important. We have The Book. I think he needs to be somewhere else. Somewhere like...*Rockwell.*"

Sandy looked panic-stricken.

"Why would he do that?"

"I just have a bad feeling. It must be getting dark back home. The lunar eclipse will be starting and..."

She stopped herself.

"I can't think about that. Our priority is to get out of here."

"But I still don't understand," Honey said vaguely, "Thalofedril is... *dead.*"

"He was," Bree replied, "but The Book fell into the wrong hands and now he's back."

"But we still have The Book, right?"

Bree nodded.

"I got it back. But unfortunately someone else got wish five."

"Who?" asked Honey.

Sandy shifted awkwardly.

"My Auntie Val."

Honey gave him a playful push.

"Very funny Greenfield. Really, *who?*"

"Sandy's telling the truth," said Bree. "It was his Auntie Val but she goes...went by another name here. She was the woman in the portrait."

"Sister of the Valley," said Honey. "I *thought* she looked familiar. Where is she now?"

"Gone. Definitely gone."

Honey scratched her head.

"I thought you said I didn't miss much," she said. "That's pretty epic news."

"Let's move," Bree said. "In case Thalofedril comes back."

With every step they took, the ceiling and walls seemed to shrink around them, and soon they had to stoop to avoid bumping their heads.

"I can see light," said Sandy, breaking into a jog. "Come on."

When Bree and Honey caught up with him he was peering over a ledge.

"We're quite high off the ground. But we should be able to jump down safely."

Bree peered over and saw a corridor with a black, marble floor. To the right it disappeared into absolute darkness, and to the left a rusty portcullis blocked their route.

"I can't see much," she said, "but the portcullis looks as if it might lead to the way out of here. I just hope we can open it."

"We'll try our best," said Honey, playfully flexing her muscles.

When they reached the portcullis they all tugged on the bars, but it was stuck fast.

Bree peered through, but she could not see much, only an extension of the corridor with the outline of something resembling a large lump of stone in the middle.

"There's something in there," she said, kicking the floor in frustration.

Honey pulled a glow stick from her satchel, cracked it in the middle and thrust it through the bars.

"It's a sundial," she said.

The yellow glow illuminated a lump of granite topped with a circular face with a metal fin sticking up from it.

"It *is* a sundial," said Sandy. "But why? I mean there's no sun down here."

"Look," said Honey, sweeping the glow stick over a section of wall where some words had been carved.

"What does it say?" asked Bree, straining to see.

Honey peered closely.

"It says...*What can fly but can also drag?*"

"It's a riddle," said Bree.

Sandy started trembling.

"It's Thalofedril. The answer is Thalofedril!"

"No," said Honey, and a smile spread across her face. "The answer is *time*."

"I suppose that makes sense," Sandy said, relaxing a little. "A sundial is basically a shadow clock."

"It's a clue," smiled Bree, "we must have to use the sundial to open the portcullis."

"But what are we supposed to *do* with it?" said Honey. "There's no sun and it's too far away to reach."

Bree stamped her foot. "Why can't anything ever be simple?"

Sandy stared longingly through the bars.

"My guess is that the gnomon is a lever of some sort."

"The whatty?" Honey asked.

"The gnomon," said Sandy, pointing to the triangular blade. "That's the part that casts the shadow."

"But even if it *is* a lever how are we going to reach it?" asked Bree.

"We're not," said Honey with a wide grin.

Bree folded her arms across her chest.

"I don't see what's so funny."

Honey tutted and rolled her eyes. She turned to Sandy.

"Do you still have that blowpipe?" she asked.

"Yeah. But it's not going to be long enough to reach the lever."

He pulled the hollow cylinder from his pocket and held it out to her.

"Excellent," she said, rummaging inside her satchel. "Now all we need are...these."

She shook a packet of gumballs in front of his face and he stared at them blankly.

"You're going to use your amazing aim to fire *these* at *that*," she grinned.

Sandy turned pale.

"But what if I just got lucky with the gargoyle?"

Honey ignored him and peered inside the packet.

"There are only three left," she said.

"No pressure then."

"You only need to hit it once," Bree said encouragingly.

Reluctantly he took one from Honey and loaded it into the blowpipe. She held the glow stick through the bars and he took aim, puffing hard on the end. It shot out at an awkward angle, hitting the wall and missing the target altogether. Sandy cleared his throat and took another gumball with trembling hands.

"Take your time," said Honey, as he aimed for a second attempt.

He blew hard and fired, narrowly missing the blade.

"Ooh so close! You'll definitely get it next time."

"What if I don't!"

Bree could not bear to look as Sandy took aim. He was shaking so much there was no way he was going to hit the target!

Puff, clink.

The gumball struck metal and the portcullis rolled up with a rusty shriek, leaving a gap wide enough for them to fit under.

The corridor was in complete darkness with only the dim light from the glow stick to guide the way. Bree searched for the slightest hint of light. And then she saw it, a flickering orange glow ahead. They quickened their pace, relieved to see an end in sight. They stopped at the bottom of a stone staircase, which was lit by burning torches on either side.

"Onwards and upwards," said Honey, taking her first, cautious step.

Sandy and Bree followed nervously. At the top of the steps two doors were held shut by a large, golden catch in the shape of a letter H. Sandy put his shoulder against one, and pushed hard. They rattled but stayed firmly shut. Bree pulled out the magic key but slumped with disappointment.

"Just our luck," she said. "*Another* door with no keyhole."

"Do you think this latch is a clue?" asked Sandy, running his finger over it. "Perhaps it's the first letter of a name or a place, like *Honey* or *home*."

"Or *hell*," muttered Bree.

"Or it could be the number eight," added Sandy. "H is the eighth letter of the alphabet."

"Let me see," said Honey, pushing them aside, and peering closely at the catch.

"*That's* not a letter," she said, her eyes bright with the thrill of discovery. "That's a symbol. A zodiac symbol to be more precise."

Sandy slapped his forehead.

"Not astrology again, that's all just gibberish."

"Actually it's *not* gibberish," Honey protested. "This particular symbol represents my star sign."

"Pisces," said Bree. "That's the fish, right?"

"*Twin* fish actually," Honey corrected. "I think we're looking for two fish."

Sandy stared around at the cold, bare walls.

"Looking *where* though?"

Honey tapped her chin thoughtfully.

"Pisces is the twelfth astrological sign of the zodiac," she said. Then she made a sudden dash down the stairs, disappearing around the bend.

Seconds felt like minutes as they waited nervously for her return.

"Right, that's it," said Bree, "I'm going after her."

Just then Honey reappeared with a huge grin on her face.

"Look what I found!"

She held up a branding iron. The design on the end matched the design of the catch on the door. Bree smiled.

"You clever thing. How on earth did we miss that on our way up?"

"It was tucked inside a deep groove that had been carved into the twelfth step. You really would have to know what you were looking for."

"Lucky we've got you then," said Sandy.

Honey ruffled his hair affectionately, and then pressed the end of the iron over the catch so the two symbols fitted together perfectly.

The doors swung inwards to reveal white marble walls that were aglow with a watery blue light, and a floor that was a jigsaw of pretty mosaic tiles.

"I could get used to this," said Sandy, staring in awe.

"It certainly beats tunnels and draughty corridors," said Honey.

"I wouldn't get too comfortable," said Bree, pointing to a wooden door in the far wall, "I've got a feeling we won't be staying here for long."

"Pisces is a water sign," said Honey, spying something of interest at the other end of the room, "so it would make sense to look for something to do with water."

They came to a small, ornamental pool filled with perfect turquoise water. Honey sat on the edge and stared down dreamily.

"Look," she said, pointing to the floor of the pool.

A giant mosaic picture appeared to move under the rippling surface. It depicted an image of a man on a horse carrying a bow and a large, circular shield. A large goldfish appeared from behind a stone and gulped lazily at the surface of the water; the silvery scales on its back formed what looked like an elongated number six.

"There's another one over there," said Sandy.

An identical fish swam over and stopped alongside its twin, facing in the opposite direction. Their bodies were perfectly still except for the ripple of their tails.

"They've made the number sixty-nine," said Bree, indicating the numbers on their backs.

"It's another zodiac symbol," said Honey. "This one is Cancer, the sign of the crab."

"Euch. I *hate* crabs," said Sandy.

"Well I don't see any around here," said Bree.

Suddenly the fish darted for cover, shattering the surface. Honey jumped up nervously.

"What is it?" Bree asked.

Honey did not answer but stood motionless, her face screwed up in concentration.

"Honey...?"

"Shh!" Her shoulders relaxed again. "It's nothing. I just thought – "

The tiles along the bottom of the walls slid up, and an army of tiny crabs poured out, hundreds of them click-clicking across the tiles until the floor was completely covered with them. Sandy yelped and jumped up onto the wall at the side of the pool.

"There's so many of them!"

Honey began kicking them out of the way, but no sooner had she cleared a space than it was filled again with a hundred more. They crawled over their feet, snapping with their serrated pincers. Bree crunched over them, carving a path to the wooden door. She pulled on the handle but it was locked. *At least there's a keyhole this time,* she thought. As she fumbled for the magic key some of the crabs climbed inside her trouser leg and pinched her skin.

"Ouch!" she yelped, shaking her legs.

She glanced over to see Honey doing a strange dance to keep them at bay.

Bree angrily kicked at the mound around her feet and some of them flipped onto their backs, revealing a soft underside with an interesting pattern.

"Honey! Look at their bellies! Is it another symbol?"

Honey glanced down and nodded.

"Yes! They've all got the same one."

Suddenly, as quickly as they had appeared the crabs scuttled sideways back into the walls, and the tiles slid back down. Bree ran over to Honey and stared down at the broken carcasses that littered the floor.

Sandy jumped down from the side of the pool. Honey put her hands on her hips and glared icily at him.

"My hero."

She bent down and picked up the remains of one. It dangled from a broken leg, turning and twisting to show the symbol on its belly.

"This is the astrological sign for Taurus," she said.

"Another astrological symbol," said Sandy. "I'll bet there are twelve obstacles dotted around this castle, one for each sign."

"Well, let's try to avoid as many as we can," said Bree.

"See the two lines coming out the top of the circle?" said Honey. She held the flattened crab up to Sandy's face.

He turned a queasy shade of green and nodded.

"Those are horns. Taurus is the bull."

She tossed the dead crab aside and wiped her hand down her trousers.

"Where are we supposed to find a bull?" asked Sandy.

"Perhaps there's another clue," said Honey, looking around the room.

She pointed to the tiles along the bottom of the wall.

"They look different," she said. "They definitely didn't have those on them before."

There was now a gold symbol in the centre of each tile.

♊

"Looks like another Roman numeral," said Sandy.

Honey shook her head.

"This is another astrological clue. That's the symbol for Gemini, the sign of the twins."

"So we're looking for twins now?" Bree asked.

"I think it's simpler this time," said Honey. "I think this is a visual clue. The next step is to find something that *looks* like it."

"A column?" Sandy suggested.

Honey screwed her nose up.

"A plinth," said Bree, "or a tall vase."

Honey clapped her hands excitedly.

"A door! Whatever's coming next I think we'll find it behind that door."

All eyes swung to the far wall.

"Come on then," said Honey. "We haven't got all day."

"It's locked," said Bree, reaching into her pocket for the magic key. "I already tried it."

Honey turned the knob and it creaked open a fraction, releasing an icy blast of air.

"Well it's not locked now."

They entered a passage so narrow that Bree wondered

whether they would fit through it. The walls on either side were smooth and regular, built from huge blocks of stone.

"It looks like the start of a maze," said Sandy, peering nervously inside. "We'll have to go in single file."

"That's the least of our worries," said Bree.

Honey looked at her with a puzzled expression.

"What do you mean?"

"We might find our way in, but that doesn't mean we'll find our way out again."

"Pity we don't have Ariadne's string," said Sandy.

"*Whose* string?" asked Honey.

"You know," he said. "From the Greek myth. Ariadne falls in love with Theseus, and she gives him a ball of thread so he can find his way out of the labyrinth."

Honey's face lit up and she dug around at the bottom of her satchel.

"I may not have Ariadne's string," she said, pulling out a rectangular box and flipping the lid, "but I've got the next best thing."

"Dental floss! What a brilliant idea."

Honey tied the end of the floss to the doorknob and gave it a sharp tug to check it was secure.

"It says on the box that there are sixty metres of this stuff. Hopefully that will be enough. Okay, who wants to go first?"

"I'll go," said Bree, mustering a thin smile.

After her first few, faltering steps she was forced to turn sideways in order to negotiate a confusing network of narrow paths. Honey and Sandy stayed close behind, following every twist and turn she took. Occasionally they came to a dead end and had to turn awkwardly to follow another path. Time and again Bree turned a corner only to find herself at another junction. To her relief the walls grew further apart the nearer they got to the centre of the labyrinth.

"I think we're almost there," she said. "How's the dental floss doing?"

"There's only a little left," replied Honey.

Bree turned a sharp corner and entered a chamber where one wall had been cut away. The stone floor felt sticky with puddles of foul-smelling water. Honey carefully tied the frayed end of the floss to a metal torch holder.

"It smells like a farm in here," she groaned.

Bree spotted a sword propped up in the corner. She picked it up and the weight of it made her arms shake.

"I wonder what we're supposed to do with this?"

Honey opened her mouth to speak, but was stopped by a low growl that came from the shadows. The sound of scraping hooves was followed by snorting and panting, as if something was preparing to charge.

Honey and Sandy backed away slowly as the muscular outline of something huge emerged, a creature with the head of a bull and the body of a man.

"A Minotaur!" Sandy gasped.

The beast roared and threw back its massive head, and Bree noticed a ring through its nose. A silver arrow with a line through the middle dangled from it. Two red eyes blazed through the darkness as it threw back its head again, its curved horns scraping the ceiling. Bree gripped the hilt of the sword with both hands, steadying herself.

"You're going to have to stab it," said Sandy, "like Theseus did in the story."

That meant getting close to it, and the thought made Bree dizzy with fear.

"Make your way back to the pool," she said, trembling. "Wait for me there."

"We're not leaving you!"

"I'm the only one with a weapon. Now *GO!*"

They turned and fled, and as she heard their footsteps recede she felt a new kind of terror – the terror of being alone. She gripped the sword tightly and edged slowly away from the beast. It began stalking forwards, stamping the floor. Her courage faltered when it let out a bellow that made the walls shake. She considered dropping the sword and making a run for it, but she knew she would not get far. Besides, something told her she needed the nose ring.

"Come on then!" she screamed, waving the sword feebly. "What are you waiting for?"

The Minotaur put its head down and pawed the ground menacingly. Bree did not wait for it to charge. She ran at it with the sword thrust out in front of her. The tip plunged into the soft, fleshy area of the Minotaur's stomach. She ran back to the exit but it jumped in front of her, the sword still hanging from its stomach. It pulled it out and threw it aside.

Bree looked down to see a tiny gash, nowhere near enough to do any lasting damage. The attack had done nothing but make it angrier. With nothing to lose she lunged at its face, grabbing for the nose ring. She felt the sickening sensation of tearing flesh, and the Minotaur bellowed a mixture of pain and rage. Seizing the opportunity she pushed past it and fumbled for the dental floss. She ran back the way they had come, smashing into walls in her panic to get away.

The Minotaur was thundering down the tunnels behind her, crashing and bellowing through the maze. Once or twice it was almost upon her, but she managed to reach the section where the walls narrowed enough that it couldn't squeeze through. She pushed herself forward with every last ounce of strength, bursting into the room and slamming the door behind her. She unfurled her fist and stared down at the silver arrow, which was warm and sticky with the Minotaur's blood.

"We made it." She turned around, expecting to see smiles of relief from Honey and Sandy; instead they were sitting side by side on the edge of the pool, pale-faced and trembling. Towering over them with an axe in his hand was Reinor.

CHAPTER 24
THE ARROW KEY

He burst into a deep, malignant laugh when he saw Bree's shocked expression.

"The look on your face," he roared gleefully. "You look like you would rather be back in there with the Minotaur! You three are as slippery as soap...been chasing you all over the flamin' place..."

He pulled out a large walnut from his top pocket, threw it in the air and caught it again with his giant fist. He might have been smiling; it was hard to tell what was lurking under his matted beard. He squatted so his face was level with Sandy's. Bree quickly slid the silver arrow into her pocket while his back was turned. Sandy gulped noisily as Reinor planted his spade-like hands on either side of his legs and cocked his head to one side.

"So young nephew of mine," he said, his voice rolling out from somewhere deep inside his chest. "What does it feel like to be related to me?"

It was obvious really. The size, the hair colour, and the beady eyes; Bree could not believe she hadn't made the connection sooner. Norrie and Reinor were one and the same.

"I'm not related to you," said Sandy, glancing down at the axe. "Not by blood anyway."

Reinor stared at him with hard, hostile eyes.

"You've found your tongue I see. Perhaps you're not the sissy I thought you were."

He stood up, put his hands on his hips and glared at Bree.

"Now I'm going to give you one chance to give me The Book, or I will open that door, throw you all in, and leave the Minotaur to finish you off."

"There's no point," said Bree. "I killed it."

Surprise flickered in his eyes but was quickly replaced with something dark and threatening.

"You must think I'm stupid!" he spat, thrusting the axe in front of him. "Even my best men cannot kill that creature."

"Perhaps they're not as clever as I am," she said boldly.

His eyes narrowed suspiciously.

"Prove it," he growled.

Bree held out her hand, still stained with the deep burgundy blood from the silver arrow. Reinor's face contorted beneath his red beard, his eyes wide and staring.

"I...I don't understand. How could..."

The shock on his face suddenly gave way to something that resembled unease.

"Did you...get the arrow key?" he asked hesitantly.

"What arrow key?" she asked innocently.

"The one that hung from the beast's nose."

Bree feigned confusion.

"I don't know what you're talking about. I was far too busy fighting a giant bull. But if it's important I can go back for it."

Calling his bluff she reached for the doorknob. To her relief he stopped her.

"No! It doesn't matter."

Reinor turned back to Sandy.

"So you *are* a big sissy. Getting a girl to do the dirty work."

Honey shot up, her eyes alight.

"Sandy is braver than anyone else I know. Leave him alone you big bully!"

Reinor shook with indignation. He stabbed a great sausage finger into her chest.

"Shut up and sit down!"

He turned away for a moment and Honey slid her hand into her trouser pocket. Bree signaled discreetly for her to stop, but Reinor's eagle eye caught her in the act. He whipped around and Honey froze with fear.

"What have you got there?"

"N...nothing," she whimpered.

"Show me."

Honey shook her head.

"*SHOW ME!*"

Honey plucked Valgus's ring from her pocket and held it up so the diamond caught the light.

"How did you get that?"

"From your friend, Hallux Valgus. Bree got rid of him and now I'm going to get rid of *you!*"

Reinor roared and stormed forwards. Honey tried to slide the ring onto her finger but she was too slow. He had already lifted his axe high over his head. Sandy grabbed her and together they rolled onto the floor a second before the sharp edge sliced into the pool surround. One clean crack and the marble split in two. Water poured out onto the floor in a steady stream. Reinor towered over them, the two goldfish flapping at his feet.

"Give it to me!" he ordered.

Honey threw the ring at him and it landed on the floor. The diamond flashed brightly and a look of fear crossed his face.

"What are you waiting for?" she screamed, pulling Sandy

to his feet. "Scared of a little ring? Ha! Who's the sissy now?"

He rushed at them, knocking Sandy to the ground, lifting his axe above Honey. She cowered in his shadow waiting for the blade to fall, but just as he was about to bring it down the heavy iron head slid off and fell behind him. He cursed loudly; his ruddy cheeks fit to burst.

Hatred had bubbled up in Bree from some dark corner of her soul, and the only voice that boomed in her head was one that shouted, *Kill him Kill him!* She ran at Reinor, grabbed his beard and tugged on it as hard as she could. He tossed the axe handle away and swatted at her like she was a bothersome insect. She threw a punch at his head but it was pathetically weak and he fended her off with ease. He caught the side of her face with a flattened hand and she flew through the air, slamming into the side of the pool. She quickly scrambled to her feet in time to see him throttling Sandy.

She looked around the room, desperately searching for a weapon. Then she saw the handle of the axe. She rushed over and grabbed it with both hands. Sandy stared up at her with glassy-eyed terror.

With a yowl she brought the thick, wooden handle down on Reinor's head. A thud and a crack melded together with a harsh *thwap* that vibrated up her arm. Through the rush of blood in her ears she heard Reinor's angry curse. He cradled his head, blood pouring out from between his fat fingers. Sandy took advantage and squirmed free. Bree brought the handle down again, even harder this time. Reinor grunted and fell onto his side.

Her legs buckled, and Sandy caught her before she fell.

"I...I killed your Uncle Norrie."

"It was self-defence," said Honey, picking up Valgus's ring.

"You had no choice."

Suddenly Reinor started breathing again through scarlet bubbles. Sandy took a deep breath and ran his fingers through his fringe.

"He's alive."

Honey slid the ring onto her finger.

"We need to finish him off! Then that'll only leave Theramonde and Thalofedril to deal with. We can do that back in Rockwell."

Sandy grabbed her hand, stopping her from pushing the ring over her knuckle.

"No! I've had enough. Now let's get out of here."

"How?" said Honey. "That door will only take us back the way we came and there is no *way* I am setting foot in that labyrinth again."

Sandy looked around the room.

"There *has* to be another way out of here."

Bree pulled the silver arrow from her pocket and held it up.

"Perhaps this might help."

Honey stared at it with an expression of utter disbelief.

"Where did you get that?"

"In the labyrinth. I pulled it from the Minotaur's nose."

"After you killed it?" asked Sandy.

"Well, I didn't actually kill it," Bree confessed.

Honey's eyes widened with shock.

"But you said – "

"I know…but I *had* to say that or he…" she glanced down briefly "…was going to chuck us back in there."

"What about the blood?" Sandy asked. "It was all over your hand."

"That came from the nose ring, and I *did* manage to stab the

Minotaur, but I wasn't strong...or brave enough to kill it."

Honey wrapped her arms around Bree's neck and squeezed her tightly.

"Bree McCready, you are better than brave," she said. "You are super-duper, *mega* brave."

Bree managed a thin smile.

Honey took the silver arrow from Bree and let it swing in front of her face.

"What I want to know is how you managed to get *this* from a real, live monster."

Bree shrugged.

"I just got lucky. I thought it looked important."

"And you were right," said Honey. "It's another symbol. This is the sign for Sagittarius. It represents the Centaur."

Bree frowned.

"The Centaur being...?"

"Part human, part horse," Sandy answered.

"Nothing too nasty then."

"Not necessarily. Centaurs were known in Greek mythology for being wild and savage."

"Great. Just what we need."

"Centaurs carried bows," Honey added. "Hence the arrow."

An image sprang to Bree's mind, and she quickly made her way over to the pool. She stared down at the mosaic pattern on the floor and a colossal grin spread across her face.

"I thought it was a man on a horse at first," she said excitedly, "but this man actually *is* a horse!"

Honey and Sandy peered into the empty pool.

"I think we've found our Centaur," Honey smiled. "Now all we have to do is work out what to do with him."

Bree studied the image. It depicted the torso of a man with

the hindquarters of a horse attached at his waist. In one hand he carried a bow and in the other a large, circular shield.

"The silver arrow is a key of some sort," said Honey, sliding it off the ring. "I heard Reinor say that. He called it the *arrow key*."

She stood over the mosaic Centaur, studying it carefully.

"Look," she said, pointing. "Right there in the middle of his shield."

She kicked away a puddle of water and pointed to a turquoise disc the size of a large coin. It was slightly raised, and at the centre there was another arrow.

"The picture of that arrow matches this key," she said, bending down to take a closer look.

She placed the silver arrow inside and found that it slotted in perfectly. The turquoise disc rose out of the floor on a glass column. Honey jumped back.

"What just happened?" Sandy asked anxiously.

Honey curled her fingers around the disc, and it came away in her hand. There was a pop and the shield slid open. The rich, cloying smell of wet earth rushed up to meet them.

"It's a trapdoor," said Sandy. "A way out."

"Look at this," said Honey, holding the turquoise stone up to the light. "It's like a compass."

Bree stepped into the pool and splashed over to Honey. The silver arrow twitched and spun erratically until the tip moved round slowly and stopped.

"It's pointing to the hole in the floor," said Honey, "as if it's telling us which way to go."

Bree peered into the hole and saw, to her relief that the ground was near the opening. A channel had been dug into the earth, and tightly packed soil walls stretched out in both directions. The earth was alive with the wriggling and writhing of worms.

"It looks awful down there," said Sandy.

Reinor moaned and tried to sit up but collapsed back down in a confused heap.

"Not as awful as up here," said Honey, ushering Sandy towards the hole.

Reluctantly, Bree jumped down behind him, landing with a soft thump on the damp earth. Honey lowered herself down with a glow stick clamped between her teeth. She slid the circular door back across and gave it a firm tug.

"Was Reinor waking up?" asked Sandy.

Honey nodded.

"I wish you'd let me get rid of him once and for all."

Suddenly the sound of heavy, staggering footsteps thundered above their heads, followed by the pitter-patter of falling soil. Honey held the glow stick over the compass.

"The arrow is pointing this way. Follow me."

The ground felt uneven and the roof was low, forcing them to crouch and crawl. Soon the earth became ridged with curling roots that hung from the earthy ceiling.

"We must be outdoors," said Sandy, pushing one out of his face.

"How do you know?"

"Well, you don't usually find trees growing *inside* a castle."

As they rounded a bend the yellow light cut a swathe through the darkness to reveal a solid wall a few metres ahead.

"It's a dead end," said Bree.

Honey ran ahead. "I don't understand, the arrow brought us this way."

Sandy followed her.

"It was probably a trick. We should've known better."

"We can't go back," said Bree. "Reinor will be waiting for us."

"Remember what Theb told us?" said Honey. "If you can't go forwards, you must go up."

"Honey, there's something you should know," Bree said.

"What?" Her eyes flicked warily between Bree and Sandy.

"It's about Theb."

"He's dead, isn't he?" she said, her eyes brimming with tears.

"No," Bree said quickly. "It's not that. He's...he's..."

"It was Theb who poisoned the cordial," Sandy blurted.

"Oh," she said numbly. "That *is* a shame. I honestly thought he was our friend."

Lost for words, Honey stared miserably at the compass. Slowly the silver arrow moved until it was pointing upwards.

All of a sudden great dollops of wet soil rained down on them. They shielded their faces until it stopped, and when they looked up they saw natural light pouring in through a ragged hole, so bright that they were momentarily blinded.

"Give me a foot up, Sandy," said Bree.

He cupped his hands under her boot like a stirrup and hoisted her up. They were in a forest. The sky was still brimming with grey light but dusk was falling. It was eerily silent except for the crows that cawed in the high branches. She could not decide in which direction they should go, and then she saw it in the distance – a flash of red against the grey.

"Your ribbon!" she said, ducking back down into the hole. "I can see your ribbon!"

"I don't believe it," Honey laughed, "we're almost back at the sloping oaks."

Bree climbed out onto a carpet of rotting ferns, focusing on the fluttering ribbon, to help keep her thoughts from whatever else was lurking in the lengthening shadows. Sandy gave Honey a foot up, and she and Bree hauled him out.

"We're almost home."

"We'll go around that pond," said Bree, pointing. "And then through those trees."

She started to run, hardly able to contain her excitement at the thought of seeing her mum and Annie again. She reached the pond first. The water was choked with leaves and the black limbs of fallen branches. She inched closer to the edge and looked down to see her reflection, but her eye was drawn to something stuck in the weeds. Curiosity got the better of her and she edged down the embankment. She peered through the murk and saw a pale oval. *A face!*

Theb floated under the surface of the water. His eyes were astonished, his lips parted as if on the verge of crying out.

Somehow, his left arm broke free and floated to the surface. For a moment she imagined he was reaching out for her. She spun around and scrambled up the embankment.

"What is it? What's wrong?" cried Honey, reaching out to help her up.

Bree jabbed a finger at the water. Sandy cautiously leaned over the edge and turned back to them, his face pale and his bottom lip trembling.

"It's Theb," he said softly. "He's...*dead*."

Honey looked shocked and then her face darkened.

"Good."

"Perhaps he slipped into the water and drowned," said Sandy.

Bree shook her head.

"No. Someone put him in there."

A chilly wind grabbed at their bare skin with icy fingers. Honey shivered and pulled up her collar.

"Let's go," she said, and turned away without so much as a final glance back at the water.

****

Bree noticed the veil looked different. The shimmer had dulled and no longer illuminated the ground below it.

"Quick! It looks like the veil is closing!"

They ran as fast as they could towards the sloping oaks. Bree could hardly make out the shimmering colours anymore. Sandy dived through as the last of the shards of light disappeared. Bree grabbed Honey and they landed on the other side with a *whoomph*. In a flash of white light the veil completely disappeared.

Bree strained her eyes against the gathering dark. She had no idea what time it was, but she knew night was coming fast. She looked up as a breeze lifted the treetops to reveal the moon, full and plump, all except for a sliver at its edge that had darkened to orange. "The lunar eclipse has started," she said miserably. "It's the beginning of the end."

"Not if we've got anything to do with it," Honey said fiercely. "We got rid of Hallux Valgus *and* The Sister of the Valley. We've got Valgus's ring and we have two wishes left. We're still in with a shot."

Somewhere in the shadows a twig snapped and the birds took to the sky in startled flight, scudding shadows across the moon. Goosebumps prickled Bree's skin.

"Time to go," she said, heading in the direction of the river.

"The log is somewhere around..." Bree tripped and stumbled forwards "...here," she said, catching her balance.

She looked down at the broken branches that spread across the embankment.

"Who wants to go first?"

Sandy sighed heavily.

"I can't see a flippin' thing. It was bad enough crossing in the daylight."

"At least the river is quieter now," said Honey.

One by one they stepped up and in no time they had reached the other side. They followed the route they had taken earlier in the day and came to the disused railway tunnel that curved into darkness.

No sooner had they ventured inside than rocks began to rain down in front of the exit. Bree shielded her head as she burst out of the tunnel, jumping clear of a large boulder as it rolled down the hill. The landslide followed with a rumble and crash. She looked back to see that the entire exit was blocked. She sat up, relieved that she had got out in time. Her relief did not last as she realised Sandy and Honey had not been so lucky.

PART THREE
THE BEGINNING OF THE END

CHAPTER 25
A STITCH IN TIME

"SANDY! HONEY! ARE YOU ALRIGHT?"

Silence.

Bree scrambled up onto the pile of rubble and clawed at the solid wall, yanking out handfuls of rock until her fingers bled. Suddenly she heard a muffled cough from inside the tunnel.

"SANDY, I'M HERE!" she called back. "ARE YOU HURT?"

She pressed her ear to the rocks and listened.

"We're okay," came Sandy's faint reply. "But there's no way out...we're going to have to go the long way home..."

"OKAY, I'LL MEET YOU BACK IN ROCKWELL."

She slid down the pile of rocks.

The moon was slowly being devoured by a deep orange shadow, and she quickened her pace until she was running at full speed, tripping over roots and stumbling through potholes. Eventually she reached a clearing that took her out onto the road adjoining Turret Shore. The wind blew through the trees, carrying the faint smell of frying onions. She saw the flashing lights of the funfair. She jumped when she felt a vibration against her hip, and when she pulled The Book from her pocket the locket was throbbing red.

"No! Not while I'm on my own!"

There was no option but to turn to the second last page and wait. Bree watched as the sixth wish appeared.

A wish this time for you alone,
What's yet to come not set in stone.
Glimpse the future, see the past,
A chance to find the truth at last.
The threads that hold this stitch in time
Now start to loosen and unwind.

Bree slipped The Book back into her pocket and ran down the hill towards Ramthorpe Junior School. When she turned the corner she found the playground in chaos. People were running blindly, trampling one another in panic. A pile of smoking grey ash was all that remained of the bonfire, and the Ferris wheel had been knocked sideways, its lights flickering.

It's all happening too fast, thought Bree. She had to get home. She pushed through the panic, shouldering people aside, using her elbows as weapons.

Against the red sky, Rockwell Tower block resembled an enormous gravestone. Suddenly, a single fork of lightning hit the rooftop garden, knocking a great chunk of stone from the corner of the building. The windows exploded, sending shards of glass onto the streets below. Flames and smoke billowed out, and flakes of ash fell around her like snow.

Something about the scene brought back a memory.

With trembling fingers she pulled Gypsy Sue's card from her pocket and flattened it. To her horror she noticed that the words CLOCKWORK BELL TOWER now read: ROCKWELL TOWER BLOCK.

"Mum!" she cried, her legs buckling beneath her.

Bree staggered and ran, not knowing where to go now that her home was gone. The roads leading out of Rockwell were clogged with cars – some abandoned. There were people everywhere, struggling to get to safety, and she searched the sea of panicked faces for Sandy and Honey. For a moment the terrible noises were drowned out by the heavy thrum of a helicopter overhead. A man hung out from the open door and held a loudhailer to his mouth.

"DO NOT PANIC. I REPEAT DO NOT PANIC!"

This seemed to make everyone panic even more.

She made a dash for Rockwell Bridge, bolting up the steps two at a time, stopping to catch her breath at the top. The moon was completely red now. Around the outside of it, light glowed like a silvery halo. Two worlds had become one. Castle Zarcalat stood in proud defiance, bright and bold as if it had been painted onto the Rockwell skyline.

And then Bree heard it – nothing more than an echo at first, muted by the wind – the sound of heavy wings stirring the air. She ran until her lungs burned, following the seething crush of people through the shopping precinct. She stopped and caught sight of herself in the dark glass of a shop window. Her hair was plastered to her head and her face looked sweaty and bruised.

A brief scream of tyres was followed by an explosion of sound. Beside her, oil spread across the pavement and steam spewed from the crumpled bonnet of a car. A horn was blaring in one long, continuous monotone.

She spotted Adam amongst the crowd and relief flooded through her.

"ADAM!" she called, waving her arms wildly to catch his attention.

He was running straight towards her, his face a picture of panic. As he got closer she stepped out into his path to stop him, but he kept running and there was no time to move out of his way. She closed her eyes and braced herself for a collision. But nothing happened – just the sensation of an icy wind passing through her.

A young man and woman stopped beside her. His face twisted in despair, and the woman threw her hand to her mouth and started to cry. A feeling grew within Bree, not quite full blown panic, but something like it. She peered into the cracked glass in the car's wing mirror and was shocked to find no reflection.

Wheeling around, Bree looked down to see what the couple were staring at. Horror swept over her when she saw her own lifeless body lying crumpled on the ground. The Book lay beside her, pages flapping in the wind like a dying bird.

"*No!*" she screamed, reeling backwards. "*I'm…I'm fine…I'm right here!*"

But the couple had gone, lost in the panicked crowd. Bree cried out for help but no-one heard. A strange feeling took hold of her, and with it came a terrible understanding.

This is how I die…

She shielded her face as a dark shadow fell over her. Thalofedril swept The Book up from the ground and disappeared. As her body started to melt away, a film reel of images raced through her mind – riding her first bike, starting school, falling out of a tree, meeting Honey, kissing Adam – and when she reached her most recent memory, the quality of the air around her seemed to intensify, to grow loud and bright until it was so powerful it lifted her from the ground.

Suddenly she was somewhere else.

The world was bathed in the peachy glow of a quiet, summer evening. The pavement was gritty with sand and a salty breeze stirred her hair. She looked up at the feathery clouds, and then over to the sea that glittered along a curve of pale, golden sand.

Bree followed a row of terraced houses, their fronts painted in different pastel shades. When she reached the end she looked up and saw a sign on a wall – thick white italics on a dark blue background – *Keves on Sea*.

She turned a corner and followed a path that led to the back of a run-down building. The place was deserted. The only sounds she heard were the faint hush of the sea as it folded itself over the shingle, and seagulls yawping and scrapping with each other.

On one side of the building there was a low window, which was bricked up. Bree glanced around, and when she looked back the bricks had disappeared, replaced by a pane of murky glass. A sense of unease settled over her.

Shielding her face from the sun she looked closely at the window. At first she thought her mind was playing tricks on her, but then she realised the glass was rippling. Slowly an image emerged. Two policemen were approaching a front door, and Bree recognised it – number 27, Granny Lissa's house.

The policemen removed their hats. When the door opened, her mother stood in the frame, heavily pregnant. Bree did not need to see the men's faces to know what they were saying. Granny Lissa appeared in the doorway in time to catch her daughter-in-law as her legs gave way beneath her.

Bree squeezed her eyes closed, and when she opened them again she was looking at a coffin being lowered into a rectangle cut into the earth. People dressed in black stood around it, their faces pale and grief-stricken. Her mother clutched her swollen belly and sobbed uncontrollably. She knew she was witnessing her father's funeral, but she felt an odd sense of detachment.

The sun disappeared behind a cloud, washing a dark

shadow across the rippling pane, returning it to normal. Bree cupped her hands and peered in to see a warehouse with high, metal shelves and steel joists along the ceiling.

Suddenly, a door slammed and she heard voices. Two men entered the room and stood with their backs to her, talking heatedly. The taller of the two turned and the sun flashed off his glasses. *Tomas Deanheart!* Bree quickly ducked under the windowsill. The men were arguing and talking over one another, and she dared to take another look.

"I trusted you," said the other man, and in an instant she knew who he was.

The grey in his hair was gone, and despite his anguished expression her father looked young and fresh-faced, like he did in all the photographs.

Without warning he swung a punch at Tomas Deanheart's head, but he missed as Deanheart dodged out of the way and punched him back hard in the stomach, knocking the wind from him. Bree covered her mouth to stop her scream escaping.

A frantic tussle ensued and for a moment it was impossible to tell where Richard McCready started and Tomas Deanheart ended. Then her father broke free and scrambled to his feet, his hair disheveled and a livid bruise forming on his cheek.

"You can beat me to a pulp if you want. But I will never hand it over!"

Tomas Deanheart pulled a knife from his belt. Richard stared down at it, fear and confusion creasing his face.

"Why?"

Tomas Deanheart stalked forwards, a sly smile lifting the corner of his mouth.

"Because I can."

"You wouldn't dare," said Richard, backing away. "If you

really are one of *them* you can't risk getting my blood on your skin."

Deanheart snarled, and Richard turned and fled, making for the exit. He yanked on the door handle, but it wouldn't open.

Panic-stricken, he scaled one of the floor-to-ceiling shelving units, and scrambled onto a girder that stretched along the length of the high ceiling. Tomas Deanheart clamped the knife between his teeth and followed him up.

"Come on then!" Richard goaded, inching backwards along the beam.

Deanheart forced him to the middle, jabbing at him with the dagger, forcing him to duck and dodge.

"To think I felt sorry for you at school," Richard spat. "Everyone called you Tomas *Freak*heart but I always fought your corner..."

He took a quick glance over his shoulder and realised the girder stopped abruptly.

"...and this is how you repay me!"

Deanheart thrust the dagger out, forcing Richard closer to the gap. His heel slipped off the end and he wobbled for a second before regaining his balance.

"Tonight you will die," said Deanheart, "but first you will tell me where The Book is."

Richard sighed.

"I will tell you, but only when you give me your word not to hurt my wife and the old woman."

Deanheart's eyes narrowed as he considered his reply.

"You have my word," he said eventually.

Richard seemed to sag with relief.

"And you have mine," he said. "So let's do this, man to man, without..." he glanced down at the dagger, "...that."

Deanheart nodded. His shoulders relaxed as he let the dagger fall to his side.

"That's better," smiled Richard. "Now come closer and I'll tell you where it is."

Behind his glasses Tomas Deanheart's eyes flashed greedily. He inched along the beam, stopping directly in front of Richard. For a fleeting second Bree imagined that the story would have a different ending; that she was witnessing a past that might come undone and veer onto a different path. But her father grabbed the dagger and yanked it out of Deanheart's hand. He swayed dangerously but somehow stayed on the beam.

"Did you *really* think I would tell you where it is?"

Blood dripped from his hand but he did not notice. Deanheart backed away slowly, with his hands in the air.

"I know you don't have it in you to use that," he said.

Richard looked down, puzzled by the pool of the blood gathering at his feet.

"I'm bleeding," he muttered, and then his dark eyes flashed. "I won't *need* to use this knife. I have a better weapon!"

"That wound was self-inflicted. The blood can't harm me," Deanheart taunted.

Richard's grip on the dagger tightened until his knuckles turned white.

Bree's eyes slid back to Tomas Deanheart. His expression had darkened and his mouth had twisted into a cruel sneer. Slowly, he removed his glasses and Richard watched uncertainly, his eyes flicking back to the gap between the joists. All of a sudden Deanheart's features transformed. His face thinned out, the skin turning pale and pockmarked. Oily black strands sprouted from his scalp, replacing his messy blonde hair. His eyes became two pieces of granite beneath heavy lids. The dagger slipped from Richard's grip.

"Who *are* you?"

A voice inside Bree's head screamed the answer. *Tanas Theramonde!*

Caught off guard, Richard was not prepared for what happened next. Theramonde ran forwards and shoved him. The breath stuck in Bree's throat as she watched her father sway from side to side, before losing his balance. He slipped off the end of the beam. Somehow he managed to grab on, but as he dangled helplessly Bree knew she was witnessing the last few moments of his life. Theramonde crept along towards him, his black eyes flashing with malicious triumph.

"Leave him alone," she whispered, her teeth sinking into her bottom lip until she tasted blood.

He knelt down and leaned over the edge so his face was close to Richard's.

"How does it feel to know you will never see your unborn child?" he asked cruelly.

Richard's fingers started slipping.

"I've made sure you will *never* get The Book," said Richard with an air of finality that made Bree's blood run cold.

Theramonde's face twitched with fury.

"Then I give you my word that one day I will kill that child of yours."

There was a glint of metal as Richard lifted his arm and sliced the blade down Theramonde's cheek. He grabbed his face and let out a heart-stopping scream. When he took his hand away a vivid scarlet slash ran from his left eyebrow all the way down to his earlobe.

Still clutching his face, he scrambled to his feet, lifted his boot and brought it down hard on Richard's fingertips. Richard

McCready's fingers left the beam and in that moment Bree's future was set.

****

Bree expected to wake up from a terrible nightmare but when she opened her eyes she was still standing next to the murky window. Her father lay lifeless on the ground. She put a hand over her mouth to try and stifle the shocking noise of her own grief. Tanas Theramonde stormed across the floor, cursing loudly as he tried to stem the flow of blood from his cheek. In a fit of rage he threw the dagger at the window – the glass exploded outwards and the dagger landed on the ground beside Bree. She stared down in horror at the dark wooden handle and the wide blade; a blade so sharp it could cut smoke into thin slices. Inside the warehouse a door slammed, and when she looked back through the broken glass Theramonde was gone.

She fumbled for her phone, her fingers clammy and desperate, but then she remembered she had left it on Annie's bedside table. She stared at her dead father, her eyes not quite managing to send the message to her brain. She could not understand anything except the need to get as far away from here as possible. She ran, slipping on the gravel, then turned back for the dagger. It felt cold and foreign in her hands and the sight of the blood made her stomach roil.

"OI!"

The shout jolted her and she spun around. A stocky man with a bald head was half-in, half-out of a taxi. Without thinking, she ran. Her legs moved slowly, her heart so heavy it seemed to pin her to the concrete. The taxi driver shouted after her but she did not look back.

It seemed so simple in that moment. She would run forever, fast enough that nothing would ever catch her – not her past, not her future, not the dark corners in her mind that she did not dare enter. Her Dad was dead and there was nothing she could do about it.

It was the cold that eventually stopped her. Night had descended, and she looked up at the moon, which was almost half-covered by a coppery red shadow. Her breath billowed out in front of her, panicky breaths punctuated by desperate sobs. She zipped up her jacket, but it did nothing to stop her teeth chattering.

She wandered down an alleyway that wound between a deserted shop and a derelict building. A collection of bulging rubbish bags had been stacked up and litter blew in circles. She was definitely back in Rockwell. *Back in the present*. A wild panic erupted within her as she caught sight of two yellow eyes peering at her from behind the bags. Savage teeth tore at the plastic, and Bree brandished the dagger with a trembling hand. Then she saw it was nothing more than a fox, scavenging for leftovers. It bolted, melting into the shadows. The mist was so thick she could not see her legs from the shins down. She slipped the dagger inside her boot and leaned against a wall, shivering wildly.

Suddenly a circle of light penetrated the mist, accompanied by the sound of some strange and hideous monster. Bree did not have the will or the energy to get up and run, so she curled into a little ball and waited to die.

CHAPTER 26
THE QUEEN OF SECRETS

Slowly, as if growing out of the mist, a tall, dark figure came into focus.

"BREE!"

With strands of hair sticking out wildly around an old-fashioned motorcycle helmet with no visor, Sandy looked every bit as astonished as she felt. She tried to get up, but the mist pinned her to the ground.

"Oh Sandy!" she sobbed. "It was terrible. I saw everything and I did nothing."

He ran over and pulled her to her feet. "We've been looking everywhere for you!"

"I couldn't save him!" Bree cried hopelessly. "I was there right in front of him and...and..."

"Who?"

"My Dad. I saw how he died."

"It's over now."

Bree shook her head and pushed him away.

"Don't you see? It's only just begun. How am I ever going to forget what I've seen? How can I ever forgive myself for not stopping it?"

"*Nobody* can change the past," he said firmly.

"I might as well have killed him myself!"

"Don't say that!"

He grabbed her hand.

"It's not possible to change what has already happened," he said, his gaze unflinching.

Bree wiped her nose along her sleeve.

"Do you really think that's true?"

Sandy looked distracted.

"Something's not right," he said, looking through the mist at Annie's motorcycle and sidecar.

Bree stared past him, the harsh light from the headlamp making her eyeballs ache. Smoky patterns of mist swirled in the beam, and it seemed to be getting thicker by the second.

"This mist...it feels like it's strangling me...quick, get in," said Sandy, guiding her towards the rusty sidecar.

"Can you drive this thing?"

"More or less."

"Well, which is it? More or less?"

Sandy strapped the spare helmet onto her head.

"After you've piloted a hot air balloon and a magic carpet, this thing is a piece of cake."

"Hurry up then," urged Bree. "Let's get out of here."

The engine, which had been ticking over, sprung to life. In the shadows two flecks of amber glinted like tiny flames.

"What's that?!" shrieked Sandy, pointing.

"Don't worry," Bree shouted over the engine. "It's only a fox."

The orange flecks widened into bright discs of liquid gold. Sandy gave Bree a nervous sideways glance, and then fixed his eyes back on the road.

"That sure is one big fox," he said, kicking the bike into gear.

The engine growled and something growled back. A huge Cleptathorn erupted through the gap between the buildings.

"GO!"

Annie's motorcycle took off with a sputter and a jerk. It shot forwards, lurching under them, as Sandy pulled it savagely to the left, whipping Bree sideways so she had to grab on to the edge of the sidecar. They skidded wildly for a moment, losing traction across the pavement before regaining control. Bree looked behind her but all she could see was a trail of exhaust fumes mingling with the fog.

"I think we lost it!"

She stole a quick glance in the rear-view mirror and saw the Cleptathorn burst through the churning mist, its muscles bunching and stretching.

"FASTER!"

She braced herself as the sidecar bumped up the kerb. Just as she righted herself Sandy took a bend too fast and swerved. She clung on. In the mirror she could see the Cleptathorn gaining on them, foam bubbling at the corners of its mouth. Sandy threw the bike around a sharp bend, and then steered hard in the opposite direction to avoid hitting a parked car. Eventually they shook the beast off. Bree was starting to feel sick and she was grateful when, after a couple of bends, Sandy swung off onto the back road that wound down towards the Rockwell Estate. All too vividly she remembered her glimpse into the future and Rockwell Tower Block crumbling in front of her eyes, flames spewing from the inside out. But for the moment it stood tall and steady, warm light spilling out from the windows.

Sandy trundled Annie's motorbike into its space and turned off the engine.

"She'll never know I borrowed it," he said, pulling off his helmet and pushing his fringe out of his eyes.

As usual, the lift was playing up so they took the stairs to the top floor. Warm and familiar, flat 8B felt like the safest place on earth. When Bree walked into the living room she saw Honey sitting at the window, grim-faced and biting the edge of her thumbnail. When she saw Bree she jumped up and ran over.

"Bree!" She hugged her tightly. "Are you okay?"

"Yeah," said Bree, managing a weak smile.

Honey was instantly suspicious.

"Are you sure? You look terrible."

"Thanks a bunch! I'm fine, really. It's just been a long day."

"And it's not over yet," Honey said gloomily. "Have you seen the moon?"

Bree nodded.

"Where's my mum?"

"She's in her bedroom getting ready for the party at my house."

"By the way, Gran is having a nap in your bedroom," added Sandy.

"I'm going to check on mum," said Bree. "Stick the TV on, I won't be long."

She crept past her bedroom and the bathroom, hoping not to disturb Annie. Madeleine was perched on the end of her bed looking through a box of photographs. The contents of her make-up bag were scattered across the quilt. She looked up when Bree walked in, offering a smile that fell away as quickly as it appeared. Her eyes were bloodshot and ringed with red.

"Hi stranger," she said, fumbling with a stack of letters held together with red ribbon. "I've not seen you all day."

"You know me, Mum," Bree said lightly. "I always come home when my belly starts rumbling."

"You didn't answer any of my calls," said Madeleine, the corners of her mouth turned down in disapproval.

"Sorry, Mum. I left my phone at Mrs Hooten's. How is she?"

"She seems a bit better. It was easier to let her stay here for a while so we could keep an eye on her."

"Where's Harry?"

"He's helping out at Mort and Saffron's. We're all having dinner there tonight. Granny Lissa is coming too. We'll be going to the eclipse party at the funfair afterwards."

"Sounds good," Bree said. "What have you got there?"

"Oh, nothing much really," she said, stuffing everything back in the box. "Just a few old memories. It was Annie's fault. She made me feel all nostalgic."

Bree cleared a space and sat down on the edge of the bed. She picked up an old newspaper clipping held together with yellowed sticky tape, and read:

Disappearance of local couple

Local couple, Michael and Jane Greenfield left their flat on the evening of July 7th and have not been seen since.

Friends say they attended a birthday party for a friend's daughter that afternoon, and appeared in good spirits as they played with their young son, Sandy, aged 3.

PC Paul Marshall said: 'Their car was found on the outskirts of Auriel Forest on the morning of the 8th July. Nothing appeared to be missing from inside but it would appear that the couple has simply vanished without a trace. We are appealing for witnesses who might have seen Jane and Michael on the night

in question and urge them to come forward with
any information.'
Jane Greenfield's distraught mother, Annie
Hooten, said: 'We want them to know they are
dearly loved and that whatever trouble they
are in it's nothing that can't be sorted. Please
come home. Sandy is asking where his Mummy
and Daddy are and it is breaking my heart.'

Bree placed the clipping back inside the box, lost for words.

"Sometimes I pull this box out and have a good old cry,"
said Madeleine. "I don't get much of a chance these days. I
wasn't really expecting anyone else to find out."

Bree looked at her mother.

"Don't worry, Mum, nobody else will know. You could say
I'm the Queen of secrets."

Madeleine smiled tenderly at her. Nestled amongst a pile of
letters was another clipping from an old copy of the *Rockwell
Gazette*. The date at the top caught Bree's eye – July the 2nd.
She picked it up and her mouth turned to dust when she read
the caption – Man found dead at Seven Oakes factory.

Madeleine reached for the cutting but Bree snatched it back
angrily, quickly scanning through the text.

Peter Gillis, a taxi driver from the Keves on
Sea area made the grim discovery at around
8.30pm on Monday evening. 'I saw a young girl
peering in through the window of the factory,'
Mr Gillis told police. 'She looked like she was
up to no good but she ran away before I could
catch her. She had something in her hand, some

kind of tool. I reckon she was trying to break
in but who knows with kids today. For all I
know she might be the one who killed him.'

"Sweetheart, please," said Madeleine, but Bree ignored her
plea and continued reading.

Police believe Richard McCready's death was
a tragic accident, but are appealing for
witnesses and urge the young girl to come
forward so they can rule her out of the
investigation.

"I want to know exactly how Dad died," she said numbly.
Madeleine wiped her eyes.
"I've told you before. It was an accident at work. A terrible
accident."
"I want to hear it again," said Bree, her voice sharper than
she had intended.
Madeleine looked at her like she was a stranger.
"Properly this time," said Bree, her tone gentler. "No half-
truths."
"Darling I -"
"*Please*, Mum, I need to know. I'm fourteen. I can handle
the truth."
Madeleine took a deep breath and reached out for her hand.
She gave it a squeeze.
"It would have been very quick," she said softly.
For a moment the words hung heavy in the space between
them.
"Who was with him?"

"He was on his own. He fell from a high beam. He didn't suffer in any way...other than a cut on the palm of his hand, which nobody could explain. I feel I should remember the last thing he said to me," she croaked. "But I don't..."

Tears leaked from the corners of her eyes and rolled down her cheeks. Bree buried her face into the soft crease of her mother's neck and cried. The reality was Richard McCready was dead. It could never be undone. Even the most powerful magic would not erase it.

"He died knowing he could live on in you," soothed Madeleine. "You were his second chance."

Bree wound her finger around the red ribbon, tilting her head to read the bold, careless scrawl with the sloping words and the disembodied circles, which floated above the letter 'i'.

"No peeking," giggled Madeleine, clutching them to her chest. "These are private."

Bree smiled.

"Why don't you go and see Annie," said Madeleine. "She'll be ever so glad to see you."

"Is she *really* okay? I'm worried about her."

"Well, she's very tired," Madeleine admitted. "She's not going to make it along to the eclipse party, but she will be coming to Mort and Saffron's for something to eat. I think she's looking forward to a good old chinwag with Granny Lissa."

Bree walked to the door, stopped and turned back. Madeleine was peering into the mirror, carefully re-applying her mascara.

"Mum?"

"Mmmm," she replied vaguely.

"Thanks."

****

When Bree opened her bedroom door Annie stirred. Bustopher, who had been curled up in a ball at her feet, stretched, and yawned in deep contentment. On the bedside table, the lava lamp glowed. The digital clock blinked 5:17pm.

"Can I get you anything?" Bree asked, fixing the edges of the quilt.

Annie sat up. Her eyes were bloodshot but she was wearing a new shade of lipstick and she was smiling.

"How about a big smile?" she said.

Bree sat down on the edge of the bed.

"How are you feeling?"

"Better after a good sleep," answered Annie. "Although that flippin' thing kept chirping away all day."

She swung her eyes to the bedside table where Bree's mobile phone sat on top of the book about Sobstoan House. Bree picked it up and looked down at the screen.

8 text messages, 5 missed calls.

Most of them were from Adam, which triggered a flurry of butterflies in her stomach. Annie slid on her gold-framed reading glasses and picked up, *Sobstoan House: Past and Present.*

"Oh and I think I found my mother," she said casually, handing it to Bree.

"What?!"

The door opened and Honey appeared. She leaned against the frame. "How's the invalid doing?" she asked with a lopsided grin.

"Oh, don't call me that," Annie groaned, "I'll be right as rain in a wee while."

Honey switched on the main light, and Annie blinked against the sudden brightness. Bustopher leapt down and disappeared under the bed.

"I come bearing gifts," said Sandy, holding out a steaming cup.

Annie patted the bed, an invite for them to sit down.

"Oooh lovely," she said. "A nice cup of tea will sort me out."

Sobstoan House: Past and Present, fell open across Bree's knee at a page that had been bookmarked by a dog-eared scrap of paper. There was a blob of bright red sealing wax on the back of it. She lifted it to reveal a double-page spread showing a collection of black and white photographs. The book smelled of dust and mothballs and past lives. Bree studied the images carefully, not exactly sure what she was looking for.

"It's the picture at the bottom," said Annie, her glasses propped halfway down the bridge of her nose, "the one with all the chambermaids in it."

"What have you found?" asked Honey, perching on the end of the bed.

"My mother," Annie replied, taking a sip of tea.

Bree stared at the grainy photograph and her eyes were immediately drawn to a skinny girl in her teens. She had a willowy figure, and she wore a neat blouse tucked into a skirt. Her hair was pinned back showing her face, young and painfully anxious. Her eyes were huge and dark, like Annie's and Sandy's. She ran a finger along the text at the bottom of the page and her eyes settled on the girl's name. A puzzle piece slotted into place as if it had always been there waiting for this moment. There it was, in black and white. All the staff names from Sobstoan House, 1938. The girl in the photograph was Agora Burton.

****

Sandy searched Bree's face, his expression one great big question mark. She could not speak. Two words had taken up all the room inside her head. *Agora Burton... Agora Burton...*

"What is it?" probed Honey.

Bree handed her the book and watched as her eyes widened, first with shock and then with delight.

"Sandy! Your Great-Grandmother was Agora Burton!"

Annie's eyes narrowed. She took a sip of tea and put her cup aside.

"I don't believe it, Annie," squealed Honey, thrusting the book in her face. "Agora Burton was your mother."

"Do you know her?" asked Annie, closing the book gently.

Bree cleared her throat.

"We met Agora a couple of years ago. I'm afraid she died not long after that. I'm so sorry."

There was a brief silence.

"I know that poem off by heart," said Annie, nodding towards the dog-eared scrap in Bree's hand, "but please read it to me."

The paper was thin and torn as if it had been read and re-read many times over many years. Bree unfolded it carefully to find a few handwritten lines. The ink had faded to a weak grey colour and was blotchy in places where rain – or tears – had landed. Bree's fingers traced the graceful swoop of the letters as she read it aloud.

"Always know I loved you so
Because of this I let you go
But in my heart you will remain
Perhaps our paths will cross again
Time won't stand still, remember this
That soon you'll feel my loving kiss
So with these words I leave for you
Think of me in all you do
And every day I'll watch the clock
And hope that soon my door you'll knock
Sweet child, there's nothing left to say
Except I'll wish the hours away"

"That's so sad," said Honey. "Your mother never knew you."

"And I never knew her," Annie replied. She peered over the top of her glasses. "How did *you* know her?"

Bree hesitated, trying to conjure up the right words.

"She was friends with my Dad for a very long time. We only met her once. We had no idea who she was, or we would have told you straight away."

Annie stared ahead, lost in thought.

"Did she have any other children? A husband. My father?"

"I don't think so," said Honey. "She lived on her own."

"Well, not quite," said Sandy. "She shared her house with ninety-three cats."

Annie made a face.

"Obviously she didn't share the family allergy then."

Bree suddenly remembered something William Hart had told them.

"Agora had a younger sister. Charlotte. I'm not sure if she's still alive though."

"Aunt Charlotte," muttered Annie, "I like the sound of her."

"The initials on your handkerchief must stand for Agora Burton," said Honey. "Not Annie Bunsfield."

"I suppose you must be right."

Bree gave Annie's hand a gentle squeeze.

"I know this might not make sense to you, Mrs Hooten," she said. "But I think your mother gave you away because she was trying to protect you from something terrible."

Annie nodded pensively.

"I can't believe I was sitting with my Great-Grandmother and I had no idea," said Sandy with a slow shake of his head.

"And I can't believe I could have met her," said Annie, her words so full of regret that they could have clouded a sunny day.

Abruptly, she threw back the quilt and swung her legs out of bed.

"No time for wallowing," she said, any hint of sadness vanishing from her face. "There's a party starting at Freesia House and I need to get my costume on."

She stood up, her knees cracking like pistol shots, and tottered over to the door.

"You're not going to believe what I'm dressing up as," she giggled as she disappeared out into the hallway.

Bree folded the letter and put it on the bedside table. She plumped up the pillow, a million thoughts spinning round in her head.

"Annie was right. Secrets always seek an ear," she said quietly.

She peered through the window at the city below. A few stars had broken sharply through the black sheet of night. A crescent of white moon was still visible behind the red shadow, but in less than two hours it would be completely covered. Her eyes settled on a dark shape perched on the edge of Guinessberry Heights, the tower block opposite. She felt the blood drain from her face as a huge bat shape flapped its enormous wings and rose into the sky. A spine-tingling howl soared into the night.

She whipped around.

"What is it?" asked Honey.

"He's back. Thalofedril is in Rockwell."

Sandy froze. "You were right."

Bree pulled the curtains shut.

"I saw something earlier – just after I left you both in the tunnel. Wish six allowed me to see the past and the future."

Her throat closed and she had to force the words out.

"The thing is I didn't just see it. I *lived* it. I know exactly what is going to happen tonight."

She paced up and down the room, chewing her thumbnail.

"I'm not sure if we can change it. This might be worse than we could ever have imagined."

Sandy sat forwards.

"Do you remember what William said about fate and our destinies being written in the stars?" he asked.

Bree nodded.

"And I told him that I preferred to believe that we could shape our future and that it wasn't all planned out for us..." he continued.

"The sixth wish said something like that too," said Bree. "Something about the future not being set in stone."

"Well there's still hope then," said Sandy. "I think we can still make a difference to tonight's outcome."

"I hope so," said Bree. "What I saw...it was *horrible*."

At that moment Madeleine breezed into the room, doing her

best to stay upright in a pair of cowboy boots. She was wearing a checked shirt, suede waistcoat and matching skirt.

"Howdy partners," she drawled, tilting her Stetson.

Bree managed a smile.

"You look great, Mum. We need to go and do something before the party starts."

"Typical," Madeleine sighed.

"Sorry, Mrs M," Honey said awkwardly, "but it's pretty urgent."

"Well, be back in time for the party," said Madeleine. "And wrap up! It's freezing out there."

Sandy stole a quick peek through the curtains.

"Can't we just stay here?" he said.

Bree shot him a sharp look.

"No, we can't. Come on you two. We've got things to do."

As they made their way down the stairs, Bree wondered whether it was possible to alter what was in store for them. Were their fates already sealed? Was the future written in the stars?

She might not have been able to change what had happened to her Dad, but she was not about to stand back and watch the world crumble around her. She would do whatever it took.

CHAPTER 27
A FINAL SHOWDOWN

The sky had turned a strange mixture of red and charcoal. As they walked past Rockwell High School the light from the fiery moon cast a faint tangerine aura around Honey's hair.

"Where are we actually going?" she asked. "How are we going to find Thalofedril? And what are we going to do *when* we find him?"

Bree shrugged. "I've no idea. How about we try the library again. That's where we got rid of him last time."

Sandy shook his head.

"We need a better plan. There's less than two hours to go. We have one wish left but there's no saying when that might – "

Bree stopped in her tracks.

"The locket! It's throbbing!"

She pulled The Book from her pocket and quickly flicked to the last page.

Honey peered over her shoulder.

"It's the last wish. What's it saying?"

"Give it a minute."

Bold letters slowly emerged and Bree read them aloud.

A fairground ride has creatures three
who've sprouted wings and now fly free.
They'll take you to a well-known place
A final showdown you must face.

> **with seven wishes now received,**
> **One more will offer a reprieve.**

The binding creaked as she closed the cover.

Honey let out an anguished moan when she felt for her satchel and realised it was not there.

"I must've left it at yours!"

"There's no time to go back for it," said Bree, returning The Book safely to her pocket. "I'm sure we'll cope without it."

"But Valgus's ring was in there," said Honey. "What if we need it?"

Suddenly, a gust of wind sent a pile of leaves swirling along the pavement. Bree glanced up. The stars seemed to jumble and collide as a shadowy figure swooped over their heads. As it circled lower, a creature the size of a horse came into focus. It had enormous wings and was covered in purple and gold scales. A scorching length of fire shot from its mouth. Honey grabbed onto Sandy's sleeve.

"It's a dragon!"

It landed on the pavement, blinked, and snorted out a rather impressive puff of smoke.

"I think he's on our side," Bree said uncertainly.

It regarded her with jewelled eyes, as she glanced nervously at its clawed feet and swishing tail.

They stared in awe as a Phoenix, ten times larger than an eagle, flew down and landed in the middle of the street. It began to preen its feathers, which were the colour of fire.

"That's only two," said Honey, her eyes searching the sky. "Didn't the wish say *three* creatures?"

Just then a white horse rose up from behind Rockwell High, buffeting the air with huge feathered wings.

"It's Pegasus," said Sandy, adjusting his glasses.

"It's the horse Mimi rode on the carousel last night," Honey pointed out. "In fact they're *all* from the carousel, just like the wish said."

Pegasus hit the ground running, and used his wings to stop alongside them. He whinnied softly, and bowed his head. The Phoenix squawked and ruffled its feathers.

"Well *there's* a sight you don't see every day," said Honey.

"I guess we're supposed to climb on," said Bree.

The dragon unfurled its wings and rested its chin on the pavement. Bree approached it cautiously, running her hand gently over scales that were arranged like roof slates.

"Nice dragon," she said softly, as she slowly swung her leg over until she was sitting astride its wide neck.

It raised its head, tossing her backwards onto its scaly back. Honey laughed.

"It's not funny," snapped Bree. "It's pretty scary up here."

Honey stroked Pegasus' velvet nose, and he whickered and swished his tail.

"This should be a piece of cake for you," said Sandy.

Honey wound her fingers through the thick mane and pulled herself up onto his back.

"I usually have a saddle," she said, patting his neck, "and I don't normally have two huge wings on either side of me."

The Phoenix ruffled its feathers and squawked at Sandy. He stepped back nervously.

"You need to climb on," said Honey, stifling a giggle.

"I *know* what to do" he scowled, circling the giant bird.

It crouched down and spread its wings across the pavement. Reluctantly he climbed up onto its back. With a *whoosh* the dragon launched into the air. Bree squeezed her eyes shut as it lifted high into the sky. After a few seconds she looked back to see Pegasus flying gracefully behind her. The Phoenix flapped furiously to keep up with them as they sailed high over Rockwell, up and up until the lights were nothing more than pinpricks on a black canvas and the twisting roads petered out into narrow lanes.

Beyond the moon-silvered fields, Bree spotted a mountain range stretching far off into the distance ahead. One rose much higher than the others, its peak resembling a huge shark fin. A thunderclap boomed and a flash of lightning illuminated the outline of Castle Zarcalat. Behind her, the lights of Rockwell twinkled. It seemed as if they were flying through no man's land. They crested the ragged mountain and circled down towards the courtyard. Bree could scarcely believe they were back here.

One by one they landed in front of the castle. Wasting no time they climbed down quickly. They scurried over the cobbles, and up the steps to the front door. When they looked back, Pegasus, the dragon and the Phoenix had disappeared. Deep inside Bree's pocket the locket stopped throbbing.

"Follow me," said Sandy.

He turned the upside down heart handle, and gave the door a heavy shove with his shoulder. It burst open and they stepped inside. Water dripped from their clothes and hair, pooling on the dark polished floor.

They made their way to the bottom of the spiral staircase. Bree peered anxiously into the shadows.

"Do you think we should go up?" she whispered.

"I don't fancy going the other way again, do you?" asked Honey.

Halfway up the stairs a door banged shut somewhere on

the top landing. They pulled into the shadows with their backs pressed to the wall.

Bree knelt down and slid Theramonde's dagger from her boot, holding it up so the blade glinted in the torchlight. Honey's hands went up to her mouth.

"Where did you get that?" she gasped.

"Don't ask," Bree replied darkly. "Someone's up there. We'll wait here until we're sure they've gone."

Suddenly a noise broke through the silence, a cheery tune that seemed very out of place. It was coming from Bree's pocket.

"It's...it's my *phone!*"

She pulled it out and held it to her chest, hoping her jacket would muffle the sound. But the tinny ringtone still sounded like a fanfare in the deathly silence. Sandy started flapping.

"Shut it up!"

"Answer it!" said Honey.

Bree stared down at the screen.

Mum calling...

She pressed the answer button and lifted the phone to her ear.

"Sweetheart? Are you there?"

"Uh-huh."

"Where are you?"

"Er, out and about."

Sandy stared at her, his eyes wide with disbelief.

"Who is it?" Honey mouthed.

"My Mum," Bree mouthed back.

"When will you be coming to Mort and Saffron's?" Madeleine

asked. "They're putting on a lovely spread for us and everyone is dressed up."

"Soon, Mum."

"Are you alright sweetie? You sound a bit far-away."

"I've got to go Mum but I'll see you soon, okay?"

"Okay darling, be good."

Bree switched off her phone and buried it deep in her pocket.

"Well, I wasn't expecting *that*," she said.

"It's good we're getting a signal," said Sandy.

"Why is that good? It means both worlds are merging into one," said Honey.

Bree pushed the dagger back inside her boot.

"I think it's safe to go up," she said.

Sandy stared at her slack jawed.

"I said, it's safe to go up," Bree said firmly, and his mouth snapped shut.

They crept up the stairs and slid into the shadows on the top landing, following the corridor until they came to a door. Bree's hand hovered over the handle for a moment and then she pushed it down.

Tanas Theramonde sat perfectly upright at the head of a long table, with a plate of steaming food in front of him. Bree resisted the urge to run, closing the door behind them instead. Theramonde shook out a napkin and smoothed it across his lap.

"I wondered when you would come back to see *me*," he said. "I was beginning to feel rather neglected."

"You don't scare us," Sandy said boldly, although his voice was quivering. "We've already dealt with some of your cronies. It's your turn next."

Theramonde's black eyes flashed.

"So, tell me, how does it feel to finally know the truth about your bloodline? *And* what happened to your dear old mother and father."

Sandy stared back at him with simmering hatred. Unfazed, Theramonde took a sip from a silver goblet, and placed it back down on the table.

"I would offer you some cordial," he said with a sly smile, "but I'm quite sure you would decline."

"I know who you are," said Bree. "You're Tomas Deanheart."

Honey threw her hands up to her mouth.

Theramonde's eyebrows arched with malicious pleasure.

"*Ah*, they did not know. I didn't think friends kept secrets from one another."

"I saw what you did," Bree said.

"Pray tell," he said, pushing himself back, rocking his chair on two legs.

"You...you..."

He leaned forwards and rested his elbows on the table.

"I killed your father," he said coldly. "But didn't we know that already?"

"I saw you do it," said Bree, her voice trembling. "You... *Tomas Deanheart*...tricked my father into going to the factory, where you murdered him."

He pushed the chair away from the table, the legs scraping noisily on the stone. He stood up and moved his hand to the hilt of his sword – Bree flinched but stood her ground.

"And even after all that you *still* didn't get what you wanted from him," she said, her tone darkening.

Theramonde circled her like a shark.

"You've got a lot of nerve for someone in your position."

Bree stayed silent.

"I was looking forward to more of a challenge," he said with a pouted lip.

"He trusted you," croaked Bree. "He only came to the factory because he trusted you."

"How sentimental," said Theramonde.

"You're nothing more than a cold-hearted murderer!"

He ran a finger reflectively down the long, diagonal scar on his face.

"He would have killed me if he'd had the chance. That makes him no different."

Bree stared into his eyes, windows to a poisonous soul.

"He was a million times more of a man than you will *ever* be," she said quietly.

She could see the rage seething underneath his calm exterior, coiling the tendons in his neck and curling his hands into fists.

"You're just like him," he said. "Stubborn and stupid."

Bree forced a cold smile.

"He can't have been *that* stupid. I mean you still don't have The Book do you?"

"Shut up! He's dead and I'm not."

With a sudden flash of defiance Bree spat in his face. His angry fingers yanked her towards him, forcing her to meet his eyes.

"Get off her!" screamed Honey. "If you hurt her…I'll…I'll…!"

Theramonde stormed towards her, his cloak billowing out behind him.

"You'll *what?* I suggest you *shut up.*"

Honey wrapped her arms tightly around herself and glared at him.

When he turned back to face Bree she had already pulled the dagger from her boot, and was holding it out in front of her with trembling hands. His black eyes fastened on the blade and the sight of it seemed to rob him of some confidence.

"Where...where did you get that?"

"I told you," said Bree. "I saw what you did."

He stared at her blankly.

"I was *there*... *when you murdered my Dad...*"

Slowly his expression changed from shock to satisfaction. A cruel smile lifted the corner of his mouth and he burst out laughing.

"As if you weren't already a bit crazy!"

"Shut up," said Bree.

"I can't imagine what it must have felt like to watch your own father die," he said with evident relish.

"*Shut up,*" she said, her hand curling into a fist so tight that her fingernails dug into her palms.

"And to die like he did," he continued, "on a cold floor, in such pain and with no-one around that he loved."

Bree fought back her tears.

"*I* was there!"

"*He* didn't know that, did he? Richard McCready died alone and in pain and you got to see every wonderful moment. I couldn't have wished for more!"

Her grip on the dagger slackened and it slipped from her hand, clattering onto the stone.

"You think you know everything, don't you?" said Theramonde. "But you don't know that I visited your mother to offer my condolences and to give her a shoulder to cry on, or that I supported your sweet Grandmother while she grieved for her son at his graveside."

Fury rose within Bree and she threw herself at him, lashing out. Her nails raked his face and he recoiled, mouth gaping. One hand gingerly probed his cheek where bright beads of blood were threading together. He lowered his hand and stared at the red smears. For a long second their eyes held, then a small smile lifted the corners of his mouth.

"You wish to give me a scar? A scar that matches the one your father gave me." His eyes dropped to the dagger on the floor. "Why don't you use the same dagger he used? Come on then!"

His knuckles turned white around the hilt of his sword, and he pulled it from the scabbard, brandishing it in a swooping arc. Bree scrambled backwards, reeling from the thrum of severed air.

"I know you wouldn't dare use that on me," she said. "I am a borrower and my blood would destroy you. Theramonde stalked towards her.

"Maybe it would be worth it to see you die...or maybe I could use it on someone who *doesn't* have the blood of a borrower," he said, looking at Honey.

Bree grabbed out, catching only his cloak. She pulled as hard as she could and it was enough to whip him round and throw him off balance. His hand flailed back, catching her full in the face. Pain shot stars behind her eyes.

She could taste blood in her mouth and felt it dribbling down her chin. Theramonde looked panicked and stumbled backwards.

"This?" said Bree, touching the sticky worm of blood. "Is *this* what you're afraid of?"

The sword slipped from his hand and hit the floor with a hollow clang.

"Stay away from me," he croaked, backing away from her.

The floor quaked and the beams in the ceiling creaked.

"I'll stay away from you, if you say sorry for what you did to my father," she said, her eyes darting at the fine cracks which were appearing in the walls.

She crept towards him, holding up her blood-smeared fingertips. He whimpered like a frightened dog and backed into the corner. The crockery on the table rattled.

"Say sorry," she said, as rubble fell around her.

Theramonde slid down the wall and cowered from her.

"I...I..."

"Go on," she said, standing over him. "*Spit it out.*"

He looked up at her and his black eyes flashed angrily.

"No."

"No?" echoed Bree, crouching down so she was face to face with him.

"NO!" he screamed, shaking with murderous hatred. "I'll *never* say it!"

Bree slapped his face, leaving a crimson smear of blood next to his scar. He gave a strangled yelp and fell onto his side, sobbing.

"Let's get out of here!" said Sandy, grabbing her arm.

Bree pulled away from him angrily.

"No! I'm staying to watch him die."

The room shook and the rafters groaned. All of a sudden Theramonde began to writhe, gasping for air. His body jerked and started folding in on itself, his head caving in like burning plastic. Honey buried her face in Sandy's chest, but Bree watched the man who had killed her father shrivel up until there was nothing left of him but his cloak.

They ran into the corridor, turning back in time to see a great mass of rubble crash down from the chamber roof. They fled back down the stairs. The castle shook, and cracks opened across the floor and up the walls.

"Hurry!" cried Sandy.

Bree opened the door and jumped back when a stone pillar fell in front of her. One by one they squeezed under it, ran across the courtyard and over the bridge, only stopping when they reached the trees that fringed the cliff. Sheltering from the rain, they watched as the roof of Castle Zarcalat collapsed, sending up a giant cloud of dust. The castle walls had taken on the red glow of a furnace. Fire clawed through the windows and smoke rose like columns of steam. The air was filled with crashes and explosions.

Sandy tried to catch his breath.

"There'll be nothing left of it after tonight."

"Good," said Bree, wiping the blood from her chin, "with any luck everyone inside will die."

"Do you think the moon is in total eclipse yet?" Honey asked anxiously.

"I guess we'll only find out when we get back to Rockwell," said Sandy. "We still have Thalofedril to deal with."

"But how are we going to get back?" asked Bree.

Suddenly, she felt a faint vibration in her pocket. At first she thought it was her phone ringing again, and then she realised it was The Book. The little window on the front cover filled with a swirl of mist and some words appeared.

> A bonus wish, oh! what a treat,
> A chance to choose one to repeat.
> Whichever one, pick carefully,
> Two, three or five, which will it be?

"I want wish five!" said Bree.

Honey and Sandy exchanged glances.

"But Bree – "

"It was the fifth wish that brought Thalofedril back to life, so surely it would bring my Dad back too. *Please!*"

Honey gripped her shoulders.

"We need to get home. You *have* to choose wish three."

Bree watched the locket's pulse grow weak. Her heart felt as if it were crumbling like the walls of Castle Zarcalat.

"Okay," she croaked.

Honey gave her shoulders a squeeze.

Under Bree's fingers the pulse reawakened as some words appeared.

> Danger nears! You must take flight,
> But first some help you should invite.
> Normal rules do not apply
> To these great beauties of the sky.

All of a sudden the rain stopped and a warm breeze blew.

The air around them burst in an explosion of light as the two giant butterflies crested the verge of the cliff, their wings brilliantly fluorescing in the dark.

They chose to ride on the same butterflies as before, and Bree took one last look at the remains of Castle Zarcalat, as the cliff top fell away and they soared into the night sky.

After a while, Bree spotted a tiny white sliver of moon hanging over the distant city of Rockwell.

"We only went and saved the world!" Honey whooped.

Bree laughed, but she would save her relief for when the lunar eclipse was completely over and Thalofedril was dead.

Far below, the lights of the funfair twinkled. Fireworks were going off all over the city. Rockwell Tower Block was approaching fast, the lights around the rooftop garden lighting the way like a landing strip. Bree turned around, expecting to see the fluorescent colours of Honey and Sandy's butterfly. She searched the darkness but they were gone.

CHAPTER 28
AN UNWELCOME GUEST

The butterfly's wings fluttered lightly as they circled Guinessberry Heights. Bree pulled gently on the reins to guide it in the right direction and they dipped towards Rockwell Tower. When the butterfly hovered gracefully above the rooftop garden Bree slid down from its back.

It rose up and disappeared into the night sky, leaving a tiny trail of blue light in its wake. Deep inside Bree's pocket the heart locket stopped beating.

She scrambled down the metal ladder that led to the balcony outside her bathroom window, pushed the window up and climbed inside. It was eerily quiet in the flat and every room was in darkness. She flicked on the living room light and saw a note on the coffee table.

Gone to Freesia House. Don't take too long! Mum X P.S I've got Honey's satchel.

She pulled out her mobile phone and dialled Sandy's number. It went straight to voicemail. She rang Honey and almost collapsed with relief when she answered.

"Thank goodness you're alright!" gasped Bree.

"You too," whispered Honey, "we couldn't see where you'd gone!"

"I'm at my flat now," said Bree, making her way into the

hallway. "Where are you?"

"At home," Honey said quietly. "I can't talk, everyone is here."

"Is Sandy with you?"

"He's making his way to your flat now to find you."

"Good," said Bree, "I'll catch him on the way to yours."

"See you soon," said Honey, hanging up before Bree could reply.

As Bree passed her bedroom, an icy draught crept around the door. She nudged it open and light oozed in from the hallway, sending a narrow line along the carpet. The window was wide open, making the curtains billow. She surveyed the scene of devastation as if from a distance; a chair lay on its side, pieces of broken ornaments lay scattered, and the carpet was pulled up in the corner, exposing bare floorboards. The bookshelf had been tipped over, its contents strewn everywhere. Her heart began to race. This was not an ordinary break-in; somebody had come here looking for something.

The hairs on Bree's arms were standing on end and she had the eeriest feeling she was not alone. She crept out of the bedroom, her senses on heightened alert. When she reached the bathroom, she heard a rustling noise coming from inside. She gave the door a tentative push and looked in. To her relief there was nothing there. Then the shower curtain twitched. Someone – *something* – was behind it.

She ran down the hallway, banging off the walls in her panic to escape. She burst out onto the landing and flew down the stairs two at a time, stopping on the next floor to hammer on Annie's front door.

"Let me in! Mrs Hooten! LET ME IN!"

There was no answer. As she fumbled with the magic key

a shadow spilled onto the stairs and spread down them like a dark stain.

Thud…slide, Thud…slide.

Bree pushed the key into the lock and Annie's door shot open. She dived inside, slamming it shut behind her. The flat was in total darkness. Through her terror she realised that Annie would be at the party too. She tore along the hallway and into the living room, searching frantically for somewhere to hide. When she heard the front door opening, something gave way inside her, a fear so great she thought she might die there and then.

Thud…slide, Thud…slide.

Slowly she backed into the kitchen, flinching when she brushed against the curtain of beads in the doorway. She hid behind them and waited.

Thud…slide, Thud…slide.

Sweat prickled her skin as the temperature in the tiny kitchen soared. Behind her flimsy defense she watched as Thalofedril's shadow spilled across the living room carpet. He stopped beside the sideboard and sniffed the air with the two gaping holes at the centre of his face. He turned her way and she threw a hand up to stifle her scream.

"Give it to me," he said, the words hissing through his fanged teeth.

She held her breath and closed her eyes.

"GIVE IT TO ME!" he bellowed.

Filled with hopeless desperation, Bree pushed the beads aside. The smell of him hit her, and she fought the urge to be sick.

"I want what is mine," he hissed.

She pulled The Book from her pocket, forcing herself not to

look into his eyes.

"Here, take it. It's over anyway. Your castle is gone. Everyone inside is dead. In a short while the veil will close again for another two hundred years."

She could feel the prick of his crimson stare on her skin.

"You have not won yet. I am still alive."

"We defeated you once before. We can do it again."

"Not without The Book," he said. "Now GIVE IT TO ME!"

She took a reluctant step forwards and held it out to him, her heart clenching when she considered how far she, Sandy and Honey had come, and how unfair it was for it to suddenly end like this. Thalofedril rasped greedily and reached out for The Book. His talons were almost touching the leather, when the cuckoo clock sounded, its cheerful tune cracking the silence. He spun around, knocking everything off the sideboard. Seizing her chance, Bree ducked out of the door, narrowly missing a cuff from his leathery wing. She stumbled down the hallway, threw herself at the lift and jabbed frantically at the button. To her relief she heard it whirr into action.

"Hurry up!" Her eyes darted back at Annie's front door, which still swung from the force of her exit.

The lift doors rumbled open and she jumped inside. She pressed the down arrow, but nothing happened.

"NO! Don't break down now!"

Annie's front door creaked open, and she jabbed the button again and again.

Thud, slide... Thud, slide...

"WORK, YOU STUPID THING!" She kicked the inside of the lift as hard as she could.

The doors juddered closed at a snail's pace. She cowered in the corner as Thalofedril slithered towards the narrowing gap.

His hand reached through the opening, searching blindly for her, but the doors closed and he pulled his hand back. The lift lurched into action and Bree shoved The Book into her pocket.

"C'mon, c'mon, c'mon…" she muttered as she watched the slow digital countdown.

Suddenly the lift jarred violently, shuddering to a stop halfway between the third and fourth floors. The lights flickered and Bree pressed her ear to the doors and listened. There was silence on the other side. Her finger hovered over the alarm button, when there was an almighty thump on the roof. She backed into the corner and stared up at the hatch, which now had a huge dent in it. Sliding to the floor she pulled her knees up to her chest. The heat was building, and sweat was starting to pool on her skin. The next thump jerked the carriage so hard it tilted awkwardly to one side. The lights went out altogether, plunging her into darkness.

THUMP!

Cables snapped and whipped like thrashing tentacles and, with a lurch and a screech, the carriage dropped. There was a brief moment of weightlessness before it slammed to a stop, throwing Bree sideways. She banged her head and pinpricks of light danced before her. The alarm was ringing, but it sounded distant and feeble. She scrambled to her feet and threw herself at the doors, prising them apart. There was a solid wall at waist level and she could see she was stuck between the first and ground floor. Summoning strength from somewhere, she hauled herself out onto the landing. Without looking back she scrambled down the last flight of stairs and burst out into the night air.

She ran and ran, only stopping to catch her breath outside Rockwell High School. She suddenly realised she had to warn

Sandy to stay away from her flat. Just as she pulled out her phone, The Evil One swooped overhead. She dashed into the school car park, throwing herself down behind a row of parked cars. The thrum of heavy wings beat the air. She closed her eyes and made herself as small as she could. The beating stopped suddenly and a terrible stench assaulted her nostrils.

Thud...slide, Thud...slide...

Thalofedril landed close by, and the car door turned hot. All of a sudden he took to the sky again, circling the school and disappearing from view.

Slowly, she stood up and was about to make a dash back to the main road when she saw something that stopped her in her tracks. He was there, in the deep shadows of the basketball court, a crouching form full of menace and savage power. He detached himself from the darkness and moved towards her. A silver Z caught the fading moonlight with a scintillating flash.

Bree ducked down and crept along the row of cars, avoiding the pools of light cast by the overhead lamps. She came to a gap and peered through it. Thalofedril had his back to her, but she could see enough of him in the lamplight to make her blood run cold. She pulled back, setting off a car alarm as she did. The noise shattered the silence, and she was sure that at any moment she would feel the grasp of his talons around her ankle. She reached the last car in the row, but the main entrance to the school was still a few metres away. It would be too risky to make a run for it, so she huddled down behind a rusty old-fashioned Mini and tried to control her breathing.

Thud...slide, Thud...slide...

She heard a snort, and then a shadow spilled out around her, a shade darker than the concrete. She pulled on the car door handle, and to her relief it opened. Wasting no time she threw herself into the passenger footwell, closed the door as quietly as she could, and curled up amongst the CD boxes and discarded apple cores. Suddenly, she realised she had not locked the doors, and slowly unfurled, stretching her hand out to the little black button under the window. Just as her finger touched it, two red eyes appeared behind the glass. She slammed it down and there was a clunk as the locking mechanism kicked in. Bree threw herself at the driver's door, pushing the lock down before he could slither round to the other side.

As she crawled back into the footwell, humming to block out the terrible sounds outside, she felt the car being lifted. It tilted and Bree was thrown into the back seat, bumping her head hard on the seatbelt buckle. When she peered out of the rear window she saw Thalofedril underneath the car, lifting it high above his head. She quickly scrambled over the seats and climbed into the driver's seat, fastening the seatbelt around her. No sooner had the buckle clipped into place than the world flew past in a blur, as the car sailed through the air before crashing into the ground. Glass shattered in an explosion of sound. The Mini had landed on its back and Bree was hanging upside down. Flames licked up the rear of the car. She turned her head and looked through the shattered windscreen, catching sight of a dark outline slithering towards her. She fumbled with the seat belt, all the time expecting the petrol tank to explode.

Thud...slide, Thud...slide...

It seemed to take forever to unbuckle her belt. Dodging the crystals of glass, she crawled towards the passenger side and pushed hard on the handle, but the door was too buckled to open. Left with no other choice, she pulled the cuff of her jacket over her hand, and pushed out the remnants of glass that hung stubbornly in the window frame. She squeezed through the hole, shielding her face from the flames. As she scrambled to her feet, she glanced up to see Thalofedril unfurl his enormous wings and take to the sky. She staggered up the front steps, fumbling for the magic key at the same time. Just as she pulled it from her pocket she was knocked to the ground by an enormous explosion. The Mini had burst into flames.

Her fingers were cold and shaking, but somehow she managed to slot the key into the door. She threw herself inside, mustering enough energy to kick the door closed. It slammed loudly and then a dark mass hit the glass. With no time to gather her thoughts she scrambled to her feet and ran along the corridor, only stopping when she was past the school office, the library, and through two sets of double doors. She collapsed behind the vending machine outside the dinner hall.

She was relieved to see that her only injury was a small cut to her lip and a painful lump in her hairline. Pulling out her mobile phone, she scrolled down to Honey's name. There was a distant slam and Bree knew Thalofedril had entered the building. The phone call would have to wait.

She made a dash to her right and followed the sign marked *Swimming Pool,* staggering through the cloakroom and out into the pool area. She stopped for a moment, struggling to catch her breath in the moist, chlorinated air. The underwater lights had been left on and the pool was lit.

A sudden drumming noise startled her and she looked up to see rain bouncing off the domed glass ceiling. She gasped when a dark shape landed on top of it. The glass misted over as steam rose from the water, and suddenly it fractured, leaving an ugly web of spidery white lines. Bree dived into the shower area just as the ceiling exploded inwards, shielding her face as great shards hit the water like bullets. Wasting no time, she ducked into the locker room and searched around for somewhere to hide. She saw that one of the lockers on the bottom row was open a fraction. Folding her body up as tightly as she could she squeezed in, and pulled the door over so there was nothing but the thinnest sliver of light entering.

Thud...slide, Thud...slide...

She peered through the crack and saw the blurry reflection of Thalofedril in the locker door opposite. He stopped and smelled the air. She was sure he would hear her pounding heart, but he turned and slithered out the way he had come in. Bree waited until she was sure he was gone before climbing out of the locker. Cautiously, she made her way back down the corridor towards the dinner hall. The gym lights had been left on and a wedge of yellow light spilled across the floor. For a moment she thought it was the vending machine that was casting a shadow onto the wall but then she caught a glimpse of Thalofedril's red eyes slicing through the darkness. She darted into the gym hall, the soles of her boots squeaking loudly on the shiny floor. When she saw her terrified reflection in the mirrored wall she remembered something and an idea came to her in a flash.

She ran over – every step she took amplified by the high ceiling – and climbed onto a chair, feeling for the button that she knew would make the heavy curtain close across the length of the mirrored wall. She found it! When she pressed it the curtain drew closed with a mechanical hum, concealing the mirror. She quickly climbed down and looked for a place to hide. The hall was empty, except for a wooden vaulting horse and a wonky pile of mats. She ran over, yanked the fire extinguisher off the wall and ran back to the wooden horse.

Palms greasy with fear she pushed the heavy top part aside, threw the extinguisher into the hollow box, and climbed in. Crouching down, she pulled the lid back over until it slotted into place.

Bree watched through the handhold as the gym door opened and Thalodefril entered. She could feel the heat of his rage as his red eyes swept the room like searchlights. His talons clicked on the wooden floor as he crept forwards. He stopped right next to the wooden horse, so close that Bree could see the reflection of the hall in his shiny claws. The heat started building up inside the box, and blood pounded in her temples as she waited for him to rip the lid off and haul her out by her hair. She grabbed hold of the fire extinguisher and braced herself.

Light flooded in when he tore the lid away. Bree sprung out like a Jack in the Box and blasted him in the face with the foam from the extinguisher. He staggered blindly, choking and gasping. She scrambled out and ran over to the curtain. As she clambered up onto the chair, Thalofedril spread out his wings and launched into the air, circling the high ceiling before perching on one of the beams. Her trembling fingers searched for the button but she did not press it. Timing was everything. She pulled The Book from her pocket and waved it in the air.

"Come and get it!"

Thalofedril turned slowly, his eyes fixed on The Book. Bree's finger hovered over the button. He flexed his wings and let out a heart-stopping roar, leaving the beam in one swift motion and swooping down towards her. She pushed the button, and with a whirr the curtain drew aside. Realising he had been tricked Thalofedril turned his head away from the mirror. But it was too late; he had already glimpsed the reflection of his crimson eyes. Still clutching The Book, Bree threw herself off the chair and rolled behind the pile of mats, bracing herself for an almighty crash. But there was no noise, no moment of impact.

After a few seconds she peered out and what she saw took her breath away. Thalofedril was trapped behind the mirror. He was roaring and hammering on the glass, but the gym hall was completely silent. Slowly, she emerged from her hiding place with a newfound courage, and tiptoed towards him. Halfway across the floor she raised her eyes and they met his for the first time. Discovering that his stare was now powerless, Thalofedril's expression changed from one of fury to confusion. Bree stopped directly in front of him.

"You can't hurt me now," she said.

Calmly, she held up The Book, pressing the cover to the mirror. He reached out for it, his talons meeting only glass.

Bree reached for the chair and pulled it towards her, the scrape of the legs on the floor momentarily shattering the silence. She stared him directly in the eyes as she lifted it off the ground. He searched around for some way to get out, but he knew he was trapped. He started gesturing wildly for her to stop; she could not hear what he was saying but she knew he would be pleading for his life. The thought made rage bubble up inside her.

"This is for my father," she said, "and for Sandy's mum and dad and Agora. This is for everyone you have ever hurt!"

She swung the chair over her head and brought it crashing down onto the mirror. There was a sound like breaking ice and then, in a burst of light and noise, the entire mirror shattered.

For a few moments the air seemed to vibrate. Bree looked up at the space where the mirror had been and saw bare brick wall. The curtain was ripped and hanging off one end of the bent rail. There was glass everywhere – great lethal shards of the stuff. But not a single piece had touched her. She reached out and picked up a large splinter, tilting it to the light. She saw one side of her tear-stained face, half obscured by her bedraggled hair. Suddenly a huge crimson eye appeared, the narrow iris darting from side to side. She scrambled to her feet and threw the shard down, stamping on it and grinding it with the heel of her boot until it looked like sugar crystals. Then she ran without looking back.

She hit the fresh air with a stitch in her side. The upturned Mini was now a burned-out shell; the flames had died but the metal carcass still cracked and glowed. She could hear the sound of approaching sirens and knew she had to get out of there before someone saw her. Running in the direction of Gillespie Gardens, she hoped that Sandy had made his way back to Freesia House. She slowed down when she spotted some children heading her way, dressed in ghoulish costumes, shouting "Trick or Treat!" Stepping off the pavement to let them pass, she spotted three small figures whizz by on the other side of the road. At first she thought it was another group of children, wearing gruesome Halloween masks, but when she looked closer she caught a glimpse of bare, red skin and yellow eyes. *Gargoyles.* As she pulled back into the shadows she realised they were not looking for *her*. They were fleeing from something. When they reached the postbox at the foot of the road there was a sudden flash and they disappeared in a puff of smoke.

She glanced up and saw that the moon was now in full eclipse – a bold, red disc with a halo of silvery light. It looked exactly as it had when she had glimpsed the future. She scanned the road in both directions but saw no police cars, no helicopters, and no hordes of panicked people. Just some excited children and a cat cleaning itself on top of a wall.

She followed the pavement that wound down to Freesia Lane. She stopped and pulled her phone from her pocket, scrolling down to Sandy's name and pressing the call button. From somewhere nearby came Sandy's ringtone. It stopped abruptly after two rings. She switched her phone off and looked around but there was no sign of him. Feeling a heavy drop of something land on her head, she touched her scalp and her hand came away red. She looked up, her breath catching in her throat. Blood dripped in slow, heavy drops, splashing onto the pavement at her feet. When she spotted Sandy's trainer poking through the branches she staggered backwards, her stomach churning. Suddenly the branches moved and he dropped down, landing with a heavy thump beside her.

"*Sandy!*"

He brushed a leaf from his shoulder and straightened his glasses.

"It was those pesky gargoyles again. They chased me all the way from Honey's house."

"I saw them," said Bree. "They ran past me like they were trying to get away from something."

Sandy held up his hand and Bree saw that his fingers were stained red.

"That would be the blood," he said, with a devilish grin.

She threw her hands up to her mouth.

"We need to get you to hospital!"

"No need," said Sandy. "It's just one of my blood capsules. But *they* didn't know that, did they?"

Bree heaved a sigh of relief.

"Where have you been anyway?" he asked, thrusting his hands deep into his pockets. "You've been gone for ages."

"I kind of got caught up with some stuff."

"What stuff?" he asked, suspiciously.

She took a deep breath.

"Well put it this way, Thalofedril won't be bothering us again," she said.

"What?! Did you see him?"

Bree threaded her arm through his.

"I'll tell you all about it on the way to Honey's."

In the sky a sliver of white appeared at the edge of the moon as the shadow began to slide off.

"The lunar eclipse is over, Sandy. We did it."

"How do you know for sure? Does Rockwell look different to how it did when you saw the future?"

They stopped outside a house where a group of excited children were on the front lawn waving sparklers. A rosy-cheeked mother leaned over the fence and offered Bree and Sandy some sweets from a plastic cauldron. Sandy took a handful and stuffed them into his pocket.

"Yes," she said, a smile lifting the corner of her mouth. "It looks *very* different."

CHAPTER 29
A TASTE OF HER OWN MEDICINE

Freesia House was a haven of warmth and light. When Bree and Sandy walked down the hallway they were met by the delicious smell of a sizzling stir-fry. Honey was sitting near the kitchen door, spooning some kind of fruity mush into baby Neil's mouth. She had changed back into her cat costume, minus the tail and ears. When she saw them standing in the doorway she flashed them a thousand-watt smile.

Madeleine and Harry – wearing matching outfits – were dancing in the conservatory, next to a large speaker which was belting out *Under the Moon of Love*.

Honey's Dad was dressed as a strongman, and was shaking vegetables in a large wok over a fierce gas flame. His tight, black curls had been gelled back from his face and he was wearing a fake, handlebar moustache. He flicked his wrist and all the vegetables took a dangerous slide, somehow ending up back in the wok.

The dining table had been set for ten people and was beautifully decorated with an assortment of goodies, including Madeleine's spicy apple squares and a cauldron filled with fruit punch.

In the far corner of the dining area, nestled amongst a forest of green plants and scented candles, Saffron stood, dressed in Roaring Twenties attire – complete with a fringed flapper dress, feather boa and headband. She was chatting to Annie who was wedged into an armchair like an overstuffed cushion. Annie's face was painted green and she was wearing a tall, pointed hat and black and green stripy tights. She propped a hand under her tightly pinned hair, which was tied at her neck like a ball of orange wool.

"Well, well, the wanderers return," she said.

Madeleine staggered through from the conservatory, cheeks aglow from her energetic dancing.

"Hi sweetheart," she said, a little out of breath. "*Please* tell me you didn't miss the eclipse!"

"No, Mum, we saw it, it was awesome." smiled Bree. "Where's Granny Lissa?"

"She's upstairs with Mimi. They're putting some finishing touches to their costumes."

Madeleine cast a disapproving eye over Bree's jeans and jacket.

"Did you not have time to change, sweetie?"

"Sorry. I forgot."

In a whirl of freckles and strawberry blonde hair, Mimi burst into the kitchen. She stopped in the middle of the room and twirled around to show off her outfit – a flowery mini dress, long white boots and a wide-brimmed hat with a huge plastic daisy stuck on the front. She had painted glittery flowers onto her cheek and was wearing little round glasses.

"Cool outfit, Meems," said Honey, wiping Neil's mouth with his bib. "What are you dressed as?"

Mimi rolled her eyes, which were framed by enormous false lashes.

"I'm a hippie, can't you tell?"

She lowered her glasses and frowned at Sandy and Bree.

"Where are your costumes?"

Bree smiled apologetically.

"Sorry Meems, we just got caught up with other things."

Just then a tall, slender woman walked into the kitchen wearing a flowing dress of white silk, which was pinched in at the waist by a gold sash studded with turquoise stones. Open-toed sandals snaked up her legs and bracelets decorated her arms. Her hair had been neatly tucked under a long, black wig with a thick fringe, and her green eyes were beautifully highlighted with thickly applied kohl.

"Granny Lissa, you look amazing! I didn't recognise you for a moment!"

"I'll take that as a compliment," she said, batting her lashes. "How are you, darling? Your mum said you were coming dressed as a pirate. What happened?"

"I feel terrible now," said Bree. "Everyone has made such an effort."

Saffron glided across the floor, stopping to wrap Bree in a perfumed embrace.

"Let's not worry about it," she said with a smile. "You can borrow something of Honey's if you want."

"How about a dress?" Madeleine said hopefully. "I'd *love* to see you in a dress."

Bree squirmed.

"I guess I'm not really a dress kind of girl," she said awkwardly.

"What if there was a special occasion," asked Madeleine, nervously. "Say...a wedding?"

Harry wrapped his arm around her shoulder, and she stared up at him affectionately.

"Mum, are you...? Did you...?!"

Madeleine held up her hand and wiggled her ring finger. A

large diamond, in the shape of an ice cube, twinkled prettily. Bree ran over, grabbed her mum's hand and squinted at it admiringly.

"Are you happy, sweetheart? *Please* say you're happy."

"Happy? I'm ecstatic! Oh Mum...Harry, congratulations."

"Yeah, congratulations Mrs M," said Sandy, taking a bite of spicy apple square.

Harry lifted his cowboy hat and flashed him a toothy smile. Over in the corner, Annie clapped her hands delightedly, but stayed firmly wedged in her armchair while everyone else fussed over Madeleine like bees around a honey pot.

"Can I be bridesmaid?" asked Mimi, wearing a grin that stretched from ear to ear.

Madeleine smiled, looking youthful and pretty.

"How about chief flower girl?" she said.

Mimi's eyes lit up.

"Do I get to choose my own dress?"

"Of course," laughed Madeleine. "Anything you like. It'll be a spring wedding," she beamed.

Harry turned to Annie who was nodding off in the chair.

"Annie...?"

She bolted awake.

"We would love it if you drove Madeleine to the registry office in your motorbike and sidecar."

"I would be honoured," she smiled proudly.

"And Lissa, I would like you to give me away," added Madeleine.

Granny Lissa looked overwhelmed.

"I...I...don't know what to say."

"Say yes," said Madeleine.

Granny Lissa nodded happily.

"Grub's up!" announced Mort. Saffron lit the candles and made a couple of last-minute adjustments to the table decorations.

"Annie and Lissa are our guests of honour, so they get the top seats," she said as everyone piled towards the table.

Annie eased herself out of the armchair with some huffs and puffs and waddled over, pulling off her hat and plonking it down on the worktop.

"Hats off for dinner," she said, eyeing Mimi's hat.

"Aw, that's not fair," scowled Mimi. "This is part of my costume."

"It's good manners," said Saffron, giving her a firm look.

Everybody sat down, and Sandy and Mort ladled some punch into glasses.

When dinner was over, Annie stretched with a sleepy smile.

"I haven't eaten this much in ages," she said, happily stroking the slight swell of her stomach. "I'm going to have to go home and sleep it off, but before I do, I'd like to make a toast," she said, picking up her glass. "To loved ones lost but never forgotten."

Everybody raised their glasses high and there was a moment of silence.

"Lissa, do you remember your hippie uncle?" asked Madeleine. "When we were kids we used to think he was the coolest person on the planet."

Granny Lissa dabbed the corners of her mouth with a napkin.

"I remember him well. He owned a fascinating little shop in Puddock Square. What was it called now...Heart of the Matter... Heart on your Sleeve...Where the Heart is..."

Bree felt the colour drain from her face.

"Hart and Soul?" she said, softly.

Granny Lissa's hand leapt to her chest.

"That was it! It had a bit of everything but mainly it was a pile of old junk."

"What was your uncle's name?" Bree heard herself ask.

"William Hart," answered Granny Lissa. "Hence the name of the shop. He was as mad as a box of frogs but such a dear old soul. He died back in 1985. Halloween in fact."

"What happened to him?" asked Sandy, who appeared to be shivering from the chilliness of Granny Lissa's revelation.

Her eyes misted over.

"Well, poor Richard arrived at his shop at the same time as the fire engines, just in time to see William being stretchered out. But it wasn't the fire that killed him. It was most likely a heart attack from the shock of the break-in."

"Break-in?" Honey probed.

Granny Lissa nodded.

"It had been completely torn apart. Goodness knows what they wanted to steal. The police told us the fire must have broken out in a passageway behind the shop. It must have been his silly old pipe, he was never without it."

Bree exchanged a furtive glance with Sandy.

"That's so sad," she said numbly.

"It must have been a horrible thing for your dad to witness," said Granny Lissa. "He was never quite the same afterwards. He was ever so fond of Uncle William."

"I remember," said Madeleine. "Richard didn't like to talk about it."

"Uncle William was the only person who ever called me Mel," said Granny Lissa. "He said it sounded much nicer to use the first half of my name rather than the last."

"Did they ever find the burglars?" asked Honey, giving Bree

a sideways glance.

Granny Lissa shook her head sadly.

"The strange thing was they never touched the till. Not that they would have found much in it. It was as if they were looking for something in particular, but the only thing that was missing from the shop was his old fob watch. It was a family heirloom but I shouldn't think it was worth much. Sad to think that was all William's life was worth in the end."

"Are you sure that was the only thing missing?" Honey probed.

Granny Lissa nodded then her brow furrowed like she had suddenly remembered something.

"His pet rat was gone but it must have run away when the fire broke out."

Annie sighed tiredly.

"I'll take you home, Annie," said Madeleine. "Kids, I can give you a lift to the funfair on the way."

Bree's stomach lurched when she suddenly remembered something.

"Er Mum, there's something you should know. I think we had a break-in."

Madeleine threw her hands up to her mouth.

"Oh my goodness! Are you sure? How? When?"

"Don't worry, Mum. I had a quick peek and it doesn't look like they took anything. It's only my room that's in a bit of a state."

"You should have come straight here, Bree! What if there was a mad axe-murderer lurking around? And why has it taken so long for you to tell me?"

"I forgot. Sorry," Bree said truthfully.

"How could you forget something like that? Harry, phone

the police and I'll get round there now."

"I'll come with you," he said, pulling his phone out of his pocket. "You don't know if it's safe."

Bree remembered something else.

"Please, nobody panic..." she said, "...but it looks like the burglars got into Annie's house too."

Madeleine slumped back down into her chair.

"Oh Annie, this is terrible," she said.

"Don't worry about it, Chickpea," said Annie, patting her hand. "Nobody was hurt, that's the main thing. I've no idea what the burglars must have thought when they saw the mess in my hallway. They probably thought someone else had beaten them to it!"

She stood up and made her way to the door, her napkin tucked into the waistband of her skirt like an orange sporran.

"Goodness, Bree," Madeleine sighed in exasperation. "You're fourteen years old. You need to start showing some responsibility."

"I know, Mum. I'm *really* sorry."

Harry came back into the kitchen.

"Apparently the police are already there. Something to do with the lift collapsing."

Madeleine gasped in horror.

"Was there anybody inside it at the time?"

"It doesn't look like it," he said. "But we'll find out more when we get there."

He disappeared back into the hall, and Bree started stacking the dirty plates in an attempt to redeem herself.

"On the bright side," she said with a tentative smile, "perhaps we'll get a brand new lift."

"Yeah, one that actually works," Sandy added.

Granny Lissa wafted her face with a napkin.

"I think I'll go and get a quick breath of fresh air."

"I'll come out with you, Granny," said Bree, reaching for her jacket.

It was cold in the garden, but the warmth from the kitchen flooded out from the French doors.

"The stars are wonderful tonight," said Granny Lissa, looking up at the sky.

"It's a perfect evening," Bree smiled. "I'm just sorry it's been spoiled by the break- in."

Granny Lissa shivered and gave her arms a brisk rub.

"I'm sure your mother didn't mean to snap at you. She was just worried, that's all."

"Are you sure you don't mind the whole wedding thing?"

Granny Lissa's face broke into a wide smile.

"Darling, of course not!"

She took Bree's hand. Her skin felt warm despite the chill in the air.

"You know, my father died when I was a baby," she said. "My mother was only nineteen when she became a widow. She never remarried and died a lonely old woman. I would never want that for Madeleine."

"Harry is really nice," Bree said.

"I know," smiled Granny Lissa. "He reminds me of your father in lots of ways."

"Really?"

"Yes. He's kind and funny. And *very* handsome."

Madeleine popped her head round the door.

"We're ready to take Annie home," she said, her breath puffing white in the cold air. "Bree, there's space in the car for two more if that's any help?"

"It's okay Mum, we'll just walk to the funfair."

Madeleine disappeared back inside the kitchen, and Bree zipped the collar of her jacket up to her nose, and hunched her shoulders against the cold.

"Have fun tonight," smiled Granny Lissa. "You're only fourteen once."

"Thank goodness," said Bree.

****

The streets of Rockwell were quieter now the children had gone home to eat their Halloween candy. Everything was etched in radiant silver light and frost sparkled like glitter on the pavement.

"There was a sketch of a boy in William's shop," said Bree. "I knew I recognised him from somewhere."

"Do you think it was your Dad?" asked Honey.

Bree nodded.

"I wish I had taken it now. It was probably destroyed in the fire."

Sandy stepped down off the kerb.

"It's weird thinking William Hart was your great, great uncle," he said.

"I know, and I'm related to Algernon Hart, too."

With this knowledge had come the confirmation of something Bree had always suspected. The Book was there in her future all along, waiting for her to find it. The very idea made the earth spin a little faster. She pulled it from her pocket and stared down at the lifeless locket, wondering about all the imprints that had been left behind – Algernon, William, Agora – all the borrowers who had come before them, and the ones who were still to come.

"I can't believe we actually went back in time," said Sandy. "I've *always* wanted to do that!"

"It explains why Douglas was nothing but dusty bones when we left the shop," said Bree.

"And it explains that girl's hideous outfit," added Honey.

"Remember when William asked us to stay in his shop so we could meet his great nephew?" said Sandy. "If we had stayed we would have met your Dad when he was the same age as us."

An icy shiver ran up Bree's spine.

"If we had stayed they would have killed us like they killed poor William."

Sandy hopped back up onto the kerb.

"Only we know the truth about what happened that day," he said.

"And that's the way it will always stay," said Bree.

As they passed the old memorial clock the sounds and smells of the funfair filled the air. Sandy licked his lips.

"Mmm. Somewhere nearby there is a hotdog with my name on it."

"How can you even *think* about food after what we've just eaten?" asked Honey.

"I'm a growing boy," he said, giving his stomach a pat.

"I'm so glad you decided to stay with us, Greenfield," giggled Honey.

"Me too," said Bree.

"How could I ever have left sunny old Rockwell?" he beamed happily. "Besides, *The Successful Others* is nothing without me."

He stopped in his tracks and stared up at the clock.

"What is it?" asked Bree.

"I totally forgot about the outdoor concert! I'm playing in less than half an hour."

"It'll be fine," said Honey. "You're a rock 'n roll star. Just act cool and nobody will know the most important night of your life slipped your mind."

Bree put her hands on her hips and frowned mockingly at him.

"Sandy Greenfield, you're fourteen years old. You need to start showing some responsibility!"

They followed the path down to Ramthorpe Junior, giggling all the way.

****

Bree held a cup close to her lips, little curls of steam veiling her face. She turned to Honey. "Remember on the frozen pond you promised me we would live to see another hot chocolate?" she said quietly.

Honey smiled. "When have I ever been wrong?"

As fireworks exploded above their heads, Mimi ran over, all bright-eyed, with cheeks like apples.

"Come with me on the carousel!" she begged, tugging on Honey's sleeve. "I want to ride the white horse again."

Honey straightened her satchel and smiled down at her.

"That white horse is no ordinary horse," she said, giving her eyebrows a mysterious wiggle.

"Why?"

Honey lowered her voice to a whisper.

"It's a magical horse with huge wings," she said, pausing for effect, "it comes to life when no-one is looking."

Mimi put her hands on her hips and rolled her eyes.

"Oh, pleeease, I'm twelve, not two."

"Look there's Mort," said Honey, spotting her Dad through the crowd. "Mort! Over here!"

He threaded his way towards them, he had changed out of his strongman costume but his hair was still slicked back from his forehead.

"Have you heard from my mum yet?" Bree asked anxiously.

"Yes. Harry phoned to say everything is fine. The police are with Annie now, and it would appear nothing has been taken from either house. They reckon the lift cables snapped due to wear and tear, but luckily nobody was inside . So you can stop worrying now and have some fun! Your mum asked me to keep an eye out for Mr Deanheart, he said he was coming along tonight."

They knew perfectly well that Mr Deanheart would not be coming. Not tonight, not ever.

"There's Adam," said Sandy, pointing to the far corner of the playground.

Bree felt a tingle of excitement when she saw him, chatting with the other band members while he tuned his guitar. He looked completely gorgeous in his jeans and black T-shirt.

"Bree! Dad!" whined Mimi. "Will you come with me to the carousel? Please, *please!*"

"Come on," laughed Mort, "just this once."

Bree waved back at Sandy and Honey as Mimi dragged her through the crowd.

Honey snuggled into Sandy's sleeve.

"Alone at last," she giggled.

"You said something," said Sandy. "You know…in the tunnel when the ceiling was coming down on us."

Honey peeled herself away from him, her eyebrows dipping.

"I don't remember." Then realisation dawned on her face.

"I probably didn't hear you right," said Sandy. "Forget I said anything."

She shifted self-consciously.

"You heard right," she said quietly, quickly adding, "but I thought you were going to die."

"It's okay. You don't have to explain anything."

"I do!"

Sandy held his hands up.

"Please. I don't want anything to change between us. I just want us to be friends."

She nodded.

"I know."

For a moment an awkward silence hung in the air between them.

"Anyway," said Honey, a smile tugging at the corner of her mouth, "I'll get over you in time."

She gave him a playful push.

"Plenty more fish in the sea, Greenfield!"

Adam appeared from nowhere, his guitar strung loosely over his shoulder.

"Sandy! There you are! You better go and tune up for the gig."

"Cool. Catch up with you later, Honey."

"Where's Bree?" asked Adam. "I wanted to see her before we go on stage."

"Here she comes now," said Honey.

"Hi," beamed Bree, her cheeks pink from the cold. "Are you ready for the big show?"

"I'm a bit nervous but I know you guys will be cheering us on," said Adam. "I better get back. Can we hang out later?"

"Sure," smiled Bree.

She turned back to watch Adam but he had already disappeared backstage. Suddenly, the crowd parted and Alice Renshaw emerged with Perpetua Andulus tottering behind her like an obedient puppy. Bree groaned inwardly when they stopped right beside them. Alice adjusted her cashmere beret and surveyed Honey with a head to toe sweep of her icy eyes.

"Look what the cat dragged in," she sneered.

"Look what the cat puked up," Honey shot back.

"Back off, ugly!" growled Perpetua.

"We don't want any trouble," Bree said. "We're here to have fun. Why don't you come and watch the band with us?"

"As if!"

"That's a shame – have it your way."

Alice's eyes burned. She pulled off her beret and threw it on the ground. Bree looked at her like she was mad.

"What did you do that for?" she asked.

Alice studied her fingernails, which were painted an electric, spangly blue.

"Pick it up," she sniffed, without looking up from her cuticle inspection.

"Go on, pick it up," repeated Alice, prodding it with the toe of her boot.

"No," said Bree.

Alice reeled back a little but quickly regained her composure.

"Pick- it- up," she said, her face stiff with fury.

Bree stayed alarmingly cool.

"NO," she said again, only this time more definite, more meaningful.

"I said – "

"I *know* what you said," interrupted Bree, "and there's no

point in repeating yourself because I'm not going to do it."

Alice turned a strange colour, as if there was an uncontrollable force blazing inside her.

"You'll do as I say!"

A wave of red-hot fury singed Bree's cheeks. All the years she had put up with this! All the snide remarks and dirty looks, all the malicious whispers, icy silences and fake smiles!

"I want you to leave me alone, Alice," she said calmly. "I don't want you whispering behind my back anymore. I don't want you spreading rumours about me, or sticking your foot out when I walk past. I don't want you pretending to be friendly when you want something from me."

The words were spilling out of her in a torrent. Perpetua's mouth opened and closed but no sounds came out.

"You are a nasty bully, Alice Renshaw," Bree continued, "but that's all you are, and you're not even very good at that without your cronies backing you up. I have friends, *real* friends, friends who would die for me. And I have real things to think about that go beyond worrying about a broken nail or split ends."

Bree waited for the dark cloud to cross Alice's face, for a lightning bolt to strike her, for the ground to swallow her whole. But apart from a little twitch in her left cheek Alice's expression remained blank.

"You've always been pretty good at ignoring me," concluded Bree, "so just do me the biggest favour and pretend I don't exist at all. Read my lips..."

She took a deep breath and spoke slowly, making each word count.

"Leave – me – alone!"

The crowd had fallen silent. Bree expected everyone to start laughing until their jawbones wiggled loose, to point and jeer at mousy Bree McCready, who had dared to stand up to Alice Renshaw. But instead something remarkable happened.

People started clapping. The claps got louder, this time accompanied by friendly cheers and whistles. Bree looked over to see Adam watching from the stage, smiling.

Alice started to twist a long strand of hair between her thumb and forefinger. For a moment Bree felt a warm glow of satisfaction, but as her rage simmered she began to wonder if she had done the right thing. To her astonishment, Alice gave her a short, cool nod and strutted off, shoulders hunched in furious humiliation. Bree wondered how it was possible to want to laugh and cry at the same time.

"Bree McCready, you ROCKED!" said Honey, hugging her tightly.

"Really?"

"Totally! But I think Ruthless Renshaw still needs a taste of her own medicine."

She flashed a quick, mischievous smile, and pulled something from her satchel. A large diamond glinted dangerously in the moonlight.

"You wouldn't dare! Please, don't *kill* her!"

"Of course I won't kill her! What I've got in mind is way more embarrassing."

She slid Valgus's ring over her knuckle, and almost immediately her expression darkened and two sinister words spilled from her mouth.

"Fundo Ventus."

Alice stopped in her tracks and an enormous burp left her lips. The crowd stopped and stared.

"BURP!"

People started laughing and pointing. Perpetua stared at

Alice, horrified by the belches coming from her mouth. But Alice could do nothing to stop them. Honey stopped her dark mutterings and slid the ring off her finger.

"There she blows!" she roared, as they watched Alice scurry away with her scarf stuffed in her mouth.

"Look! There's Sandy! They must be starting their set."

A discordant blast of electric guitar boomed from two giant speakers next to the stage. Bree and Honey started dancing as *The Successful Others* broke into their version of *Smells Like Teen Spirit*, much to the delight of the audience.

"I can't believe Perpetua called you ugly!" Bree shouted over the music. "I mean look at you. You could have any guy you wanted!"

Honey stopped dancing for a moment and watched Sandy strut confidently around the stage. She lowered her lashes and hid her true feelings behind a turbulent fall of blonde curls.

"Not any guy," she muttered.

CHAPTER 30
IN THE END

The path that snaked alongside the river was mulchy with rotting leaves.

"Looks like rain is on the way," said Bree, zipping up her jacket.

"Well it *is* the first day of November," said Annie, her cheeks pink with the cold.

The path curved gently to the right and led them up to an opening in a line of fir trees, the entrance to a lane bordered with creeping thyme.

"Where are we?" asked Annie, glancing up at the thick fretwork of branches.

"This is the old pathway where nobody goes," said Bree, remembering the last time they had been here.

"Except *we're* here now," said Annie with a twinkle in her eyes.

"This path will take us to Agora's cottage," said Honey, her breath swirling out in white clouds around her.

After a while they came to a small clearing through which they could see a small white house at the far end of a field.

"It looks like the house in Hansel and Gretel," beamed Annie.

"Well, let's hope there isn't a witch inside waiting to cook us," Sandy said dully.

"Don't be so silly!" she scolded, cuffing him with

her handbag. "Goodness, you have such an over-active imagination."

"So this is where my mother lived," she said thoughtfully.

Bree suddenly realised how difficult this must be for her, how strong her sense of loss and regret must be.

"We can turn back if you want."

"Nonsense," Annie said curtly. "We'll do nothing of the sort."

"We should never have made you walk so far," Sandy said worriedly.

"Nobody *made* me do anything," Annie replied sternly. "I wanted to see this place for myself."

She held on tightly to his arm as they traipsed across the marshy field. In little less than two years the front of Agora's cottage had been devoured by ivy, and the pretty garden had been left to fall sadly into decay. Wooden planks had been nailed over the windows. Bree wondered how long it would take before this little house disappeared forever; simply merged into the surrounding fields and forest.

When they reached the garden gate, Annie stared ahead with an expression so wistful and sad it twisted Bree's heart.

"What an enchanting house. I used to dream of one exactly like it when I was a child."

"Maybe you've been here before, Gran?"

Annie thought about this for a long, hard moment.

"Perhaps I have," she replied as she lifted the rusty latch.

They crunched up the stony path where weeds thrived unchallenged on either side.

"Look, it's for sale," said Sandy, pointing to a squint sign. "Perhaps we should put in an offer."

"How cool would that be," gasped Honey, "I'd *love* to live

here."

"It needs a lot of work," Annie frowned.

As they approached the front door, Bree thought about all the secrets and memories that occupied this place. This was where Agora Burton had shared her knowledge about The Book for the first – and last – time. This was the last place Jane and Michael Greenfield had been before they disappeared from this world – and Sandy's life – forever. On the front window sill a terracotta box trailed withered plants and long dead twig-like weeds.

"I don't believe it," said Sandy. "The bike is still here!"

Sure enough, Agora's old bicycle was propped against the side of the cottage. The chain and spokes were orange with rust and the basket on the handlebars was mouldy and tattered. Honey grimaced.

"Let's face it, no-one in their right mind would nick *that*."

Annie turned away for a moment, and Bree quickly slid the magic key into the lock. The front door creaked open. Annie looked surprised.

"Someone must have left it unlocked," she said, trying to peer through the crack.

Bree stepped aside and gestured for Annie to go in.

"I'm sure nobody would mind if we had a quick look inside," she said.

Annie hesitated and then stepped up onto the doorstep, wiping her feet on the welcome mat with the black cat asking them to, PLEASE KNOCK.

"I shouldn't think a bit of mud will matter now," Sandy said.

"It's still nice to show some respect," said Annie, throwing him a disapproving glare.

One by one they stepped inside. The house was as quiet

as a grave, which Bree supposed in some ways it was. The floorboards creaked as they made their way down the narrow hall. A large Grandfather's clock stood proudly at the end, its hands stuck at 4 o'clock. Everything had been suspended in time. The living room was exactly as they had left it. All the clocks were in the same positions, each with the hands stuck at 4 o'clock. Wallpaper hung limply, damp and peeling in places. Shards of glass from the broken lampshade crunched under their feet. The shoebox lay on its side, the contents scattered like rubbish. Some of the photographs had muddy footprints on them, most likely from whoever had come to board up the windows and chimney. The rocking chair sat in the corner with the oversized bag still hanging from the arm.

"I wonder if the Hoochie Koochies are still in there," said Sandy.

"We won't be taking anything," Bree said firmly. "We're only here to look."

She stepped back out into the hallway, turning left into the kitchen. A green tarpaulin had been stretched over the windows, shrouding everything in mouldy shadows. Spiders had made their webs between the shelves, and the glass in the back door was still a jagged hole, boarded up from the outside. Dust, as thick as snow, carpeted the linoleum.

Bree walked back up the hallway. She paused for a moment at the bottom of the stairs. The carpet had seen better days – threadbare, stained and frayed at the edges. She imagined her father touching this banister, his fingerprints still ingrained in the wood. Bree was not the only one seeing ghosts. Annie had appeared beside her and was looking up towards the second floor landing.

"I'd like to see where she slept," she said softly.

Afternoon sun slanted in through a window at the top of the stairs. Annie inhaled deeply as if savoring the atmosphere, but her eyes looked heavy and sad, a damson smudge of exhaustion under each one. Bree wondered if she was thinking about what life might have been like had those before her chosen a different path.

Agora's bedroom was unevenly lit courtesy of a skylight, which had been partially boarded up from the inside. Bree flicked a switch, and a naked bulb spread a feeble glow over a room with a sloping ceiling.

A heavy, mahogany dressing table with a three-sided mirror sat along one wall and a mantelpiece, covered in clocks, along the other. There were logs and scrunched up balls of paper stacked up inside the fireplace. Dust smothered everything and moths had clearly been gorging on the curtains. The wallpaper was old, a repeated pattern of summer flowers, faded on the far wall where the sun had sucked the colour from it. In the corner, a curious forest of white mushrooms grew out of the bare floorboards.

"My goodness," said Annie, setting her handbag down on the bed. "This place really does need a good old scrub."

She turned her head but not before Bree had caught the glimpse of sorrow in her eyes.

"It's such a shame," Bree sighed, "it was such a pretty little house when Agora lived here."

Annie sat on the edge of the bed. She smiled ruefully as she studied a collection of framed photographs on the bedside table. She picked one up and tilted it towards the light.

"I think this might be your Dad," she said. "It's difficult to tell."

Bree looked at the framed drawing behind the glass; the

hastily sketched face of a teenage boy with eyes like hers. Her heart did a somersault as she traced the lines with her finger. This was the same sketch she had seen in William's shop. She placed the frame on the table and picked up another. A black and white photograph showed a young Agora Burton holding a fussily dressed baby. Behind her smile was a terrible sadness that came with the knowledge that this child would not stay in her arms for long. She turned the frame over to find a tiny lock of red hair had been stuck down on the back. Annie stared at it with glassy eyes and patted down her wispy hair absent-mindedly.

"So she had a little piece of me with her all those years," she said, her voice cracking painfully.

Bree placed the frame down gently on the table.

"I'm sorry you never met her, Mrs Hooten. You must feel so sad."

Annie smiled feebly.

"You know how I feel about regrets. Everything that has happened in my life has made me who I am. In the end all that matters is love, and I have had a heart full of love for a very long time."

Sandy appeared in the doorway and let out an enormous sneeze.

"Bless you," said Annie, her face creasing into a fond smile.

"Agora liked to say *Spatangalam*," said Bree, and Annie chuckled.

"It's the dust," wheezed Sandy. "It's playing havoc with my allergies. It's like a time capsule in here. This must be how Agora left it."

The floorboards creaked as he crossed them. When he reached the window he pulled back the faded, moth-eaten curtain and grey light flooded in.

Bree sat down next to Annie and the mattress sunk low.

"I think the springs have lost their spring," she joked.

"A bit like me then," Annie said tiredly.

The sun came out from behind a cloud, painting everything in the room a shade of gold. Annie tilted her face to the warmth, looking almost too frail to bear its blast. She reminded Bree of a dried flower that had once been full of colour and life but was now withered and fragile.

"I'm worried about you, Mrs Hooten. You look really upset."

Annie took her hand; she felt cold and clammy despite her several layers of clothes.

"When you learn something it always feels at first like you've lost something," she said.

Bree understood only too well.

"My heart will adjust with time," added Annie, "although something tells me I don't have much of that left."

"You mustn't talk like that," Bree scolded. "It upsets me."

Honey sailed into the bedroom, dodging a loose floorboard near the fireplace. She swiped a finger along the clocks on the mantelpiece and pulled a face.

"Everything is so grotty," she said, picking up a box of matches and giving it a shake. "Poor Agora would be upset to see it like this."

Sandy looked out of the window. It had begun to pour and the rain was lashing off the roof and gutters.

"Perhaps we could come back tomorrow and give it a clean," he suggested.

"We're not supposed to be here," Bree reminded him. "It's up to whoever buys this place to sort it out."

"But what about all her things?" said Honey. "Her

photographs and belongings."

"It wouldn't feel right taking anything," said Bree. "I think we should leave the past in the past now."

"That's a very good idea," said Annie.

The house seemed to settle around them, its pulse calm and steady.

"I wouldn't have believed a house could have a heart," said Sandy, fiddling with a damp curl of wallpaper, "but this one definitely has."

"Ooh yes," said Annie. "Every house has a heart. One that has sung, one that has loved, one that has been broken."

Honey struck a match and held it to a scrap of paper. The flame curled around it, filling the fireplace with flickering light. Bree turned back to Annie. Her expression was so far away, so sad, it was as if she had forgotten who and where she was.

"Mrs Hooten?"

"I just need to lie back for a moment," croaked Annie.

With a grunt of effort she swung her legs up onto the bed. Sandy rushed over and knelt down beside her.

"Do you want to go home now, Gran?" he asked anxiously.

Annie closed her eyes and shook her head.

"We're worried. You don't look at all well."

"I'm just tired," Annie sighed, as her head sunk deeper into the pillow.

Honey stood with her back to the fire. "Perhaps she's just having a woozy episode. You know, connecting with Agora or something."

Sandy took Annie's hand in his. The room was almost dark now; the firelight cloaked the corners of the room in shadows.

Annie struggled to say something but her lips would not co-operate. Sandy held the back of his hand to her forehead, but she tossed her head from side to side to shake him off.

"I think we might need to get some help, Sandy," said Bree.

He looked at her numbly for a moment and then nodded reluctantly.

"No," said Annie, wincing as she heaved herself onto her side. "I don't want any fuss."

She pointed to her handbag with some urgency. Obediently, Bree placed it beside her.

"I want you to have what's in there."

She thrust the bag back at Bree as though the contents were the most important thing on Earth.

"I don't want your money," said Bree. "I just want you to be okay."

Annie shook her head, frustrated by her inability to speak properly.

"*Not...money...*" she gasped, struggling for breath.

"What then?"

"I couldn't leave without giving you presents could I?" she said weakly.

Sandy looked panic-stricken.

"What do you mean *leave?* Where are you going?"

Annie did not answer, but the look she gave him made Bree's heart buckle. She was suddenly filled with an overwhelming need to tell Annie everything. What did it matter now? Wherever she was going she would be taking their secrets with her.

"Jane and Michael," she blurted, "we saw them."

Honey gasped, but Bree continued, undeterred.

"...they're well and happy and Jane misses you *so* much."

Sandy let out an anguished moan and rested his forehead against the bed. The words came rushing out of Bree in an incoherent ramble, but she no longer cared.

"Sandy nearly stayed with them but he couldn't leave you. He loves you too much. I know it all sounds strange, Mrs Hooten but you *need* to know the truth!"

Annie's eyes stayed shut, but Bree could tell she was soaking in every word. Sandy lifted his tear-stained face.

"They didn't want to leave you, Gran!" he cried. "None of it was their fault. You have to say you believe me!"

Annie's eyes fluttered open.

"I believe you, Chickpea," she croaked as she stroked his fingers.

In the fire the logs hissed and spat. The colour had left Annie's face and she looked shrunken and papery.

"My darling boy," she said, "I have loved you forever. The same invisible thread that connects me to my birth mother connects you to me. Nothing will ever sever it. Not even death."

Sandy was too upset to speak. Annie winced as she turned her head back to Bree and reached for her hand.

"You know all about the invisible thread, don't you pumpkin?"

Bree swallowed.

"Yes. It will tie me to my dad forever."

Annie suddenly turned a terrible colour, so pale it looked like she was lit up from the inside.

"Mrs Hooten...?"

"My time has come now," said Annie.

Sandy held his head in his hands.

"You're scaring me!" But Annie did not hear him.

Her eyelashes blinked rapidly as she mustered up the energy to squeeze Bree's hand.

"Stay strong..." she whispered. "...Stay you."

"Annie," she said bravely, "we love you so much."

Annie tried to laugh.

"At last," she whispered. "You called me Annie."

A flash of lightning turned the room white. Everything went quiet in the house, as if even the walls were holding their breath. Bree laid her head on Annie's chest. She expected to find the strong, steady beat of a heart filled with adventure; a heart crammed full of kindness, love and laughter. Instead all she found was silence.

****

The sky flared and the rain came down in streams against the window. The shadows made it look like Annie's face was moving, but Bree knew it could not be. Annie was gone.

"Gran?" croaked Sandy, his face torn into a ragged expression of disbelief.

Bree touched his arm.

"She's gone, isn't she?" he said simply.

He pulled away from her angrily. Tears blurred her eyes and spilled over onto her cheeks.

"Sandy, I – "

She stopped, knowing no words would ever be enough.

He paced the room like a trapped animal. "She *can't* be dead," he said, his breath coming out in frantic sobs. "I mean she was dressed up as a witch less than twenty-four hours ago! What's going on? Wake up Gran! I can't bear it!"

He sobbed, clutching his chest. "It hurts too much!"

Bree wished her mother was there; she would know what to do. Annie's hair spread out across the pillow like a blanket of coppery thread. Her skin was as thin and pale as a moth's wing, and her hand felt cold and smooth. It was hard to connect this small, white figure with the vibrant, exciting, slightly cookie Annie Hooten.

Super Granny Annie.

"It's hard to imagine what life is going to be like without her," said Honey as she picked up Annie's handbag.

Sandy stopped crying and looked up at her like she was a stranger.

"How can you be so calm?"

"I'm *not* calm," she said, fiddling with the clasp. "I just know that Annie would not have wanted us to be sad." She opened the bag and there was a waft of Annie's perfume. "We'll survive this like we've survived everything else...because we're strong and because we've got each other. Everything will be alright. I promise."

Bree nodded.

"What's in there?"

Honey shrugged awkwardly.

"I dunno. It feels kind of wrong rummaging about in it."

"Gran said we could," Sandy said hurriedly, hopefully.

Honey fished around inside, finding Annie's embroidered handkerchief with the initials stitched into the corner.

"There's something for you," she said, handing Bree a small paper bag with string handles.

Tied to them was a label with a glittery letter B at the centre. Bree turned it over and her heart flipped when she saw a handwritten message from Annie.

For Bree. The oak is the greatest of trees and is symbolic of strength and wisdom. It is there to remind us that we build our character through patience and endurance and that we are never alone. The branches of an oak tree rarely move unless there is a strong wind. Mighty oak trees grow from tiny acorns. An acorn is simply the oak tree's way back into the ground for another try. A second chance."

A log slipped in the fire, producing a shower of crimson sparks. Bree opened the paper bag and pulled out a wooden oak leaf that had been painted dark green and red.

"I absolutely love it, Mrs Hooten," she said in a voice choked with tears. "Thank you."

"This one is for me," said Honey.

She pulled a serrated wooden leaf from a white paper bag. The label, which had a love heart on the front, was tied to the string handles with a bright red ribbon.

She flipped it over and read Annie's message aloud.

"The Elm tree likes to lead and not obey. Honest and generous it symbolises strength of will and intuition. The leaves of the elm provide protection and strength to all who stand near it. Though firmly anchored in the earth, this tree will stretch its branches all the way up to the clouds."

Big tears balanced on her lower lids as she carefully placed the elm leaf back into the paper bag.

"One left," she said quietly, pulling out a cream coloured bag with a bright yellow label on the front.

She handed it to Sandy and he opened it carefully. Inside was a large yellow leaf with five points that had been tipped with red and green. He ran his finger over the glittery star on the label and started to read the message, but his voice cracked and he had to stop. Bree felt her bottom lip start to tremble. She peered down at her lap to avoid his eyes.

"Read it to me," he said, handing the bag to Honey.

She took it from him and cleared her throat.

"For Sandy. The sycamore stands proud and knows itself well. It is a tree which struggles through the hardest times to reach its potential. Its leaves are a reminder of what is needed to stay strong in the years to come. The sycamore tree grows high but the falling leaves will always return to their roots. Sink those roots firmly into the earth but let your branches wander in all directions."

"It's beautiful," said Bree, without looking up.

The ordeal of crying seemed to have exhausted Sandy. His face was puffy and red and he was limp and shivery. Grief had smashed the strength from him. He took the bag from Honey and held it to his face, inhaling the scent of Annie's perfume, which still lingered on the paper.

Suddenly all the clocks in the house started up again, ticking and chiming as if they had awoken from a deep sleep. It was a soothing sound – a sound that marked the end of something but also the beginning. Sandy seemed to be lulled by it, his hiccupping sobs slowly lessening, the spaces between them growing longer.

The logs crackled in the fireplace, the only noise in the heavy silence. Sandy let his eyes rest on his Gran. She looked like she was sleeping but they all knew the essence of her was gone.

"She must have known she was going to – " Sandy stopped.

Honey threw herself at him and squeezed the breath from his chest.

"You know Annie," she said. "As deep as an ocean and full of mystery."

They sat like that for some time. Bree watched Sandy's grief flare and fade as Honey soothed him with soft words. Eventually Bree pulled her mobile phone from her pocket and dialed 999. Her finger hovered over the call button.

"Wait!" said Sandy. "I just want some more time with her."

Bree nodded and switched her phone off. She had no idea how long they stayed there; long enough for the fire to die, long enough to say their goodbyes. Long enough to listen to the soft breathing sounds of the cottage; the clocks ticking, the tiny pitter-patter tune of rain hitting the roof, the noise it made as it filtered through the guttering choked with leaves. The bones of the cottage creaked and groaned, seeming to expand against the pressure of feeling, the weight of grief and love – a love too big for this little room.

was sure the little house was smiling.

Although the sun was high in the sky a ghostly disc of full moon was still visible. Sandy would be coming back to school on Monday and there was the wedding to look forward to next Spring. Everything felt like it was returning to normal – as normal as it could be without Annie around.

Bree smiled at the postman as he did his rounds, and stopped to stroke a cat that popped up from behind a fence to say hello. This was a world away from castles, monsters and riddles. And it would stay that way – as long as nobody ever found what was hidden under the floorboard.

It was a chilly morning despite the clear blue sky – not quite cold enough for her to pull up the hood of her sweatshirt – but brisk enough for her breath to turn to puffs of white in front of her. In many ways it was a day like a hundred others, but as her trainers pounded the concrete she grew more aware that something inside her had changed.

She had let go.

On a day like this it was easy to believe in magic and hope and possibilities. To believe that the world was out there waiting for her and that life was for the taking.

The wind blew back her hair and wrapped itself around her. She knew the crack in her heart would always be there, but it was what made her who she was. She could not change the past but she could shape the future.

As she passed the allotments on Turret Shore, great floods of sun swooped over the rooftops and warmed her from the outside in.

This is the first day of the rest of my life, she thought as she made her way towards Kimbalee's Café. *I am Bree McCready - friend, daughter, Queen of secrets. Just an ordinary girl.*

pulled Algernon Hart's fob watch from her pocket and tilted it to the light so she could read the inscription around the rim. The words made more sense to her now than ever. Next, she carefully removed the sketch of her father from the frame on the bedside table. She could see that the fire in William's shop had singed the bottom corners of the paper. She snapped the two halves of the locket from the slot on the front of The Book and slid them into her pocket, then wrapped it in the sketch, placing the package beside the fob watch. As she brought the corners of the material up to meet in the middle, Bree felt satisfied that a little piece of everyone would be left behind in this house where it had all begun. She tugged on the loose floorboard until it broke free. Underneath was a secret, dusty cavity into which the package fitted neatly. Bree replaced the floorboard and stamped on it until it slotted firmly into place. She hoped when the new people moved in, a carpet would be laid in this room and nobody would ever know what secrets lay hidden beneath it. In the hallway the Grandfather's clock struck 11 o'clock.

When she reached the foot of the stairs her mobile phone chirped.

Meet us @ Kimbalee's Café in half an hour.
Hot Chocolates on me! Honey :)

Bree smiled as she closed the door behind her, locking it with the magic key. As she made her way back to Auriel Forest she knew she would never set foot inside the cottage again, but it felt like the right time to say goodbye, not only to The Book but to Agora, her father, William and Annie. She turned back only once; it might have been a trick of the light but she pasted across the For Sale sign. It was hard to imagine anyone else living in Agora Burton's cottage now. But it was nice to see all the boards had been taken down from the windows.

Just as she slotted the magic key into the front door, the sun burst free from behind a blanket of cloud, splitting the trees and framing them in a hundred different shades of fire. Birds chirped – not crows, but songbirds that flitted gracefully from twig to twig. She stepped inside the house, and made her way up the stairs. She had to brace herself before opening the bedroom door. Although so much had happened in the last two weeks the memory of losing Annie was still fresh in her mind.

In the quiet, Bree could feel all the secrets in this little room, secrets as deep as the dust and as dark as the shadows in the corners. She swallowed when she saw the dent in the quilt where Annie had lain.

"We miss you," she whispered.

The sun came in through the window, spilling light across the floor, and Bree's eyes were drawn to the loose floorboard near the fireplace. It made sense to her now. This was the floorboard Algernon Hart had referred to when he told them the story about hiding The Book in an attempt to keep it separate from the locket. How could he have known that they would be reunited years later by a twelve-year-old William Hart and a teenage Agora Burton? Bree pulled The Book from her pocket and gently traced the outline of the gold heart locket with her finger. This tiny, ancient book held the future of the world in its pages, but at the same time it held Bree's past in there too. It felt right that it had found its way back here.

She sat down on the saggy mattress and laid out three things on the quilt. The Book, then Annie's embroidered handkerchief, which she smoothed out until it was flat. She

EPILOGUE

Bree made her way towards Ramthorpe Junior. The weather was unusually mild for a Saturday morning in the middle of November.

She was content to be by herself for a while, immersed in her own thoughts. Honey was spending the day helping Sandy move some of his things into Freesia House; a temporary stop for him while something more permanent could be arranged. Mort and Saffron had welcomed him with open arms, and it made sense that he stayed with them because of the extra space. Honey had been thrilled by the idea, but not as thrilled as Mimi who had almost burst with excitement at the thought of Sandy living under the same roof as her.

As she walked past the memorial clock, Bree remembered what her dad had once said. *The Book is not safe until all seven wishes have been used and it has been returned to its rightful place.* She felt for the outline of The Book in her pocket and a thought sprung to her mind. What if its rightful place was not aisle 142 after all? What if it belonged where William Hart had discovered it all those years ago? Filled with a new and unexpected certainty, Bree took a sharp left towards Auriel Forest.

****

She felt a pang of sadness when she saw the SOLD banner

EPILOGUE

Bree made her way towards Ramthorpe Junior. The weather was unusually mild for a Saturday morning in the middle of November.

She was content to be by herself for a while, immersed in her own thoughts. Honey was spending the day helping Sandy move some of his things into Freesia House; a temporary stop for him while something more permanent could be arranged. Mort and Saffron had welcomed him with open arms, and it made sense that he stayed with them because of the extra space. Honey had been thrilled by the idea, but not as thrilled as Mimi who had almost burst with excitement at the thought of Sandy living under the same roof as her.

As she walked past the memorial clock, Bree remembered what her dad had once said. *The Book is not safe until all seven wishes have been used and it has been returned to its rightful place.* She felt for the outline of The Book in her pocket and a thought sprung to her mind. What if its rightful place was not aisle 142 after all? What if it belonged where William Hart had discovered it all those years ago? Filled with a new and unexpected certainty, Bree took a sharp left towards Auriel Forest.

****

She felt a pang of sadness when she saw the SOLD banner

pasted across the For Sale sign. It was hard to imagine anyone else living in Agora Burton's cottage now. But it was nice to see all the boards had been taken down from the windows.

Just as she slotted the magic key into the front door, the sun burst free from behind a blanket of cloud, splitting the trees and framing them in a hundred different shades of fire. Birds chirped – not crows, but songbirds that flitted gracefully from twig to twig. She stepped inside the house, and made her way up the stairs. She had to brace herself before opening the bedroom door. Although so much had happened in the last two weeks the memory of losing Annie was still fresh in her mind.

In the quiet, Bree could feel all the secrets in this little room, secrets as deep as the dust and as dark as the shadows in the corners. She swallowed when she saw the dent in the quilt where Annie had lain.

"We miss you," she whispered.

The sun came in through the window, spilling light across the floor, and Bree's eyes were drawn to the loose floorboard near the fireplace. It made sense to her now. This was the floorboard Algernon Hart had referred to when he told them the story about hiding The Book in an attempt to keep it separate from the locket. How could he have known that they would be reunited years later by a twelve-year-old William Hart and a teenage Agora Burton? Bree pulled The Book from her pocket and gently traced the outline of the gold heart locket with her finger. This tiny, ancient book held the future of the world in its pages, but at the same time it held Bree's past in there too. It felt right that it had found its way back here.

She sat down on the saggy mattress and laid out three things on the quilt. The Book, then Annie's embroidered handkerchief, which she smoothed out until it was flat. She pulled Algernon Hart's fob watch from her pocket and tilted it to the light so she could read the inscription around the rim. The words made more sense to her now than ever. Next, she carefully removed the sketch of her father from the frame on the bedside table. She could see that the fire in William's shop had singed the bottom corners of the paper. She snapped the two halves of the locket from the slot on the front of The Book and slid them into her pocket, then wrapped it in the sketch, placing the package beside the fob watch. As she brought the corners of the material up to meet in the middle, Bree felt satisfied that a little piece of everyone would be left behind in this house where it had all began. She tugged on the loose floorboard until it broke free. Underneath was a secret, dusty cavity into which the package fitted neatly. Bree replaced the floorboard and stamped on it until it slotted firmly into place. She hoped when the new people moved in, a carpet would be laid in this room and nobody would ever know what secrets lay hidden beneath it. In the hallway the Grandfather's clock struck 11 o'clock.

When she reached the foot of the stairs her mobile phone chirped.

Meet us @ Kimbalee's Café in half an hour. Hot chocolates on me! Honey ;)

Bree smiled as she closed the door behind her, locking it with the magic key. As she made her way back to Auriel Forest she knew she would never set foot inside the cottage again, but it felt like the right time to say goodbye, not only to The Book but to Agora, her father, William and Annie. She turned back only once; it might have been a trick of the light but she was sure the little house was smiling.

Although the sun was high in the sky a ghostly disc of full moon was still visible. Sandy would be coming back to school on Monday and there was the wedding to look forward to next Spring. Everything felt like it was returning to normal – as normal as it could be without Annie around.

Bree smiled at the postman as he did his rounds, and stopped to stroke a cat that popped up from behind a fence to say hello. This was a world away from castles, monsters and riddles. And it would stay that way – as long as nobody ever found what was hidden under the floorboard.

It was a chilly morning despite the clear blue sky – not quite cold enough for her to pull up the hood of her sweatshirt – but brisk enough for her breath to turn to puffs of white in front of her. In many ways it was a day like a hundred others, but as her trainers pounded the concrete she grew more aware that something inside her had changed.

She had let go.

On a day like this it was easy to believe in magic and hope and possibilities. To believe that the world was out there waiting for her and that life was for the taking.

The wind blew back her hair and wrapped itself around her. She knew the crack in her heart would always be there, but it was what made her who she was. She could not change the past but she could shape the future.

As she passed the allotments on Turret Shore, great floods of sun swooped over the rooftops and warmed her from the outside in.

This is the first day of the rest of my life, she thought as she made her way towards Kimbalee's Café. *I am Bree McCready - friend, daughter, Queen of secrets. Just an ordinary girl.*